WE INSTALL

WE INSTALL

and other stories

HARRY TURTLEDOVE

OPEN ROAD
INTEGRATED MEDIA
NEW YORK

"Father of the Groom" first appeared in John Joseph Adams, ed., *The Mad Scientist's Guide to World Domination* (Tor Books: New York, 2013).

"We Install" first appeared in *Analog*, January-February 2013.

"Alternate History: the How-to of What Might Have Been" first appeared in Michael Knost, ed., *Writers Workshop of Science Fiction & Fantasy* (Seventh Star Press: 2013).

"Drang von Osten" first appeared in Martin H. Greenberg, ed., *First to Fight* (Jove Books: New York, 1999).

"Hoxbomb" first appeared in *Alien Crimes*, Mike Resnick, ed., (SFBC: New York, 2007).

"Logan's Law" appears here for the first time.

"The Ring and I" first appeared in Karen Haber, ed., *Meditations on Middle Earth* (St. Martin's: New York, 2001).

"Birdwitching" first appeared in Esther Friesner, ed., *Witch Way to the Mall* (Baen Books: New York, 2009).

"Down in the Bottomlands" first appeared in *Analog*, January 1993.

"The Thing in the Woods" first appeared in Martin H. Greenberg and Sarah Hoyt, eds., *Something Magic This Way Comes* (DAW Books: New York, 2008).

"Perspectives on Chanukah" appears in print here for the first time.

"Under St. Peter's" first appeared in Darrell Schweitzer, ed., *The Secret History of Vampires* (DAW books: New York, 2007).

"It's the End of the World as We Know It, and We Feel Fine" first appeared in *Analog*, March 2013.

Copyright © 2015 by Harry Turtledove

Cover design by Mauricio Díaz

978-1-5040-0942-3

Published in 2015 by Open Road Integrated Media, Inc.
345 Hudson Street
New York, NY 10014
www.openroadmedia.com

CONTENTS

FATHER OF THE GROOM

One of the quaint and curious tribal customs of the United States is that, when there's a wedding, the bride's family makes the arrangements and foots the bills. As the father of three girls, I have had occasion to ponder this custom. The groom's family has an easier and more relaxed time of it. That, obviously, was part of what went into "Father of the Groom." Since it is a mad-scientist story, there are also a few echoes of Theodore Sturgeon's classic "Microcosmic God" running around loose. And let me state for the record that when our dear Rachel got married, she didn't go even slightly Bridezilla.

No, it isn't Professor Tesla Kidder's name that marks him as a mad scientist. It isn't the ratty, chemical-spotted lab coat or the shock of uncombed gray hair or the gold-rimmed glasses or the electrically intense blue eyes behind those glasses. It isn't even the fact that he has an assistant named Igor (who'd been in grad school at the University of Moscow when the Soviet Union imploded, and who'd split for greener pastures right afterwards).

No, indeed. It's none of that. By his works shall you know him.

Consider, if you will, the stop light. Perhaps I should say, consider if you can. The stop light plunged an area with a radius of 1.378 miles around his Tarzana laboratory into darkness illimitable, absolute, and—it rapidly transpired—unrelieveable. That circle might be a black hole yet if the cheap AAA battery with which he powered his gadget hadn't run out of juice after a couple of hours.

Or consider his room-temperature super conductor. Professor Kidder was convinced the world would beat a path to his door (now that it could see the way again). Better he should have stuck to mousetraps. No matter how super his conductor was, who needed the poor android in an age of automated trains?

Then again, you might—or, if horror disturbs you, you might not—want to contemplate his motion censor. It did just what it was designed to do, and froze the Ventura Freeway into utter immobility at morning rush hour. Once people noticed (which, given the usual state of the Ventura Freeway at morning rush hour, took some little while), an irate CHP officer pounded on his door and demanded that he turn the goddamn thing off. Traffic eventually resumed the uneven baritone of its ways.

I'm not even going to talk about his microcosmic green goddess. That's a whole 'nother kettle of sturgeon. And some things are better left to the imagination.

I *will* tell you that lately Professor Kidder has got more and more interested in DNA and genetic engineering. This worries you? Let me tell you something—it even worries Igor.

You might imagine that, with such splendors on his *curriculum vitae*, Tesla Kidder lives alone, cooking in Erlenmeyer flasks over a Bunsen burner. You might, but you would be mistaken. He is happily married to Kathy, a smashing blonde, and has been for lo these many years.

How? you ask. How? you in fact, cry. Well, to put it as simply as possibly, Kathy is a bit mad, too, or more than a bit. Proof? You want proof? She breeds Weimaraners for a living. What more proof do I need?

They have a son. He looks like Tesla Kidder, except his shock of uncombed hair is brown and he wears contact lenses instead of mad-scientist specs. His name is Archimedes. Some people would get a complex about that. Young Kidder just goes by Archie. He smiles a lot, too. He's the most normal one in the whole family—not *normal*, mind you, but the most normal.

He majored in physics and minored in chemistry at UCLA. Maybe they'll issue him those gold-rimmed glasses when he starts going gray. Or maybe not. He's head over heels in love these days, not trying to cypher out the best way to turn the moon into a giant economy-sized bowl of guacamole for God's next Super Bowl party.

His beloved is a smashing blonde named Kate. Like father, like son? Well, yes and no. For one thing, Kate is allergic to Weimaraners—and other dogs, and anything else with four legs and fur. For another, she's about as far from mad as you can get. While Archie's doing the research for his doctorate, she's finishing her MBA.

But she sure said yes when he popped the question. The two-carat rock in the engagement ring he gave her didn't hurt, no doubt. And if Archie didn't explain that his father had synthesized it from two carrots, well, can you blame him? When the wind is southerly, he knows which side his bread is buttered on.

Kate and her folks (he does real estate; she's an investment banker) immediately started planning the wedding. The German General Staff may have worked harder planning Hitler's invasion of the Low Countries and France. Then again, they may not have. This was going to be The Way Kate Wanted It To Be.

Or else.

You might think such elaborate—even anal—preparations would put Professor Tesla Kidder's wind up. Mad scientist, after all, is traditionally a (small-L, please) libertarian kind of job description. For the longest time, he just smiled and nodded and went along.

And why the hell not? All he was was the father of the groom.

At a wedding, the father of the groom is as vestigial as your coccyx (unless you happen to be the non-baboon sort of monkey, anyhow). All he has to do is show up at the rehearsal and the ceremony and drink. That's it. He's not even drinking booze he's bought, because the bride's family foots the bill.

Oh, he has to get a tux, too, in case he doesn't have one or eleven hanging in a closet. But that's okay. Mad scientists tend to look dashing and distinguished in formalwear. Here, for once, Professor Kidder conforms to a rule. He'll try not to let it happen again.

Sadly, Kate also conforms to a rule. The daughter of a real-estate whiz and an investment banker is much too likely to think she has the world wrapped around her finger. Sure as the devil, dear Kate owns a whim of iron.

Archie Kidder has noticed this, proving he isn't quite blind with love or some other related four-letter word. He labors, however, under the delusion that getting away from her folks and alone with him will cure her of this, proving he is as near blind with love or some other related four-letter word as makes little difference.

His cousin Stacey has also noticed this, since she is going to be one of the bridesmaids. She is not blind with love or some other related four-letter word for Kate, even though she introduced her to Archie (which is why she is a bridesmaid). In fact, now she is rather regretting that. The more Kate issues *diktats* about bridesmaids' dresses and such-like wedding arcana, the less in love (or some other related—oh, hell, you know) with Kate she becomes. She's starting to get pissed off instead.

Now, bridesmaids' dresses could piss off a saint. And if you are currently visualizing a pissed-off saint in a bridesmaid's dress, you are indeed the kind of person for whom this tale is intended, you poor sorry sod, you. But I digress. Bridesmaids' dresses have the twin virtues of being expensive and, more often than not, wearable only once, because bridesmaids' dresses look exactly like, well, bridesmaids' dresses, and like nothing else under the Andromeda Galaxy. Most bridesmaids' dresses come in one of two categories: the Bad and the Worse.

In Stacey's opinion, Kate was innately oriented toward the Worse. What's more, since it was her wedding, she was damn well going to ram the Worse down everybody else's throat come hell or high taxes. Attempts to reason with the daughter of a real-estate hotshot and an investment banker went the way you would imagine: into a stone wall at high velocity.

Stacey was not pleased. Which is putting it mildly. "She's going Bridezilla on us, is what she's doing," she said at a family gathering.

Now, Stacey is, all things considered, a sweet kid. She made a point of *not* saying this where Archie could hear it. But she didn't make a point of not saying it where Professor Tesla Kidder could hear it.

Oops. Major oops, as a fatter of mact.

Up till then, Prof Kidder had been occupying himself the way he usually did at family gatherings: comparing and contrasting the flavors of various single-malt scotches. After comparing and contrasting enough of them, he could forget he was at a family gathering. And Kathy could pour him into her van and drive him home. He'd get hair from Weimaraners' coats on his own coat, but there are worse things. A few, anyhow.

If he'd done a little more comparing and contrasting, he wouldn't have notice Stacey's snarking. If he had noticed, he wouldn't have cared. But he did, and he did, respectively.

You could see his ears quiver and come to attention. (No, he hasn't genetically engineered himself. Mad scientists *like* being mad scientists, except when they turn themselves into giant tarantulas or something. This is a mad writer's trick called hyperbole—I think.)

"Bridezilla?" he murmured in tones that spread nervous indigestion from Woodland Hills all the way to North Hollywood and beyond. "A metaphor perhaps worthy of reification. Yes, indeed." He's not the kind of mad scientist who goes in for *mwahaha*, but if he were he would have thrown one in there.

At most family gatherings, he would have been the only one there who had any idea what the hell *reification* meant. And the terror that, uh, terrorized the Northridge Mall might have been averted. But Igor, who was along because the story kind of needs him to be there (and also because he kind of has the hots for Stacey), hadn't learned English halfway. Armed with his rich vocabulary, he proceeded to ask precisely the wrong question: "Are you sure that's a good idea, boss?"

It was precisely the wrong question because mad scientists are always sure their ideas are good ones. It's part of what makes them mad scientists. "Of course I'm sure that's a good idea, dammit," Professor Tesla Kidder declared, at something over twice his usual volume.

"Well, I think we'd better be going," Kathy said brightly. She could tell when the comparing and contrasting might be getting a touch out of hand.

But all the way home Prof Kidder kept muttering "Reification" under his single-malt breath. Since his smashing blond wife didn't know what the hell it meant (she rather thought it had something to do with East and West Germany getting together not long before Igor escaped the XSSR), she didn't worry her pretty head about it. She didn't worry about Weimaraner hair, either. She *likes* Weimaraners, remember. Nope, Tesla isn't the only mad Kidder running around loose.

A bride and a bunch of bridesmaids constitute a giggle, which is something like a gaggle but shriller and squeakier. You can recognize giggles because they descend on bridal shops and malls with open credit cards. They are going to have fun, and somebody else is going to pay for it. But, to quote from the Gospel according to Theodore, don't worry; I'm not going political on you.

Instead, I'm going to the Northridge Mall with Kate and Stacey and the rest of the girls. And at the same time, thanks to the miracle of narrative, I'll also go to Professor Tesla Kidder's laboratory.

Kate is saying, in a voice that puts some of the bridesmaids in mind of a slightly off-center grinding wheel working its slow way through a fat nail, "No, you're not going to use those handbags. You're going to use these over here." *These over here* are larger and homelier and cost more. One of the bridesmaids has the gumption to point this out.

Kate's face curdles into an expression that would make even love-addled Archie think twice if he were there to see it. She wheels out the heavy artillery: "It's my wedding, and we're going to do it the way I want to."

Stacey's mouth forms the word "Bridezilla" once more, silently this time. Two other bridesmaids read her lips and . . . giggle. What else?

Professor Kidder reads her lips, too. Hooking his laboratory up to all the surveillance cameras in the mall is child's play for a mad scientist. Hell, Igor handled half the design work on the device that lets him do it, and Igor isn't even a mad scientist. He's just an Igor. (And of course Professor Kidder reads lips. Read lips? Professor Kidder practically *writes* lips. He's a mad scientist's mad scientist, Tesla Kidder is.)

He frowns. "Someone should do something abut this personage," he says. No, he's not talking about Stacey. "Something . . . instructive." He nods to himself, liking the word. "Yes. Instructive." And he remembers another word he likes: "Reification."

"You shouldn't take too much on yourself, boss," Igor says quickly. "Once the strain of the wedding is over, she'll be fine."

But Tesla Kidder isn't listening any more. Not listening is another hallmark of mad scientists. Professor Kidder thinks. Then he explodes into experimentation. No, no, not literally. It has happened to a mad scientist or three, sure. Not to Prof Kidder. He's a *carefully* mad scientist.

He pulls a mouse out of his lab-coat pocket to test the genetic recodifier he's cooked up. You don't keep mice in your pocket? Too bad. I already told you the lab coat was ratty.

Everything works at least as well as he hoped it would. Igor has the privilege of hunting down the recodified mouse. A fire extinguisher keeps him from suffering anything worse than second-degree burns.

He passes on to Professor Kidder a piece of advice from his student days in the vanished Soviet Union: "Make sure they can't trace it back to you."

"Interesting," Tesla Kidder replies. "I don't believe they know I'm working on a long-range genetic recodifier."

"Urk," says Igor. He hadn't known that himself. He hadn't imagined such a thing was possible. He is, after all, only an Igor.

"I didn't plan to field-test it so soon. Still and all, under the circumstances, no doubt it's justified. No doubt at all." As I've mentioned before, Prof Kidder doesn't come equipped with doubts. It's . . . a lodge pin, like.

Being only an Igor, Igor does have them. "What about Stacey?" he asks. He also comes equipped with the usual male ductless glands. Anything happening to Archie Kidder's cousin would be a great waste of natural resources, as far as he's concerned.

"Tcha!" Tesla Kidder says, which may mean anything or nothing—he's a master of mad-scientistspeak. He pulls from a shelf not anything or nothing, but something, definitely something. To Igor, it doesn't especially look like a long-range genetic recodifier, but who the devil knows what a long-range genetic recodifier is supposed to look like?

Prof Kidder flicks a switch on the something. He adjusts a dial, then another one—fussily, till they're both just right. Then he punches a button. The something makes a noise. It isn't a great big noise. Then again, it isn't a great big something. A beam of light shoots out. Professor Kidder scowls. That isn't supposed to happen. He pushes another button. The light vanishes. He checks the rest of the instrumentation. By his satisfied grunt, the something still works.

Which means we return to the mall. Kate and the giggle of bridesmaids are in Bed, Bath and Beyond, discussing scented soap. (Testing the recodifier on the mouse and calibrating the long-range version do take a little while, you know.) To be precise—which we'd better be, in a story involving a mad scientist—Kate is discoursing about scented soap. A bad habit, discoursing. Kate is firmly convinced of the superiority of lime to frangipani, sandalwood, or any other scent in the explored universe. Very firmly convinced.

One of the other bridesmaids whispers to Stacey, "She's even starting to look like a lime."

"It's just the fluorescent lighting." Stacey, after all, has spent time around a mad scientist. She's tried to explain impossible things before.

But it's not just the fluorescent lighting, and things keep right on getting impossibler. Kate's complexion goes from lime to Hass avocado: dark green and bumpylumpy. More and more bumpylumpy. Scaly, even. Where has that muzzle come from, with all those sharp teeth? To say nothing of the tail? No, we have to tell some kind of tale of the telltale tail, but not much.

Kate starts to say something else, presumably more about the magnificent wonderfulness of lime. What comes out, however, isn't exactly English. It isn't even approximately English. It's a bubbling shriek of about the volume you would use if you wanted to set Mount Everest running for an air-raid shelter.

What else comes out is a blast of fire. It's Kate's very first one, so it's not a *huge* blast of fire. But it's plenty to set several cardboard boxes burning, and it's plenty to make the giggle of bridesmaids stop giggling and start running. Running like hell, if, once more, you want to be precise.

The Bed, Bath and Beyond sales staff also opt for Beyond, and at top speed, too. Their customer-service training does not involve dealing with dinosaurian monsters, even ones that just stop in for soap.

Kate follows them out of the store. She hasn't fully figured out what's happened to her. Well, neither has anyone else but Professor Tesla Kidder, and he's off in another part of the narrative somewhere. She tries to complain. More bubbling shrieks come forth. So does more flame. Lots more flame. She's getting the hang of it.

When you are on fire, a man once said from agonizing personal experience, people get out of your way. And they get out of your way even faster when you breathe fire. Panic roars through the clothed mall-rats of Northridge.

"Run for your life!" a woman screams. "It really is Bridezilla!"

How can she tell? Simple. On the second digit of Kate's left forepaw (not the fourth, because the forepaw has only two digits once the genetic recodifying gets done) still sparkles Archie Kidder's two-carat rock.

And when people aren't running, they're aiming cell-phone cameras at Kate and zapping the stills and videos to every TV station and newspaper in town (lots of the former; not much left of the latter). Some of them even think to call the police, the fire department, and the SPCA.

Media frenzies have been built from less. From much less, to tell you the truth. Cars, vans, and all the helicopters not covering the latest freeway chase—say, about as many as the Brazilian Air Force owns—converge on the Northridge Mall. "Dinosaur runs amok!" a blow-dried airhead shouts breathlessly into his mike. "Details after this message!"

Before the impotence-drug commercial can even finish, Professor Tesla Kidder's cell phone blorps. Mm, how would you describe the noise a theremin makes? And what else would a mad scientist use for a ring tone?

"Yes?" he says.

"No," his wife tells him firmly. "I don't know what you've done, but stop doing it. Undo it, if you can—and you'd better be able to." She hangs up before he can get out even one more word.

And, before he can put the phone back in his pocket (no, not the pocket the mouse came from—mice gnaw on phones), it blorps again. Once more, he raises it to the side of his head. "Yes?"

"Dad!" Archie sounds reproachful, not firm. That may be even worse. "Fix it, will you please? Kate'll be fine as soon as the ceremony's over and the pressure's off. C'mon!"

So much for *Make sure they can't trace it back to you*. His family sure doesn't have any trouble. The police and fire department don't know him as well. Even so . . . How much damage can a real Bridezilla do in a mall? How expensive will that damage be? Tesla Kidder is a mad scientist, but he isn't a stupid scientist. No way, José.

His calculations take but a moment. "Oh, all right," he says, and, if he sounds a trifle sulky, it's only because he is. Back into the pocket goes the phone.

He recalibrates the long-range genetic recodifier. The police don't call. The fire department doesn't, either. No one pounds on the laboratory door. (Remembering Moscow nights, even Moscow nights under *perestroika* and *glasnost*, Igor is relieved.) No reporters show up asking for comments. They're all too busy trying to sound blasé about this Mesozoic irruption into the bastion of modern American capitalism.

Prof Kidder pushes the button on his device again. No annoying extraneous beam of light this time. Tesla Kidder beams himself. He's fixed that, anyhow.

We return, then, to the mall to await developments. The Kateosaurus with the flashy engagement ring has just flamed a Cadillac Escalade in the parking lot. The SUV's fuel tank, a reservoir containing the essence of Lord knows how many dinosaurs, sends a column of greasy black smoke into the sky to mark their final return to the environment.

After a roar of triumph, the Creature from the Lime Soap Lagoon advances purposefully on a van even bigger than the Escalade (and they said it couldn't be done!). On the side of the van is blazoned EYEWITLESS NEWS. Another burbling roar. Another blast of flame. But—disappointingly, at least to Prof Kidder—only a small one. The news van gets scorched, but does not become as one with Nineveh and Tyre and the unmourned Escalade.

Kidder sighs. "I should have waited another minute or two. Oh, well."

For Bridezilla is undergoing another transformation—another recodification, if you will. Not from real-estate whiz and investment banker's kid to fire-breathing monster, but the reverse. To Tesla Kidder, who is thinking about Archie, going this way may be the more frightening. With a fire-breathing monster, at least, you know ahead of time what you're getting. You don't have to find out later, the hard way.

In the Northridge parking lot, Kate—yes, she's Kate again—looks vaguely confused. She doesn't remember a whole lot of what just happened. As Bridezilla, she had a brain about the size of a walnut. Most MBA candidates come with a little more cranial capacity than that.

Most reporters? It's an open question. Anyone watching the subsequent interview between the TV guy and the recently ex-dinosaur would doubt that the intelligence level of the planet's dominant species has changed much over the past 65,000,000 years.

Professor Tesla Kidder puts the long-range genetic recodifier back on the shelf. Maybe he'll need it again one of these days. "Well, Igor," he says, "what shall we work on next?"

Igor is still watching the aftermath of chaos on TV. Maybe staying in Moscow would have been better than this, or at least less wearing. But maybe not, too. That may be the scariest thought of all.

The wedding is a great success. If everything smells a bit too strongly of lime, well, you can live with lime. After the vows, before the minister tells Archie he may kiss the bride, he beats the guy to the punch. "Kiss me, Kate!" he says, and she does. If she doesn't quite grok why he's got that kind of smile on his face while he says it, you have to remember she's only someone who's finishing an MBA.

At the reception, Kate's mother comes up to Tesla Kidder, champagne flute in hand. "Hey, listen," she says, "you didn't have anything to do with the, ah, unfortunate incident, didja?" That's what Kate's family—and their lawyers—have taken to calling the scaly, incendiary rampage through the mall.

"How could I possibly?" Professor Kidder answers. "I was in my laboratory the whole time. You can ask Igor, if you like. He was there with me."

Actually, Kate's mom *can't* ask Igor right this second. He's out on the dance floor with Stacey (who smells, defiantly, of frangipani). Kate's mother nods, as if in wisdom. "Okay," she says. "That's what I already heard, anyways." You have to remember, she's only an investment banker. Mad scientists? They're right out of her league.

WE INSTALL

This one is my daughter Rebecca's fault. Living in sunny Southern California, we put up with visits from, among other people, solar-power-company salespeople hawking their outfits' products door-to-door. After I sent yet another one of them away without buying, I noticed that she was giggling.

"What's funny?" I asked.

"Didn't you hear what he said?" she answered. "He said, 'We install solar systems.'"

I thought about that. "Oh." I laughed, too, and went on, "Well, if I write the story, I'll give you a chunk of the check." A few days later, I wrote it, and she did get a piece of what I got for it.

So the doorbell rings. So for a wonder it's twenty minutes before dinner, not during. So okay, I heave my butt out of the recliner and go to the door. There's a kind of dweeby-looking guy on my front porch. Khakis. Dark blue polo shirt with a company logo on the left breast. Plastic badge on a lanyard around his neck. Clipboard.

Not likely to be a home-invasion robber. Possible, sure, but not likely. So I open the door. "Yes?" I say.

"Hi." He smiles almost like he means it. "My name's Eric." He holds up his badge. The badge's name is Eric, anyway.

I nod. I say, "And?" I wait.

"I'm with Superior Solar." He taps the logo on his chest. "We install solar systems, and we're going through your neighborhood now offering some very attractive discounts. Putting in a new solar system can save you some serious money, you know."

When I open the door, I expect I'll listen to his spiel and go *We're not interested, thanks.* It's like there's a tape in my head. A salesman comes, I listen to his spiel, I go *We're not interested, thanks,* and I shut the door. Spiel runs long, I shut it before he finishes.

Only not today. I turn and I yell, "Debbie! Hey, Debbie!"

"What?" my wife yells from the kitchen. That's where the good smells come from. Twenty minutes till dinnertime, remember?

"There's a guy from Superior Solar on the porch." When she's in the kitchen, she can't hardly hear the bell ring. "He says they got good deals on new solar systems."

"Well, talk to him, for crying out loud," she says. "The one that came with this place is old as the hills, and it's a piece of junk."

She's right, no two ways about it. She is. That old solar system's given us nothing but trouble ever since we moved in here. And when she goes *talk to him,* that means we can finally afford to replace the miserable thing. Debbie minds the checkbook around here. Tell me it's not like that at your house, pal.

So okay, I say, "C'mon in, Eric. Let's talk abut these deals of yours."

So he spreads his pictures and his price list out on the dining-room table. And right away I see a system I like. It's got good power, and the price looks okay to me. I call Debbie over to make sure I'm not getting us in too deep. She thinks for a minute. Then she says, "Yeah, we can swing that."

"We *will* swing that," I tell Eric. "How soon can you install it?"

"We've got a tech crew in the neighborhood," he says. "We'll start tomorrow morning. If it's a straightforward job, we should be done by late afternoon. Any chance I can get up on your roof now so I can see what we'll have to do in the replacement process?"

I ask Debbie a question with my eyebrows. She goes, "I'll turn supper down."

I lean the ladder against the side of the house. We both go up there (I check to see Eric's insured first). He's good and careful on the slope; it's not like he's never done this before. He steps over the oorts and kuipers out at the edge (smart—those little bastards'll freeze your ankles off if you give 'em half a chance) and bends down to take a look at the power unit in the center of the system.

He kinda grunts. "You could do with a new one, all right. This one here's gotta be close to 5X10E9."

"I told you—this system was in place when we bought the house," I say.

"They don't usually last past 1X10E10, not ones this size. They blow up on you, make all kinds of trouble. You're smart to replace while it's still kinda working." Eric takes out a loupe and inspects the sixth wanderer. "What happened here? What's up with the ring?"

"A couple of the outliers smashed together a while ago and broke up. Didn't seem to hurt anything much, so I just left it alone."

"Sloppy workmanship, though." Eric switches to another loupe, one with a longer lens. "Same with this grit between Five and Four. We make 'em a lot better now, we really do. You'll like your new one. It's *clean*, man."

"Cool," I say. "Um, could you take a peek at Three? It's been kinda funny-like for a while."

He does, with the strongest lens yet. He's frowning when he looks up. "Hate to tell you, but I think it's gone moldy."

"I was afraid of that. Now I'm extra glad we're ripping this one out."

"Yeah, that stuff can be nasty," Eric agrees. "Sometimes it even spreads to systems up and down the block." He writes on his clipboard. "Gotta make sure we sterilize it before we recycle."

I nod. "Sounds like a plan." He fiddles around up there while I get hungrier. So I say, "You want to have dinner with us? Debbie always makes plenty."

That gets him moving. "No, thanks," he says. "Still got more ground to cover today. Let's go down, shall we?" And we do.

I stow the ladder in the garage. We go into the house again. Debbie says, "I heard you guys clomping around up there. Everything all set?"

"Sure is," Eric answers. "Good thing I went up. Wanderer Three's got mold on it, and it'll need steam cleaning before they can reuse it."

"Ewww." Debbie hates gross stuff. She asks, "No extra charge?" She hates that, too.

But he says, "Nah—comes with the install. The crew'll be here between nine and eleven tomorrow. It'll be kinda noisy, but not too bad. Look, here's my card." He sets it on the table. "Any trouble at all, call me, hear? Now I'm gonna run. Thanks, folks." And away Eric goes. He's got more solar systems to sell.

ALTERNATE HISTORY: THE HOW-TO OF WHAT MIGHT HAVE BEEN

When Michael Knost put together his *Writers Workshop of Science Fiction & Fantasy* (Seventh Star Press, 2013), he asked me for a piece on how to write alternate history, since I've done a fair amount of it. The question faintly alarmed me, since I usually don't think about how I do what I do, any more than a centipede thinks about how it keeps all those legs going. I just do it. I worried that, if I started taking apart what I did, I might start having trouble doing it, the way a contemplative centipede might end up with its feet all tangled together. But the prospect of a check got me going again, as I suspected it would. And I'm still writing stories, too, which is nice.

It's mildly surprising that, these days, alternate history is mostly a sub-genre of science fiction. Up through the first third of the twentieth century, it was the province—more accurately, the playground—of historians and politicians on a lark. As far as I know, it was invented by a historian on a lark, and not one notorious for larkishness, either. Writing around the time of Christ, the Roman scissors-and-paste specialist Livy wondered what might have happened had Alexander the Great not died in 323 BC, but turned west and loosed his Macedonians against the Roman Republic. Livy's opinion was that his long-dead ancestors would have handled Alexander's hoplite band just fine. My opinion is that Livy was a wild-eyed optimist, but that's neither here nor there. He wrote about not what had been but what might have been, and the die, as another Roman said, was cast.

More recent examples also have authors better known for things other than cranking out alternate history. In 1931, Winston Churchill published "If Lee Had Not Won the Battle of Gettysburg" in editor J.C. Squire's *If It Had Happened Otherwise: Lapses into Imaginative History*. Churchill wasn't in the British government at the time, but he had been, and, as some of you will recall, he would be again. Three years later, Arnold J. Toynbee, a historian of considerably greater acumen than Livy, wrote "The Forfeited Birthright of the Abortive Western Christian Civilization" as part of the second volume of *A Study of History*. This examines what a world where Celtic Christianity triumphed over the Roman variety and the Muslims succeeded in invading the Frankish Kingdom could have looked like. Both of these essays are party tricks, games intellectuals play.

So how did a-h become part of sf, then? Well, for one thing, sf writers have written a devil of a lot of alternate history. Those in our field who've turned their hand to a-h include Murray Leinster, L. Sprague de Camp (whose "The Wheels of If" dramatizes the results of Toynbee's speculation), Poul Anderson, H. Beam Piper, Philip K. Dick, John Brunner, yours truly, S.M. Stirling, Kim Newman, William Sanders. . . . I could go on, but you get the idea.

And it's not surprising that this should be so, either. Alternate history uses the same extrapolative technique as other science fiction. It just plants the extrapolation at a different place on the timeline. Most sf changes something in the present or the nearer future and works out its consequences in the more distant future. A-h, by contrast, changes something in the more distant past and examines the effects of that change on the nearer past or the present. The tools are identical. Their placement, though, makes for different kinds of stories.

Outsiders still do pick up these tools every now and again. Over the past couple of generations, interesting alternate histories have come from writers as diverse as MacKinlay Kantor, Len Deighton, Richard Harris, and Philip Roth. In comments about *The Plot Against America*, Roth made it plain that he thought he was inventing something new and different with this whole what-might-have-been thing. He wasn't, but he produced an important book anyhow.

So you've decided you're going to write an alternate history this time around. How do you go about writing a good one, one that will entertain and interest your readers (without which, all else fails) and, with luck, make them think a bit, too? The first thing I need to warn you of is, it's not about Being Right. By the nature of things, you can't know if you're right. You are conducting a *Gedankenexperiment*, nothing more (and nothing less). You can reasonably hope to be plausible. Often—though not always—in this kind of story you will want to be plausible. We'll talk about how to manage that in a little bit. First, though, another word of warning.

Who and what you are will influence what you find interesting. This is not a hot headline; it is, in fact, inevitable. All fiction—not just a-h, not just sf, but all fiction—is not about the world you're creating. It's about the world you're living in. It's no accident that Livy speculated about an Alexandrian-Roman encounter. It's no accident that several nineteenth-century French novelists wondered what the world would have looked like had Napoleon won. It's no accident that Americans write so much a-h about their Civil War: it shaped who and what our country became. It's no accident that everybody seems to write a lot of alternate history about World War II; it's drowned out World War I in public perception of what made the rest of the twentieth century (and now the twenty-first) the way it is. Look at a different war and you look at a different world. A-h gives you a funhouse mirror in which to examine the real world and distort it in ways you can't do with any other kind of fiction.

Okay. Well and good. You can't help being who and what you are. History—real history—made you that way. Neverthenonetheless, using your a-h story to bang a big drum for your political views has about as much chance of succeeding as using any other kind of story for the same purpose. People who already agree with you will go "Well, sure!" or, if they're old farts, "Right on!" People who don't will say less kindly things. Converting them ain't gonna happen. And selling your birthright for a pot of message (thank you, Ted Sturgeon) is almost always a bad idea. On second thought, delete "almost."

What should you do, then? The same thing you would do for any other kind of story: write the best piece you can. Even if you're writing something that seems to you far removed from your essential convictions, they will shine through anyhow. They can't help it. This is the famous realization that then-*Galaxy* editor H.L. Gold passed on to—once more—Theodore Sturgeon. He knew what he was talking about, too.

Let's look at some of the pieces that go into writing that best piece you can. A breakpoint for an alternate-history story needs to be both significant and interesting. The battle of Teutoberg Wald in 9 AD, which ensured that Germany would not become part of the Roman Empire, is one of the most significant in history. Europe looks profoundly different today because of what happened there then. If it had turned out otherwise . . . well, who cares? Too long ago, dammit. It took me more than twenty years to come up with a story to follow on changing things there. The breakpoint also needs to be something that believably could have gone the other way. This is why writing a story where, for instance, the Native Americans fend off the Europeans is so hard: the conquistadors and their English and Dutch brethren simply had too big a head start on the people they found on this side of the Atlantic.

To figure out what you might change and to have an idea how you might change it and what would spring from that, you should be interested in real history and know something about it. You don't have to be professionally trained in history to write a-h, any more than you have to be an astronomer to write an sf piece involving one of Neptune's moons. If you are professionally trained, as I happen to be, that's an asset. But it's not a prerequisite. Still and all, you're unlikely to write a good story about Neptune's moons if you first have to hit Wikipedia to find out how many moons the planet has and how big they are. And you're unlikely to write an interesting a-h piece on early modern Europe if you have to look up the order of the Hundred Years' War, the Thirty Years' War, and the Seven Years' War. Doesn't mean you can't try something else. But that particular period might not be ideal for you.

When you look at what happens when you make your breakpoint go the other way, the way it didn't really go, you have to remember that you are *changing* things. You are changing them in all kinds of ways, and those changes will radiate out from your initial alteration. *Everything* will change, not just the stuff you're looking directly at. The farther from the breakpoint you go, the more different stuff will be. If Germany successfully gets incorporated into the Roman Empire, no way in hell Constantine the Great gets born in an obscure provincial town more than two and a half centuries later. And double no way in hell he fulfills a role in the changed world similar to the one he had in the real world.

This is one of those places where you can cheat. If you've got a world where the American Revolution never happened, Richard Nixon won't get born (one possible advantage to learning different words to the tune of "America the Beautiful"). But if you need a used-car sales-man called Tricky Dick in the late twentieth century of that world, go ahead and stick him in. Just be aware that you *are* cheating, and then sin proudly. Don't drop him in there for no better reason than that you haven't thought through the consequences of your change.

Because if you are sloppy that way, people will spot it. There's always someone out there—usually, there are lots of someones out there—more knowledgeable about your topic than you are. In many ways, alternate history is still an intellectuals' parlor trick. Like any good fiction, it should evoke an emotional response. But it should also evoke one in the thinking part of the brain. And if your carelessness makes somebody crumple under the weight of disbelief that can no longer be suspended, you've lost that reader forever. You'll hear about it, too, in great detail. The Internet has made this easier and quicker, but it happened before, too.

A while ago, I said that you didn't have to be right when you were creating an alternate history: that by the nature of things you *couldn't* be right. It's still true. It has a back-asswards corollary, though. You'd better not be wrong about stuff you aren't changing deliberately. If you have British fighters accompanying British bombers on air raids over Germany in the early years of World War II, you *will* get letters—those alarmingly detailed letters—telling you those fighters couldn't have done that because they lacked the range. Again, someone will have failed to suspend disbelief and probably won't want to read on. Same thing goes for the shape of a '57 Chevy's tail fins and the price of shoes in 1902—or 1602.

If you aren't changing it on purpose and you can't be sure you're right about it, leave it out. A-h is a research-intensive subgenre; you need to resign yourself to that. If you can't, you'd once more be better off taking a swing at something else. This leads me to another point. The more of your research you do but don't show, the better off you are. "I've done my homework and you're gonna suffer for it" is one of alternate history's besetting sins. Expository lumps, friends, are right out. Research ought to be like an iceberg: ninety percent of it should stay under the surface of your story. If and when it crops out, it should do so in a few telling details, ones that make your reader feel *Well, of course he knows all that other stuff!* Tolkien, writing a fictitious history rather than an altered one, was particularly good at this.

One important difference between alternate history and other forms of sf and fantasy is that, with a-h, you aren't projecting onto a blank screen. If you're writing about the future or about a wholly created world, readers know only as much as you choose to tell them. The same goes for the people who inhabit your city on Tau Ceti II or in the imaginary Empire of Bebopdeluxe.

But what if you're writing about Chicago in 1881 in a world where the Confederacy won the Civil War? What if you're putting Abraham Lincoln in Chicago in that world in 1881? Everybody has ideas about Chicago. Everybody has ideas about what things were like for real in 1881. And everybody has ideas about Lincoln, too. In this altered world, what are some of the things you need to think about?

Chicago will probably be diminished economically to some degree, because a Confederate victory puts a national frontier halfway down the Mississippi. But it will still be an important east-west hub, definitely a big city. Overall life in the new world's 1881 likely won't be much different from how it was in ours. Again, because of losing the war and being divided, the rump of the USA may well be poorer than it was in reality. If that's relevant to the story you're telling, you can find ways to indicate it.

But Abraham Lincoln, Lincoln in 1881, *there's* your challenge as a writer. In the real world, of course, he was dead, and a revered martyr north of the Mason-Dixon Line. Here, he'll be past seventy. Is Mary Todd Lincoln still alive? If she is, what's she like? That will affect her husband. If she isn't, how and when did you have her die? (Isn't playing God fun?) That will also affect Lincoln.

He's not a martyr in the alternate world, obviously. Chances are he's not revered, either. After all, he's the President who led the USA into war against the CSA—and then lost it. Would he have won reelection in 1864, assuming the war was over by then? Chances are he wouldn't; you'll have to do more explaining if you say he did. What did defeat do to the Republicans? In real history, they dominated politics in the last third of the nineteenth century. Would they now? How do things look in Washington in the changed world (assuming you've left Washington in the USA)? What's Lincoln doing in Chicago, and how many people care?

And how does the brave new world he never really lived to see look to Lincoln? What does he think and feel about it? That's liable to be the crux of your story. He's watched laissez-faire capitalism take hold in the USA (and, don't forget, in the CSA) after the war. What does he think about it? He wrote some sharp things about the relationships between capital and slave labor. What would the relationships between capital and wage-slave labor look like to him? Has he ever heard of Karl Marx? What does he think about him, if he has?

I've offered answers to some of these questions in my novel, *How Few Remain*. The ones I proposed there certainly aren't the only ones possible. To me, alternate history is always more a game of questions than of answers, anyhow. The questions you come up with show what concerns you in the real world, even more than your answers will.

Real historians still play this game, too. Now they call it "counterfactuals." In my admittedly biased opinion, counterfactuals are much less interesting than alternate-history stories and novels. Why? Simple. Counterfactuals are illustrations of broad historical forces. Stories and novels are illustrations of character. People fascinate me; I have to confess that broad historical forces don't. You need both for any reasonably serious approach to the world's workings, but more people care more about people—a clumsy sentence, but true, and important to a writer.

Changing wars is an easy way to generate alternate histories. It's far from the only way. Altered history can spring from changed diseases. What would the world look like today if the Black Death had killed off ninety percent of Europe's population in the fourteenth century rather than "only" a third? What would it look like if HIV had spread out of Africa three hundred years before it really did?

You can play with geography, whether Earth's or the Solar System's.

If the lump of rock in the next orbit out from the Sun had been big enough to hold a reasonable atmosphere, our Viking probe might have got a humongous surprise when it touched down there. Or—who knows?—their probe might have discovered us instead. If the Mediterranean Sea had never refilled after evaporating when the gap between Gibraltar and Africa closed up five million years ago, what might that part of the world look like now? If glaciations and migration patterns had worked out differently, the Americas might have been settled by *Homo erectus*, not *Homo sapiens*. How would Europeans have treated subhumans when they found them here? (This notion, and my book called *A Different Flesh*, spring from a speculation by the late Stephen Jay Gould. Inspired by exactly the same speculation, Roger MacBride Allen wrote the fine *Orphan of Creation* at about the same time. Each of us was fascinated to see how the other used very similar research materials—and we've been friends ever since, not least because of the coincidence.)

If gold hadn't been discovered on Cherokee lands in the late 1820s, the Trail of Tears might never have happened, treaties between the USA and Native American tribes might have been more respected, and things might not have turned out quite so bad for our original immigrants. Might—you can't be sure.

And if that fender-bender hadn't made you an hour late for your job interview, you wouldn't have drowned your sorrows at the place next door to that office . . . and now, twenty years later, you wouldn't be married to your spouse. This is alternate history on what you might call the microhistorical level. Everyone has such stories. In a lifetime, you accumulate piles of them. It's so easy to imagine your life being different if you'd made another choice back then. And if it could happen to you, couldn't it happen to your country? Your world? Maybe Livy was pondering *his* long-ago fender-bender when he set pen to papyrus to talk about Alexander and the Romans.

I've mentioned researching a-h stories a few times. How do you go about that? If you want to capture the look and feel—and, most important, the language and attitudes—of a bygone time, use primary sources as much as you can. Primary sources are written by the people you're researching. A collection of Lincoln's speeches and writings is a primary source. A modern biography of him isn't—it's a secondary source. The advantage to using primary sources is that, with them, you are the only person standing between your source and your reader. Secondary sources add another layer of distancing, which isn't what you want. (Just in case you're wondering, it also isn't hard to find reprinted or plain used 1880s travel guides that will tell you more than you ever wanted to know about contemporary Chicago—what it was like before you went and changed it, at any rate.)

On this same principle, do as many things related to your novel yourself as you can, too. Nothing tells you more about what riding in an airship feels like than talking your way aboard the Goodyear blimp. You may not own an AK-47 yourself, but I wouldn't be surprised if you know someone who does. If you need to write about field-stripping one, watching where your friend has trouble will tell you where your characters may, too. If you set a novel in Hawaii, you should go there if you can possibly afford to; seeing the place first hand will tell you more about weather and smells and such than you can get from a zillion books. (The same is no doubt true of Buffalo, but the temptations are fewer there.) And remember, for a working writer such travel is deductible. Save those receipts!

If you're working on something contentious, you will often find out that one side says one thing, the other side says something else, and if you didn't know better you'd be positive they were talking about two different incidents. How do you decide who's telling the truth and who's lying? How do you decide if anyone's telling the truth? You do it the same way you do when two of your children are squabbling over the last cookie: you weigh the available evidence, you make up your mind, and you take your best shot. Sometimes, when your kids are going at it hammer and tongs, you feel like smacking both of them, though I hope you don't. Sometimes you feel like smacking your sources, too. Most of the time, you can't, which is bound to be a good thing.

To sum up, you need to make up your mind about what your change is and what it means to things that follow upon it, and you probably need to do a not-too-obtrusive job of establishing it in the front end of your story. (You can do this too well. I had a story bounced by an editor who couldn't tell where the real history left off and the a-h began. I had, honest, made this Perfectly Clear—to me, anyhow. Not to him/her. The story eventually sold elsewhere, so I don't think the beam was entirely in my own eye.)

And, most important, you need to have your changes matter to the people in your piece, whether those people are real ones in new circumstances or figments of your imagination. If you don't do that, you may have yourself a cool counterfactual, but you won't have a story. People, what they do, what happens to them, and why, are what make stories. One reason alternate histories are hard to do well is that your need to do the background stuff can make you look away from the people in the foreground. Especially at the shorter lengths, you just don't have room to do that, so try not to.

The rewards are the flip side of the difficulties. A good alternate history can make your readers look at the ordinary, mundane world in a whole new way. The urgent desire to blow somebody's mind is a very Sixties thing, you say? Okay, I plead guilty to that. But in closing, I will note that a good friend of mine once said writing a-h was the most fun you could have with your clothes on. I don't know for sure that she was right, but I don't know for sure that she was wrong, either. Your next assignment, should you choose to accept it, is to find out for yourself.

DRANG VON OSTEN

This story was written just as the Soviet Union was coming to pieces in the late summer of 1991. Yes, it's one where I was working from the headlines. It's a story that starts out looking like one thing and ends up—I hope—looking like something else. Science fiction isn't and isn't supposed to be prophecy, but I have to say that, more than twenty years after I did this piece, it looks at least as probable as it did when it was new. Maybe more so, or maybe, again, I'm judging from current headlines. Eventually, we'll all find out.

Buckets of rain poured down from the autumn sky. They turned the endless Russian plain into an endless swamp. The thick, gluey mud tried to suck the boots off *Gefreiter* Jürgen Sack's feet at every weary westward step he took.

The clouds and the deluge shut down visibility, too. The lance-corporal never knew the ground-attack plane was near until it screamed past just over his head, almost close enough for him to reach out and touch the big red star painted on the side of the fuselage. He threw himself face-down into the muck. A few of his comrades had the presence of mind to fire at the aircraft, but to no effect.

Half a kilometer west of Sack, the plane vomited cannon fire and rockets into the Germans retreating across the Trubezh. He swiped a filthy sleeve across his equally filthy face. "God help us," he groaned. "We'll never make it back to Kiev alive."

Beside him in the mud lay a staff sergeant who'd been at the front since the push east began in '41. *Wachtmeister* Gustav Pfeil said, "If you think the Reds are going to get you, they probably will. Me, I figure I'm still alive and they haven't got me yet." He pushed himself to his feet. "Come on. The sooner we cross the Trubezh, the safer we're liable to be."

Sack stumbled after him. You had to stay with your comrades, no matter what. Get cut off and dreadful things were likely to happen. Like too many other German soldiers, he'd seen what the Reds sometimes did to men they caught. Some of the roadside corpses had their noses cut off, others their ears. Others had their pants pulled down and were missing other things.

The lance-corporal lifted his face against the rain, letting it wash some of the dirt away from his eyes. Here and there, through the downpour, he saw other hunched figures tramping west.

A squeal in the sky, different from any aircraft noise. "Rockets!" he screamed, his voice going high and shrill as a girl's. He dove for the mud again, in an instant redestroying a couple of minutes' approach to cleanliness.

He was near the rear edge of the salvo of forty truck-mounted artillery rockets; no doubt they were all intended to slam down on the Germans struggling to cross the rain-swollen Trubezh. The noise and the blast were quite dreadful enough where he lay. He felt as if he'd been lifted and then slammed back to earth by a giant's hand. Fragments of rocket casing screeched past his head. They could have gutted him like a carp.

More rockets rained down on the crumbling German position east of the river. The enemy must have lined up a whole battery of launcher trucks axle to axle, Sack thought with the small part of his mind not terrified altogether out of rationality. To either side of him, wounded men's screams sounded tiny and lost amidst the shrieks and explosions of the incoming rockets.

Just when he was certain his company's hellish fix could not grow worse, shells began landing along with the rockets. Mud and dying grass fountained up into the weeping sky, then splashed down on men and on pieces of what had been men.

Then German artillery west of the Trubezh—the last defensive positions in front of the Dnieper and Kiev—opened up in counterbattery fire. The eastbound shells sounded different from incoming ordnance; instead of growing louder and shriller, their track across the sky deepened and got fainter as they dopplered away. But any response to the barrage under which he suffered was lovely music to Jürgen Sack.

The enemy fire slackened: maybe the counterbattery work had smashed the rocket launcher trucks. Sack didn't care about wherefores; the only thing that mattered to him was that, for the moment, the heavens were raining only water, not steel and brass and high explosive.

"Up!" he yelled, scrambling to his feet. "Up and get moving!"

At the same time, *Wachtmeister* Pfeil was shouting, "Come on, you lice! Head for the river! We have a chance to hold them there."

Between them, the two noncoms bullied almost all the huddled, terrified Germans into motion. A few did not move because they'd never move again. One or two more, still alive and unhurt, refused to get up even when Sack kicked them with his muddy boots. They'd taken all they could; even capture by the enemy, with its prospects of Siberia at the best, horrid death at the worst, could not stir them from their fatal apathy. Sack hurried on. Delaying to force the laggards up would only have meant dying with them.

A ragged German rear guard—men in flooded foxholes, three or four mechanized infantry combat vehicles, a couple of panzers—held a line on a low rise a couple of hundred meters this side of the Trubezh. A grimy lieutenant, his helmet knocked askew on his head, squelched toward Sack. The lance-corporal gulped, fearing he was about to be ordered to help hold that unholdable line. But the lieutenant just waved him toward the river. "Go on, go on. Get as many across as you can, while we keep the *verdammte* Asiatics off your backs."

Sack nodded and stumbled on. But when he started to come down from the rise toward the Trubezh, his feet for a moment refused to carry him forward. The ground-attack plane had caught German rafts in the water. Wreckage drifted downstream. So did dead men, and their fragments. Sack had read of battles where streams flowed red with blood. Till that moment, he'd thought it a novelist's conceit. No more.

Living soldiers still struggle in the Trubezh, too; a couple of rafts and barges that hadn't been hit wallowed up onto the western bank. Men in camouflage cloth and field-gray mottled and filthy enough to serve as camouflage cloth scrambled off, glad to put any water barrier, however small and flimsy, between themselves and the uncountable Asiatic horde swarming out of the east.

The boats started back toward the eastern bank of the Trubezh. Sack

dispassionately admired their crews, just as he admired the worn lieutenant in charge of that doomed rear-guard line. He admitted to himself
that he lacked the courage required to stick his head deliberately into
the tiger's mouth and leave it there while the fanged jaws closed.

Boots splashing at the marge of the river, *Wachtmeister* Pfeil posi-
tioned himself where one of the barges looked likeliest to ground. Sack
stood at his left shoulder, as if he were a feudal retainer. But chivalry in
the east was dead, dead. This war had room only for ugliness.

An old soldier, Pfeil knew all the tricks. As soon as the barge got
close, he splashed out into the Trubezh and helped drag it to shore. As
if by magic, that entitled him to a place on board. His big, rough hands
pulled Sack in after him.

Germans swarmed on until the rough water of the Trubezh was
bare centimeters from the gunwale. Even as the sergeant at the engine
threw it into reverse and backed the clumsy vessel away from the riverbank, more men reached out beseechingly, though they had to know
they'd swamp it if they managed to get aboard.

The cannon of one of the panzers posted on the eastern rise roared.
A moment later, a couple of MG-3 machine guns opened up. With
their rapid cyclic rate, they sounded like giants ripping enormous
sheets of canvas. However many bullets they spat, though, there always
seemed to be more short, stocky men who wore the red star on their
fur caps.

Some of the Germans by the riverside turned and ran back toward
the rearguard line to help buy their comrades time. Others threw down
weapons, stripped off clothes and boots, and plunged naked into the
chilly Trubezh: drowning looked to them a better risk than waiting
for another boat where they were. They swam almost as fast as Sack's
overloaded barge made headway across the river.

The lance-corporal became aware of an unfamiliar feeling. "Great
God, I'm almost warm!" he bawled into Pfeil's ear.

"I shouldn't wonder," the senior noncom answered. "We're packed
together tight as steers in a cattle car." Pfeil managed a worn grin. "I
just hope we're headed away from the slaughterhouse."

Sack tried to laugh, but after what he'd been through the past few
months—and especially the past few days—he couldn't force himself

to find it funny. Hardly more than a year before, German motorized patrols were operating east of the Volga and pushing toward Astrakhan over a steppe that seemed empty of foes. Now the Volga line was long forgotten. If the army couldn't hold the Reds along the Dnieper . . . if they couldn't do that, where would they stop them?

Deciding such questions was not a lance-corporal's concern. Sack watched the western bank of the Trubezh ever so slowly draw nearer. How long could crossing a couple of hundred meters of water take?

Too long—the barge was still wallowing toward the far shore when he heard another fighter-bomber screaming in on an attack run. Cannon shells whipped the river to creamy foam; underwing rockets lanced down on tongues of flame. Sack's scream was lost in those of his comrades.

One instant he was huddled in the barge, the next flying through the air, and the one after that floundering in the cold, muddy Trubezh. He must have swallowed a liter of it before he clawed his way to the surface and sucked in a lungful of desperately needed air. Then his boots touched bottom. He realized he was just a few meters from shore.

He splashed up onto the western bank and threw himself down at full length, more dead than alive. Or so he thought, till a roar in the sky warned that the enemy plane was coming back for another pass. He scrambled on hands and knees toward a shell hole that might offer some small protection.

He rolled in on top of another man who'd beaten him to it. "I might have known it would be you, *Wachtmeister*."

Pfeil grunted. "You can get hurt around here if you're not careful."

Both men buried their heads in the wet dirt, waiting for another dose of guns and rockets. But it didn't come. The Red fighter-bomber sheered off and streaked away eastward, two *Luftwaffe* fighters hot on its trail. Moments later, a blast louder than shellfire said one enemy aircraft, at any rate, would never harass German ground troops again.

Sack and Pfeil both shouted like men possessed. They pounded each other on the shoulders, clasped hands. "The air force *is* good for something!" the lance-corporal yelled, in the tone of an atheist suddenly coming to Jesus.

"Every once in a while," Pfeil allowed. "Haven't seen much of those bastards the past few weeks, though." Sack nodded. Too many hundreds of kilometers of front, too few planes spread too thin.

The two battered soldiers used the momentary respite to get away from the riverbank. Sack spotted an abandoned farmhouse, half its roof caved in, that looked like an ideal spot to curl up and rest for a while before getting back to the war. When he pointed it out to Pfeil, the staff sergeant grinned. He hurried past his junior to take the lead in exploring the retreat.

He and Sack both entered with rifles at the ready, in case partisans were lurking inside. And indeed, the farmhouse was occupied—but by German soldiers in too-clean uniforms with the metal gorgets of the military police round their necks. "What unit, gentlemen?" one of them asked with a nasty smile.

"First platoon, third company, second regiment, Forty-First *Panzergrenadiers*," Sack and Pfeil answered in the same breath.

"Where's the rest of it?" the military policeman demanded.

"Back in the hospital, dead on the field, drowned in the f— in the Trubezh," Pfeil said. "Oh, I expect some of our comrades are still alive, but we got separated. It happens in battle." His tone implied, as strongly as he dared, that his questioner had never seen real combat.

If the military policeman noticed the sarcasm, he didn't show it. One of his companions might have, for he said, "At least they have all their gear, Horst. Some of those fellows have been coming back without a stitch on them."

"As if the quartermasters didn't have enough problems," Horst snorted. Sack wanted to pump him full of bullets—here he was in his dog collar, with a safe post back of the line, making the lives of fighting men miserable. But Horst went on, "You're right, Willi, we have worse things to worry about. You two—there's a road, of sorts, about a hundred meters west of here. A kilometer and a half, maybe two, down that road are more *panzergrenadiers*. Attach yourself to their *Kampfgruppe* for the time being."

"Yes sir," Sack and Pfeil said, again together. They got out of the farmhouse in a hurry; the military police had almost certainly taken possession of it knowing it would attract tired soldiers.

The road, like too many Russian roads, was nothing more than a muddy track. Pfeil swore at the military police as he tramped along. Sack echoed him for a while—like any real soldier, he had only scorn for the dog-collar boys—but then fell silent. He didn't like what he'd heard back at the farmhouse. A *Kampfgruppe* was like papier-mâché: bits and pieces of defunct units squashed together in the hope they'd hold. Also like papier-mâché, battle groups fell apart when handled roughly.

Somebody in a foxhole shouted, "Halt!"

Sack and Pfeil obediently halted. "We're friends," Sack called. He stood still to let the sentry see his uniform.

"Stay," the sentry said. They stayed—he had the drop on them.

He didn't get out of the hole to check them himself, but called to someone else. The other soldier approached from the side, careful not to get between the foxhole and the two Germans. He too kept his assault rifle at the ready as he carefully examined Sack and Pfeil. But when he spoke to them, what came out of his mouth was gibberish, not German.

Now the two noncoms exchanged glances. "Should he worry about us being the enemy, or should we worry about him?" Pfeil muttered.

Then sack saw the rampant lion on the fellow's collar patch. "Norway?" he asked, pointing to it.

"*Ja!*" the other soldier exclaimed, and then more in his own language. Sack eyed him with increasing respect. Several western European nations had sent contingents to hold back the Red Asiatic flood, and those outfits had solid fighting reputations. Sack just wished their soldiers had picked up more German.

The Norwegian was a big blond fellow who might have posed for a recruiting poster if he'd been cleaner. He and Sack soon discovered they'd both taken English in school. Neither of them was fluent, but they managed to understand each other. The Norwegian said, "There is a—how do you say it?—a canteen? a kitchen?—down the road not far." He pointed to show the direction.

That cut conversation off at the knees, or rather at the belly. The German supply system had worked well for a while, with everyone having plenty of food and field kitchens keeping pace with the advancing armies. The armies were no longer advancing. Enemy aircraft had taken their toll on truck columns and supply trains. The long and short of it was that Sack hadn't eaten for more than a day.

The big bubbling pot smelled wonderful. Most of the soldiers gathered around it were Scandinavians of one sort or another: Norwegians, Danes who wore a white cross on a red shield, or Swedes with blue and gold emblems that were almost the same shades as those of the Ukraine's national colors. Some spoke German; more knew English. They all had the worn look of men who'd been through a good deal.

But the stew in the pot was thick and rich, full of cabbage, potatoes, and meat. Sack wolfed down a big bowl. "It's horsemeat," a Dane said apologetically in English. The corporal didn't quite take that in, so someone else translated: "*Pferdfleisch*." In civilian life, the idea would have revolted him. Now he just held out his bowl for more. The Scandinavians laughed and fed him.

He'd hardly begun his second helping when firing to the east picked up. Gustav Pfeil looked grim. "Eat while you can. I think the Reds are trying to force the river."

As if on cue, a German artillery battery not far away fired a salvo. Then Sack heard the heavy diesels of the self-propelled guns roar into life to move them into a new position before Red artillery could reply.

The Norwegian who'd led him to the field kitchen handed him a mug full of hot instant coffee. He gratefully held it under his nose. Even the rich aroma was invigorating. And the aroma was all he got, too, for a whistling in the air said the Germans hadn't knocked out all the enemy guns. Soldiers shrieked "Incoming!" in a medley of languages. Some, who'd been around here for a little while, knew where the slit trenches were and dove for them. Sack threw his coffee away and flattened out on the ground. The burst were thunderous, and less than a hundred meters from where he lay. Splinters flew by with deadly hisses; mud splattered down on top of his helmet.

Still on his belly, he pulled out his entrenching tool, unfolded it, and started digging himself in. The Red shells kept falling; it might as well have been a World War I bombardment. If it was going to be like that, Sack wanted himself a nice World War I trench in which to endure it.

Then Gustav Pfeil screamed.

Sack rolled out of his half-dug hole, crawled snakelike over to where the *Wachtmeister* lay writhing on the ground. Pfeil had both hands clenched to his thigh. His trouser leg was already reddish-black, his face gray.

"Medical officer!" Sack shouted. Then, more softly, he said to Pfeil, "Here, let me see it." His hands shook as he moved the staff sergeant's away from the injury. Pfeil had never been scratched, not in more than two years of hard fighting. How could he be wounded now? And if he was, how could anyone hope to come through this war intact?

The wound sliced cleanly into the meat of the thigh. Pfeil's flesh looked like something that ought to be hanging in a butcher's shop, not like part of a man at all. "I don't think the femoral artery's cut," Sack said inanely.

"Of course not," Pfeil replied with the eerie calm of a man in shock. "If it were, I'd already have bled out."

Sack dusted the wound with sulfa and antibiotics from his aid kit, wrapped a pressure bandage around it. One of the Danes came up to help a moment later. Along with his white cross on red, he wore a red cross on a white armband. He looked under the pressure bandage to see what Sack had done, nodded, and then rolled up Pfeil's left sleeve. He gave the *Wachtmeister* a painkiller shot, then said in good German, "Make a fist." When Pfeil obeyed, the Dane stuck the needle from a plasma unit into the bend of his elbow.

The medical officer turned to Sack. "I wish we could airlift him out, but—" A fresh barrage of incoming artillery punctuated the *but*. The Dane stood up anyhow, shouted, "Stretcher party!" first in German, then in English.

"I'm one," Sack said.

The Norwegian who'd guided the two Germans back to the kitchen came out of his hole. "I'm the other," he said in English. "I know the way back to the field hospital."

The medical officer pulled telescoping aluminum stretcher poles from his pack, extended them, and strung them with mesh. He fixed an upright metal arm to one of them to hold the plasma bag. Together, he and Sack got Pfeil onto the stretcher. "He should do well enough," the medical officer said, "unless, of course, we're all overrun."

Sack, for one, could have done without the parenthetical comment. He and the Norwegian stooped, lifted the stretcher, and started for the field hospital. Though they headed away from the fighting, no one could question their courage, not with artillery shells still falling all around. They would have been safer staying in their foxholes than walking about in the open.

Wachtmeister Pfeil was not a big man; he weighed perhaps seventy-five kilos. By the time Sack had hauled him through mud for more than a kilometer, it might as well have been seventy-five tonnes. He marveled that his arms didn't drag the ground like an orangutan's by the time he reached the aid station.

All the tents there were clean and white, with red crosses prominently displayed on the cloth. They wouldn't necessarily keep away artillery fire, but Sack did notice no bigger bombs had hit in the immediate vicinity of the tents. That raised some small measure of relief in him; too often, the godless Reds respected nothing.

An orderly took charge of Pfeil. Sack stood near the hospital tents for a couple of minutes. He windmilled his arms, trying to work the soreness out of them. The Norwegian did the same; they traded weary grins. The lance-corporal wondered what the devil to do next. He supposed he ought to go back to the *panzergrenadiers*; if any officer asked what he was doing there, he could say the military police had sent him.

The Norwegian rolled himself a smoke with old newspaper and coarse Russian *makhorka*. He offered Sack the tobacco pouch. Sack shook his head. "I never got the habit."

"Better for you," the Norwegian answered. He lit his own cigarette—no easy feat in the rain—and took a deep drag. "I like it, though."

"However you wish." Reluctantly, Sack started back toward the Trubezh River. Still puffing happily, the Norwegian followed. They hit the dirt whenever an incoming round sounded as if it might be close, but otherwise gave the bombardment only small heed.

Then a shell landed almost right on top of them, so suddenly they had no time to duck. The blast left Sack half deafened, and also with the feeling someone about the size of God had tried to pull his lungs out through his nose. Otherwise, though, he wasn't hurt. He looked around to make sure his new friend had also come through all right.

His stomach lurched. Only a burial party needed to worry about the Norwegian now, and they'd have to spoon him into a jar if they intended to sent his remains home. It was worse than butchery; it was annihilation. The only good thing about it was that the Norwegian couldn't have known what hit him.

Dazed and sickened, Sack staggered on. This wasn't how he'd pictured war when he first donned the German uniform. It wasn't so much that he hadn't imagined the death and injury that went with combat. He had, as well as one can without the actual experience. What he hadn't imagined was the horror and terror and dread they left in their wake, nor the filth and exhaustion of long combat, nor, most of all, that Germany, having pushed her frontier east almost two thousand kilometers, would ever see the line begin to shift west once more.

Trucks rumbled past him, heading away from the Trubezh. One of them stopped. Its driver was one of the Scandinavians with whom Sack had eaten. He poked his head out the window and said in English, "How goes your friend? And where is Olaf?"

"My friend will make it, I think," Sack answered, also in English. "Olaf—" He grimaced, turned. "Back there, a shell—" Speaking of death in a foreign language helped distance him from it, make it feel unreal, as if it could not possibly touch him.

"Shit," the driver said, and then, as if English did not satisfy him, he spoke several sharp sentences in Swedish or whatever his native tongue was. After he spat into the mud, he said, "You'd better climb inside. We're pulling back toward the Dnieper."

"Already?" Sack said, dismayed.

The driver only answered, "*Ja*. That is how my orders are."

The men in the back of the truck helped pull the lance-corporal aboard. He sat on somebody's lap the whole way. He was not the only one packed in like that, either, and the truck grew more crowded the further west it went. The compartment stank of unwashed men, mud, and damp.

The Scandinavians told different stories. Some thought the Reds had forced the line of the Trubezh in large numbers, while others claimed the enemy was sweeping down from the north and threatening to cut off all the German forces still on this side of the Dnieper. Whichever was true—if either was—it meant another retreat.

"When will it end?" asked the medical officer who had worked on Gustav Pfeil. No one answered him. The silence was in itself an answer of sorts, but not one to ease Sack's foreboding.

It was indeed another retreat. Over the rear gate of the truck, Sack saw panzers, mechanized infantry fighting vehicles, and self-propelled guns rumbling westward crosscountry, heading no doubt for the still intact bridges (he hoped they were still intact, at any rate) and the ferry links between the eastern bank of the Dnieper and Kiev on the far shore.

He'd passed through Kiev in the summer of '42, on his way to the front. German arms had still been winning victories then. He remembered the blue-and-gold Ukrainian flags everywhere in the city. He remembered the smiling girls who'd greeted and fed him at the soldiers' canteen across from the old Intourist Hotel on Vladimirskaya Street, some of them in the elaborately embroidered blouses, skirts, and headdresses of native Ukrainian fashion, others wearing dresses that had been the very latest styles in Berlin in the early thirties.

He wondered how many flags would be flying now, how many girls would want to have anything to do with soldiers who might have to pull out of their city at any minute. Not many, he suspected. Victory had a thousand fathers; defeat was always an orphan.

Just getting to Kiev looked like more of an adventure than he'd ever wanted. A shell hit the truck right behind his in the convoy, turned it into a fireball in an instant. He looked down at the tattered knees of his trousers, not wanting to watch his comrades burn. It could have been he as easily as they, and he knew it. Had the trucks not kept the ordained fifty meters' separation even in adversity and retreat, it could easily have been he *and* they.

One of the Scandinavians, a big burly Dane, pulled out a mouth organ and started playing American country songs. Sack was not the only one to smile when he heard them. Their incongruity here on a plain vaster than any in the United States somehow brought home the absurdity of war.

After jounces and jolts and halts where everyone scrambled out to put a shoulder to a wheel to get the truck out of the mud, it pulled to a stop not far from the Dnieper. "All out," the driver called over the intercom. "I'm going back for another load."

"Good luck to you," Sack called as the driver put the truck back into gear. The Scandinavian waved to him and drove off. He never saw the fellow again.

If the bank of the Trubezh had been crowded, that of the Dnieper fairly swarmed with men. Panzers and other fighting vehicles still crossed over into Kiev by way of the motor bridges still standing, but that way was closed to mere infantry, who might clog traffic and impede the flow of the precious armor. Military police directed foot-soldiers toward the boats boarding by the river.

The two biggest, the *Yevgeny Vuchetich* and the *Sovietskaya Rossiya*, were four-deck Dnieper excursion boats, seized when the Germans first took Kiev more than two years before. Along with a host of smaller craft, now they ferried German soldiers back to guard the city against recapture by the Reds.

The big boats each took aboard hundreds, maybe a thousand or more at a time. The smaller vessels added dozens, more likely hundreds, to that total. But the riverbank remained packed as men from the crumbling German positions east of the Dnieper streamed back to try to hold the line west of the river.

Such a concentration of men, unfortunately, also offered a delicious target for planes painted with the red star. Antiaircraft batteries fired furiously at the raiders, but bold pilots bored through to strike even so. The casualties were horrendous, but Germans still kept pressing down toward the bank. As at the Trubezh, the only alternative was to stand and fight, and that seemed a worse bet than trying to escape.

A ground-attack plane roared low overhead, firing cannon and rockets into the crowd of men. Just above Sack, it also let go with its chaff cartridges. But instead of strips of aluminized foil to baffle radar, the cartridges were filled with leaflets. They fluttered down on the Germans like warnings of doom from the heavens themselves.

Sack snatched one out of the air almost in front of his own nose. He read it quickly, before the cheap paper it was printed on turned soggy in the rain. THERE'S MONEY IN WAR . . . FOR SOME, the headline read. Sack snorted. "Not for me," he said aloud. He collected 108 Deutschemarks a month, including his combat pay bonus.

He read on: *For others, this war can only mean death and mutila-*

tion. Maybe you think Berlin is fighting for the European values your propaganda so loudly proclaims. The hard fact is that you are carrying out Berlin's vicious orders, and those of Mercedes, Siemens, I.G. Farben, and other capitalists who drink your blood to fatten their dividend checks. Where will that get you? Your armies are marked down for defeat; all your sufferings are futile. Your blood is worth marks on the stock exchange— but what cost to your folks at home?

Sack's folks had been bombed out of their homes a few weeks before. With rising anger, he finished the leaflet: *We have common enemies. Every member of the People's Liberation Army hereby guarantees: if you lay down your arms, you will not be harmed or humiliated. Your personal belongings will not be touched. You will receive any medical treatment you need. You will surely get home. Come on over, soldier. Just put down your weapon and say—*

Growling, Sack crumpled the paper and stuffed it into his pocket. He didn't care how the Reds said "surrender." But one of the other *panzergrenadiers* gave him a half-curious, half-suspicious look. "Why are you keeping that *Scheisse?*" the fellow asked.

"*Scheisse* is right," Sack answered. "How many better arsewipes have you seen lately?"

"None around here," the other fellow admitted. "Last time I dumped, I scraped my backside raw with dry grass."

The attack run of another Red fighter-bomber ended abruptly when a *Gepard* self-propelled antiaircraft cannon shot off its left wing. The plane slammed into the Dnieper with a tremendous splash. The Germans on the bank and on the boats cheered like wild men.

Little by little, Sack drew nearer the concrete stairway that led down to the embarkation point. As he filed down to the river, he fearfully watched the heavens—hemmed in as he was, he couldn't hope even to duck if shells or rockets started coming in or if another plane strafed the landing. He saw other faces also turned up to the rain. Knowing comrades shared his fright made it easier to bear.

Down by the river, military police with submachine guns kept the troopers boarding the boats in order. When a man in camouflage gear tried to shove his way onto an already crowded boat, they did not argue with him. One of them fired a short burst from point-blank range, then rolled the corpse into the Dnieper with the toe of his boot. After that, the line stayed orderly.

"This way! This way! This way!" a big fellow with a metal gorget shouted. Sack was among those whom he directed "this way": aboard the *Yevgeny Vuchetich*. The men packed the boat's four decks so tight no one had room to sit down. Combat engineers had mounted a 20-millimeter antiaircraft gun at the bow and another on the third deck at the stern, but the lance-corporal doubted their crews had room to serve them.

The old boat's overloaded diesel roared flatulently to life. Slowly, so slowly, it pulled away from the riverbank. The *Sovietskaya Rossiya* was a couple of hundred meters ahead. It had drawn close to the colonnaded mass of the river station when a bomb or a big rocket struck it amidships.

The excursion vessel seemed to bulge outward, then broke apart and sank like a stone. Hundreds of soldiers must have gone down with it. More hundreds thrashed in the chilly water. Many of them quickly sank, weighted down by their gear.

The *Yevgeny Vuchetich* slowed to throw lines to survivors and pull aboard those they could. Sack stared in horror as men drowned within easy reach of a line because they were too stunned to reach out and grab it. The boat did not save as many as it might have under other, more peaceful, circumstances, both because it was already overloaded itself and because stopping would have left it even more vulnerable to an attack like the one that had sunk its sister.

At the Pochtovaya Ploshchad river station, more military police lined the docks. Like their fellows on the east bank, they screamed, "This way! This way! This way!" As he followed their pointing arms into the station, Sack wondered if they knew how to say anything else.

Milling men in grimy uniforms filled the main hall. Still more men in dog collars profanely urged them on their way. One of the herd, Sack shambled sheeplike past wall panels depicting big blond men in chain mail (Varangians, he supposed), men with guns under red and gold hammer-and-sickle banners entering Kiev in triumph, and factories pouring smoke into the sky under the same Soviet emblem. The lance-corporal deliberately looked away from those. He had seen all the red flags he ever cared to look at.

The German military police *did* know how to say more than "This way!"—the ones at the rear of the station were shouting, "To the subway station! To the subway station!" That was an order Sack obeyed gladly; the farther underground he went, the safer he felt from Red air attacks.

More crowds of wet, stinking, dazed soldiers jammed the platform. When he'd been here last, the station had been immaculate. It was a long way from immaculate now. The trains did not run on time, either. Advancing as much from the pressure of the men behind him as by his own will, Sack moved toward the track.

After a longish while, he boarded a train. It rumbled through the darkness of the tunnel, then came to a jerky stop at Kreshchatik Station, only two stops south of Pochtovaya Ploshchad. The few Ukrainian flags that draped the inside of the station were faded and stained; he'd have guessed they were the identical banners he'd seen when he came through Kiev heading east to the front. Now he was back, and the front with him.

When he walked outside into the rain, he met only silence. He looked around in confusion, then turned to the soldier nearest him and said, "Where the devil are the boys in the dog-collars? I figured they'd be screaming at us here, same as everywhere else."

"Do you miss them so badly, then?" the other fellow asked, tugging at the straps of his pack. He and Sack laughed. They both knew the answer to that.

The lance-corporal started to say something more, but a public address system beat him to the punch and outshouted him to boot: "German soldiers detraining at Kreshchatik Station, report to Dynamo Stadium in Central Recreation Park. The stadium is north of the station. Signboards will direct you. German soldiers detraining at Kreshchatik Station—"

The recorded announcement ran through again, then shut off. Sack turned to the other soldier. "There, you see what they've done? They've gone and automated the bastards."

Sure enough, signs with arrows pointed the way up Zankovetskaya Street. Sack and his new companion, whose name, he learned, was Bruno Scheurl, ambled toward the park with other weary men coming up out of the subway.

He glanced over at the Moskva Hotel, which had taken shell damage when the Germans forced their way into Kiev. It looked as good as new now, all the rubble cleared away, all the glass in place. He wondered how long that would last. If Germany held the line of the Dnieper, it might survive intact a while longer. If not—if not, the hotel would be the least of his worries.

The Palace of Culture was similarly pristine; the Museum of Ukrainian Fine Arts on Kirov Street had not been damaged when Kiev fell. Across Kirov Street from the museum lay Central Recreation Park. The trees, green and leafy when Sack last saw them, now were skeletons reaching bony branches up to the dripping sky. The grass in the park lay in dead, yellowish-white clumps.

"Ugly place," Scheurl remarked.

"It's nice in summer," Sack said. "But I'm damned if I know how even Russians—excuse me, Ukrainians—live through winter hereabouts, especially when winter seems to run about eight months out of the year."

Near the entrance to Dynamo Stadium stood a granite monument more than twice the height of a man. In low relief, it showed four stalwart-looking men in the short pants and knee socks of footballers. A nearby plaque told who they were, but its Cyrillic letters meant nothing to Sack. He jerked a thumb at it, asked, "Can you read what it says?"

"Maybe. I did some Russian in school." Scheurl studied the plaque, then complained, "Ukrainians spell funny. I think it says these fellows were part of a team of Russian prisoners who beat a crack *Luftwaffe* team in an exhibition match during the last war—and got executed for it. The death match, they call it."

"Ha!" Sack said. "I wonder what really happened."

Shrugging, Scheurl headed into the stadium. Sack followed. Signs of all sorts in the stands and on the football field directed soldiers to their units. The rows of colorful seats were rapidly filling with field-gray. Military policemen served as ushers and guides. "What unit?" one of them asked Sack.

"Forty-First *Panzergrenadiers*, second regiment," the lance-corporal answered.

The fellow with the gorget glanced down at a hastily printed chart. "Section 29, about halfway up. Haven't seen many from your division yet."

Sack believed him. Too many comrades hadn't made it back over the Trubezh, let alone the Dnieper. He and Scheurl parted company, one of a thousand partings with brief-met friends he'd made since he came east.

The people who made the signs hadn't left a division's worth of room for the Forty-First *Panzergrenadiers*. Maybe they knew what they were doing; only a company's worth of men rattled around in the area, so many dirty peas in a pod too big for them. Sack found a couple of real friends here, though, men he'd fought beside for more than a year. They all looked as worn and battered as he felt. He asked after others he did not see. Most of the time, only shrugs answered him; once or twice, he got a grim look and a thumb's-down.

Somebody asked him in turn about Gustav Pfeil. "He took a leg wound, not too bad," he said. "I got him to a doctor. He should be all right, unless"—he found himself echoing the Danish medical officer— "the field hospital gets overrun."

"He may be luckier than all of us," somebody else said. "If he does make it, they'll fly him all the way back to Germany." Everyone in earshot sighed. Germany seemed more a beautiful memory than a real place that still existed. Reality—mud and blood and rain and fear—left scant room for beautiful memories.

Sack nervously looked around at the ever-growing crowd. "If they land a salvo of rockets in this place, they'll kill thousands," he said.

"We've got our own rocket batteries in the trees east of here, on the far side of the square," one of the other *panzergrenadiers* assured him. "They've knocked down everything the Reds have thrown so far."

Sack nodded and tried not to think about the potentially ominous ring of those last two words. "I notice there aren't a whole lot of vehicle crews here," he said. "Did the damned Asiatics take out that many panzers and combat vehicles?"

"No, that's not as bad as it seems," the other *panzergrenadier* said. He was a little skinny fellow named Lothar Zimmer, and seemed to have been born without nerves. "There's a big vehicle park north of here, and most of the crews are trying to get their machines serviced. The fellows you see here are just the orphans, the ones who had theirs blown out from under them."

"That's a relief, anyhow. I was beginning to wonder if we had any armor left at all."

One thing the Germans knew almost instinctively was how to organize. Without that skill, the campaigns across the vast distances of European Russia would have been impossible to imagine, the more so as the Reds had more machines and far more men than did Germany or even Europe as a whole. Even with it, the tide was flowing west now, not east.

Still, as he watched Dynamo Stadium fill, Sack had to believe Germany would hold the onrushing Communist hordes out of Europe. Each of the men here was worth two, three, four of his foes, thanks to the combination of discipline and initiative the German army had mastered better than any other. Given a spell to regroup and breathe a little behind the barrier of the Dnieper, they'd surely halt the Reds and keep most of what they'd won in these past bloody two and a half years.

Yet no sooner had the sight of so many Germans sorting themselves out by unit boosted the lance-corporal's confidence than whispers began running through that crowd of soldiers. Sack could almost watch them spread by the way the men turned toward each other like so many stalks of wheat bending in the breeze. Where the whispers had passed, silence lay heavy.

They came piecemeal to the Forty-First *Panzergrenadiers*, a word here, a word there: *balkas* (the gullies that crisscrossed the country on both sides of the Dnieper), helicopters, Reds. By now, Sack had had a lot of practice at joining a word here with a word there and making a whole rumor of it. "They've crossed the river," he said. He sounded almost as stunned as *Wachtmeister* Pfeil had after the shell fragment laid open his leg.

Another word came: bridgehead. Then another: breakthrough. Lothar Zimmer could paste them together, too. "If they break through here, where do we stop them next?" he said. No one answered him.

The stadium loudspeakers began to bellow, ordering units to report to concentration points scattered all through Kiev. Chatter stopped as men listened for their own assignments. Eventually, Sack's came: "Forty-First *Panzergrenadiers* to vehicle park seventeen, Forty-First *Panzergrenadiers* to vehicle park seventeen!"

"Is that the one you were talking about?" the lance-corporal asked Lothar Zimmer. The little swarthy fellow nodded. He got to his feet and trudged off. Sack followed, glad to be with someone who knew where he was going.

What he found when he got to the vehicle park dismayed him. Only a fraction of the division's panzers, self-propelled guns, and mechanized infantry combat vehicles stood there. To eke them out and give the Forty-First *Panzergrenadiers* a fraction of the mobility they'd once enjoyed, a motley assortment of captured Red equipment and impressed civilian cars and trucks sprawled across the asphalt. Maintenance personnel were still slapping hasty tape crosses onto their doors and sides to identify them as German.

"Look at all this soft-skinned junk," Sack blurted. "The Reds won't need missiles to take it out. They won't even need machine guns. An officer's pistol ought to do the job nicely."

"They'll get some of us there, wherever 'there' is," Zimmer said, shrugging. "Once that happens, we're on our own, but that's the way it always works."

To Sack's relief, a lieutenant waved him into a mechanized infantry combat vehicle. He peered out through the *Marder*'s firing ports as it began to roll. At least he had a modicum of armor between himself and the unfriendly intentions of people in the wrong uniforms.

Somebody inside the *Marder* came up with a name for where it was heading: Perayaslav, about eighty kilometers south and east along the Dnieper. *An hour's drive on the Autobahn*, Sack thought. It took the rest of the day and all night. Not only did the alleged highway stop being paved not far out of Kiev—which slowed the impressed vehicles to a crawl—the enemy had it under heavy bombardment from artillery and rockets both.

An antitank missile fired at extreme range from across the Dnieper took out the lead panzer and forced everyone else to detour around its blazing hulk. That made delays even worse. Jets blazoned with red stars arrogantly screamed past overhead. They raked the column with cannon fire and more missiles. The *Luftwaffe* was nowhere to be found. The Germans expended their whole stock of surface-to-air missiles before they got halfway to Perayaslav. As far as Sack could tell, they hit nothing.

He must have dozed in spite of the racket and the rough ride, for he woke with a jerk when the *Marder* stopped. He had to piss so bad, it was a miracle he hadn't wet himself while he slept. Artillery boomed ahead. He licked his lips. The firing sounded heavy. It was almost all incoming.

Somebody banged on the combat vehicle's entry doors with a rifle butt. Lothar Zimmer was sitting closest to them. When he opened the metal clamshell, whoever was outside handed him a bucket full of stew. He took it with a word of thanks and set it down between the two facing rows of seats. Everyone dug in with his own spoon. It was vile stuff, mostly potatoes and grease by the taste, but it filled the belly.

Sack took advantage of the lull to leap out and empty his bladder. Another *Marder* had stopped in the mud a few meters away. One of its crewmen—likely the driver, judging by his fancy helmet packed full of electronics—stood by his machine doing exactly the same thing as Sack. The little the lance-corporal could see of his face looked gloomy. "We're for it now," the fellow said.

"What do you know?" Sack asked eagerly. Nobody bothered telling infantrymen anything, but a driver couldn't help but get the word over the radio net.

The man answered, "The Reds are pushing hard. You can hear the guns, can't you?" He didn't give Sack a chance to answer. "Their field engineers have done something sneaky, too. They've built their pontoon bridges half a meter *under* the surface of the fucking Dnieper. Makes 'em harder to spot, a lot harder to knock out, but men and panzers just keep on coming across."

"Bad," Sack said. The driver grudged him a nod, then climbed back into his fighting vehicle through the front hatch. He slammed the hatch down after him. The *Marder*'s diesel roared. Its tracks spat mud as it headed toward the fighting.

When Sack returned to his own *Marder*, he passed on the news the driver had given him. His comrade's faces said they were as delighted as he had been. The combat vehicle got moving again.

A roar from the turret announced the launch of an antitank missile. Sack clutched his assault rifle and hoped it hit. If it didn't, the Red panzer would return fire, and the *Marder* wasn't armored against the big, fast, hard-hitting shells a 150-millimeter panzer cannon threw.

The *Marder* didn't blow up in the next few seconds, so the missile must have done its job. The combat vehicle stopped about a minute later. "This is where you get out, lads," the driver announced over the intercom. "Good luck. *Gott mit uns.*"

"*Gott mit uns,*" Sack echoed as he reluctantly left the relative safety of the *Marder*. He and his mates formed a skirmish line, each man six or eight meters from his comrades. The driver let them get a couple of hundred meters ahead, then followed, his cannon ready to deal with any threats their personal weapons could not handle.

Glancing left and right, Sack saw more men heading up into the front lines with his squad, more combat vehicles moving with them to provide covering fire. He and his comrades were pushing through the battered German trench lines when the real Red artillery bombardment began. He leaped into a hole (he had endless variety from which to choose), held his helmet on his head with one hand, and waited for the nightmare to end.

It lasted two solid hours that seemed two years long. The ground shook and jerked, as if in unending earthquake. The Reds were giving it everything they had, rockets, shells, all different calibers, every weapon firing fast as it could. They wouldn't have much ammunition left when the barrage was over, Sack thought dazedly somewhere in the middle of it, but that might not matter, either.

The pounding let up at last. When Sack raised his head, he saw the German lines, already cratered, now resembled nothing so much as a freshly plowed field. Through the rain, through the mud, through the rubble, seemingly straight for him, came the Red ground attack.

It was, in its way, a magnificent sight. The green-clad troops stormed forward almost shoulder to shoulder, assault rifles blazing, a wave of men to swamp the Germans who still survived. Panzers and armored fighting vehicles rumbled forward in their wake; jets and assault helicopters roared overhead with missiles and cannon to engage German armor.

Sack wanted to empty his magazine into the onrushing horde. But if he and his comrades opened up too soon, the Asiatics would just dive for cover before enough of them could be slaughtered. "Fire discipline," he said out loud, reminding himself.

He and his comrades showed their training. Almost everyone started shooting at the same instant. The pieces of German artillery that hadn't been knocked out added their voices to the fire fight. The infantry in green went down like wheat cut too soon. But as the first wave fell, another took its place.

A brilliant white flash marked an enemy panzer brewing up; some infantryman's wire-guided missile had struck home. But it was like fighting the hydra; for every head cut off, two more took its place. Sack scrambled backwards to keep from being outflanked and cut off.

He looked back toward the *Marder* that had brought him into action. It was burning. How many divisions had the Reds managed to crowd into their fucking bridgehead, anyhow, and how much heavy equipment? *Too many and too much* was all he could think as he retreated past the combat vehicle's corpse.

Something moved behind the *Marder*. As if it had a life of its own, his assault rifle swung toward the motion. But before he squeezed off a burst, he saw it was Lothar Zimmer. He pointed the muzzle of his weapon at the ground. "You still alive, Zimmer?" he croaked.

"I think so," the other German said. He looked as battered, as overwhelmed, as Sack felt. Staring at the lance-corporal as if Sack had all the answers, he asked, "What do we do now?"

"Try as best we can to get out, I guess," Sack answered. It wasn't going to be easy; firing came not only from in front of them and from both flanks, but from the rear as well. While their little piece of the battle hadn't gone too badly, overall the Reds were forcing the breakthrough they'd sought.

The two Germans started north, back toward Kiev. Sack hoped the enemy would take no special notice of them in the rain and the confusion. For a couple of kilometers, those hopes were realized. But just when he began to think he and Zimmer really might get away free, a burst of machine-gun fire sent them diving into a ditch.

The fire let up for a moment. "Surrender or die!" a Red yelled in mangled German.

"What do we do?" Zimmer hissed.

"What *can* we do?" Sack said hopelessly. But if he stood up, even with his hands in the air, he was afraid the machine gunner would cut him in half. Then he remembered the propaganda leaflet he'd stuffed in his pocket, intending to use it for toilet paper. He dug it out, scanned it quickly. "*Tow shong!*" he shouted, as loud as he could. "*Tow shong, tow shong!*"

"*Tow shong?*" The Red pronounced it differently; Sack hoped he'd been understood. Then the enemy switched to German: "Surrender?"

"*Ja*, surrender. *Tow shong!*" Now Sack did stand. After a moment, Zimmer followed his lead. Their assault rifles lay in the mud at their feet, along with their dreams.

Several green-clad soldiers ran up to them. Grins on their flat, high-cheekboned faces, their almond eyes glittering with excitement, they searched the Germans, stripped off their watches, their aid kits, and everything else small and movable they had on their persons.

One of the Reds gestured with his weapon. Hands high, Sack and Zimmer stumbled toward captivity. A soldier of the Chinese People's Liberation Army followed to make sure they did not try to escape.

HOXBOMB

We've built our technology on chemistry and physics. We're just starting to get a handle on genetics and biochemistry. Most of the coming century's big advances will probably be in those areas, and chances are people alive now would have no more idea what to make of what they'll have in a hundred years than someone from 1850 swept forward a hundred years would know what to do with a television set . . . or an atomic bomb. And aliens who based their civilization on biotech would be just as wary of our mastery of the other stuff as we would by what they could do. This is a story of that kind of meeting.

They met by twilight.

The hours when day died and those when night passed away were the only ones humans and Snarre't comfortably shared. Jack Cravath thought it was a minor miracle humans and Snarre't shared anything on Lacanth C.

You had to try to do business with them. Everybody said so. Everybody, in this case, was much too likely to be right. If the two races didn't get along, they had plenty of firepower to devastate a pretty good stretch of this galactic arm. Black-hole generators, ecobombs, Planck disruptors, tailored metaviruses . . . The old saying was, they'd fight the war after this one with rocks. Not this time around—there'd be nobody left to do any fighting, and the rocks would be few and far between, too.

By one of those coincidences that made you think Somebody had it in for both species, they'd found Lacanth C at the same time 150 years earlier. They'd both liked the world. What was not to like? It was a habitable planet, as yet unscrewed by intelligent life of its own. They both wanted it. They both needed it, too. In lieu of a coin flip, stone-paper-scissor, or that spiral-arm-wrecking war, they decided to settle it jointly.

Codominium, they called it. On Earth, such arrangements went back to the seventh century CE—ancient days indeed—when the Byzantines and Arabs shared Cyprus for a while. The Snarre't had precedents of their own. Jack Cravath didn't know the details about those; he just knew there were some.

And he knew codominium worked—as well as it worked, which often wasn't very—only because all the alternatives that anybody could see were worse. His own alternatives were none too good right this minute, either. By choice, he would have closed his scooter dealership when the sun set and gone home to dinner with his newly pregnant wife. But that would have shown interspecies insensitivity. You didn't do such things on Lacanth C, not if you had anywhere close to your proper complement of marbles you didn't.

He sat in his office instead, while darkness deepened around him. The ceiling lights began to glow a dull, dim orange. As far as anybody could tell, that amount and shade of illumination annoyed both races equally.

In a little more than an hour, when it was full dark outside, he could legitimately close. Then he could use his IR goggles to get out of the interspecies business district in Latimer and back to the human residential zone, where such perverse curiosities as street lights were allowed. His stomach growled. Beverly's good chicken stew tonight. He was hungry, dammit.

He could watch the street from his dealership. Humans went by on scooters or, occasionally, on Snarre'i drofs or caitnops. Far more Snarre't rode their beasts, but some of them sat on scooters. That was why—aside from law and custom—he kept the dealership open into their hours. Every so often, he did business with them. He wasn't allergic to fattening up his credit balance, not even a little bit.

That wasn't the only reason he was always happy when he unloaded a scooter on a Snarre'. Drofs and caitnops creeped him out. They looked like nothing so much as Baba Yaga's house, only with most of the house part gone: oversized yellow scaly legs with a platform for the rider and handholds through which he controlled his drof. Press here, and it went forward. Press *here*, and it stopped. Press here, and it turned right. Press *here*—left. Press here and *here*, and it opened its mouth so you could give it some yummy drof treats.

He shivered. The Snarre't had a technology that mostly matched and sometimes outdid humanity's. But theirs was biotech from the ground up, with mechanical gadgets as relatively recent high-tech innovations. It wasn't the way humanity had done things, but it worked.

Caitnops and drofs did what they did about as reliably as scooters did the same thing. Human programmers and engineers had loudly insisted biocomputers could never come close to electronic gadgets . . . till the Snarre't showed they were talking through their hats.

For their part, the Snarre't thought the idea of the Turing test was the funniest thing they'd ever heard. Of course computers were intelligent, as far as they were concerned. How not, when they were built from neurons? And the Snarre't had left in the pain response, even amplified it, to make sure their servants didn't turn into masters. Jack shivered again.

He looked at his watch. Half an hour till he could bail out. He thought about chicken stew, and about Bev, and about the baby due in 270 days or so (talking about months was pretty silly on a world without a moon—Lacanth C's year was divided into neat, tidy tenths). Beverly'd found out within hours that she'd caught. That was a Snarre'i-derived test; humanity's reagents weren't nearly so sensitive. He smiled. The baby would be their first.

The door opened. Two Snarre't walked in. Jack muttered under his breath. Bev wouldn't be happy if he came home late. But she would if he made a sale. "I greet you," he called to them in Snarre'l.

"Hello," they chorused in English. Using the other race's language first showed you had manners.

Returning to English himself, Jack asked, "What can I do for you today?"

Both Snarre't showed their teeth in the gesture that meant they were amused. They had more teeth, and sharper ones, than humans. Their noses were three vertical slits in their round faces, their eyes enormous and reflective, as suited nocturnal creatures. They had big ears that twitched, ears that put the legendary Alfred E. Newman to shame. They didn't wear clothes; they had gray or brown pelts. All in all, they looked more like tarsiers than any other earthly beasts . . . but they didn't look a hell of a lot like tarsiers, either.

"We would like to buy from you some meat," the taller one said in—probably—her own language. The babelfish in Cravath's left ear translated the word. The wider rictus on the other Snarre's face translated the sarcasm.

Thinking of Beverly, Cravath answered, deadpan, "I can give you a good deal on chicken stew."

He didn't know exactly how the Snarre't turned English into their tongue. Maybe a worm in their brains—and, with them, it would be a literal worm, not a gadget—did the translating. Maybe . . . Well, since he didn't know, what point to worrying about it?

The shorter Snarre' said, "We are interested in trying the Model 27 two-seater. If we like it, perhaps we will also get from you some chicken stew."

They both thought that was pretty funny. Jack Cravath dutifully smiled. Were they a mated pair? Jack thought so, but he wasn't sure. Among Snarre't, females were usually taller than males, but not always. Their sex organs were neatly internal unless they were mating, and females had no boobs: despite the fur, they weren't mammals, but fed their young on regurgitated food like birds.

"A Model 27, you say?" the dealer echoed. Both Snarre't splayed their long, spindly fingers wide: their equivalent of a nod. Cravath went on, "Well, come with me, and I'll show you one. What sort of payment did you have in mind?"

There was the rub. Humans had a burgeoning economy, and the Snarre't had a burgeoning economy, and the two were about as much like each other as apples and field hockey. Each species' notion of what constituted wealth seemed strange, stranger, strangest to the other. That turned every deal into a barter—and a crapshoot.

"Knowledge, perhaps," the taller alien said. "We have a brain that is getting old but is not yet foolish with age. This might be a good enough price, yes?"

"It might, yes." Jack tried not to sound too excited. How much good did that do? If they got a whiff of his pheromones, they'd know he was. Snarre'i brains intrigued human scientists the same way human electronics fascinated the aliens. Different ways of doing the same thing . . . He was pretty sure he could get more for even an old one than a Model 27 was worth. "Step into the showroom with me, why don't you?"

"We will do that," the taller one said, and they did.

He made his best pitch for the Model 27. He talked about its speed, its reliability, and its environment-friendly electric motor. "You don't have to clean up after it, either, the way you do with your drof."

"We don't mind. Drofshit is for us pleasant—more than pleasant—to eat," the shorter Snarre' said. Jack kept his face straight. You couldn't expect aliens to act like people: the oldest cliché in the book, but true. They weren't asking *him* to eat candy turds. *A good thing, too*, he thought. But they'd bred their animals to do that, which was not the sort of thing people would ever have thought of . . . he hoped.

"May we test drive?" the taller one asked.

"Sure," Jack said. "Let me check the headlight to make certain it's not up too bright." In the human part of Latimer, people needed headlights when they drove at night. The kind of light levels humans preferred would have blinded Snarre't, though. When the aliens had to go out by day, they wore sun goggles even more elaborate than the IR jobs humans needed to see at night without raising havoc among the Snarre't.

"Thank you for your courtesy," both aliens chorused, and he could hope they meant it.

The headlight was okay. Cravath asked, "Whichever one of you is driving is allowed to use a scooter? You are of the proper age and know how?"

"Oh, yes," the Snarre't said together. The taller one pulled what looked like a caterpillar out of its fur and breathed on the thing, which glowed a faint pink. "You see?" When a Snarre' asked if a human saw, the alien always sounded doubtful. To them, humans *didn't* see very well, and being adapted to do best in daylight didn't count.

But Jack Cravath nodded. That response on that thing meant the same as a green light on a human computer reader scanning a driver's license. He didn't know why, but he knew it did.

"Shall we try it, then?" the shorter one said. "Our drof is yours if we fail to return the scooter."

Jack wanted a drof like a hole in the head. But what could he say? "Go ahead," he answered. "Come back in twenty minutes."

"Agreed," the two Snarre't said. The taller one got on the scooter in front. The shorter one sat behind. Jack held the door open for them. Out they went. They turned the headlight on. The orange glow was just bright enough to warn humans who weren't wearing IR goggles. That was what interspecies law required, and they lived up to it . . . barely.

Out on the street, the drof's big eyes—much like those of the Snarre't themselves—swung to follow the scooter as it purred away. How smart *were* drofs? Humans had acquired a good many, just as the Snarre't had a fair number of scooters by now. It remained an open question, though. Some scientists maintained they were only bundles of reflexes; others insisted more was going on.

As for the Snarre't, they weren't talking. Nobody human was even sure the question meant anything to them.

Jack pulled his phone off his belt to warn Bev he'd be late. "What? You've got Furballs in the office?" she said.

"Well, they're taking a test drive now." Jack was glad the two Snarre't were, too. If their translator picked up what his wife said, they could nail her on a racism charge—or threaten to, and screw him to the wall on the scooter deal. The two races sharing Lacanth C didn't have to love each other, but they did have to make nice where the other guys were listening. Cravath continued, "Anyway, I'll get back as soon as I can. Go ahead and eat. I'll nuke mine when I come in."

"Okay," Beverly said. She was so freshly pregnant, she hadn't even started morning sickness yet. Her appetite was still fine. "Don't be too long."

"I'll try not to. It isn't just up to me. Love you, babe. 'Bye." Jack stowed the phone.

He looked at his watch. Naturally, the Snarre't didn't use hours and minutes; they had their own time units. Translators were usually pretty good about going back and forth with those. But if this one had screwed up . . .

Nineteen minutes and forty-one seconds after they left, the two aliens drove back into the showroom. "It is a very different sort of conveyance," the taller one said. "Less responsive than a drof—you cannot deny that."

"But peppier," the shorter one said. "Definitely peppier."

The taller Snarre's big googly eyes swung towards its partner or friend or whatever the shorter alien was. Jack didn't know for sure, but he guessed that meant the same it would have with people. *Don't praise what we're shopping for. You'll run up the price.*

If the shorter one noticed, he—she?—didn't let on. "The price we proposed before is acceptable?" the Snarre' asked Jack. "For the scooter, our aging but still functional brain?"

The babelfish translation made that sound pretty silly, as if the aliens would open up their heads and pour out whatever was inside. But Jack Cravath spoke formally: "Yes, the price you proposed before is acceptable."

"Draw up the contracts, then," the taller one said.

"How old is the brain you want to trade for the scooter?"

"Six years. Six years of Lacanth C."

"Okay." Jack spoke into the office business system. It spat out contracts in English and in Snarre'l. Jack reviewed the English versions to make sure they had the deal straight. He signed all the copies, thumbprinted them, and added a retinal scan to each one. The aliens also signed in their angular squiggles. They pressed a special area on each contract to an olfactory gland under the base of their stumpy tails. Those chemical signatures were supposed to be even more distinctive and harder to counterfeit than retinal scans.

"I will get the brain." The smaller Snarre' went out to the drof and stroked it. A pouch opened. If Baba Yaga were a kangaroo instead of a chicken . . . But the edge of the pouch had teeth, or something an awful lot like them. The Snarre't discouraged drof thieves.

Back came the alien. He—she?—put the brain on the counter. It looked up at Jack out of disconcertingly Snarre'-like eyes. *Have to keep it in the dark*, he thought. A tagline floated through his mind: *and feed it bullshit.* It was about the size of a basketball, with two little arms and four little legs. Its fur was molting here and there. It looked like something that had seen better days.

"What *do* I feed it?" Jack asked.

"Here is about ten days' worth of brain food." The Snarre' set a membranous sack on the counter by the brain. "You can get more from any of our merchants." Another, smaller, sack went by the first one. "And here, because you have shown yourself to be congenial, are some spices for flavoring your food. They are not harmful to your kind. It is likely—not certain, for taste is never certain—you will find them flavorsome. They are a gift. We ask nothing in return for them."

That was also polite. Even so, Jack said, "Well, thank you very much. Let me give you my stapler here." It was the first thing he saw on his desk. He showed them what it was for, and threw in a box of staples.

They seemed happy enough with the theoretically optional return gift. He wondered how they held papers together. Pointy twigs? Bugs with sharp noses? Something biological—he was sure of that.

They took their copy of the contract. One of them got on the scooter. The other tethered the drof to the new purchase. Away they went. Jack got on the phone. "Made the sale. On my way. See you soon."

"Oh, good," Bev said. "I didn't start after all, but I was going to pretty soon."

"Back as quick as I can," Jack told her. "'Bye."

His own scooter was parked out front. He eyed the brain, which was sitting on the counter. It looked back at him. Did it know it belonged to him now? If it did, what did it think of that? Rather more to the point, how was he supposed to get it home without hurting it?

He found a cardboard box and put the brain into it. To his relief, it didn't kick up a fuss. It said something in Snarre'l. The babelfish gave Jack gibberish. "It'll be okay, honest," he said in English, and hoped he wasn't lying. Did the brain understand? Whether it did or not, it kept quiet. That would do.

Jack set the box between his knees as he got on the scooter. That was the best way he could think of to keep it safe. As soon as he put in the key, the scooter's electric motor whispered to life. Getting home to Bev made him want to speed up. Protecting the brain made him want to slow down. He probably ended up somewhere in the middle.

He could tell the second he left Latimer's mixed-race central business district and got back to the human-settled east side of town. Street lights became bright enough to be useful. He turned the rheostat on the headlight switch and lifted his goggles onto his forehead. Now he could really see where he was going. The Snarre't might be nocturnal, but he wasn't.

The brain was. As the lights brightened, it made a small, whimpering noise. It was taking in more glare than it could handle. He put his riding jacket over the top of the box. The brain stopped whining, so he supposed he'd done the right thing.

He stopped at a traffic light—one more reminder he was in the human part of Latimer. Another scooter pulled up alongside his. "Hey, Jack!" the man on it said. "How you doing?"

"Oh, hello, Petros," Jack answered. Petros van Gilder lived around the corner from him. He sold a rival firm's scooters. They forgave each other their trespasses. Jack went on, "I'm tolerable. How's by you?"

"Fair to partly cloudy," van Gilder answered. "What's in the box?"

"Snarre'i brain. I sold 'em a two-seater, and this is what I got for it."

"Not too shabby." Petros stuck out his hand, which he'd kept in the pocket of his riding jacket. "Way to go. I had a near miss with the Furballs the other day, but I couldn't close the deal. Congrats."

"Thanks." Jack shook hands with him. "Yeah, that ought to make the firm a tidy little profit once I sell it to the right people. Some left over for me, too."

"There you go," Petros said. The light turned green, and he zoomed off. Jack would have, too, if not for the brain in the box. He followed more sedately. Van Gilder would get home ahead of him tonight.

He parked in front of the house when he did arrive. One of Lacanth C's big selling points for human colonists was that it was roomy enough for every family to enjoy its own house and lot. That was one more thing the Snarre't didn't grok. Most of them lived in apartment warrens. They liked crowding together. Smells meant more to them than they ever would to humans.

Come on now, dear. Let's sniff the Hendersons' butts. To humans, the talking dogs made a classic T-shirt. The Snarre't wouldn't have got the joke, because they really did stuff like that.

Cravath carried the box to the house. He kept his jacket over it, because the lights were bright—if you were something (someone?) the Snarre't had bioengineered. He unlocked the front door and let himself in. "Hi, hon!" he called. "I'm home!"

"What have you got there?" Beverly asked. She was short and blond and plump, and worked for a quantum-mantic outfit that would have to learn to do without her before too long.

He explained about the brain again. She was suitably impressed. He told the house to turn down the lights. "Now I can uncover it without hurting its eyes," he said.

He tossed the jacket on a chair. Bev peered down at the brain. "It looks so sad," she said.

"I thought the same thing. I'll give it some food. Maybe that'll perk it up. Would you get some water for it, too, please?"

Bev did, in a plastic cup. The brain ate and drank. It still looked sad after it finished. Jack was happy after chicken stew and a bottle of beer. He tried some of the Snarre'i spices in the stew. He liked them. Bev stayed away from them even so, for fear that anything alien wouldn't be good for a rapidly growing fetus. She didn't drink any beer, either, and she liked it.

They celebrated the sale of the scooter back in the bedroom. The brain stayed in its box in the kitchen. Did it know what was going on at the other end of the house? If it did, it couldn't do a damn thing about it. *Poor thing*, Jack thought.

Did brains mate with other brains to make more brains? Or did the Snarre't clone them one at a time from a genetic template marked *brain*? Cravath had no idea. Was the brain in the box male or female? Or, if it was a clone, had the Snarre't bioengineered all the complications of sexuality out of it? If they had . . . *Poor thing*, Jack thought again.

Well, he was going to sell it to the humans best equipped to take care of it. How well would the Snarre't have cared for an aging indoor cat? That comparison didn't occur to Jack, or he probably would have thought *Poor thing* one more time.

He got almost as much for the brain as he hoped he would. The retail price for which he would have sold the scooter to humans went into the firm's account. The rest went into his. Were the tall Snarre' and the shorter one making similar arrangements? Had they bought the scooter for themselves, or were their engineers tearing the tires and the power-pack to pieces, trying to figure out how they worked?

That wasn't his worry. Neither was the brain, not any more.

He and Bev used the extra credit in his account to take a South Coast vacation. They lay in the sun and swam in the sea. He drank drinks with plastic rocketships in them. She stuck to fruit nectars and occasional sips stolen from his mugs. She was being good for the baby's sake. He admired her for that.

When they got home, a genetics scan showed that it was a boy, and that it suffered from none of the 400 commonest genetic syndromes. That scan came free with their medical coverage. If they wanted to check for the next 400, they would have to pay for the test. Beverly looked up the incidence rate of syndrome 401. It was named for four twenty-first-century doctors, and occurred, the data net said, once in every 83,164,229 births.

"What do you think?" she asked Jack.

"Your call, babe. We can afford it if you want to do it," he said. If, God forbid, anything really rare was going on, he didn't want her blaming him for not looking into it.

But she smiled and shook her head. "If you worry about odds like that, you probably snap your fingers to keep the elephants away." Jack snapped his. They both laughed. The closest elephants to Lacanth C were a lot of light-years away, so snapping your fingers worked like a charm there.

And that secondary scan wouldn't have picked up what was going on, anyhow. Neither would a tertiary scan, or a quaternary. . . .

The ultrasound very clearly showed the baby's heart. As for the rest . . . The tech examining the image frowned a little. "You've got a wiggly kid," she said. "He twisted himself into a really funny position."

"Is everything all right?" Bev asked.

"Yeah, I think so," the tech answered. "Maybe you want to come in for another check a little closer to term."

"Well, maybe I will," Beverly said. But she didn't. The tech didn't make it sound like a big deal, and so she didn't worry about it. Her OB seemed to think everything was fine. The fetal heartbeat came in loud and clear. Junior—she and Jack were going to name him Sean—sure kicked like a soccer player.

Both new parents were as ready as new parents could be when labor started. It took a long time, but they were braced for that. It hurt, too, but Bev knew ahead of time that it would, which made a lot of difference. When she finally got the urge to push, the OB told her to go ahead.

"Won't be much longer," the woman said cheerfully from behind her mask. Bev made a noise somewhere between a grunt and a squeal—she might have been trying to lift a building off her toe. The OB nodded approval. "That's good! Do it again!"

Jack thought his wife would explode if she did it again. But then, that was the point.

Bev bore down once more. Her face turned a mottled purple. That couldn't be good for her . . . could it? The obstetrician seemed to think so. "The baby's crowning," she said. "I can see the top of its head. Push hard. One more time!"

And Beverly did, and the baby came out, and that was when the screams in the delivery room started.

Sergeant John Paul Kling was in the shower when the telephone rang. Swearing under his breath, he turned off the water and plucked the phone out of the soap dish. "Exotic Crimes Unit, Kling here," he said.

"This is Dr. Romanova. I'm at Tristar Hospital." The woman on the other end of the line sounded like someone biting down hard on hysteria. *And she's a doctor*, Kling thought. *Whatever this is, it isn't good.*

"Go ahead," he said out loud, while water dripped from the end of his nose and trickled through the mat of graying hair on his chest.

"I think . . ." Dr. Romanova had to pause and gather herself. "I think we've had a hoxbomb here." There. She'd said it.

"Good Lord!" Kling didn't know what he'd expected, but that wasn't it. "Are you sure?"

"I'll send you the image," she said, and she did.

For a few seconds, Kling thought he was seeing what he was seeing because his phone screen had drops of water on it. He wiped it clear with his thumb, and what he saw then was even worse.

It was a newborn baby. Well, it couldn't be anything else, but whoever'd put it together hadn't looked at the manual often enough. Parts sprouted from places where they had no business being. He'd heard of sticking your foot in your mouth. Now he saw it—either that or the kid's tongue had toes. Which would be worse? He had no idea.

"Sergeant? Are you there, Sergeant?" Dr. Romanova asked. "They put me through to you, and—"

"I'm here." Kling got rid of the photo, but it would haunt him forever. And he was going to have to see the model in a few minutes. "Tristar Hospital, you said? I'm on my way. Shall I notify the Snarre't, or do you want to do it?"

"You're the police office in charge," she answered, which was a polite way of saying, *You're stuck with it, buddy*. "A hoxbomb *could* be purely human, of course."

"Yeah. Right," John Paul Kling said tightly. He was a cop. Like any cop with two brain cells to rub against each other, he went with the odds, not against them. A hoxbomb didn't have to mean the Furballs were involved, but that was sure as hell the way to bet. They were the ones who really knew how to do that stuff: a lot better than humans did, anyhow.

He got out of the shower, put on his clothes, and called headquarters. He would have to show them visuals, and naked just didn't cut it. Lieutenant Reiko Kelly took the call. "I thought it would be you, John Paul," she said. "A hoxbomb, the doctor told me."

"Uh-huh. I'm about to head for Tristar now. Reason I'm checking in is, I want to involve the Snarre't." He was doing things by the book. Being only a sergeant, he needed formal permission before taking care of what everybody—even the doctor, or maybe especially the doctor—could see he had to take care of.

Lieutenant Kelly sighed, but she nodded. "Yes, go ahead. With a hoxbomb in the picture, you don't have much choice. If it turns out they aren't involved, we can always peel them out of the investigation later."

"Okay. We're on the same page, anyhow," Kling said. "I'll make the contact. Boy, that'll be fun. Fun like the gout, is what it'll be. So long, Reiko. Talk with you later." He hopped on his scooter and headed for the hospital.

The Snarre'i investigator's name was a collection of screeches and smells that don't translate well into human-style phonemes. We can call her Miss Murple. The name is similar but not identical to that of a legendary human investigator. What she did was similar but not identical to what a human investigator might do, too, so Miss Murple works well enough as a handle.

She didn't want to be investigating just then. She was right in the middle of an exciting lifey. Again, the name is approximate, but it will do. Since it was daytime out, she'd told her windows to exclude most of the ambient light. She sat in her darkened living room, her eyes closed, her brain's little hand wrapped around her left index finger.

A special nerve patch there connected with the brain. The genetically engineered creature spun out the story, which was set in the Era of the Three Queendoms. They hadn't know much about biology back then, but they'd had amazing adventures. She was living this one, with all her senses involved. When the character from whose viewpoint she was experiencing the action walked across the grass, she smelled it and felt it on the bottom of her feet. When the character got hurt, she felt that, too. And when the character mated, it was as good as the real thing—better, if you'd run into some of the clumsy males Miss Murple had met lately.

She had to deliver the spice package before sunup if she wanted her love interest to keep blinking when. . . . "I'm sorry," the brain said as it abruptly returned Miss Murple to the mundane world. "You have an urgent message from Investigation Thumb."

"A stench!" she said. Of course the brain stayed connected to the rest of the neural net while it entertained her. But why did Thumb have to come in right at the most exciting part of the lifey? She was an investigator. She knew why. Because things worked that way—that was why. Hadn't she already seen it too many times? "Connect," she told the brain resignedly.

Instead of the trees of the homeworld, she saw the unlovely offices of the gripping organ of the Snarre'i self-protection agency. Her superior's name was as unpronounceable as hers, so we can call him Sam Spud. "A Baldy requires communication with you," he said without preamble.

"A Baldy!" Miss Murple said in dismay. That was too much! The aliens *didn't* communicate, not at any truly important level. That was a big part of what was wrong with them. "What's this about?"

Sam Spud's pupils narrowed to slits, even though the offices were also darkened against the day. "A hoxbomb," he answered grimly. "You'd better talk to the human, sweetheart. That's trouble with a capital T." Not quite the idiom he used, but humans don't have the odor receptors they'd need to appreciate his to the fullest.

"A hoxbomb? Used on the Bald Ones? Is someone out of her mind?" Miss Murple said. Antagonizing weird, dangerous aliens had to be a maniac's game . . . didn't it? She hoped so. Humans could do things with ordinary, boring inorganic matter that the Snarre't had never imagined possible. They could blow up a world. They could, very possibly, blow up a star.

Sam Spud waggled his ears to show he wasn't kidding. The brain in his office caught the scent of his agitation and relayed it to Miss Murple through the neural net. "Yes, a hoxbomb. No possible doubt. I've seen the image. That's one scrambled baby Bald One."

It showed up in his mind, which meant it showed up in Miss Murple's. She winced. He wasn't wrong. A baby that distorted was good for nothing but euthanasia. "A hoxbomb," she agreed. "All right, we need to get to the bottom of this before the humans break out in assholes." A Snarre' who said something like that meant it literally. Reluctantly, Miss Murple went on, "I will activate my telephone. You may—I suppose you may—give the code to the Bald One investigating."

"Right." Sam Spud would have given it to the human anyhow. Miss Murple knew that. And he would have overridden her if she tried to keep the telephone inactive. He was her boss, so he had the right. And he was a son of a bitch, so he would have used it without compunction. He broke the connection.

A very little while later, the telephone made a horrible noise. Gingerly, Miss Murple picked it up. It didn't quite fit her hand. It felt unnaturally smooth and slick. It smelled funny, to say nothing of nasty. Even with shielding, its little screen lit up too bright to suit her.

The human who appeared on the screen was, like any human, a bad caricature of Snarre'kind: bare face, tiny eyes, pointy beak with only two round breathing orifices, small mouth with niggardly teeth. "I greet you," it said in Snarre'l.

"Hello," Miss Murple replied in English. How were you supposed to get anything important across when all you could use were sound and sight? She didn't know, but she'd have to try. Returning to her own language, she said, "A hoxbomb?"

His translator—a mechanical thing, cousin to the mechanical thing she was holding—must have worked well enough, for he said, "That's right." That was what *her* translator said he said, anyhow. It gave his impoverished speech all the overtones it would have had in Snarre'l. Whether those overtones were really there in English . . . was a question for another time. The human went on, "The victim's mother and especially father dealt with Snarre't about the time the pregnancy began."

"You don't know one of us used the hoxbomb," Miss Murple protested.

"I didn't say I did," the human replied. "But that's more your kind of weapon than ours. And even if it was one of our people who did it, you're liable to be better than we are at tracking it down. And I hope you want to help, because you know our news media will start screaming it was all your fault."

He might be ugly—he *was* ugly. He might—he *did*—speak an impoverished language. Impoverished or not, he made too much sense in it. From everything Miss Murple knew of human news reporters, they were at least as simplistic and sensational as those of her own folk. She couldn't think of anything worse to say about them, especially when their yattering might help uncoil an interstellar war.

She sighed. Another Snarre' would have smelled the resignation coming off her. Not only would she *not* have a chance to finish the lifey any time soon, but she *would* have to work with this alien. For its benefit, she had to put what she was feeling into plain old ordinary words, too: "I'll do what I can."

Miss Murple wanted to put on eyecovers and go out by daylight the way she wanted to come down with the mange. What choice did she have, though? Crime happened when it happened, not when it was convenient. More resignation poured from her, not that the human could notice. "I'm coming," she said, and hung up. She didn't deactivate the telephone, though. She knew she would have to keep using the stinking thing.

Hospitals gave John Paul Kling the willies. Maternity wards were supposed to be better than the other units. Happy things happened there. Mostly healthy women went in, and they mostly came home with healthy babies.

Yeah, mostly. Not this time, though. Tristar was treating the birthing room as a crime scene. Kling didn't tell the doctors and nurses not to. But this was only where the crime was discovered, not where it had happened. Kling didn't know where that was yet. But he could make a damn good guess about when: just about 280 days earlier.

He talked with the victims. Mrs. Cravath was in no condition to help yet. It wasn't only that she was devastated by what had happened. Going through labor made her look as if she'd just stepped in front of a truck. Kling couldn't really question her.

Her husband wasn't in much better shape. "Why would anyone do this to us?" he asked.

"I don't know, sir," Sergeant Kling answered. "That's one of the things we have to look into. Do you have any personal enemies? Any business enemies? Did you ever do anything to offend the Snarre't?" *Did you ever do anything to really, really piss off the Furballs?* was what he wanted to ask, but this was being recorded, so he didn't.

Jack Cravath just looked bewildered. "I sell scooters. What kind of business enemies am I going to have, for crying out loud? I'm not important enough to have enemies like that. I haven't been in a fight with anybody since the fourth grade, and I lost then. The Snarre't buy scooters from me every once in a while. You never can tell for sure, but I don't think I ever got 'em mad at me."

"Okay," Kling said, a little wearily. Cravath sounded as ordinary as he looked. But he wasn't, not to somebody—not unless the perpetrator hoxbombed his wife for the hell of it. *Isn't that a lovely thought?* Random criminals were a lot tougher to catch.

"Detective Sergeant Kling, please report to the reception desk. Detective Sergeant John Paul Kling, please report to the reception desk," came from a speaker on the wall.

Kling jumped out of the uncomfortable hospital chair on which he'd perched. "Excuse me," he said. Getting away from what should have been a proud new papa was nothing but a relief.

Going out by day, going into the human part of town, Miss Murple felt as if she'd fallen into a lifey of light. Back when lifeys were fairly new, those had been all the rage for about twenty years. Ambitious directors still turned one out now and then, but the modern imitations didn't come close to the originals.

Part of the allure about lifeys of light was the seamy side of things they portrayed. The other part was the way they portrayed it. As their name implied, they were *daytime* dramas, showing what went on while honest, ordinary Snarre't slept. They blasted you with light, and you couldn't even squeeze your pupils into tight slits against it, because it was *inside* your head. And all that light didn't just wash out the details of what you saw. It somehow mashed down smells, too, and made hearing seem less distinct. Part of that was the director's postproduction work, of course. But part of it was the endless, inescapable, brutal glare.

Humans live this way all the time. It's as natural to them as night and shadow are to us, Miss Murple reminded herself. Another thought followed hard on the tail of that one. *No wonder humans are so stinking weird.*

Her eyecovers and her narrowed pupils warded her from the worst of the daylight. A human with a machine would have insisted that the light level Miss Murple actually experienced was only very slightly higher than it would have been in the middle of the night. But the Bald Ones, again, were stinking weird. The human and the machine wouldn't have understood about the heat of the sun on her fur, or about the way the air felt and smelled when she breathed it, or the simple fact that she was up and about and doing things when she should have been asleep. A lifey of light, all right.

Street signs in the human part of town were also lettered in Snarre'l characters, just as those in the Snarre'i area had transliterations—of a sort—in the odd letters humans used. Most human buildings weren't marked in any way that made sense to her, though. Humans assumed no Snarre' would want anything to do with them . . . and the humans were likely to be right.

Tristar Hospital was an exception. *Area for the Infirm of Three Stars,* read the Snarre'l translation of the English name. No olfactory cues or anything, but what could you expect from humans? At least they made some effort, anyhow. Only in the direst of emergencies would Miss Murple have wanted a bungling, ignorant human physician—but she repeated herself—coming anywhere near her, but the possibility of such an emergency was there.

Another sign in Snarre'l got her to the reception desk. A human behind a machine—one of the devices that were a little like a brain—said, "I greet you," and then, still in Snarre'l, "How may I help you?"

Miss Murple needed a few heartbeats to realize this human actually did speak some of her language. That was a nice touch. "I am looking for Detective Sergeant John Paul Kling," she said, hoping she wasn't mangling the name past comprehension. "It told me we were to meet here."

"One moment, please," the human said, again in Snarre'l. The Bald One spoke in English into something that looked a little like a telephone: "Detective Sergeant Kling, please report . . ." The human looked at something Miss Murple couldn't see, then reported, "He is on the way."

So this Kling was a male. Well, it could only matter to another Baldy. Miss Murple wondered how the functionary knew King was coming. Did the humans have something like Snarre'i hearers that could pick out the male's footsteps from among all the others. Or did they . . .? Miss Murple's fur rippled in a gesture of uncertainty. When it came to inorganic technology, she knew how little she knew.

Hoxbombs were a different story. The Snarre't had used them for thousands of years, and hadn't needed long to discover they worked on humans, too. It made sense that they should. Even humans understood how tightly biochemistry constrained biology. If things were going to work at all, they needed to work within certain narrow limits.

Creatures with front ends and back ends, for instance, needed hox genes to order their endedness. If you scrambled the sequence of those genes and added a couple in places where they didn't belong . . . If you did something like that, you got a monstrosity like the one that had been born here.

Easy to make hoxbombs—too stinking easy. All you needed was a little technique and a whole lot of malice. Sometimes ideology would do in place of malice. If you wanted to grab attention, not much worked better than a hoxbomb.

"I greet you," said a human with a voice of familiar timbre.

"Hello," Miss Murple replied, glad to get jolted out of her gloomy reverie. She returned to Snarre'l: "You are the human detective, aren't you?"

"That's right. Easier for me to recognize you here than the other way around. I wouldn't have such an easy time in your part of town."

"No, I suppose not." Miss Murple thought telling her own folk apart the easiest thing in the world. Why were humans so inept? That she'd also had trouble recognizing him never crossed her mind.

"I talked to the couple who had the damaged baby—mostly to the father, because the mother's still wiped out," the human said.

Miss Murple had heard somewhere that delivering a baby was difficult and unpleasant for a human female. She'd never expected to *need* to know that, but life was full of surprises. "Any leads?" she asked.

"No known enemies or business rivals. No known trouble with the Snarre't," the other detective replied. "They got blindsided, in other words."

She heard the human idiom as *The sun rose in their faces.* "That doesn't make this any easier," she said.

"Tell me about it!" the human replied. "It'll take lots of legwork, trying to nail down everybody they dealt with around the time she got pregnant."

"That may not have anything to do with it," Miss Murple said. "Some hoxbombs are planted in a parent's genes years before the affected offspring are born."

"Oh, my aching back!" the human detective said. "How do you ever catch a perp in a case like that?"

"You said it yourself," Miss Murple replied. "A lot of legwork—and a lot of lab work."

"This is a mess, Kling," Reiko Kelly said. "You've got to pin it on somebody, or there'll be hell to pay."

"Okay," Kling said obligingly. He stabbed out a forefinger at the lieutenant. "Why'd you do it?"

"What?" Then Lieutenant Kelly got it. "Oh. Funny. See? I'm laughing. How about nabbing the bastard who really did it?"

"Yeah. How about that?" John Paul Kling was not a happy man. "From what the Furball says, it could be anybody who ever had anything to do with the Cravaths. That's sure what it sounded like, anyhow. Happy day, happy day."

"It could be anybody, uh-huh. It could be, but it isn't. It's *somebody*, somebody in particular. Who had a reason to give them grief? Grief!" Kelly shook her head. Long auburn hair flipped back and forth. "What do you do with a kid like that? What do you do *for* a kid like that? You know the worst part? No matter how scrambled it is, it's pretty much healthy. It could be around for a lot of years. How would you like to be Mommy and Daddy, knowing what Junior's like all that time?"

"How's it supposed to eat or talk? You see that thing it's got for a tongue?" Kling said.

"I saw." The lieutenant shuddered. "But surgery can probably fix that. Surgery can fix . . . quite a bit, maybe." She sounded like someone trying to make herself believe it.

John Paul Kling *didn't* believe it, not for a minute. "And all the king's horses and all the king's men / Couldn't put Humpty Dumpty together again," he quoted grimly.

"Yeah, well, if we don't solve this one, that's what Lacanth C is liable to be like," Kelly said. "Plenty of humans will want to pay the Snarre't back for this. Then they'll have an excuse for paying us back, and then. . . ." She spread her hands.

"We don't even know they did it," Kling pointed out.

"No, but everybody human here will sure think they did. A hox-bomb? My God!" Kelly rolled her eyes. "Do you want to risk escalation?"

"Nope. If this is such an important case, how come a dumb sergeant catches it?" Kling asked.

"So I can cut your nuts off if you screw up," his superior said brutally.

"You sure know how to pump a guy up so he'll work hard," Kling said.

"What? You think my nuts—well, my tits—aren't on the line, too? Get real," Kelly said.

"Happy day," Kling said again. "Okay, I'll start the legwork. I'm going to assume Beverly Cravath caught the hoxbomb around the time she got pregnant—"

"What if she didn't?" Kelly broke in.

"Then either we're screwed or the case takes a lot longer to solve unless we get lucky," Kling answered. "But I can get a pretty good handle on who all they both had anything to do with from surveillance cameras and stuff. I'll do that first, check those people out, and see what the lab can figure out about the hoxbomb. Maybe they'll be able to work out if it's one of ours or straight from the Snarre't, and how long it was in Mrs. Cravath and Junior." He flinched. No, he didn't like thinking about Junior. Who would?

Grimacing, the lieutenant nodded. "Yeah, go ahead. That's about all you can do, I guess. You think the Snarre't will really help, or are they just blowing smoke?"

"Well, they sent a Furball over in the middle of the day, so that's something," Kling replied. "He—she—it—whatever—didn't seem to like the idea of a hoxbomb much. I sure hope like hell they help. Their genetics labs beat ours six ways from Sunday."

"You're not supposed to say stuff like that," Kelly told him.

"Why not? Isn't it true?" Kling made as if to spit in disgust. "You didn't see us inventing goddamn hoxbombs, did you?"

"We're as smart as they are," Lieutenant Kelly insisted.

"Sure we are. Who says we're not? We do some stuff better than they do. But they do some stuff better than we do, too. Electronics? Yeah, we wallop the snot out of them. Biotech? You know the answer as well as I do."

Reiko Kelly didn't argue with him. Maybe that meant he was unquestionably right. Maybe it meant he'd stuck himself in deep kimchi. Maybe it meant both at once. Sergeant Kling was mournfully certain which way he'd bet.

Miss Murple managed to obtain a tissue sample from the baby human who'd been hoxbombed. The human doctors wouldn't let her take the sample herself—as if she could do anything to the baby now that hadn't already happened to it! She wasn't happy when they did it. Bald Ones knew about as much about genetics as Snarre't knew about popup-blocking software. She only hoped they wouldn't mess up the sample.

She rode her caitnop—a faster though slightly stupider beast than a drof—back to the Snarre'i side of town with nothing but relief. The laboratory, of course, stayed open all hours of the day and night. She turned over the sample to the chief technician on duty: we can call him Louie Pasture. He smelled unhappy when she told him the provenance of the sample.

"Why didn't you take it yourself, so we'd know it was done right?" Louie demanded.

"Because I damn well couldn't," Miss Murple answered. "It was their jurisdiction. It was their chemical-stinky, glareblind hospital. One of their physicians did it. They don't like us any better than we like them."

"Chemical-stinky is right," Louie Pasture said scornfully. "They try to do analysis like that, you know? With machines and electricity and I don't know what. They make everything as complicated as they can. Amazing they ever got anywhere, when they don't understand bacteria at all."

The Snarre'l word for *bacteria* actually meant something more like *one-celled chemical factories you can train to do your work for you.* That's a lot to pack into one word, but the Snarre't packed a lot into the technology. Bacteria, on their home planet and on Earth, were much more versatile biochemically than plants or animals or fungi or slime molds. From a bacterium's point of view, all the bigger, more highly organized forms of life represented a couple of boring variations on a theme. Either they photosynthesized or they ate things that photosynthesized. But there were more tricks in heaven and earth than were dreamt of in their philosophies.

Some varieties of bacteria used oxygen. Some got along without it very nicely. Quite a few preferred temperatures close to that of boiling water. Those were some of the most valuable, because their biochemistry was so robust. If it weren't, they would have cooked. When you used enzymes and other proteins derived from them down at room temperature, those were often much more potent than the ones taken from less thermophilic beasties.

Miss Murple's race had understood that for a lot of years, and centered an elaborate technology of selective breeding and deliberate mutation on it. Human DNA analysis had scratched the surface of such techniques. From a Snarre' perspective, that was about all humans had done along those lines.

"Well, we'll see what we've got," Louie Pasture said, and placed the sample in a preliminary checking bath, one that searched for contaminants. His nostril slits widened as he sniffed the bath. "Not . . . too bad." His voice was grudging. "And they gave you a big enough sample, didn't they?"

"They measured it by their standards," Miss Murple answered. "If they need this much to know anything—"

"Then they aren't likely to find much no matter what kind of sample they take," Louie finished for her. "Makes it easier for us, though."

He prepared several more baths. Each was a culture of a bacterium primed and tweaked to react to the genetic presence of a particular hoxbomb that hit humans. Miss Murple didn't know whether the bacteria were originally from her own homeworld or from Earth. For all she cared, some could have come from one planet and some from the other. The only thing that mattered was what they told her—or rather, told Louie Pasture.

The lab tech muttered to himself as he diluted some of the tissue sample from the victim and put a small amount in each bath. "How long do we have to wait for results?" Miss Murple asked. She didn't have much experience with hoxbomb labwork.

"Depends," Louie said. "If it's a common one, we'll find out right away. If it's not one I'm set up for with these baths, we'll have to try some others."

He passed a sniffer over each bath in turn. Its nostril slits were vastly more sensitive than his own—for this purpose. The little animal was bred to detect the metabolic byproducts the bacteria in the test bath gave off when they came up against genetic material from their particular hoxbomb type. Humans would have used machines to do the same job. Humans, in Miss Murple's opinion, were fools. Of course natural selection, given several billion years, could come up with more sensitive detectors than engineers could in a few centuries starting from scratch.

For brute force, on the other hand, engineering had advantages over natural selection. Human weapons weren't subtle, which didn't mean they weren't strong. Humans might not be able to ravage a biosphere the way the Snarre't could. But if you could take out a whole planet, or maybe even the star it orbited, what price subtlety?

The sniffer squeaked. "Ha!" Louie Pasture said. "Was it this bath or that one?" He slowly passed the sniffer above each of them in turn. When it went over the second bath, it squeaked again. He stroked it and gave it a treat. It wiggled with delight in his hand.

"Which hoxbomb is that?" Miss Murple asked.

Louie looked at the label on the side of the container, which was a shell bred for internal smoothness and sterility. (The animals that secreted the shells were bred to be tasty. Waste not, want not.) "It's called Scrambled Egg 7—one of the oldest ones around," he answered.

"Could humans have got their hands on it?"

"Oh, absolutely," Louie said. "And if they got a sample, they could probably make it themselves. It's that old and that simple."

"Which doesn't mean it doesn't work," Miss Murple said. "All right—thanks, Louie. I'll pass this on to the Baldy who's tackling the case from their end. And I'll see if he's come up with anything for me."

"Good luck," Louie said. "You know how come humans are bald? 'Cause they're so dumb, they'd get shit on their fur if they had any."

Miss Murple thought that was funny, too. But she did wonder what kind of jokes humans told when no Snarre't were around to hear them.

"Scrambled Egg 7?" John Paul Kling wrote it down. When he got a chance, he would google it and see what humanity knew about it. In the meantime . . . "How common is it?"

"Very," the Snarre'i detective answered. "It could have been used by one of our people or by one of yours."

"Okay." Kling respected the Furball for mentioning her—his?—own folk first. "Do you have to use it when the pregnancy is new, or is it one of the ones that can sit for a long time before it does what it does?"

"You asked the right questions, anyhow." The alien sounded as uncertain about his competence as he was about its. "Scrambled Egg 7 is designed to damaged a very young fetus, not to lie in wait in an ancestor's germ plasm for years or centuries."

"Okay," Kling repeated cautiously. *An ancestor's*, the Snarre' said, not *a parent's*. The human detective sergeant thought again about a hoxbomb lying dormant not just for years but for centuries. He shivered. That sounded like Revenge with a capital R. It also made him think that, even if you were sure you'd whipped the snot out of the Snarre't, you would be smart not to count your chickens before they hatched and you could make sure they didn't have wings growing out of their eye sockets or eighteen legs or anything delightful like that.

"What have you got for me now?" Even through the babelfish, the Snarre' sounded challenging.

"I've been making a list of everybody who was in contact with the Cravaths around the time the hoxbombed baby was conceived," Kling answered.

"Yes, that seems sensible," his opposite number allowed. "May I ask you something else? What is the present status of the youngster?"

"They're planning surgeries to repair as much as they can," Kling said.

"Surgeries?" Either the Snarre' couldn't believe what it was hearing or Kling's babelfish was letting its imagination run away with it. The Furball went on, "I know you do more cutting than we would, but surely not even your surgery can repair everything wrong with that baby."

"I'm no expert, but I wouldn't think so, either," Kling agreed.

"Then why do it? Why not put the poor thing out of its misery? Why not make sure its distorted genes—and with Scrambled Egg 7, they are—never enter your gene pool?"

"Well, I wonder if they're doing the kid a favor, too," the detective said. "But if there's a sound mind inside that—"

"That mess of a body," the Snarre' broke in.

The alien wasn't wrong, either. All the same, Kling said, "Machines—and maybe helper animals—can do a lot. The kid'll never be pretty, but we don't get rid of people for being ugly. If we did, there'd be a lot fewer humans than there are."

"I hardly know where to begin," his opposite number said. "What you call helper animals . . . You don't know the meaning of the words." That was bound to be true. Humans trained animals to help the disabled. The Snarre't didn't just breed them for that—they bioengineered them. This Snarre' continued, "As for ugly . . . well, each species has its own standards. But if you are saying you don't deliberately improve your own looks and smells—why not? We've been working on it for thousands of years, and the results are striking."

You still don't do a thing for me, sweetie, John Paul Kling thought. But the Furball was right; that went species by species. He said, "Each race has its own customs. Different societies in the same species can have different customs."

What came from the Snarre' was unmistakably a sigh. "No doubt." That had to mean he—she?—figured these human customs were odious or stupid. Well, too damn bad. The alien said, "We should discuss this all another time, at leisure. In the meanwhile, tell me about the people who came into contact with either the male or female parent at about the time the latter discovered she was pregnant."

"Here's the list." Kling sent it to her phone. "As you'll see, most of them are human, but some are, uh, Snarre't." Calling Furballs Furballs in front of a Furball could and would damage your promotion chances.

He watched his opposite number's big, bulging eyes go back and forth as the other detective read the names. The Snarre's phone was supposed to render not only the Roman alphabet but also Snarre'l characters. He hoped it was working up to spec.

After going through the list—or so Kling presumed, anyhow—the Snarre' said, "This is exceedingly comprehensive. How was it generated?"

"Partly by questioning the Cravaths. That wasn't such a good bet, though, because so much time's gone by. The rest came from going through surveillance camera records."

"That must have taken a lot of time."

John Paul Kling shrugged. "A lot of computer time. Not so much for me. The real art is generating the algorithm that makes the computer identify the victims' faces and body dimensions. We had a few false positives a real, live human had to sift through, but not that many."

"False positives?" the Snarre' asked.

"People who looked like the Cravaths to the computer but turned out not to be."

"I see. If you added a smellchecker, you could reduce those to zero, or very close to zero."

"Maybe," Kling said. "We haven't had such an easy time getting our hardware and software to handle smells, though."

"You would do better not to involve machines at all," the Furball said. "If you're trying to detect organic compounds, you need organic detectors."

"Oh, yeah, like I'm really in a position to change policy," Kling said. "We've got a job to do here, not fix the damn world. Suppose you question the Snarre't on the list, and I'll take care of the humans. Then we can talk again—compare notes, you know? Do you think you can do it in four days? You don't have as many of 'em as I do."

"I'll try," the other detective said. "I will speak to you then." The screen on Kling's phone went blank.

Dealing with her own species, Miss Murple at least got to keep civilized hours. She could go out and talk to people while it was decently dark. She didn't miss eyecovers, not even a little bit.

Most of the stalls in the garage of the fancy apartment block where Sharon Rock and Joe Mountain (again, the names are approximate, but they beat the hell out of transcribing funny noises and trying to transcribe smells) lived had caitnops or drofs in them, the way they would have on a Snarre' night back on the homeworld.

But the shiny new scooter in Sharon and Joe's stall would have announced that they dealt with Bald Ones, even if Miss Murple hadn't already known as much. Everything about their apartment screamed *money*, from the scooter to the way the front door dealt with her.

On the homeworld, a servant might even have opened that front door. But that sort of thing hadn't come here. Miss Murple didn't miss it a bit, either. But she *was* surprised when a voice spoke in English after she used the knocker: "Hi! With you in a minute!"

She had to wait for the worm in her brain to translate before she understood. Almost any Snarre' would have. Did Sharon Rock and Joe Mountain have more human guests than those of their own kind? Or were they just infatuated with everything the Baldies did? Miss Murple knew which way she would bet.

The door opened. There stood Sharon Rock. Miss Murple had experienced her in any number of lifeys. The real thing was even more depressing. Nobody in real life ought to have such big eyes or such soft fur, or to smell quite so sexy. How did this female get through the night without distracting everyone around her?

"You must be the detective," she said, and her voice really was like pearly bells. "Come in, please." She raised her voice: "Joe! The detective's here!"

"I'm coming." Joe Mountain had been retired for fifteen years, but if you paid any attention to sports you remembered the days when he wasn't. He'd put on a little weight since his athletic days, but not a lot, and he still smelled like a younger male. That was distracting, too.

So was their flat. It was full of human-made gadgets, many of them replacing perfectly ordinary Snarre'i equivalents like heat sensors. There was even a television set from the Bald Ones: a demon's tool if ever there was one, as far as Miss Murple was concerned.

"You're fond of humans, aren't you?" she remarked.

Sharon and Joe looked at each other. "Yes," Sharon answered. "And do you know why?"

"Tell me, please," Miss Murple said.

"*Because they leave us alone.*" Both Snarre'i celebrities spoke together. Sharon went on by herself: "When we deal with the Bald Ones, we're nothing but funny-looking aliens to them. You have no idea how wonderful that is."

"We have privacy with the humans," Joe agreed. "They aren't always sniffing and touching and staring at us. It's—"

"Peaceful," Sharon finished for him. He splayed his fingers in agreement.

"All right." They'd led Miss Murple straight to what she wanted to ask: "Is that why you purchased a scooter from the human named, uh, Jack Cravath most of a year ago?"

"If that's what the human's name was," Sharon Rock said. "We like the scooter."

"We really do," Joe Mountain said enthusiastically. "It's faster than a drof, and cheaper to maintain, too." He'd done a lot of selling pitches, capitalizing on his fame as a sports hero. This sounded like another one.

"Do you know that Jack Cravath's mate was just the victim of a hoxbombing?" Miss Murple said. "She gave birth to one of the most scrambled offspring I've ever had the misfortune of seeing." *And they're trying to keep it alive, too. I don't begin to understand that.*

"How awful!" Sharon Rock breathed. She really sounded and smelled shocked and dismayed. But how many lifeys had she made? She was used to having other people looking over her emotional shoulder, so to speak. Lifey performers got so used to projecting emotions, some of them even gave sniffers trouble.

"We had no idea," Joe said. Miss Murple had to remind herself that he was an experienced actor, too. "Why would anybody want to waste a hoxbomb on a Bald One?"

"That's one of the things we're trying to find out," Miss Murple replied.

Sharon Rock's voice took on a certain edge: "Why are you asking us about all this, exactly?"

"Because you bought your scooter from the male of the family at about the same time as the female became pregnant," Miss Murple said. "This is all routine. You aren't suspects, or even persons of interest, at the present time."

"We don't know much about hoxbombs." Joe Mountain spoke with more than a little pride. He might have said, *We don't know much about anything.* Some people suspected that athletes *didn't* know much about anything.

"I was in a lifey about them once." Now Sharon Rock sounded almost apologetic, and smelled that way, too. "I liked the plot outline, and the payment was good, so I did the production."

What was *she* saying? *I do know something about hoxbombs, but it's not my fault?* It sounded that way to Miss Murple.

"Your statement is that you weren't involved in conveying the hoxbomb to the human?" the detective said.

"That's right," Sharon and Joe chorused. They didn't sound like liars. They didn't smell like liars, either. Miss Murple sighed. They were performers. If they were performing now . . .

Shoe leather. John Paul Kling looked at the soles of his own shoes. They weren't leather, though the uppers were. Leather or not, they'd taken their share of wear and then some. He tramped along the streets of Latimer's central business district, the part of town that catered to both humans and Snarre't. It was daytime, so not many Furballs were out and about. He did see a few, the way he would have seen a few humans at two in the morning.

He would have wondered what the humans were doing up at two in the morning. He did wonder what the Snarre't were doing now. Unless it looked obviously illegal, it was none of his business.

He checked the map unscrolling on his phone. He needed to turn left at the next corner. After he did, he nodded to himself. There it was, in the middle of the block on the far side of the street. SUNBIRD SCOOTERS, the sign said. He crossed without getting run over by scooters or trampled by caitnops (which tended not to pay attention to humans) or drofs.

A very pretty young woman smiled at him in a friendly way when he walked into Sunbird Scooters. "May I help you, sir?" she said.

"You're not Petros van Gilder," Kling said regretfully. He displayed his badge, after which the young woman didn't look so friendly any more. He sighed to himself. It never failed. Well, he'd stick to business, then: "I need to ask him a few questions."

"Hold on. I'll get him." She paused. "What shall I tell him this is about?" Kling didn't answer. No, the woman didn't seem friendly at all now. He shouldn't have been surprised. Hell, he *wasn't* surprised. That didn't mean he was happy.

She went into the back part of the building. When she came back, she had a short but well-built man not far from her own age with her. "You're Petros van Gilder?" Kling asked.

"That's right. And you are . . .?"

"Sergeant John Paul Kling, Exotic Crimes Unit. I'm here because of the hoxbombing suffered by Jack and Beverly Cravath."

"I heard about that. Terrible thing. But what's it got to do with me?" van Gilder said.

"Maybe nothing. Probably nothing, in fact," Kling said. "Just routine right now. I'm trying to contact everyone who had anything to do with either one of them around the time Beverly Cravath got pregnant."

"If it's a hoxbombing, shouldn't you be concentrating on the Snarre't?" van Gilder said. "I mean, they're the ones who're mostly likely to do something like that."

"Believe me, we're looking at that angle, too. So are their own police officials," Kling said.

Petros van Gilder had a fine—almost a professional—sneer. "Oh, yeah. I'm sure they're looking real hard."

"We don't have any reason to believe they're not," said Kling, who worried about the same thing. "Catching whoever did it is in their interest, too."

"It is if a human did it," the scooter salesman said. "One of their own people? Fat chance."

"I'm not here to argue with you. I'm here to ask you about the time you saw Jack Cravath." Kling gave the date and time, adding, "I gather you were both coming home from work."

"I've got to tell you, I don't remember this at all," van Gilder said. "Maybe that makes me a suspect or whatever, but I totally don't."

"You were stopped at a traffic light, together. You said something to each other and shook hands, and then the two of you separated," Kling said.

"How about that?" van Gilder said. "Well, if you've got it recorded, I can't very well tell you you're wrong, but it sure doesn't ring a bell."

"You had your hands in your pockets before you shook hands with Jack Cravath," Kling said. "Why would that have been?"

"Beats me. Probably because it was cold. What's the big deal?" the younger man asked.

"The big deal is that that might have been when you delivered the hoxbomb." Kling took a print from the surveillance footage and showed it to Petros van Gilder. "Do you recognize this jacket? Do you still have it?"

"Is that me?" Van Gilder eyed the photo. It was him, all right—no possible doubt. "Yeah, I've still got that jacket. It's back at my apartment. How come?"

"Because we'd like to examine it for possible presence of the hoxbomb agent called Scrambled Egg 7," Kling replied. "We could get a warrant, but it would be simpler without one."

"You wouldn't have any trouble getting a warrant, either, would you?"

John Paul Kling shook his head. "Not even a little, not on a case like this."

"Go on, then," van Gilder said bleakly. "I don't have anything to do with a hoxbomb."

Pulling his phone out of his pocket, Kling poked a button and spoke into it: "Go ahead, Vanessa." He put the phone away. "Okay. That's taken care of. And believe it or not, Mr. van Gilder, I hope you're telling me the truth."

"I am!" Van Gilder bristled.

Kling held up a placating hand. "Honest to God, Mr. van Gilder, I hope so. But that hoxbomb didn't happen all by itself. Somebody planted it on the Cravaths. And that means somebody is lying to me—or maybe to my opposite number on the Snarre'i side of town. Whoever it is, we'll catch him, or her, or them."

"Evidence? You have evidence?" Miss Murple said eagerly.

The human detective's head went up and down on the little telephone screen, by which he meant yes. "That's right," he said. "A jacket taken from a man who talked with and touched Jack Cravath early enough in his mate's pregnancy to make him a possible hoxbomber. We're taking it to the lab to check for traces of Scrambled Egg 7."

"Don't!" Miss Murple exclaimed. The human had called her in the middle of the day, so she wasn't at her best. But no matter how sleepy she was, the protest automatically rose to her lips.

"Why not?" Even heard through the worm in Miss Murple's brain, John Paul Kling didn't sound happy.

"Will you believe me when I tell you I speak without offense?" Miss Murple waited till the human nodded again before she went on, "I want one of our own labs to do that analysis. We can detect much smaller traces of organics than you can."

"Maybe so," he said. "But it's in your interest to pin this on a human, regardless of who really did it. How far can we trust your lab results?"

Miss Murple bared her teeth in a threat gesture he might or might not understand. She was too angry to care whether he did. "If you don't trust us, why are we working on the same side? For that matter, why should we trust you or anything your labs do?"

She didn't anger him in return. She'd gathered that he wasn't easy to anger—or, at least, that he didn't show his anger. Miserable human telephones wouldn't let her smell him, and humans used nasty chemicals to try to defeat their own odors anyhow. It was as if they wanted to play guessing games with one another.

"Well, you've got a point," Kling said. "Can we share the cloth from the pocket that the hoxbomb would have been in if it was there at all?"

"Why would it have been in that pouch and not some other one?" Miss Murple asked suspiciously.

"Our greeting gesture involves clasping right hands. You will have seen this." The human waited. Miss Murple waved for him to go on; she *had* seen the gesture. Kling continued, "The suspect's right hand would have been in his right jacket pocket. It *was* in his right jacket pocket. We have video confirming that."

They had video for everything, near enough. A human criminal had to be clever and intrepid, or else very stupid. Well, the same held true for her own species. "All right—we can share," she said. "But if we find something and you don't, it isn't necessarily because we're cheating, you know. Your laboratory simply may not be good enough to sniff out what it should."

"Maybe." John Paul Kling didn't seem convinced. "I'll send you the cloth as soon as I can. 'Bye." His picture winked out.

Miss Murple called Sam Spud to let him know what was going on. When the neural net connected the two of them, she didn't just see and hear him at headquarters. She smelled how tired he was, smelled on his breath the cragfruit grub that let him go on longer than he could have without it. She had a real conversation with him, in other words, not the denatured excuse for one she was reduced to with humans.

"Part of this cloth is better than none, anyhow," he said after she summed up what she'd got from Kling. "Maybe the human really did it, and that will wrap things up for everybody."

"We can hope so, anyhow," Miss Murple said. "The next most likely candidates are Sharon Rock and Joe Mountain."

Sam Spud winced as if an impacted anal gland suddenly pained him. "I wish I could pretend I never heard that. Their solicitors have bone hides and giant fangs. The mere idea that they could be suspects is an insult. And what's their motivation?"

"If I knew, I would tell you," Miss Murple said.

"Besides, I think they really are innocent," her superior went on. "They gave the male parent spices as a parting gift when they bought the scooter from him. Our lab and the Baldies' excuse for one both analyzed what's left of those spices. No hoxbomb. I would eat from that spice pack myself."

"Stench! I hadn't heard that." Miss Murple muttered to herself. Then she asked, "Did they ever have anything to do with this other Baldy before, the one the humans suspect?"

"You're reaching, Murple," Sam Spud said. Miss Murple spread her fingers; she knew she was. Sam went on, "Why are you asking me, anyway? Let the miserable Bald Ones figure it out. They're so stinking proud of all their pictures. . . ."

The humans had reason to be, too, at least when it came to gathering potential evidence. Bald Ones made all kinds of boastful noises about how free they were. Whether the way they lived measured up to their claims might be a different story.

"I wouldn't be surprised if Sharon and Joe did," Miss Murple said. "They like human gadgets—one sniff at their flat will show you that. And their brain will let us know the truth even if they can lie well enough to beat the sniffers."

"They just got a new one," Sam Spud said. "They used the old one to pay for their fancy new scooter."

"They did?" Miss Murple's ears came erect. "That's interesting. How did you find out?"

"Oh, they were open enough about it," her superior said. "It's in their contract with the Bald One. They know humans keep trying to figure out how brains do the things they do."

"Yes," Miss Murple said uncomfortably. She wouldn't have given humans even an old brain. The unhappy little creature would think it had done something dreadful. Brains were terrific at storing information and passing it along, not nearly so good at figuring out what it meant. They would have been people if they could do that, so the ability had been bred out of them. Well, most of it had, anyway. "So the humans have had it all this time, then?" Miss Murple asked.

"If it's still alive, yes. I don't even know that it is," Sam Spud said.

"If it is still alive, it's probably not sane any more, poor thing," Miss Murple said. "I'd better find out, though, don't you think?"

"Bound to be a good idea," Sam Spud replied. "Maybe it doesn't know anything interesting, but getting rid of it like that sends up a bad smell."

"Sure does. Makes you wonder what Sharon and Joe are hiding. Even if they aren't hiding anything, it still makes you wonder." Miss Murple sighed. "After the neural net, the human telephone seems worse and worse."

"Well, you're stuck with it." Sam Spud sounded glad he wasn't stuck with it himself. And well he might, too. He took his finger away from the brain on his desk, vanishing from Miss Murple's perceptions. She called Kling again. "Yeah? What is it?" the human asked.

"We're trying to find out if there was ever any connection between our couple who bought the scooter from the father of the hoxbomb victim and the human you're interested in," Miss Murple said.

"*Are* you? That could be interesting, couldn't it?" John Paul Kling said. "Well, we may have video to let us know."

"Our . . . individuals of interest's brain could have told us, but they used it as the price for the scooter," Miss Murple said. "It may be valuable even now, if it's still alive and close to sane in your hands."

"Ha!" Kling said, a noise the worm in Miss Murple's brain didn't translate. The Baldy went on, "You think they got rid of the evidence on purpose."

"It's a possibility," Miss Murple agreed. Kling could smell which way she was going, anyhow. He might be alien, but he wasn't stupid. That was worth remembering.

"I'll see what we can find out from Cravath," he said. "Talk with you pretty soon. So long." He disappeared as abruptly as Sam Spud had.

Jack Cravath had to check his own credit records before he could tell Sergeant Kling the name of the outfit that bought the Snarre'i brain. The detective showed up at Intelligent Designing with a search warrant, but also with the hope that he wouldn't have to use it.

"We don't see police around here every day," the receptionist remarked. By the way she looked at Kling, she might have just noticed him on the bottom of her shoe. If he had an hour's pay for every time he got that look, he could have quit the force a long time ago. She also sounded dubious as she went on, "What's this all about?"

"It's in connection with the hoxbombing a few days ago," Kling answered.

That made her sit up and take notice. The crime was all over the news. Such things weren't supposed to happen on Lacanth C. Well, what was crime but something that wasn't supposed to happen but did anyway? "How are we involved in that?" she asked.

"I'd rather discuss it with one of your principals, if I could," Kling said coolly. He might have gossiped if she were friendlier. He was as human as anybody else on Lacanth C except the Furballs . . . and even they were closer to apes than angels.

Dr. Brigid Singh was a small, precise blond woman who wore a tailored lab coat. "Oh, yes, I remember that brain," she said. "We're always pleased to acquire them, however we do it." The Snarre't didn't encourage humans to learn more about their technology. Some of the deals Intelligent Designing made were probably under the table.

"Have you still got it?" Kling asked.

"I don't believe so. Let me check." Dr. Singh spoke to a terminal. She turned the display so Kling could also read it. "Unfortunately, we don't. That's getting on towards a year ago now. The brain was old then, which has to be why the Snarre't traded it to Mr. Cravath. And brains never do as well with us as they do with their creators. We lost this one within thirty days."

"Well, hell," Kling said. What he thought was considerably less polite. "Did you learn anything worthwhile from it?"

"We think so. That's proprietary information, though." Dr. Singh was polite, anyhow. If she weren't, she would have told him it was none of his goddamn business.

"Proprietary. Right," he said. "Did you learn anything from it that has anything to do with the hoxbombing at all? No information stays proprietary in the middle of a criminal probe." That wasn't strictly true, not if the people who wanted to hide things had a good lawyer. But it came close enough.

Brigid Singh shook her head. "No, Sergeant. Please accept my assurances that we didn't."

Kling decided he would accept them—for the time being. He went off to the crime lab. One look around was plenty to remind him that Intelligent Designing wasted more money than the department spent. People like Dr. Singh probably looked down their noses at the lab almost as much as the Snarre't did. But, even if it cut corners, it did pretty good work.

"Any signs of hoxbomb material on the pocket I got from van Gilder?" he asked the tech on duty.

"I don't think so," she said. "Let me check." She spoke to the computer, then nodded to herself when it coughed up an answer. "Nope. Far as we can tell, it's clean."

"Okay. Thanks." John Paul Kling wondered what to make of that. The lab did pretty good work, yeah. When it came to genetic material, though, the Furballs did better. Everybody and his stupid Cousin Susie knew that. Of course, the Snarre't had reasons of their own for wanting to find Scrambled Egg 7 in Petros van Gilder's pocket. If he hoxbombed the Cravaths, their people were off the hook. How far could he trust any positive they got?

I'll burn that bridge when I come to it, Kling thought. Then he wondered how he was supposed to cross if he burned the bridge. Things were really screwed up when you couldn't trust your own clichés.

"Ah, yes." Louie Pasture looked as pleased as a toleco chewing pintac leaves. "The human did it. We have a match. We have an unmistakable match, a double match. Scrambled Egg 7, or I'm a Baldy. The humans can't argue with us."

"Their detective said their laboratory didn't find any," Miss Murple told him.

Louie Pasture emitted a rude smell. "Oh, yes, and a whole fat lot humans know about these things, too."

"They aren't dumb," Miss Murple said. "They don't do things the way we do, but they aren't dumb."

"When it comes to stuff like this, they are." The lab tech pointed to a vat with a soft yellowish glow. "That wouldn't be there if my bacteria didn't detect Scrambled Egg 7. I got a smell check from the sniffer, and confirmed it with the light emitters. I don't waste time with the droppers and reagents and I don't know what all other kinds of foolishness the Bald Ones use. I have the right bacterial strains, and I don't need anything else."

"They'll say your bacteria are wrong. Or they'll say you planted the hoxbomb material. They don't want to believe one of their own could be guilty." Miss Murple didn't want to believe one of her own could be guilty, either. She recognized the possibility all the same.

Louie Pasture gave forth with an even ruder odor. "Yeah, nothing's ever their fault. Now tell me another one."

Humans thought Snarre't were sneaky. Snarre't thought humans were self-righteous. As often as not, both species were right. "I'll pass the report on to their detective," Miss Murple said. "He won't like it, though."

"Too stinking bad," the tech retorted. "Long as they give the unlicked cloaca what he deserves, they don't have to like it. They just have to do it."

"Well, you're right," Miss Murple said.

"But I'm innocent!" Petros van Gilder squawked.

"You're under arrest anyway," Sergeant Kling answered. "I don't much like this, but I've got to do it."

"I didn't do anything to the Cravaths. I didn't have any reason to do anything to them," the scooter salesman said.

"You're a business rival. Maybe that's reason enough. It would be for some people." Kling nodded to the uniformed cops who'd come with him. "Take him away. We'll see what happens when he goes to trial."

"Right, Sergeant," the police officers said. They led van Gilder out of the dealership and into a *rara avis* on Lacanth C: a fully enclosed car. Doing the perp walk wouldn't help his business any, even if he got off in the end. Sergeant Kling swore under his breath. Sometimes things felt neat and tidy when he closed a case. This wasn't one of those times.

Which didn't necessarily prove anything. Sloppy cases could be as solid as elegant ones. But he liked clean patterns, and he didn't have one in front of him. Well, maybe things would neaten up later.

Next interesting question was where Petros van Gilder got the hoxbomb in the first place. Unless he had a biochemical lab or some trained Snarre'i bacteria back at home—and he didn't, because the police had searched the place—the thing had to come from somebody else.

From a Furball, Kling thought. Maybe from the Furballs his Snarre'i opposite number was already suspicious about.

But even if that was true, what did it mean? Did van Gilder approach them so he could do something horrible to a competitor? Or did they want to do something horrible to a human for reasons of their own? Why would they? Did Cravath do something to them?

Those were all interesting questions. Kling had answers for exactly none of them. He—or rather, the DA—didn't have to prove motive, of course. Opportunity would do, especially if nobody else had that opportunity. That felt sloppy, too, though.

He wondered what he could do about it. Only one thing occurred to him: see what was in the endless hours of surveillance video. Even with computer help, he'd spend a lot of time in front of the monitor for a while. He looked forward to that the way he looked forward to a salpingectomy with nerve enhancement.

Which didn't mean he wouldn't have to do it, like it or not. It was all part of the day's work. It was why the city put credit in his account twenty times a year. Routine *did* solve cases. It wouldn't have become routine if it didn't. That didn't make it any less a pain in the ass, only a necessary as opposed to an unnecessary pain in the ass.

Kling was opposed to all kinds of pains in the ass, necessary and unnecessary. He wondered why the hell he'd ever thought being a cop was a good idea. Somewhere back down the line, he'd been pretty goddamn stupid.

Now, instead of being stupid, he'd be bloody bored. Monitoring surveillance video? About as exciting as pulling up a chair and watching a blank screen. Who didn't know better than to do anything openly nefarious—or even openly interesting—where the cameras were rolling? The Snarre't used different surveillance methods, but over on that side of Latimer you literally couldn't fart without somebody knowing about it.

Back to the office. Kling went through the digital stream from van Gilder's scooter dealership first. He had to identify everybody who came in. The computer helped a lot there. It had—or at least was supposed to have—ID photos of all the humans on Lacanth C. Matching them to faces should have been a piece of cake for software engineers.

And so it was . . . but it was a piece of cake with the occasional pebble in the dough. People were just flat-out better than machinery at recognizing faces. Evolution had been working on it a lot longer than software engineers had. (And hadn't the Snarre'i detective said something like that, in another context?) Instead of naming *a* name, sometimes the computer would spit out two or three or six and let Kling figure out whose photo that really was.

Sometimes he could—and sometimes he damn well couldn't. So he would have several possibilities here and there, and he'd have to track down which of them really had seen van Gilder back most of a year earlier. Half of them wouldn't remember, and half of the other half would lie. Long and bitter experience made him sure of that.

Just to make things even more enjoyable, van Gilder *had* dealt with Snarre't, too. Human technology fascinated some of them. If they decided riding overgrown drumsticks wasn't cool any more, they went scooter shopping. If they didn't visit Jack Cravath, they visited Petros van Gilder. Often, they visited both of them.

Algorithms for computer recognition of Furballs were light-years behind the ones for recognizing humans. Evolution didn't give John Paul Kling a hand with the aliens, either. He called his opposite number to see what the Snarre't could do.

Miss Murple didn't even try to sound happy. "How am I supposed to recognize Snarre't if I can't smell them?" she demanded.

"Sorry," the human detective said. "We don't record smell. I'm not sure we can record it."

"I understand that," Miss Murple said. "But it's possible—it's likely—that you expect too much from me. I hope I'm a reasonably good investigator. I don't work miracles, though."

"Well, neither do I," the human said. "Can you recognize *any* of your people by sight alone?"

"Maybe." Miss Murple didn't want to say even that much. It would build up the Baldy's hopes. She was much too likely to dash them again right afterwards.

He kept trying. He had the virtue, if that was what it was, of stubbornness. "Audio goes with the visuals," he said.

"That may help—a little," she admitted, and sighed. "Well, go ahead. Transmit. This will be dull, won't it?"

"I sure think so. I'd be amazed if you didn't," he said. "Our species are different, but they aren't *that* different."

One thing she quickly discovered: she couldn't identify anybody on a phone screen. There were times when she had trouble telling her own kind from humans. If that didn't say the job was hopeless, nothing ever would.

"Wait!" she told Kling. "You can make these images larger, can't you?"

"Oh, sure," the human detective said. Snarre'i records, like Snarre'i communication generally, were much more involved. The Bald Ones just looked at things and sometimes listened to things. Snarre't experienced sensory records as if taking part in them themselves.

Miss Murple sighed again. "I'd better come over to your side of town to view them properly, then. Can we do this after nightfall?"

The worm in her head interpreted the noise the human made as yet another sigh. "All right," he said. "Come ahead. I'll wait for you. You understand I wouldn't usually be working then?"

"Yes," Miss Murple said. "One of us is going to be unhappy. I would rather not be the one."

"Well, you're upfront about it, anyhow. Have it your way," her counterpart said. "Come before it gets too late, if you possibly can."

"I will do that." Miss Murple broke the connection with nothing but relief.

She enjoyed the smooth rhythm of her caitnop's strides as it hurried toward the humans' police headquarters. She had to wear eyecovers even after sundown, because the Bald Ones lit up their district so they could pretend daytime never ended. The caitnop narrowed its eyes to cut down the glare. She stroked the carefully bred creature, and reproached herself for not giving it eyecovers, too. She hoped it wouldn't come to harm.

Humans on scooters stared at her. She'd ridden scooters a few times. To her, the motion seemed unnaturally smooth. And the machines stank of metal and plastic. If Sharon Rock and Joe Mountain wanted one so badly, they were welcome to it, as far as she was concerned. What did a scooter do that a caitnop or drof didn't except break down at random? There wasn't any yummy scootershit to gather up, either.

She had the caitnop wait in the best-shadowed spot she could find near the police headquarters. Things proved even brighter inside the human-filled building than they were outside. Even with eyecovers, she started getting a headache.

Kling was considerate enough to wait for her in a dark room. Would she have given a Baldy the converse courtesy? She doubted it. "Let's have a look at these images," she said without a great deal of hope.

The screen where the human displayed them was much larger than the one on the phone. The sound quality was much better, too. All the same, Miss Murple was so conscious of the alien presentation, she was sure she wouldn't be able to identify any of the Snarre't on the video.

She was sure, but she was wrong. She thought she would have recognized Joe Mountain if he weren't with Sharon Rock. But Sharon Rock, even by herself, even without her preposterously sexy aroma, would have been unmistakable. If she wasn't a perfectly made female, Miss Murple had no idea where she fell short of the ideal. Seeing her made the Snarre'i detective all too conscious of her own shortcomings.

Kling sat there watching the stunner without being stunned. Miss Murple would have thought Sharon Rock could stimulate even someone of a different species. Evidently not. The lifey performer had said she and Joe Mountain liked to get away from the constant attention their own kind gave them. She must have meant it.

"These are the Snarre't who bought a scooter from the parent of the hoxbombed infant," Miss Murple said, and then, "Why *don't* you dispose of the malformed thing, anyway? It's horrible."

"To look at, yeah," Kling said. "But its brain seems to work." Miss Murple bared her teeth. It didn't seem reason enough. The human detective went on, "I will tell you something interesting about these images. Do you see the jacket on the chair behind van Gilder? Behind the human suspect, I mean?"

"I see something on the chair. Is it a, uh, jacket?" Miss Murple said. The worm in her brain had trouble with words like that, words that stood for things human used and her own kind didn't.

"It's a jacket, all right," the Baldy said. "And unless I'm very much mistaken, it's the jacket with the pocket that had the hoxbomb material inside."

"Really?" Miss Murple said. Kling nodded instead of spreading his fingers, but she knew what that meant. She watched a little more. "There is no sign that the Snarre't are tampering with the jacket in any way."

No sooner had she spoken than the human on the screen said, "Excuse me for a moment. I have to go void some waste." That was how the worm in Miss Murple's head turned his words into Snarre'l, anyhow. He hurried away, leaving Sharon Rock and Joe Mountain alone in his bare little office.

No sooner had he gone than Joe Mountain picked up the jacket. "What a silly thing," he said. "See what happens when you don't have hair?" He admired Sharon Rock's soft, silky pelt. Well, who wouldn't?

"Bald Ones are pathetic beasts," Sharon agreed. Miss Murple found herself thinking the performer was right. But what did that have to do with the price of grubs? Sharon Rock gestured imperiously to Joe Mountain. "Let me see that thing."

"Here. You're welcome to it." He handed it to her.

The human detective stared at the video screen with Miss Murple. "Do the Snarre's hands go in the pocket? Hard to be sure, isn't it?"

The Snarre'. He hasn't the faintest idea who Sharon Rock and Joe Mountain are. Maybe he's lucky. "It is hard, yes," Miss Murple said. "Can we get a better view? Will that give us what we need to know?"

"Can't tell till we try," the human answered. He spoke to the plastic-stinking computer as if it were alive. It responded as if it were alive, too. The image of the jacket and then of that one pocket slowed down and grew till it almost filled the screen. It stayed center, too, no matter how Joe Mountain and Sharon Rock moved it. This technology might be inorganic, but it was formidable in its own way. "Hold it right there!" her opposite number said sharply, and the image froze.

"Well, well," Miss Murple said. Two of Sharon Rock's fingers—the fur on them was noticeably darker and thicker than it was on Joe Mountain's—did find their way inside that flap of cloth. "Isn't that interesting?"

"Interesting. Yeah." Kling told the computer to take special note of that sequence. Miss Murple had no idea how it would, but she believed that it would. The human gave his attention back to her. "Looks like it wasn't our boy after all."

"You don't know that yet," Miss Murple said. "The visual shows fingers in there, yes. It doesn't let us smell or taste those fingers to know for sure what's on them. I should also let you know that these Snarre't are celebrities." *Oh, yeah. Just a little.* "They are rich and famous. They will have the best barristers around. They won't be easy to convict."

To her surprise, the human detective started to laugh. To her even greater surprise, he seemed to have trouble stopping. At last, shaking his head, he succeeded. "Some things really don't change between species, do they?" he said. "The ones who are rich and famous think they can get away with anything *because* they're rich and famous."

"That happens with us, yes," Miss Murple agreed. "Does it happen with you, too?"

"Oh, just a little," he answered.

She needed a moment to smell out the sarcasm. Then she went on, "As I said, though, we still don't know for sure that it happened here."

"Let's watch the rest of this sequence," Kling said. Miss Murple wondered if he'd got his name because of the way he clung to a case. He spoke to the computer once more. The image shrank to the usual size of the surveillance video. The speed at which it moved also returned to normal.

Joe Mountain's ears twitched. "I hear him coming back," he said.

Quickly, Sharon Rock returned the jacket to the chair where it had lain. It wasn't quite in the same position it had been in before, but Petros van Gilder never noticed. When the human suspect walked into his office, all he cared about was selling the two Snarre't a scooter. Even without smell, he radiated disappointment when they declined to buy.

"Maybe you'll come back another time," he said as Sharon Rock and Joe Mountain made their good-byes.

"Maybe we will." Sharon Rock wasn't laughing, but she wasn't far from it. She and Joe Mountain left the office. Van Gilder kicked at the floor. A Snarre' wouldn't have shown frustration the same way, but Miss Murple knew it when she saw it.

"You say that isn't proof?" the human detective. "Well, maybe it isn't, not by itself, but it sure smells funny, don't you think?"

So even noseblind Bald Ones used a phrase like that! Miss Murple's fingers spread to show she thought he was right. "It is not proof. It sure does smell funny."

"All right. What's our next move?"

"You can bring this record with you, right?"

"Oh, sure."

"Good. I think you'd better show it to my superiors."

Kling sighed again. "I ought to be going home," he grumbled, perhaps more to himself than to her. "Well, I'll put it on a laptop. If we can wrap this up, we'd better do it."

"You think like an investigator, sure enough," Miss Murple said.

John Paul Kling didn't like night-vision goggles. If you went over to the Furball side of town, though, you needed them—which was putting it mildly. The Snarre't didn't believe in street lights. They didn't believe in a big way. It was as dark as the inside of a cow over there.

The Snarre't didn't think so, and neither did their genetically engineered mounts. Their big eyes (which glowed in the dark like cats') glommed on to every available photon. Human scientists insisted that night-vision goggles grabbed even more, but you couldn't have proved it by Kling.

"Here we are," the detective said. Kling could read Snarre'l pretty well, even if he didn't speak it worth a damn. The sign in front of the low, sprawling building said PURSUIT AND CAPTURE OF CRIMINALS. The last word literally meant *stinkers*. The Snarre't thought with their noses a lot of the time.

A Furball sat just inside the entrance. His pose bespoke boredom. If he didn't look like every desk sergeant ever born . . . He stopped looking bored as soon as he saw—and probably smelled—Kling. "What the—?"

"This is my associate on the hoxbomb case," said the detective with whom Kling was dealing. "He has evidence the ones high in the tree need to smell right away."

"How can you smell human evidence?" Either the sergeant didn't know Kling was wearing a babelfish or he just didn't care. Kling would have bet on number two. The Snarre's wiggle was the Furball equivalent of a shrug. "Well, go on. You're supposed to know what you're doing." Even through the babelfish, his tone said it wasn't his problem.

Neither Snarre'i eyes nor night-vision goggles could work with *no* photons. Dimly glowing plates—bioluminescence—set into the walls and ceiling every so often doled out a few. Snarre'i cops bustled along the hallways much like their human equivalents. Some of them stared at Kling. Some just ignored him. He didn't know what that meant. He wasn't real anxious to find out, either.

"Here." His Snarre'i—colleague?—walked through an open door. "This is my boss."

John Paul Kling went in, too. By size, the new Furball was a male. "I greet you," Kling said in Snarre'l.

"Hello," the male replied in English, then went back to his own language: "What have you got? Hoxbomb business, yes? Yes, of course." He answered himself. "Why else would a human be here?"

"Yeah, it's hoxbomb business, all right." Kling opened the laptop, made sure the screen was set to a brightness level Snarre't could stand, and fired it up. He ran through the surveillance video in Petros van Gilder's office, and especially through the part where the two Snarre't handled van Gilder's jacket.

"You sniff out—well, you see—who they are," his opposite number said to her boss. "But we have to drop on them just the same." Kling hid a smile. How many times had he heard conversations just like that back at his cop shop? More than he could count—he was sure of that.

"Are you sure we can, with just human evidence?" the boss cop asked.

"Once we interrogate them, we'll get the stench of lying soon enough," Kling's counterpart said. "Then they're ours."

"But she's a lifey performer," the boss cop said. "She can fake those odors."

"Well enough to fool you or me, maybe. I'll be damned if I believe she can fool a sniffer for long." The other Furball seemed very sure of herself.

"Hmm." The boss cop thought it over. "Yeah, I guess you're right." He didn't sound thrilled about it. A human lieutenant would have decided the same thing, and would have sounded the same way, too. High-profile cases always meant trouble. The boss cop swung his big eyes toward John Paul Kling. "Want to come along for the bust? Maybe you'll intimidate them."

"Sure. Why not?" Kling found himself grinning. Not many of his fellow bulls would have a story like this one. That was almost as good a reason to go with the Furballs as the chance to close the case. He wondered if the aliens would see—or smell—things the same way. He thought they would. Plainly, they were cops, too.

The human-made scooter wasn't in the garage at Sharon Rock and Joe Mountain's apartment house. Miss Murple muttered under her breath. That meant the suspects were out doing whatever important people did.

Miss Murple had started muttering when she discovered that reporters were at the apartment house ahead of her and her comrades and Kling. Somehow, the newsies always sniffed out stories. Somebody back at the station was probably counting her sweetener right now.

"What are you doing here?" one of the reporters called. "Sharon and Joe are at Famous Janus' party."

"*Whose* party?" Sam Spud asked. Famous Janus wasn't famous to him. As far as Miss Murple could tell, Famous Janus was famous for being famous, not for anything he'd actually done. To a lot of Snarre't, that didn't seem to matter. Miss Murple wondered whether humans were so foolish. She doubted it. Maybe not being driven by odors had occasional advantages. Famous Janus *smelled* as if he ought to be important, so people naturally thought she was.

"Do you know where Famous Janus lives?" Miss Murple asked the reporters.

They laughed at her. She'd known they would. But they told her where, too, and then they set out to beat her over there. Sam Spud turned to the Baldy. "Can your gadget go faster than drofs and cait-nops?" he asked.

"And how many can it carry?" Miss Murple added.

"It will take both of you, if you want to ride with me," Kling said. "I don't know whether it will go faster than your animals or not. Shall we find out?"

"Yes!" Miss Murple and Sam Spud said together.

"Hop on behind me, then," the human told them. "You'll have to let me know when to turn. This isn't my part of town, remember."

"We'll do it," Miss Murple promised. "Just hurry."

"Right," Kling said. "Grab the handholds. Are you ready? . . . We're going, then."

Go they did. Maybe scooters were faster than caitnops. They were certainly smoother. The sheet of clear stuff in front of the human kept the wind from buffeting the riders the way it would have on a caitnop at full gallop. The remaining breeze was almost enough to sweep away the stench of metal and plastic that clung to human-built machinery. Miss Murple could see why Sharon Rock and Joe Mountain might want a scooter. What she couldn't see was why they'd hoxbombed the male who sold it to them.

Had the Baldy somehow offended them? If he had, then the human suspect was working with them and not their dupe. Did they do it because Cravath *was* a human and they thought they could get away with it? Was it a thrill crime? Maybe answers would come out one of these days. In the meantime . . .

"Go right!" she shouted. Kling swung the scooter into a tight turn. It raced past a reporter on a tired old drof. The female looked and no doubt smelled unhappy. Miss Murple yelled for another turn. The human made that one in the nick of time, too. He started passing caitnops, even though they were running flat out. If you wanted to get somewhere in a hurry, a scooter could do the trick.

"Stop!" Sam Spud said. The human did, so abruptly that Miss Murple was squeezed against his back for a moment. It wasn't pleasant. Like most of his kind, he wore chemicals to mask his odors. They made contact with him less pleasant than his natural aromas would have, even if those were sharply alien. Humans didn't just ignore their noses. They seemed to go out of their way to torment them.

A large, muscular bouncer advanced on the scooter. "Who are you people?" she demanded. "And what are you doing with a Baldy?"

"Don't get personal, Furball," Kling snapped. Humans could be speciesist, too.

"We are investigators," Miss Murple said. "We are seeking two people said to be at Famous Janus' party. You will be sorry if you interfere."

"Very sorry," Kling put in, drawing his hand weapon. The noise it made when it went off might kill a Snarre' even if the pellet it hurled missed. Bald Ones more readily survived such shocks. They were a coarse-grained race.

The bouncer recognized the weapon for what it was. She retreated in a hurry. Miss Murple and Sam Spud uncurled their ears as the human stowed the vicious thing once more.

"What's going on?" someone shouted as a caitnop panted up. "Have they dropped on Sharon and Joe yet?"

"Sharon and Joe!" the bouncer exclaimed.

"Don't warn them," Miss Murple said. *Her* weapon launched a casing full of paralyzing spores. It took a couple of heartbeats to kill, but no longer than that. The bouncer didn't warn anybody.

Miss Murple, Sam Spud, and the human rushed up the stairs and into Famous Janus' flat. Several different illegalities were going on there. *Another time*, Miss Murple thought. The music was almost as loud as Kling's weapon would have been. Joe Mountain was licking the ear of a female not a quarter as attractive as the one he had. Sharon Rock was dancing with a weedy little male; if they'd danced any closer, they would have been mating.

"I arrest you," Sam Spud told Joe Mountain. "Go quietly, or else." Joe looked astonished. He smelled that way, too. He hadn't even noticed the investigators coming in.

Miss Murple, then, had the pleasure of seizing Sharon Rock. The lifey performer looked and smelled amazed, too. "You'll never pin this on us," she said.

"That's what you think," Miss Murple said. "We have plenty of human evidence to convict you. Come along quietly, or you'll stay quiet for good."

"Human evidence," Sharon Rock said scornfully. "What's human evidence worth?"

"Your neck," Miss Murple answered. "Nobody takes kindly to hoxbombing. You won't get away with it, even if you passed the stuff on to a Bald One."

"We didn't do anything." Sharon rather spoiled that by adding, "You haven't met our solicitors and barristers yet, either."

"Quietly, I told you," Miss Murple said. And Sharon Rock, who was used to taking direction from the finest lifey visualizers on Lacanth C, took it from a no-account investigator, too.

Once Miss Murple and Sam Spud and Kling brought their prisoners out onto the lawn in front of the apartment house . . . things got no easier. By then, the reporters had got there. The brains they carried recorded the images of the captured stars and sent them into the neural net. All the jaded sensation-seekers would be stinking up their flats in excitement.

How much trouble *would* Sharon and Joe's attorneys be able to kick up? Once the sniffers decided they smelled guilty, not much. It didn't matter how famous you were, not if you smelled like someone who'd done it. If the sniffers *didn't* think Sharon and Joe had done it, Miss Murple knew what her career was worth, and Sam Spud's with it.

Attorneys being what they were, the Snarre't might even go after the human investigator. Could they get him? Miss Murple didn't know, but she had her doubts. If he was wrong about Sharon and Joe, he'd made an honest mistake. The Bald Ones wouldn't be upset about it, not when he was dealing with Snarre't.

Miss Murple's big boss wouldn't care whether her mistake was honest or not. Who would have imagined that humans might have better sense than her own folk?

"You helped us. You truly did," Sam Spud told Kling. He sounded startled. Miss Murple couldn't blame him. She also had trouble believing a human could be worth anything. But this one had pulled his weight. He really had.

"Yeah, well, you guys did all right, too," he replied. Maybe it was the imagination of the worm in Miss Murple's brain, but he also seemed surprised. She wondered why. Didn't he know the Snarre't had a strong sense of justice? And if he didn't, how ignorant *were* humans, anyhow?

"Looks like you're off the hook," John Paul Kling told Petros van Gilder as he set the scooter seller free. "You were just a sucker for the Furballs."

"I said so," van Gilder replied with as much dignity as he could muster. "I don't have anything against Jack and Beverly. I feel bad things turned out the way they did." He shook his head. "I don't feel bad. I feel awful. That poor kid."

"Yeah." Kling didn't like thinking about the Cravaths' baby. He wished he'd never set eyes on it. By all accounts, it was healthy and showed every sign of being smart even if it was a monster. The Snarre't still thought humans were crazy for not getting rid of it. They had a point, too. Could any kid be smart enough to make up for what the hoxbomb had done to this one's flesh? It wasn't easy to believe.

"I talked with my lawyer," van Gilder said.

That snapped Kling's attention back to the here-and-now in a hurry. "Yeah?"

"Yeah." Van Gilder nodded. Then he sighed. "He said you had probable cause to arrest me, so suing you wouldn't go anywhere. But some people will think I did it whether you let me go or not. This is bound to louse up my business. How do I get my good name back?"

Unfortunately, that was a damn good question. Kling did the best he could with it: "The people who matter to you know you're innocent. For the others, for the yahoos, you're a nine-days' wonder. They'll forget you as soon as something else juicy hits the news. You may get hurt for a little while, but I don't think it'll last long."

"I hope not." Van Gilder didn't sound convinced. Kling didn't push it, because he wasn't a hundred percent convinced, either.

He led the scooter dealer to the station's front door. A police vehicle waited outside to take van Gilder home. He could get on with his life—as much of it as he had left after getting busted for a really nasty crime. He was liable to be right; the stain from the arrest wouldn't vanish overnight.

A few minutes after van Gilder disappeared, Kling's phone rang. He pulled it out of his pocket. "Sergeant Kling speaking."

"This is Jack Cravath, Sergeant." Sure enough, Cravath's face looked out of the phone screen at Kling. "I just called to say thank you."

That didn't happen every day, or even every tenth of a year. "You're welcome," Kling answered. "I'm only sorry we had to meet the way we did."

"Yeah, me, too," Cravath said. "So the Snarre't turned the hoxbomb loose for the hell of it, did they? And it found somebody it could bite?"

"That's what they're saying," Kling answered. "Maybe I believe 'em, maybe I don't. It puts the best face on what they did—that's for sure."

"Why would anybody do such a horrible thing?" Cravath asked.

"My guess is, because they thought they could get away with it," John Paul Kling said. "Maybe they didn't figure the hoxbomb would find anybody vulnerable. Maybe. But why put it in van Gilder's pocket if that wasn't what they wanted?"

"Why do it at all?" Jack Cravath repeated.

"Most likely, they didn't think we could catch them. They like our machines, remember," Kling said. "They probably guessed we couldn't figure out what was going on, because we didn't have the right kind of technology to handle it. If we'd tried by ourselves, they might have been right, too. But hoxbombing is so evil, their own people got involved, and that made the difference."

"A lot of humans wouldn't admit it," Cravath said.

"Yeah, well . . . You know what else?" Kling said. "The Furballs think we're just as dumb and weird as we think they are. And a lot of the time, they're right. So are we. But I'll tell you something funny. That one Snarre'i detective, I wouldn't mind working with her again. How's that for peculiar?"

"I deal with them all the time," Cravath said. "They aren't so bad. They're no worse than we are."

"Come on—which is it?" Kling asked. Cravath didn't see the difference. But then, he wasn't a cop.

LOGAN'S LAW

This story appears here for the first time. It's one of my occasional lunges at mainstream fiction. I first started playing with it in the 1980s, when some of the events on which it's based were fresher in my mind. That should be obvious from the technology, and lack of technology, involved. It is fiction, though. Of course it is. It says so right here on the box.

He sat in the sixth-floor office, glumly grading finals. It was a bright spring Berkeley Thursday outside, but fluorescent no-time in there. A file cabinet cut off most light and all the view from the window. The desk faced away from it anyhow, toward the books stacked everywhere. Good solid stuff: the *Cambridge Medieval History*, the *Monumenta Germaniae Historiae*, journals like *Speculum* and *Viator*, dictionaries and hagiographies, the tools of a medievalist's trade.

Why did he come up to campus? Working at his place would have been just as easy. His stuff was unpacked, into closets, onto shelves, boxes folded flat and stowed for his next move. But the apartment was a worse tomb than this, and at night the queen-sized bed felt way too big. He wasn't used to sleeping alone, not these last eight years.

He bent to the bluebook in front of him. Somebody walked past the door. He noticed out of the corner of his eye. A minute or two later, he caught another flick of motion: same jeans, same top somewhere between rust and maroon. Someone who wanted to know what was up with in his High Middle Ages class next quarter?

He sighed and put down the pen. But this was part of the job, too. "Help you?" he called.

He thought for a second she didn't hear him. Then she cautiously stepped into the office after all.

What was she doing here? She wasn't one of the bright, eager, unprepared undergrads who filled his courses. Like him, she was gaining hard on the tired side of thirty. "What can I do for you?" he asked, and felt like an ass the second the words were out of his mouth.

He got lucky—she wasn't listening. Her eyes wandered from the map of thirteenth-century Germany half-unrolled and leaning against a bookcase to the boxes full of back numbers of *Byzantinische Zeitschrift* (one on a chair, the other on its side underneath) to the two shelves solid with black-spined paperbacks: Penguin Classics.

While she checked out the office, he did the same with her. About five-four, slim, with hair as black as the Penguins, tied behind her head. Hazel eyes, very fair skin. She carried herself like a dancer.

"What a lot of books," she breathed, a grad student's lust for the printed page in her voice.

"Wish they were mine," he agreed.

"No?"

"Christ, no. This is old Blaustein's office—my chairman, I mean—but he's teaching in Hamburg this year. I've got his classes, and he lets me use the office. He drops dead over there, I'm out in the hall with my brother's pickup, you betcha."

"Don't blame you. This is an incredible collection. Not my field, but incredible."

He glanced at her left hand: no ring. *Whoa, boy, down*, he told himself. He remembered what his buddy Ed Logan said a couple of years back, when Ed's divorce was fresh and new. Ed was having a tough time connecting as a new single, and they were both pretty drunk. Ed sat on his couch—a couch he didn't have any more—looking down into a glass of gin and ice, and solemnly declared, "Man, the good ones are all taken."

After a while, they made a joke of it: Logan's Law, to go with Newton's and Murphy's and Sturgeon's and the rest. Now his own marriage was egg on his face, and it wasn't so funny any more.

She took a couple of deep breaths, then blurted, "Does writing a dissertation make everybody hostile?"

"I'm single because of mine." It wasn't the whole truth, or even half, but it wasn't a lie, either. The months at the Mac, and before that fighting sources and lexica and secondary literature, sure hadn't helped.

She accepted the words without surprise. "I was talking with my friend Liz Martin—she's in Near Eastern studies; do you know her?"

"'Fraid not."

"Oh. Well, anyway, I was talking with Liz and she said something totally innocuous, and I screamed in her face."

"It's crazy-making," he agreed. "I'm Steve, by the way."

"Oh," she said again. A beat later: "I'm Jen."

"Hi." *More inanity*, he thought. To cover it, he asked her what her thesis topic was.

"Dutch administration in the East Indies—Indonesia, now—between the two World Wars." It was no stranger than the study of Manfred Hohenstaufen's struggle against the thirteenth-century papacy that earned him this temporary spot behind a desk. Jen went on, "I was on my way to give Teske my second chapter, but he doesn't act like he cares when he gets something—he took three months to read chapter one. Even when he did, he hardly had anything to say about it."

"You don't know when you're well off. Blaustein fought me comma by comma all the way through."

"It'd be nice to find out," she said wistfully.

"Ha! Change this, revise that—then put it back the first way again."

They bitched for a while: not enough money, not enough time, probably no fulltime job at the end anyway, and a workload that made you a hermit to survive. Grad students' gripes seemed pretty much the same in modern Southeast Asian studies as in medieval Europe.

She looked at her watch. "I've got to run."

He hesitated, then plunged: "Could I—dammit, I don't know how to do this any more—could I ask you for your phone number?"

She smiled, maybe at the awkward parenthesis. "Sure." She took a scratchpad and pen from her purse. "Here."

"Thanks." He looked at the little sheet. *Jen Barkman*, she'd written. She crossed her sevens like a European. "Call you tonight?"

She was already at the door. "Okay," she said, and disappeared.

The phone rang four times before she answered. "Hello?"

"Jen? Hi, this is Steve."

"Oh, hi. How are you?"

"All right. Um—have anything planned for tomorrow night?"

"Translating tax records, maybe. Besides that, diddly."

"Well, do you like Japanese food? There's a good place not far from my apartment. Best sushi on the East Bay, I think. And have you seen 'Trouble All Over' yet?"

"No, and I want to," she said. "Where are you?"

"Up in Martinez."

"Martinez has sushi?" She sounded amazed. "I'm in the Oakland Hills. That's a long way for you to make the round trip picking me up. How do I get to your place?"

"Take the 80 up to Carquinez Scenic Drive. . . ." He finished the directions.

"About seven?"

"Say, six-thirty. The movie starts at twenty past eight."

"Sounds good. Give me your number in case something goes wrong." When she had it, she asked, a little sheepishly, "Um, Steve—what's your last name?"

That startled a laugh out of him. "You didn't read it on my door card? It's Whortleberry."

She giggled, then said at once, "Sorry."

"It's okay. Everybody does that. Actually, the name's kind of useful now—people remember me by it. No fun at all when I was a kid, though."

"I can imagine," Jen said, and then, "I'd better get back to it. The tax registers are calling."

"I'll let you go." He knew how a thesis could drive somebody. "See you tomorrow."

"'Bye."

He was standing naked in front of a steamy mirror, trimming his mustache, when the cell phone chirped. He grabbed it. "Hello?"

"Steve? This is Jen."

"Hello." His stomach lurched as if he were on a rollercoaster, one he hadn't known he was riding. "What's up?" But he feared he could guess. She had to be crazy to go out with somebody freshly single. What kind of excuse would she come up with?

"I don't think I can get up there tonight. Clio—Clio is my dog, named for the Muse of History, you know—Clio has something wrong with one of her paws, and I don't want to spend a whole evening away from her. I'm sorry to mess things up, but—"

"It's okay," he said, biting the bullet as gracefully as he could. "Maybe another time." Now she'd come back with *Maybe* in the drone that meant *Not on your life*.

But she went on, "I was thinking you could have dinner down here where I'm staying. The movie's at the Eightplex, and I wouldn't feel so bad about going off for a couple of hours."

Reprieve from the governor ran through his mind. "How do I get there?" The directions were more complicated than the ones he'd given her. "Can I bring anything?" he asked. "Beer? Wine?"

"Beer, I think," she said. He grinned like an idiot—his ex hated the stuff.

"When do you want me?"

"Whenever. If dinner runs late, we can always catch the 10:45 show."

"See you soon, then."

He dressed quickly and threw on the rumpled herringbone jacket every male one-time grad student seems to own. Just on the off chance, he stuck a Trojan in his wallet. He hadn't worried about anything like that since high school. As he locked the deadbolt, the ugly furnished apartment felt surprisingly like home.

His old Nissan didn't like the Oakland Hills, or any others. He managed to drive past Jen's street and had to double back. Even when he found her address, he thought he had it wrong. Most of Oakland was tough and working-class, but this. . . . The house was a mansion, set well back from the street. His car coughed climbing the steep driveway, then sighed into silence when he killed the ignition.

Jen came out on the deck and watched him unfold. "I didn't know you were so tall," she said.

"I guess I was sitting down the whole time when we talked before." His angular six-three and odd last name were usually the first two things people noticed about him. Funny she'd missed them both.

He went around to the other side of the Nissan for the beer. "Quite a place," he said, climbing the narrow flagstone stairway toward her.

"Isn't it? I'm housesitting. The owners' last daughter just went off to college, and they bought a smaller place in Sausalito."

"Wow, life's tough."

"Yeah. They want someone here till they sell this one. It's a great deal—no rent, I have all the privacy I need, and a pool and sauna besides."

"I'm so jealous."

"Come on in. I'll show you around."

She led him to the side door. It opened onto the kitchen, which was the size of his living room. He put the beer in the refrigerator, met Clio—a big black retriever who did limp—and walked through several rooms with cathedral ceilings and a forest's worth of wood paneling.

"Had enough?" Jen asked.

"You're staying in a place like this and you still want to be a grad student in history?"

"Might as well enjoy it while I have the chance. Let's go back to the kitchen. I'll put you to work."

"I'll open a couple of those beers before you do."

"Sure."

They drank most of a bottle each. Then she said, "It's chicken breasts and stir-fry vegetables—you get to cut up the veggies. Told you I'd make you work."

"I'm easy. Where's the knife?"

"In that drawer there." She got out fresh broccoli, mushrooms, an onion. He bought the same mix, but quick-frozen in a plastic bag. She said, "Cut everything thin. They're not supposed to be in the skillet long."

"Gotcha." The knife thocked on the cutting board. Steve was functional in the kitchen—and cooking for himself was cheaper than eating out every night.

They talked while he chopped and she fiddled with the chicken. She was twenty-nine, from Milwaukee, divorced herself: "Three years now. Yeah, I went through the wars."

"I thought you might have."

Her laugh rang sour. "Scars still show?"

"No, no. Just—you seem to know where I'm coming from, is all."

"Well, sure. Divorced people are the only ones fit to talk with other divorced people. Nobody else knows what you mean."

He remembered his parents' pained incomprehension when he told them he and Elaine were breaking up, his married friends' sympathy—tinged with alarm, as if divorce were something catching, like the flu—and the barely concealed amusement of a couple of bachelor buddies. Nothing from any of them had touched the sudden aching emptiness the collapse left inside him.

"Why don't you bring those vegetables over here if you're done with them?" she said.

It was the first time he'd stood really close to her for more than a couple of seconds. Wondering if he should touch her made him as nervous as a tenth-grader. In a way, that was about what he was. Who knew how the rules had changed when he was out of circulation?

"Penny for 'em," she said, out of the blue.

His cheeks heated as he told her.

"Oh, that." She fed strips of chicken into the pan with the vegetables. "No rush, is there?"

Having no good answer, he let her tend the stir-fry. Some of his nerves went away.

The chicken came out fork-tender. The vegetables were perfect, too: hot clear through but still crisp, juicy, full of flavor. Soy sauce and a touch of something he couldn't quite name only added to them.

"What's that, mm, tang?"

"Fresh-grated ginger."

"Uhwishush," he said with his mouth full, then tried again. "Delicious."

They were nearly through when she asked the question he'd half hoped for, half dreaded: "Want to talk about what went wrong?"

"I suppose." But he took a long pull at his beer before he went on. "My fault as much as Elaine's, I guess. She always wants to be out and doing stuff. A party, a play, a concert, dancing, shopping, just driving around. Me, I'd sooner curl up with a book or have a couple of friends over and talk all night. If we'd worked right, maybe we would've split the difference. But she got speedier and I dug in my heels. . . . Does that make any sense at all?"

"Oh, yes," she said softly. "Remember, I've been there." She ate a last bite, then leaned back in her chair and stretched. "Now, do you want to wash or dry?"

"Wash. I hate drying. Tell me where the john is first, though. The one drawback of beer."

"That hall there, first door on your left."

When he got back, he did put his arm round her shoulder. "Thank you," he said. "This is all wonderful."

"What, doing dishes?" Her tone was sharp, but she didn't move away.

"Sure. That, too." He let her go, turned on the hot water, and got to work.

"Amazing what enthusiasm can do," she said a few minutes later as she put away the last fork. She folded the dish towel and hung it up. "Now what?"

"I don't know. Do I have better things to be enthusiastic about than dishes?" Small and slight, she felt strange in his arms as he kissed her; Elaine was a full-bodied five foot nine.

"I should stand on a stool," she said against his chest. "You'll give me a crick in the neck."

"Sorry."

"Don't be. . . . I, ah, sort of like the man to take the lead at a time like this."

"Um, I would, if I knew where to lead you to."

"Well, yeah, that helps, I guess. Same way you went before, only a little farther."

So he led. As they passed the bathroom, she slipped free. "With you in a second." When she came out, her cheeks were puffed up like a chipmunk's, trying to hold in laughter that got loose anyhow. "It's so nice to have a man around the house," she caroled.

"Huh?" He went red as realization hit. "I left the goddamn seat up!"

"You sure did. Good thing I noticed—talk about cooling things."

"Sorry."

"Not to worry. No harm done." They walked down the hall. "Here we are," she said. "Close the door after you so Clio can't get in."

Afterwards, they lay together, side by side. She traced a scar on his belly with her finger. "Appendix?"

"Uh-huh. Seven years ago."

"Ah." Lazy silence for a while. Then she said, "Penny for 'em," again. She seemed to do it for a game, to see what would come out.

"Really want to know?"

She nodded.

"Well, I was thinking that not very long ago I was wondering what it would be like with someone new—and whether I could at all."

She leaned up on an elbow and looked at him in surprise. "You mean you never—?"

"No, never." He didn't know how to feel about that, proud or embarrassed or what. He'd had chances, a time or two, but it never quite happened.

Her forehead creased. "Interesting," was all she said, but the bitterness behind the word told of memories dragged into the light.

He didn't want that. He reached around her and started to rub her back. She grunted with pleasure and flopped over onto her stomach. He straddled her to do a proper job. "You give massages, too?" Jen said, her voice muffled by the pillow.

"Well, I try."

"Not half bad." A few seconds later, she added, "The lady was a fool."

Something crunched under his hands. Jen purred. "Nice," she said when he got to the base of her spine. "I feel limp as a jellyfish, but good." She stirred. "What time is it?"

He looked over at the alarm clock on the nightstand. "A few minutes past ten."

"We can still make the late show, then. Want to?"

"Why not?" He got off the bed and started climbing into his clothes. "Where is your, uh, Eightplex? I don't know Oakland real well."

"Just drive—I'll get us there. I'm a hell of a navigator."

"You got yourself a deal."

The Nissan wheezed up the driveway again. Steve was glad for his jacket when he got out. The night was very clear, but chilly. His breath smoked.

He went around to let Jen out. They stood together for a few seconds. "Where do we go from here?" he asked.

She shrugged; she was older at this game than he was. "Who can tell yet? Maybe nowhere, maybe . . . Wherever we take it, that's all."

"Okay."

She yawned, then laughed. "Sorry to be rude and crude, but I'm going to get some sleep." She tilted her face up for a kiss.

He watched her go up the stairs and into the big house, then fired up the car. It caught on the first try, as if it knew the way back was mostly downhill. He put it in gear and started home.

It was almost two when he got in. He was too keyed up to think of going to bed himself. Instead, he poked buttons on the phone.

"H'lo?"

"Ed?"

"Who—? Steve?" The poor devil sounded like somebody talking under water. "What's going—?"

"Ed, you know the Law? Logan's Law? It's wrong!" Was there even a fifty-fifty chance he wasn't full of it? He had no idea. But, right now, any chance at something good seemed a miracle of rare device.

Sleepy outrage filled Ed's voice. "Are you out of your mind? You call me up in the middle of the—what time is it, anyway?—to tell me that?" The line went dead.

Steve didn't care. He sat with the phone in his hand, smiling at the dial tone.

THE RING AND I

One more nonfiction piece here. Everyone who has written fantasy in the past sixty years owes J.R.R. Tolkien an enormous debt, of course, not least for popularizing the genre so others could hope to make a living from it. In "The Ring and I," I was able to spell out some of how much more than that I owe him. It's been almost fifty years since that tall, skinny kid picked up a paperback and decided to spend a dollar to find out what kind of story the author was telling. The rest, as they say, was history.

I discovered *The Hobbit* and *The Lord of the Rings* in summer 1966. I was seventeen; I had just graduated from high school, and was about to head off to the California Institute of Technology. I liked *The Hobbit* pretty well: well enough, at any rate, that I bought the trilogy to see what else J.R.R. Tolkien had written.

With *The Lord of the Rings* I was utterly entranced, and have been from that day to this. What struck me most about the trilogy was the astonishing depth of Tolkien's creation. He had not simply imagined the fictional present in which his characters were living, but also a history thousands of years deep as well as not one but several fictional languages. And what had happened in the dim and distant past of this created world kept bubbling up and remaining intensely relevant to the fictional present, in much the same way as Arminius the German's defeat of the Roman legions at the Teutoberg Wald in 9 A.D. remains intensely relevant to the history of Europe during the twentieth century.

I read *The Hobbit* and the trilogy obsessively. In the year after finding them, I must have gone through them, appendices and all, six or eight times. This was, of course, my freshman year at an academically demanding institution. Falling head over heels in love with *The Lord of the Rings* isn't the only reason I flunked out of Caltech. It isn't even the most important reason. But the time I spent with Frodo and Sam and Merry and Pippin was time I didn't spend—and should have spent—with physics and calculus and chemistry.

Nor was I the only one at Caltech caught up in Tolkien's spell. There were about ten of us, three or four, as luck would have it, in my residence house. We would get together when we could to try to stump one another with obscure quotations, to seek to work out the meanings of Elvish words, and to argue about things as abstruse and unprovable as how well a Roman legion suddenly transported to the universe of *The Lord of the Rings* might fare: of this last, more anon.

We searched through the books for hints about how the unwritten history of the Fourth Age might go as diligently as fifth-century theologians went over the New Testament for clues as to the nature or natures of Christ. I came to the conclusion that the chief evil power of the Fourth Age would be the Lord of the Nazgûl. This is, no doubt, heresy of the purest ray serene, but, like the Arians or Nestorians of early Christendom, I had some texts on my side.

Consider. The Fourth Age is to be the Age of Man, with the Elves and other ancient races vanished or much reduced in power. The Nazgûl, proud men ensnared by Sauron's schemes, are the great bane of mankind. When Merry hamstrung the Lord of the Nazgûl, he did so with a blade from the Barrow-downs, a blade specially made with charms against Sauron's chief lieutenant, who had been the Witch-king of Angmar in the north. But when Éowyn struck the blow that finished the Ringwraith, what sword did she use? Only an ordinary weapon of the Rohirrim. And when the Nazgûl's spirit left him, it "faded to a shrill wailing, passing with the wind, a voice bodiless and thin that died, and was swallowed up and was never heard again *in that age of the world* [italics mine]." Not in the Third Age, certainly. But what of the Fourth?

I may also note that, having thus been disembodied, the Lord of the Nazgûl was not caught, as were the other eight of his kind, in the incinerating eruption of Mount Doom after the Ring went into the fire. And, in a footnote to letter 246 in Carpenter's collection, Tolkien, who had been talking about how Frodo would have fared had he faced the remaining eight Nazgûl, writes, "The Witch-king [the Lord of the Nazgûl] had been reduced to impotence." Tolkien does *not* say the Ringwraith was slain, so I have, at least, a case.

Such was my reasoning. I should also note at this point that I was already trying to become a writer. I'd tried to write three different novels, and had actually finished one (none of this work, I hasten to add, came within miles of being publishable). The summer of 1967 was among the blackest times of my life. I had no idea how to cope with academic failure—thinking I could excel without studying much, as I had in high school, was another contributing factor, and not such a small one, to my flunking out of Caltech.

And so I plunged into a new novel. It was, of course, an exercise in hubris complete and unadorned. I realize that now. I did not realize it when I was eighteen. There are a great many things one does not realize at eighteen, not least among them being how very many things one does not realize at eighteen. Taking some of the arguments from the Caltech dorms, my own growing interest in history, and my belief that the Lord of the Nazgûl survived, I dropped a couple of centuries of Caesar's legionaries (and one obstreperous Celt) into what I imagined Gondor would be like during the Fourth Age.

God help me, I still have the manuscript. The one thing I can truthfully say is that I meant no harm. (I take that back. I can say one other thing: I am *not* the individual mentioned in letter 292 of *The Letters of J.R.R. Tolkien*, the chap who not only aimed to write a sequel to *The Lord of the Rings* but sent Tolkien a detailed outline of it. That letter dates from December 1966, before part of the same bad idea occurred to me.)

I wrote it. I finished it: something close to 100,000 words, far and away the longest project I'd ever undertaken up till then. Even had all the inspiration come from my own mind, I couldn't have sold it. Neither the style nor the characterization—such as that was—measures up to anything anyone else would ever want to read. To this day, though, I can say the plot was not disastrously bad. I had a tolerable story, but I didn't yet know how to tell it or where to set it.

A dozen years passed. I did a lot of the things most people do going from eighteen to thirty. I found something that interested me and pursued it. (In my case, it happened to be the history of the Byzantine Empire, which I admit is not a subject reckoned universally fascinating.) I fell in love several times. Sometimes this was mutual, sometimes not, which is also par for the course. Once, when it was, I got married. That lasted a little more than three and a half years. Not too long after my first wife and I broke up, I met the lady to whom I'm married now. In short, I grew up, or started to.

After I got my doctorate in Byzantine history, I taught for two years at UCLA while the professor under whom I'd studied had a guest appointment at the University of Athens. I had kept writing, and I began to sell an occasional piece: a science-fiction novelette to a magazine that expired before the piece saw print; a fantasy novel that owed nothing to Tolkien except, of course, a debt of gratitude for vastly broadening the market for fantasy novels of all sorts.

In the autumn of 1979, I was engaged to the woman now my wife, unemployed—a combination always especially endearing to a prospective father-in-law—and hoping to find a job, any sort of job, before my savings ran out and I faced the ultimate indignity of my generation: having to move back into the house where I'd grown up. Being unemployed, I had time on my hands. I decided I would go to work on another fantasy novel. If all went extremely well, that would even help me pay my bills.

In pondering what to write, I remembered that novel I'd worked on in an earlier time of crisis, the one that dropped Romans from Caesar's legions into Fourth Age Gondor. By the time I reached thirty, I was smart enough to figure out that using someone else's universe—especially without his permission—was not the right way to go about things. I'd also spent all that time and effort acquiring specialized knowledge of my own. This time, I dropped the legionaries into a world of my own creation rather than Tolkien's. I should have done that in the first place, but better late, I hoped, than never.

The world I built was modeled on the Byzantine Empire in the late eleventh century, at the time of the crucial battle of Manzikert, except that magic worked. Into it I brought my Romans—and one obstreperous Celt. The broad outlines of the plot of what became *The Videssos Cycle* are the same as those of my earlier act of unauthorized literary appropriation. This is why *The Misplaced Legion*, the first book of *The Videssos Cycle*, is dedicated to my wife, to the professor under whom I learned Byzantine history, to L. Sprague de Camp (whose *Lest Darkness Fall* first interested me in Byzantium) . . . and to J.R.R. Tolkien. My own cast of mind and my work usually resemble de Camp's far more than Tolkien's, but I felt I needed to note all the origins of the series. Attention must be paid.

Stretching and cutting the plot to fit the new situation wasn't that hard. I had envisioned Gondor in the Fourth Age as being in a situation the Byzantines would have understood: ancient; proud; diminished in territory from earlier days; in constant conflict with neighboring peoples, some of them nomads off the plains. (To this day, that seems reasonable to me. Tolkien himself, in letter 131 of the Carpenter collection, writes, "In the south Gondor rises to a peak of power, almost reflecting Númenor, and then fades slowly to decayed Middle Age, a kind of proud, venerable, but increasingly impotent Byzantium." The analogy was in his mind, too. The difference is, it had a right to be in his, but not in mine, not in his universe.)

One problem I had with *The Videssos Cycle* was the nature of my villain. The Lord of the Nazgûl was, as I mentioned, the chief evil power in my imagined Fourth Age. When he appeared among men, he necessarily went veiled and masked, as he had no face he could present to the world. I incorporated this feature of his appearance into the new world I was building: incorporated it without first asking myself, *Why are you doing this?*

By the time I did think to ask myself that question, my masked and veiled villain had become an integral part of the world I'd created. That meant I had to devise some reason for his concealing himself, and one that needed to be far removed from the reason the Nazgûl never showed themselves. I hope I succeeded in this. Had I not transposed quite so thoroughly from the Tolkien-based world to the one I was creating myself, the difficulty never would have arisen. And, indeed, it shouldn't have.

Aside from strip-mining my unpublishable *hommage* to *The Lord of the Rings* to help form work I might legitimately show the world, I've used Tolkienesque motifs only once that springs to mind, in a short story called "After the Last Elf Is Dead." There, the borrowing was intentional and, I believe, necessary. Tolkien and many of his lesser imitators depict the struggle of Good and Evil, with Good triumphant, at some cost, in the end.

This is, of course, how we want the world to work. The question I looked at in "After the Last Elf Is Dead" is, what happens if it doesn't work that way? What does the world look like if Evil defeats Good? Turning common tropes on their ear is often one of the most enjoyable and thought-provoking things a writer can do.

One of the more *profitable* things a writer can do, however, is to repeat those tropes. Tolkien's influence on fantasy since the publication and enormous success of *The Lord of the Rings* has not been altogether beneficial. This is not his fault, I hasten to add. But he has had many imitators, and imitators of imitators, and imitators of imitators of imitators, until some heroic-quest fantasies resemble nothing so much as blurry sixth-generation xeroxes of his great work, borrowing not only structure but bits of background such as noble, immortal elves and wicked, bestial orcs as if they sprang from lore long in the public domain rather than from the imagination of a writer not yet thirty years dead!

One very successful imitator—at least in financial terms—stated quite openly in an interview that his method was to emulate all the elements of adventure in *The Lord of the Rings* and to suppress the mythological, theological, and linguistic themes: every bit of the lore and scholarship and depth that informed the original. I read his words in astonished disbelief and dismay. And yet, he proved a shrewd judge of what a substantial part of the reading public wanted, or was willing to settle for. His books outsell those of all but a handful of other writers in the field.

The essential difference, I think, is that Tolkien created his world for himself first, and for others only afterwards. He began building the lays and legends of Middle-earth more than twenty years before even *The Hobbit* saw print. Almost twenty years more passed before *The Lord of the Rings* appeared. Everything in these books is a product of long reflection, long refinement. It shows. How could it help but show?

Because of that, it is unique, and is likely to remain so. Most books come into being far more quickly, and with at least one eye toward the market. It has always been so, ever since the earliest days of the printing press. Several of Shakespeare's plays, for instance, were first published as what we now call Bad Quartos—hasty, pirated editions designed to make a printer a fast buck. If we had only the Bad Quarto of *Hamlet*, the Prince of Denmark's immortal soliloquy would read,

> "To be, or not to be. Ay, there's the point,
> To die, to sleep, is that all? Ay, all:
> No, to sleep, to dream, ay marry there it goes,
> For in that dream of death, when we awake,
> And borne before an everlasting Judge,
> From whence no passenger ever return'd,
> The undiscovered country, at whose sight
> The happy smile, and the accursed damn'd.
> But for this, the joyful hope of this,
> Who'd bear the scorns and flatteries of the world,
> Scorned by the right rich, the rich cursed of the poor?"

The difference between that sorry text—probably set in type relying on the shaky memory of one of the actors in the play—and what Shakespeare actually wrote is the same sort of gulf that lies between those who would imitate Tolkien and the man himself. It is the difference between haste and care, between commerce and love. (I don't mean to suggest that Tolkien was immune to concerns about commerce; any examination of his letters proves otherwise. But he had built his world long before commerce became a concern. It is not often, and cannot often be, thus.)

As I've noted before, perhaps the greatest debt of gratitude fantasists of all stripes—emphatically not just the imitators—owe to J.R.R. Tolkien is what his success did for the genre as a whole. A couple of generations ago, speaking in broad terms, fantasy was something sf writers occasionally turned out in between novels full of spaceships. Science fiction normally outsold it by a considerable margin.

It isn't like that any more. Fantasy novels, these days, appear on bestseller lists far more regularly than their counterparts from science fiction. And a rising tide lifts all boats. Fantasies that could not have hoped to find a home in the 1950s or 1960s now have a better chance of seeing print, because—in no small measure due to Tolkien's work—fantasy has become a recognized category of its own. It is no accident that the professional organization for those who produce speculative fiction recently changed its name from the Science Fiction Writers of America to the Science Fiction and Fantasy Writers of America.

The next question to ask is, why has this happened? What has made Tolkien so enduringly popular? What has made fantasy in general so popular, besides Tolkien's example? Part of the answer, I think, lies in the ongoing, ever more rapid, changes in American life—indeed, in life throughout the industrialized world—during the course of the twentieth century, and especially after the end of the Second World War. We are all time travelers nowadays. When we look back to our childhoods, we remember a world quite different from the one in which we live today.

Take me as an example. I am, as I write these words, fifty-one. Things we take for granted nowadays but either did not exist or were in their infancy when I was born include television; vaccines for polio, mumps, measles, and chicken pox (I had all but the first, though I didn't come down with chicken pox till the age of forty-three); frozen foods; jet airliners; no-fault divorce; most though not all antibiotics; audio- and videotapes; space travel and most of what we know of astronomy (in the 1950s, the canals of Mars and oceans of Venus were legitimate topics for hard science fiction); birth-control pills; microwave ovens; the civil-rights, women's-rights, gay-rights, and environmental movements; freeways and the interstate highway system; rock 'n' roll; lasers; CDs; Mass in the vernacular rather than Latin; computers; legal pornography; e-mail; the hydrogen bomb; organ transplants; and the World Wide Web. The list is brief, and far from comprehensive.

No wonder, then, that every so often we are tempted to stop and wonder, *What the hell am I doing here?* Throughout almost the entire course of human history, people lived in much the same world at the end of their lives as at the beginning. Change did happen, but incre- mentally, even glacially. Medieval artists dressed the Roman soldiers around the crucified Jesus in the armor of their own day, and saw nothing incongruous in doing so. That styles and techniques in such things had altered through time was beyond their mental horizon.

Only in the past couple of hundred years has change become rapid enough to grow visible in the course of a single human life. It is no accident that historical fiction—fiction emphasizing the differences between past and present—came into being at about the same time as the Industrial Revolution took flight. The smooth continuum between past and present was broken; the past became a separate country, and interesting specifically because of that.

And I also think it no accident that fantasy has become so popular in an age of unprecedented change. It offers the reader a glimpse of a world where the verities underlying society endure, where moral values are strong (and, returning directly to Tolkien here, those who neglect the moral underpinnings of his work blind themselves to a large part of the world he built), where choices between good and evil are simpler than in the real world, and where good may reasonably be expected to triumph in the end. It's an anchor on a wildly tossing sea. Sometimes, it can be a crutch.

Few of us, I think—I hope!—would care to live permanently in such a world. But, especially when presented as magnificently as Tolkien does, it is a wonderful place to visit. We can enjoy the intricate adventure for its own sake, and for the respite it gives us from the complications and frustrations of mundane life. And perhaps, even after we set the books aside, we find ourselves a little more ready to face with good heart the world in which we do live. What more could one possibly ask of a work of the imagination?

BIRDWITCHING

My first daughter, Alison, is a serious birder. My wife and I are birders, too, though somewhat less passionate about it. And so, when Esther Friesner asked me for a story of suburban fantasy for a book to be called *Witch Way to the Mall*, this was what I came up with. In any competition, somebody's gonna cheat. The how and why may vary; the fact won't. That's what makes the story.

Lucy Parker was a birder. So was her son, Jesse. Lucy was a witch. It wasn't obvious whether Jesse had the Talent; he was only nineteen, and it didn't manifest itself till people got into their mid-twenties. John Parker, Lucy's husband and Jesse's father, was terminally mundane and had no interest in birds except dark meat. These character flaws not-withstanding, he did have other talents, and the three of them lived happily enough in Sunset Grove.

Fred O'Neill was also a birder. So was his daughter, Kathleen. Fred was also a witch, as well. Kathleen was only eighteen, so nobody knew whether she had the Talent, either. Her mother—Fred's wife—Samantha was every bit as mundane and at least as uninterested in birds as John Parker (though she liked white meat). So you can pretty much forget about her and John.

You do need to remember that the O'Neills lived in Fernwood, just over the barony line from Sunset Grove. You also need to remember that Lucy Parker couldn't stand Fred O'Neill, and that it was mutual. Who done what to whom? It all started a long time ago, and they tell different stories. They both sound sincere when they do, too. By now, that hardly matters. They ain't friends, and they ain't ever gonna be.

Jesse Parker, on the other hand, thought Kathleen O'Neill was pretty cute. She had red hair and freckles and everything else an eighteen-year-old girl ought to have—and Svarovski binoculars besides. She didn't think Jesse was half bad, either. This horrified and amazed his mother and her father. Not Montague-Capulet country, maybe, but you could see it from there. Also not your basic California Dreamin'.

And you need to remember that the annual Yule Bird Count was coming up. Sunset Grove and Fernwood birders would have been rivals even if Lucy Parker and Fred O'Neill were thick as thieves (which each thought the other was). They lived next door to one another, for cryin' out loud. If you can't brag on yourselves and woof on your neighbors, well, what's a heaven for?

So every year there was a mad scramble to spot as many different sparrows and raptors and waterfowl and other feathered critters that happened to lurk anywhere close by, and to publish same, and to laugh at the neighboring birders whose count happened to come up short. About every other year, there were charges that Sunset Grove's birders—or Fernwood's, depending—counted birds they didn't really see, just to make their numbers bigger.

Everybody denied everything, of course. Of course. Nobody would stoop to such evil, underhanded tactics, of course. Of course.

"We'll get 'em this year," Jesse told Lucy as the big day approached. Fernwood had outcounted Sunset Grove the year before. Suspicions of cheating were more than usually rampant—among Sunset Grove's birders, anyhow. Jesse was a competitive kid. It all added up.

"You'd best believe we will, kiddo," Lucy answered. She was even more competitive than her son. It wasn't easy, but she managed. "We'll whip 'em good. You can count on it."

"Cool." Jesse grinned. Then, perhaps incautiously, he added, "Kathleen says—"

"What does Kathleen say?" Was that frost in Lucy's voice? As a matter of fact, it was ice. A competition with Kathleen was a competition she'd lose. Come to that, a competition with Kathleen was a competition where she couldn't even compete. She knew it, too. She hated it, but she knew it.

For his part, Jesse knew something wasn't quite right there, but his hormones made sure he didn't know what. "She says some of Mr. O'Neill's birding buddies were talking with him the other day. They were asking him what he could do about, like, finding some extra birds for the Yule Count."

"Oh, they were, were they?" Lucy's ice turned into a glacier and started overrunning a continent. "Magicking birds into place for the count is immoral and unethical." She paused. If you listened near the edge of the glacier, you could hear woolly mammoths trumpeting. "And I wouldn't put it past Fred O'Neill for a minute."

"Kathleen says that they said that some of them thought that maybe you'd done some birdwitching before," Jesse said.

It was a good thing he needed three dependent clauses to get where he was going with that, or the whole glacier—and probably the poor woolly mammoths, too—would have flashed to superheated steam. As things were, what Lucy said made Jesse's jaw drop. Moms weren't supposed to talk like that.

"I haven't," Lucy continued, biting syllables off between her teeth. "I didn't. But if Fred O'Neill is crooked enough to think he can get away with pulling that kind of stunt, he'd better think twice. Those nearsighted yahoos in Fernwood won't cheat their way past us again. Not a chance."

"Cool," Jesse said again. Then, even more incautiously than before, he started another sentence with, "Kathleen says—"

"What?" Lucy barked.

Her son flinched. When he got his nerve back, he finished, "She says her dad says he won't let us win by cheating, either."

"Oh, he does? Oh, he won't?" Lucy echoed ominously. "Well, we'll just have to see about that, won't we?"

Yule dawned clear and cool. It would get up into the high sixties later on, maybe even to seventy. Winter in Southern California. Lucy, who'd been born in Cleveland, loved it. Jesse, a native, took it for granted, the way he did his upper-middle-class lifestyle. Lucy and John (maybe you can't *quite* forget him) had busted their humps for years so he could do exactly that.

The Parkers had a big back yard, full of trees and flowers. Flowers at Yule? Sure. Why don't *you* pack up and move here? Everybody else has. It was also full of hummingbird feeders full of sugar water, of seed feeders on poles with big iron baffles to keep squirrels away (there were even bigger ones to keep raccoons away, but the coons didn't come around very often), of suet left out for woodpeckers and other birds that found it tasty, and little fountains so the feathered beasties could sing in the shower.

Behind the Parkers' yard were fields and scrubby chaparral. Plenty of birds that wouldn't come into a yard on a bet liked it fine out there. Some of them were even willing to be spotted.

Even though it wasn't *very* cold, John (yeah, there he is again) had set the Yule log burning in the fireplace at midnight. Tradition? Tradition! It was down to coals when Lucy and Jesse got up a little before sunrise. She smiled as she lurched into the kitchen to make coffee. The embers and the smell reminded her this was a holiday.

Holiday or not, it would also be a small war. She needed no witchy Talent to figure that out.

Jesse hated coffee. He bounced around anyhow. Nineteen did that for you, or to you. He peered out the kitchen window. An early-rising Anna's hummingbird that was about to tank up at the feeder hanging outside buzzed away instead.

"One Anna's," he sang out.

"Well, we're started." Lucy poured sugar into her cup. Her mix had less sweetness and more caffeine than hummer water. Hummingbirds were speedy enough—they didn't need caffeine. She darn well did.

"You ought to note it down," Jesse said, reproof in his voice.

"I will—once I get to the bottom of my mug here. I don't think I'll forget till then. If you can't stand to wait that long, do it yourself, Charlie," Lucy said. He sighed. He was no good at waiting. Along with being able to function in the morning without coffee, that went a long way toward tagging him by age.

Something moved in the magnolia not far from the window. Jesse stared intently. "Yellow-rumped warbler," he said after a couple of seconds.

"Okay. An Anna's and a butterbutt," Lucy said. Even half a cup of coffee started to clear the cobwebs.

"Butterbutt," Jesse echoed. "That's a silly name."

"I know. So what?" his mother answered. "Birders have their own secret lingo, same as witches, same as any other bunch of people interested in the same thing." There were differences, of course. Misusing birders' jargon wouldn't get you toasted by a salamander or drowned by an undine. But it would show the people you were trying to impress that you didn't really belong with them. As often as not, that was the main function of jargon.

Lucy thought about a second mug of coffee, at least as much to annoy Jesse as to get herself up to speed. It could wait, she decided, not without regret. She went over to the kitchen crystal and attuned it to the Cosmos-Spanning Consortium. Mystically linking all the crystals in the world was the greatest sorcerous achievement since the megamagics that had swept two Nipponese cities off the map at the end of the Second Great Slaughter. And CSPANC had a lot more peaceful possibilities than sorceries of mass destruction any day.

She quickly steered to the CSPANC scroll that recorded birds seen in the Sunset Grove Yule Count. Other local birders had already identified house finches, house sparrows, white-crowned sparrows, and a California towhee. All of those, like her Anna's and yellow-rump, were completely unsurprising, which didn't mean they didn't count.

"Oh!" she said, spotting another check on the list.

"What's up?" Jesse came over to see for himself. "A barn owl! That's pretty neat."

"It is," Lucy agreed. Barn owls lived over most of the world—they had one of the widest ranges of any bird—but weren't common anywhere. You sure couldn't rely on conveniently spotting one for Yule. Somebody'd done it, though: somebody who'd crawled out of bed too bloody early, odds were.

"What have they seen in Fernwood?" Jesse asked.

Murmuring a charm, Lucy shifted to the rival town's CSPANC scroll. They must have had somebody out at the lagoon early in the morning, because they were reporting double-crested cormorants and a pied-billed grebe and a northern shoveler, which was a duck with a bill shaped like a serving spoon. And they'd spotted a California scrub jay and some American robins.

"Nothing they shouldn't have," Lucy said grudgingly. "Not yet, anyhow." She trusted Fred O'Neill as far as she could punt him. Since she was no football player, and since *dear* Fred weighed about 250 pounds . . .

A flock of tiny, twittering birds flew into the leafless apricot tree from the yard next door. Then, one by one and two by two and several by several, they fluttered into the magnolia. They hopped around the branches, looking for bugs. A moment later, they were gone, as abruptly as they'd appeared.

"Bush tits," Lucy said.

Her son nodded. "Tree fleas," he said scornfully—the birders' nickname for the bouncy little birds.

"Hey, I like 'em," Lucy said. Jesse looked at her as if she were dribbling marbles out her ears. Most birders thought bush tits were nothing but nuisances that disturbed less common, more interesting birds. They reminded her of a pack of first-graders turned loose on the playground for recess. They were fun. If you couldn't have fun with your birds, why watch them?

To keep track of how many different kinds you've seen. Plenty of birders, Jesse among them, would have given the answer without even pausing to think. He was a good kid, so good she almost forgave him for liking Kathleen O'Neill. No denying he could be too serious for his own good, though.

Another quick spell brought Lucy back to the Sunset Grove Yule list. "How many bush tits would you say there were?" she asked. "Maybe twenty-five?"

After careful consideration—he was Jesse, after all—her son nodded. "Sounds right."

"Okay." The bush tits they counted would get added in with all the others Sunset Grove birders spotted today. Somewhere behind the scenes at CSPANC, a sprite with an abacus would draw overtime.

Lucy did pour herself another cup of coffee then. She split a bagel and put honey on one side and jam on the other. Then she slapped them together and started eating breakfast. Jesse scrambled eggs. He was young enough so he didn't have a healer clucking reproachfully whenever he did something like that.

His pocket crystal made a noise like a rhythmic kangaroo as he was sitting down at the kitchen table. Till he started using that particular ringspell, Lucy hadn't imagined there was any such thing as a noise like a rhythmic kangaroo. But there was, and Jesse was far from the only kid with that ringspell. Hip-hop music was all the rage these days. You could either put up with it or wear earplugs, one.

"Hello?" Jesse said, and then, on an altogether different note, "Oh. Hi!"

Kathleen, Lucy thought unhappily. She knew that note, all right. *He's talking with fat Fred O'Neill's daughter. Talking with the enemy's daughter. With the enemy.* Was Jesse sleeping with the enemy? Lucy didn't know. She couldn't very well ask. Parents who snooped on their pretty-much-grown children's love lives deserved the trouble they landed in. Lucy did know one thing: if Jesse wasn't sleeping with Kathleen, he sure wanted to. He was male. He was nineteen. He had a pulse. 'Nuff said.

"Nothing real exciting here so far," he was saying. "Tree fleas, a but-terbutt, an Anna's . . . Oh, wait. A couple of stoogebirds just landed on the platform feeder."

"A couple of *what?*" Lucy could hear Kathleen's voice coming out of the pocket crystal.

Stoogebirds was family slang, not regular birders' slang. Jesse had to explain it: "You know. Mourning doves, on account of their wings go *woob-woob-woob-woob* whenever they take off. Just like Curly, right?" He paused, listening, then answered with more than a little pride in his voice: "Sure I'm weird. Like you didn't already know." He listened one more time, then said "'Bye" and stuck the crystal back in his pocket.

Lucy checked the Fernwood scroll on CSPANC again. As soon as she did, something way more strident than a hip-hop kangaroo went off inside her head. "They can't get away with that!" she yipped.

"With what?" Jesse ambled over to see what she was talking about.

"With *that.*" Quivering with indignation, Lucy pointed out the offending entry. "Yellow-billed magpie? Here? Or in Fernwood, I mean? No way, Jessay." She pronounced his name so the phrase rhymed, which made him wince. She went on, "No way unless Fat Freddy magicked it in, I mean. Well, if he's gonna play that way, we can play that way, too. *Oh*, yeah!" So much for immoral and unethical. What were rules, in war?

"What'll you do, Mom?" Anticipation and alarm jangled in Jesse's voice.

"I'll make sure those no-good, lousy cheaters in Fernwood don't steal this year's count, that's what." Lucy stormed out of the kitchen and into her study. She came back with several grimoires and an armload of *materia magica*—oh, and a few birders' guides, too. She paged through one of them, then smiled carnivorously and nodded. "We'll have people down by the old slough, right?"

"We always do," Jesse answered.

"Right," Lucy said again. "Now we find out whether they're awake." You could conjure in a bird—sure. But if you did and nobody spotted it, you might as well not have bothered.

Lucy's *materia magica*, unlike those of a lot of witches, included feathers of all different colors . . . just in case. She pulled out a dark green one, and a little bronze crown that might have graced a doll's head once upon a time. She knew where her target birds lived. She knew where she wanted to put one. The charm and the passes that got the bird from A to B were second nature to her. After umpty-ump years of training and practice they were, anyhow.

"What exactly did you do?" Jesse asked. "I mean, I can guess, but—"

"Go ahead and guess," Lucy said. "We'll find out if it worked pretty soon." If it didn't, if the loafers at the slough were standing around yawning or just not paying attention . . . Well, she'd find some other way to make sure they weren't asleep over there next year, by God!

She made herself sit there for fifteen minutes before she checked the Sunset Grove scroll on CSPANC again. That was at least fourteen minutes longer than Jesse wanted to wait. By the time they finally looked, he had a bad case of the wiggles.

His grin almost made the top of his head fall off. "Green kingfisher!" he whooped. "I thought that's what you were up to!" Belted kingfishers, larger and blue-gray, were common over water. Green kingfishers barely came north of the Rio Grande, and never visited California—not unless a friendly witch lent a hand.

Not two minutes later, his pocket crystal made hip-hop noises again. "If that's Kathleen bitching—" Lucy began.

Her son waved her to silence. A call on the pocket crystal was *important*. A parent standing right there? Fuhgeddaboutit. "Hello?" he said, and then, "Hi!" His face got all goofy. It was Kathleen, all right. He listened, then looked at Lucy. "She says her dad's not real happy about the kingfisher."

"T. S., Eliot," Lucy answered. "What about the yellow-billed magpie?"

Jesse asked the question. He listened some more, then reported: "She says her dad says it just happened to be there. He didn't have anything to do with it."

"Yeah, right," Lucy sneered. "And the check is in the mail."

"Uh, my mom's not so sure of that." Talking to a girl he was sweet on, Jesse was more polite than Lucy had been. He listened to Kathleen. To Lucy, he said, "She says her dad says the magpie was legit. But if you want to play that way, he can play that way, too."

"Tell Kathleen to tell him to bring it on," Lucy answered. Only later did she realize there were ways to say things like that, and then again there were ways. One particular fellow who'd used almost her exact phrase was still trying to shovel his way out of Mesopotamia.

But the Great Yule Bird Count in Sunset Grove and Fernwood was never the same again.

WATCH THE SKIES! the old posters shouted—as if there could be life on other planets, when magic had proved that planets were nothing but lights attached to moving crystal spheres. But weird-looking invaders from Mars were fun to tell stories about, even if they couldn't be real.

Fernwood and Sunset Grove got invaders, too, but they didn't come from Mars. And if you weren't watching the skies, you'd miss them. Birds that hadn't been seen there in a long time—birds that had *never* been seen there—showed up one after another. It was a life lister's heaven on earth (appropriate enough for Yuletide, after all). And it was one of the worst cases of Anything You Can Do, I Can Do More Of in the history of American witchcraft.

Lucy couldn't watch the skies, or even the back yard, as much as she would've liked. She was too busy checking the Fernwood scroll on CSPANC to find out what Fred O'Neill was up to and the Sunset Grove scroll to make sure the birds she magicked in got properly counted. She could picture Fat Freddy doing the same thing, only back-asswards.

Four black vultures spiraled above Fernwood. They had no business being there, not when the nearest sighting of a black vulture was an accidental bird right by the California-Arizona border. Did Fred O'Neill give a rat's patoot? Not when he had a chance to win the bird count, he didn't.

When Lucy saw the report of the black vultures, she called Fred a son of a witch, or something like that. Then she pulled a big black feather and a little yellow one out of her *materia magica*. She incanted like nobody's business.

Some Sunset Grove birders at a park were surprised and delighted to spot black-backed woodpeckers drilling on pines. Black-backed woodpeckers didn't live within hundreds of miles of Sunset Grove. Well, hey, if you were going to fuss about every little thing . . .

Lucy waited to see what Fred O'Neill would come up with next. It was like a prizefight, with all the punches in extremely slow motion. *Sure*, Lucy thought. *A featherweight prizefight*. She poured herself more coffee. By all the signs, she was pretty punchy herself.

Fernwood birders declared they'd seen a smew at a pond. "What's a smew?" Jesse asked, reading CSPANC over her shoulder.

"I don't know. What's smew with you?" Lucy returned. Yeah, she was punchy. Her son sent her a reproachful look. She tried again: "A kind of merganser—a diving duck. It lives in Europe. Once in a blue moon, one gets over here by itself."

"You don't think this is a blue moon?"

"Now that you mention it, no."

"What'll you do about it?"

Lucy was already thumbing through guides, deciding exactly what she'd do about it. She plucked a black feather, and then a shiny blue one, from her *materia magica*. The charm she chanted had a Latin rhythm.

Something started squawking raucously in the magnolia tree. Crows and ravens and jays aren't very musical, but the noises they make show they all come from the same family. This raucous squawking was corvid racket, too, but it wasn't the kind of corvid racket Lucy'd ever heard before.

Jesse grabbed his binoculars. "Whoa!" he said, nothing but admiration in his voice. "What *is* that thing?"

"Black-throated magpie-jay," Lucy answered, not without pride. It was a jay the size of a crow or bigger, with a fancy crest and a long, droopy tail. It flew away, skrawking as it went.

"Whoa!" Jesse said again. "Where's it from?"

"Middle of Mexico," Lucy answered, recording it on the Sunset Grove SCPANC scroll.

Jesse got another call from Kathleen as soon as she and her father saw the claim for the new bird. "She says her dad says you aren't gonna beat him," Jesse reported.

"He started it. I'll finish it," Lucy said grimly.

The next exotic bird reported from Fernwood was a condor. That left Lucy unimpressed for a moment. Thanks to captive-breeding programs, California condors weren't impossible to spot these days, but a lot of birders didn't count them because they weren't truly wild. *Even a lamebrain like Fred ought to do better*, she thought.

And Fred had. It was an Andean condor. It was even bigger than a California condor, and even uglier. Lucy showed Jesse a picture in a book about Chilean birds. The head was large and naked and pink, with wattles and a comb. You were in no danger of mistaking it for any other bird ever hatched.

"What are you gonna do now, Mom?" Jesse was caught up in the competition, too.

"You'll see. I'll bring in several of these, 'cause I've always liked them," Lucy answered. "Maybe they'll hang around once the count is over." That intrigued her son, as she'd hoped it would. She got busy spellcasting.

Bringing in a bunch of birds was a lot harder than bringing in just one. She was good, though. One of the birds appeared in the backyard apricot tree. Crest, brown belly and back, black-and-white striped wings. *"Poo! Poo! Poo!"* it called.

"A hoopoe!" Jesse exclaimed in delight. "Awesome!"

Maybe it heard him. It flew off, skipping through the air like a butterfly. "The Bible says it's not kosher," Lucy said. "Twice, in fact. I bet I know why, too."

"Why?" Jesse asked when she didn't come out with it right away.

Lucy wrinkled her nose. "Because it smells like *poo-poo-poo*, that's why."

She didn't post the hoopoe on the Sunset Grove Yuletide scroll. Before long, some other local birder did. The mundanes in the birding crowd had to be talking to themselves about all the weird stuff going on. They wouldn't be complaining, though. Oh, no. She knew birders well enough to be sure of that.

She didn't know Fred O'Neill well enough to guess how he'd retaliate. She only knew he would. And he did. Not fifteen minutes after Sunset Grove reported hoopoes, Fernwood reported Carolina parakeets.

"Wait. I've heard of those." Jesse flipped through the Sibley guide. "Why doesn't this book have a picture?"

"I'll tell you why—they're extinct." For the first time in the contest, Lucy felt shaken. Reaching across space was one thing. Reaching across time was something else again, something much harder. She hadn't believed Fred could. She wasn't sure she could herself. Trying not to think about that, she went on, "They've been extinct for almost a hundred years. There's a wonderful Audubon painting, if you want to know what they looked like."

Jesse nodded eagerly. "I've seen it. But now they're back, huh? How cool is that? What are *you* gonna do now, Mom?"

Lucy wasn't sure how cool it was. Didn't it cross a line somewhere? But, assuming it didn't, what *was* she gonna do? Whatever it was, it was liable to take just about all the witchcraft she had in her.

Then she started to laugh. If she was gonna do it, she'd go all-out. She gathered herself. She chose her feathers. She chose her spell. She took one moment to wonder if she'd gone off her rocker. Well, if she had, it was a grand madness. After a deep breath, she started.

It took everything she had, all right. The lights flickered. The CSPANC crystal went black. She'd have to rebless it later.

John came in (see?—you couldn't quite forget him). "What's going on?" he said. "How much crowleyage are you using, babe? What'll our magictrixity bill look like next month?"

Lucy waited till she'd finished the Summoning to answer. Then she gave him three words: "I don't care." They'd been married a long time. He looked at her, nodded, turned around, and walked away.

Jesse was peering out into the back yard. "What did you call up, Mom? All I see are a bunch more stoogebirds."

"Take another look," Lucy said wearily. If she'd just turned herself inside out for the sake of more dirt-common mourning doves . . . In that case, Fred O'Neill and Fernwood would win the Yule Count, that was all.

"They're funny-looking stoogebirds," Jesse said. "Kinda salmony breasts, red eyes . . . No. They can't be."

There were lots of them. That was part of what had worn Lucy out—and made the lights flicker. The other part was reaching back through the years. She eyed them through binoculars. No, they sure weren't stoogebirds. "Passenger pigeons," she said proudly. They all flew off together.

By the time Lucy had CSPANC up again, someone else had already spotted them (and recognized them, which also impressed her). And Jesse had got another call from Kathleen. "She says her dad won't quit, no matter what," he said.

"Big deal," Lucy declared. Later, she wondered if she should have sounded so arrogant. That was later. In the middle of a war, you only cared about winning. You'd figure out what it all meant later.

They didn't hear about the newest Fernwood bird on the CSPANC scroll. John (here he is again!) called them in to look at the news crystal. "Some kind of monster's loose," he said.

That rated a look, all right. And he wasn't wrong. People were sending pictures from a flying carpet. The thing stalked through a park labeled FERNWOOD in the bottom left of the news crystal. It was taller than a man. It had chickeny feet, about the size of the ones that would have walked around under Baba Yaga's house. Its wings were useless, except for flapping to show it was ticked off. It had a big feathery crest on top of its head and a hooked beak that looked as if it could bite through steel bars. The only people in sight wore Tilly hats and carried binoculars, which made them birders. Even they had the sense to keep their distance.

One of the flying carpets swooped low. The monster bird snapped at it and let out a loud, furious screech. "Wow!" Jesse said. "Oh, wow! What *is* that thing?"

As if on cue, an announcer said, "A paleo-ornitholologist has identified this creature as a *Titanis*, a flightless predatory bird previously believed extinct for almost two million years. Witchcraft is suspected in its strange resurrection."

"Right on, Sherlock!" Lucy laughed, but shakily. She hadn't dreamt Fred O'Neill could do *that*. He was just lucky it hadn't taken a bite out of one of the Fernwood birders. Yet.

Her son's thoughts ran in a different direction. "How can you top him this time, Mom? A *Pteranodon?*"

"NFF," John said. Lucy stared at him. All these years together, and she hadn't imagined he knew *that* bit of birders' slang. He was right, too. A *Pteranodon* didn't have any feathers. If she was going to top Fred, she had to come up with something that did.

She laughed again. This time, hysteria—or maybe just plain lunacy—lay under the mirth. If you were gonna go for it, you should *go* for it. "One thing," she said. "If I bring this off, Fred's whupped." If she didn't, chances were the spell would toast her. She tried not to think about that. The crowleyage? The magictrixity bill? Count the cost later. That kind of thinking was probably why people did so many really stupid things during wartime—one more point Lucy did her best not to think about.

Back to her *materia magica*. Which feathers to choose? She had no idea. But Fred wouldn't have known what color the *Titanis* was, either. He'd managed. If he had, so could she. She hoped.

The form the spell would take would resemble the ones she'd used before, especially the charm that brought the passenger pigeons up to be counted. But reaching back over a hundred years was one thing. Reaching back a million times that far . . .

"It's the same principle," she said, and hoped she was right. Discovering she was wrong in the middle of the incantation wouldn't be much fun.

Do I really want to try this? she wondered. She'd already started by then, though. It was either this or admit Fred O'Neill had won. She was damned if she'd do that. . . . A moment later, she wished she'd phrased that differently. One more thing it was too late to worry about.

Lights didn't just flicker—they went out. So did the CSPANC crystal. John's yelp from the family room said he couldn't watch *Titanis* any more, either. Lucy noticed all that as if from a hundred million miles—or a hundred million years—away. She was deep in the spell by then. Backing out would be worse than going forward.

"Come forth! Come forth! Come forth!" she commanded. Then she slumped to the floor. She'd never fainted before. Outside of women with the vapors in Victorian novels, who did? When she woke up—it couldn't have been more than a few seconds later—she felt silly. Her head spun as she stood up, but she made it.

Jesse hadn't even noticed. He was scanning the yard with binoculars. "See anything?" Lucy asked. Her voice seemed shaky—to her, anyway.

Again, Jesse didn't notice. "Nooo," he said slowly. Lucy's heart sank. Had she half-fried her brains for nothing? Would Fred O'Neill and Fernwood spend the next year gloating? But then her son stiffened like a bird dog pointing. "Holy crap! There! In the magnolia." Darned if he didn't point, though not with his nose.

Lucy went over to the window and stared. For a second, she didn't see it. She was looking for purple and white or something else gaudy, the way artists always showed it. The real critter, though, was brown and green. Which made sense, when you thought about it. Even way back then, protective coloration mattered.

It was about the size of a crow. It didn't look like one, though, and wouldn't have if it were all black. It looked like a lizard that had decided to play bird. Trouble was, the poor lizard might've heard of birds, but it had never seen one, so it got stuff wrong. It didn't have a beak—it had a a mouthful of teeth. It had a long, lizardy tail. But feathers sprouted from the tail, and from the wings, too, even if those also had claws to remind everybody they weren't done being arms yet.

"I did it. I really did it." Lucy sounded amazed, even to herself. "*Archaeopteryx.*"

"*Archaeopteryx,*" Jesse agreed, awe in his voice. "There's one for the life list! Can it really fly?"

"Don't know," Lucy replied. She got her answer a moment later. An Anna's hummingbird dive-bombed the funny-looking stranger. The *Archaeopteryx* snapped at it, but missed. It had a long, lizardy tongue. Another dive-bomb persuaded it not to hang around. Off it flew. Not gracefully, maybe, but it flew.

Jesse was talking on his pocket crystal. Lucy's spell hadn't blasted that, anyhow. "No way!" she heard Kathleen exclaim when Jesse told her what they'd just observed.

"Way," he assured her, and then said to Lucy, "She's telling her dad."

"An *Archaeopteryx*?" That was Fred O'Neill's bull-in-a-china-shop bellow. "Well . . . fudge. I'm not gonna top that this year."

You'll never top it, Lucy thought. *You can't, not till they find an older bird. If they ever do.* Even so, he'd come up with *something* next year, sure as sure. He always did. This time around, though, the Yule Bird count belonged to Sunset Grove. and, as far as Lucy was concerned, that was just how things were supposed to be.

DOWN IN THE BOTTOMLANDS

This story was lucky enough to win the Hugo for novella at the 1994 Worldcon in Winnipeg. Charles Sheffield's novelette, "Georgia on My Mind," which appeared in the same issue of *Analog*—not just the same magazine, mind you, but the same issue—won the Hugo for novelette at the same convention. Stan Schmidt, the longtime boss man of *Analog*, didn't win the Hugo for editor that year. Go figure. I owe him major props for his suggestions about the story, though, and I'm delighted to say as much here. I also owe my youngest daughter, Rebecca. She was just a toddler at the time, but she gave me the idea for the koprit bird. Thanks, hon.

A double handful of tourists climbed down from the omnibus, chattering with excitement. From under the long brim of his cap, Radnal vez Krobir looked them over, comparing them with previous groups he'd led through Trench Park. About average, he decided: an old man spending money before he died; younger folks searching for adventure in an overcivilized world; a few who didn't fit into an obvious category and might be artists, writers, researchers, or anything else under the sun.

He also looked over the women in the tour group with a different sort of curiosity. He was in the process of buying a bride from her father, but he hadn't done it; legally and morally, he remained a free agent. Some of the women were worth looking over, too: a couple of tall, slim, dark Highheads from the eastern lands who stuck by each other, and another of Radnal's own Strongbrow race, shorter, stockier, fairer, with deepset light eyes under heavy brow ridges.

One of the Highhead girls gave him a dazzling smile. He smiled back as he walked toward the group, his wool robes flapping around him. "Hello, friends," he called. "Do you all understand Tarteshan? Ah, good."

Cameras clicked as he spoke. He was used to that; people from every tour group wasted pictures on him, though he wasn't what they'd come to see. He went into his usual welcoming speech:

"On behalf of the Hereditary Tyranny of Tartesh and the staff of Trench Park, I'm pleased to welcome you here today. If you haven't read my button, or if you just speak Tarteshan but don't know our syllabary, my name is Radnal vez Krobir. I'm a field biologist with the park, doing a two-year stretch of guide duty."

"Stretch?" said the woman who'd smiled at him. "You make it sound like a sentence in the mines."

"I don't mean it like that—quite." He grinned his most disarming grin. Most of the tourists grinned back. A few stayed sober-faced, likely the ones who suspected the gibe was real and the grin put on. There was some truth in that. He knew it, but the tourists weren't supposed to.

He went on, "In a bit, I'll take you over to the donkeys for the trip down into the Trench itself. As you know, we try to keep our mechanical civilization out of the park so we can show you what all the Bottomlands were like not so long ago. You needn't worry. The donkeys are very sure-footed. We haven't lost one—or even a tourist—in years."

This time, some of the chuckles that came back were nervous. Probably only a couple of this lot had ever done anything so archaic as getting on the back of an animal. Too bad for the ones just thinking about that now. The rules were clearly stated. The pretty Highhead girls looked particularly upset. The placid donkeys worried them more than the wild beasts of the Trench.

"Let's put off the evil moment as long as we can," Radnal said. "Come under the colonnade for half a daytenth or so and we'll talk about what makes Trench Park unique."

The tour group followed him into the shade. Several people sighed in relief. Radnal had to work to keep his face straight. The Tarteshan sun was warm, but if they had trouble here, they'd cook down in the Trench. That was their lookout. If they got heatstroke, he'd set them right again. He'd done it before.

He pointed to the first illuminated map. "Twenty million years ago, as you'll see, the Bottomlands didn't exist. A long stretch of sea separated what's now the southwest section of the Great Continent from the rest. Notice that what were then two lands masses first joined in the east, and a land bridge rose *here*." He pointed again, this time more precisely. "This sea, now a long arm of the Western Ocean, remained."

He walked over to the next map, drawing the tourists with him. "Things stayed like that until about six and a half million years ago. Then, as that southwest section of the Great Continent kept drifting northward, a new range gradually pushed up *here*, at the western outlet of that inland sea. When it was cut off from the Western Ocean, it began to dry up: it lost more water by evaporation than flowed into it from its rivers. Now if you'll come along . . ."

The third map had several overlays, in different shades of blue. "The sea took about a thousand years to turn into the Bottomlands. It refilled from the Western Ocean several times, too, as tectonic forces lowered the Barrier Mountains. But for about the last five and a half million years, the Bottomlands have had about the form we know today."

The last map showed the picture familiar to any child studying geography: the trench of the Bottomlands furrowing across the Great Continent like a surgical scar, requiring colors needed nowhere else on the globe to show relief.

Radnal led the tourists out to the donkey corral. The shaggy animals were already bridled and saddled. Radnal explained how to mount, demonstrated, and waited for the tourists to mess it up. Sure enough, both Highhead girls put the wrong foot in the stirrup.

"No, like this," he said, demonstrating again. "Use your left foot, then swing over."

The girl who had smiled at him succeeded on the second try. The other balked. "Help me," she said. Breathing out through his beaky nose in lieu of sighing, Radnal put his hands on her waist and all but lifted her into the saddle as she mounted. She giggled. "You're so strong. He's so strong, Evillia." The other Highhead girl—presumably Evillia—giggled too.

Radnal breathed out again, harder. Tarteshans and other folk of Strongbrow race who lived north of the Bottomlands and down in them *were* stronger than most Highheads, but generally weren't as agile. So what, either way?

He went back to work: "Now that we've learned to mount our donkeys, we're going to learn to dismount." The tourists groaned, but Radnal was inexorable. "You still have to carry your supplies from the omnibus and stow them in the saddlebags. I'm your guide, not your servant." The Tarteshan words carried overtones of *I'm your equal, not your slave.*

Most of the tourists dismounted, but Evillia stayed up on her donkey. Radnal strode over to her; even his patience was fraying. "This way." He guided her through the necessary motions.

"Thank you, freeman vez Krobir," she said in surprisingly fluent Tarteshan. She turned to her friend. "You're right, Lofosa; he *is* strong."

Radnal felt his ears grow hot under their coat of down. A brown-skinned Highhead from south of the Bottomlands rocked his hips back and forth and said, "I'm jealous of you." Several tourists laughed.

"Let's get on with it," Radnal said. "The sooner we get the donkeys loaded, the sooner we can begin and the more we'll see." That line never failed; you didn't become a tourist unless you wanted to see as much as you could. As if on cue, the driver brought the omnibus around to the corral. The baggage doors opened with a hiss of compressed air. The driver started chucking luggage out of the bins.

"You shouldn't have any problems," Radnal said. Everyone's gear had been weighed and measured beforehand, to make sure the donkeys wouldn't have to bear anything too bulky or heavy. Most people easily shifted their belongings to the saddlebags. The two Highhead girls, though, had a night demon of a time making everything fit. He thought about helping them, but decided not to. If they had to pay a penalty for making the supply donkeys carry some of their stuff, it was their own fault.

They did get everything in, though their saddlebags bulged like a snake that had just swallowed a half-grown humpless camel. A couple of other people stood around helplessly, with full bags and gear left over. Smiling a smile he hoped was not too predatory, Radnal took them to the scales and collected a tenth of a unit of silver for every unit of excess weight.

"This is an outrage," the dark brown Highhead man said. "Do you know who I am? I am Moblay Sopsirk's son, aide to the Prince of Lissonland." He drew himself up to his full height, almost a Tarteshan cubit more than Radnal's.

"Then you can afford the four and three tenths," Radnal answered. "*I* don't keep the silver. It all goes to upkeep for the park."

Grumbling still, Moblay paid. Then he stomped off and swung aboard his animal with more grace than Radnal had noticed him possessing. Down in Lissonland, the guide remembered, important people sometimes rode stripehorses for show. He didn't understand that. He had no interest in getting onto a donkey when he wasn't going down into Trench Park. As long as there were better ways of doing things, why not use them?

Also guilty of overweight baggage were a middle-aged Tarteshan couple. They were overweight themselves, too, but Radnal couldn't do anything about that. Eltsac vez Martois protested, "The scale at home said we were all right."

"If you read it right," Nocso zev Martois said to her husband. "You probably didn't."

"Whose side are you on?" he snarled. She screeched at him. Radnal waited till they ran down, then collected the silver due the park.

When the tourists had remounted their donkeys, the guide walked over to the gate on the far side of the corral, swung it open, and replaced the key in a pouch he wore belted round his waist under his robe. As he went back to his own animal, he said, "When you ride through there, you enter the park itself, and the waivers you signed come into play. Under Tarteshan law, park guides have the authority of military officers within the park. I don't intend to exercise it any more than I have to; we should get along just fine with simple common sense. But I am required to remind you the authority is there." He also kept a repeating handcannon in one of his donkey's saddlebags, but didn't mention that.

"Please stay behind me and try to stay on the trail," he said. "It won't be too steep today; we'll camp tonight at what was the edge of the continental shelf. Tomorrow we'll descend to the bottom of the ancient sea, as far below mean sea level as a medium-sized mountain is above it. That will be more rugged terrain."

The Strongbrow woman said, "It will be hot, too, much hotter than it is now. I visited the park three or four years ago, and it felt like a furnace. Be warned, everyone."

"You're right, freelady, ah—" Radnal said.

"I'm Toglo zev Pamdal." She added hastily, "Only a distant collateral relation, I assure you."

"As you say, freelady." Radnal had trouble keeping his voice steady. The Hereditary Tyrant of Tartesh was Bortav vez Pamdal. Even his distant collateral relations needed to be treated with sandskink gloves. Radnal was glad Toglo had had the courtesy to warn him who she was—or rather, who her distant collateral relation was. At least she didn't seem the sort who would snoop around and take bad reports on people back to the friends she undoubtedly had in high places.

Although the country through which the donkeys ambled was below sea level, it wasn't very far below. It didn't seem much different from the land over which the tourists' omnibus had traveled to reach the edge of Trench Park: dry and scrubby, with thorn bushes and palm trees like long-handled feather dusters.

Radnal let the terrain speak for itself, though he did remark, "Dig a couple of hundred cubits under the soil hereabouts and you'll find a layer of salt, same as you would anywhere in the Bottomlands. It's not too thick here on the shelf, because this area dried up quickly, but it's here. That's one of the first clues geologists had that the Bottomlands used to be a sea, and one of the ways they map the boundaries of the ancient water."

Moblay Sopsirk's son wiped his sweaty face with a forearm. Where Radnal, like any Tarteshan, covered up against the heat, Moblay wore only a hat, shoes, and a pocketed belt to carry silver, perhaps a small knife or toothpick, and whatever else he thought he couldn't do without. He was dark enough that he didn't need to worry about skin cancer, but he didn't look very comfortable, either.

He said, "Were some of that water back in the Bottomlands, Radnal, Tartesh would have a better climate."

"You're right," Radnal said; he was resigned to foreigners using his familial name with uncouth familiarity. "We'd be several hundredths cooler in summer and warmer in winter. But if the Barrier Mountains fell again, we'd lose the great area that the Bottomlands encompass and the mineral wealth we derive from them: salt, other chemicals left by evaporation, and the petroleum reserves that wouldn't be accessible through deep water. Tarteshans have grown used to heat over the centuries. We don't mind it."

"I wouldn't go that far," Toglo said. "I don't think it's an accident that Tarteshan air coolers are sold all over the world."

Radnal found himself nodding. "You have a point, freelady. What we get from the Bottomlands, though, outweighs fuss over the weather."

As he'd hoped, they got to the campsite with the sun still in the sky and watched it sink behind the mountains to the west. The tourists gratefully descended from their donkeys and stumped about, complaining of how sore their thighs were. Radnal set them to carrying lumber from the metal racks that lined one side of the site.

He lit the cookfires with squirts from a squeeze bottle of starter fuel and a flint-and-steel lighter. "The lazy man's way" he admitted cheerfully. As with his skill on a donkey, that he could start a fire at all impressed the tourists. He went back to the donkeys, dug out ration packs which he tossed into the flames. When their tops popped and began to vent steam, he fished them out with a long-handled fork.

"Here we are," he said. "Peel off the foil and you have Tarteshan food—not a banquet fit for the gods, perhaps, but plenty to keep you from starving and meeting them before your time."

Evillia read the inscription on the side of her pack. "These are military rations," she said suspiciously. Several people groaned.

Like any other Tarteshan freeman, Radnal had done his required two years in the Hereditary Tyrant's Volunteer Guard. He came to the ration packs' defense: "Like I said, they'll keep you from starving."

The packs—mutton and barley stew, with carrots, onions, and a heavy dose of ground pepper and garlic—weren't too bad. The two Martoisi inhaled theirs and asked for more.

"I'm sorry," Radnal said. "The donkeys carry only so many. If I give you another pack each, someone will go hungry before we reach the lodge."

"We're hungry now," Nocso zev Martois said.

"That's right," Eltsac echoed. They stared at each other, perhaps surprised at agreeing.

"I'm sorry," Radnal said again. He'd never had anyone ask for seconds before. Thinking that, he glanced over to see how Toglo zev Pamdal was faring with such basic fare. As his eyes flicked her way, she crumpled her empty pack and got up to throw it in a refuse bin.

She had a lithe walk, though he could tell little of the shape of her body because of her robes. As young—or even not so young—men will, he wandered into fantasy. Suppose he was dickering with *her* father over bride price instead of with Markaf vez Putun, who acted as if his daughter Wello shat silver and pissed petrol . . .

He had enough sense to recognize when he was being foolish, which is more than the gods grant most. Toglo's father undoubtedly could make a thousand better matches for her than a none-too-special biologist. Confrontation with brute fact didn't stop him from musing, but did keep him from taking himself too seriously.

He smiled as he pulled sleepsacks out of one of the pack donkeys' panniers. The tourists took turns with a foot pump to inflate them. With the weather so warm, a good many tourists chose to lie on top of the sleepsacks rather than crawling into them. Some kept on the clothes they'd been wearing, some had special sleep clothes, and some didn't bother with clothes. Tartesh had a moderately strong nudity taboo: not enough to give Radnal the horrors at naked flesh, but plenty to make him eye Evillia and Lofosa as they carelessly shed shirts and trousers. They were young, attractive, and even well-muscled for Highheads. They seemed more naked to him because their bodies were less hairy than those of Strongbrows. He was relieved his robe hid his full response to them.

Speaking to the group, he said, "Get as much sleep as you can tonight. Don't stay up gabbing. We'll be in the saddle most of the day tomorrow, on worse terrain than we saw today. You'll do better if you're rested."

"Yes, clanfather," Moblay Sopsirk's son said, as a youngster might to the leader of his kith grouping—but any youngster who sounded as sassy as Moblay would get the back of his clanfather's hand across his mouth to remind him not to sound that way again.

But, since Radnal had spoken good sense, most of the tourists did try to go to sleep. They did not know the wilds but, with the possible exception of the Martoisi, they were not fools: few fools accumulated for an excursion to Trench Park. As he usually did the first night with a new group, Radnal disregarded his own advice. He was good at going without sleep and, being familiar with what lay ahead, would waste no energy on the trip down to the Trench itself.

An owl hooted from a hole in a palm trunk. The air smelled faintly spicy. Sage and lavender, oleander, laurel, thyme—many local plants had leaves that secreted aromatic oils. Their coatings reduced water loss—always of vital importance here—and made the leaves unpalatable to insects and animals.

The fading campfires drew moths. Every so often, their glow would briefly light up other, larger shapes: bats and nightjars swooping down to take advantage of the feast set out before them. The tourists took no notice of insects or predators. Their snores rang louder than the owl's cries. After a few trips as tour guide, Radnal was convinced practically everyone snored. He supposed he did, too, though he'd never heard himself do it.

He yawned, lay back on his own sleepsack with hands clasped behind his head, looked up at the stars, displayed as if on black velvet. There were so many more of them here than in the lights of the big city: yet another reason to work in Trench Park. He watched them slowly whirl overhead; he'd never found a better way to empty his mind and drift toward sleep.

His eyelids were getting heavy when someone rose from his—no, her—sleepsack: Evillia, on her way to the privy shed behind some bushes. His eyes opened wider; in the dim firelight, she looked like a moving statue of polished bronze. As soon as her back was to him, he ran his tongue over his lips.

But instead of getting back into her sack when she returned, Evillia squatted by Lofosa's. Both Highhead girls laughed softly. A moment later, they both climbed to their feet and headed Radnal's way. Lust turned to alarm—what were they doing?

They knelt down, one on either side of him. Lofosa whispered, "We think you're a fine chunk of man." Evillia set a hand on the tie of his robe, began to undo it.

"*Both* of you?" he blurted. Lust was back, impossible to disguise since he lay on his back. Incredulity came with it. Tarteshan women—even Tarteshan tarts—weren't so brazen (he thought how Evillia had reminded him of smoothly moving bronze); nor were Tarteshan men. Not that Tarteshan men didn't enjoy lewd imaginings, but they usually kept quiet about them.

The Highhead girls shook with more quiet laughter, as if his reserve were the funniest thing imaginable. "Why not?" Evillia said. "Three can do lots of interesting things two can't."

"But—" Radnal waved to the rest of the tour group. "What if they wake up?"

The girls laughed harder; their flesh shifted more alluringly. Lofosa answered, "They'll learn something."

Radnal learned quite a few things. One was that, being on the far side of thirty, his nights of keeping more than one woman happy were behind him, though he enjoyed trying. Another was that, what with sensual distractions, trying to make two women happy at once was harder than patting his head with one hand and rubbing his stomach with the other. Still another was that neither Lofosa nor Evillia carried an inhibition anywhere about her person.

He felt himself flagging, knew he'd be limp in more ways than one come morning. "Shall we have mercy on him?" Evillia asked—in Tarteshan, so he could understand her teasing.

"I suppose so," Lofosa said. "This time." She twisted like a snake, brushed her lips against Radnal's. "Sleep well, freeman." She and Evillia went back to their sleepsacks, leaving him to wonder if he'd dreamed they were with him but too worn to believe it.

This time, his drift toward sleep was more like a dive. But before he yielded, he saw Toglo zev Pamdal come back from the privy. For a moment, that meant nothing. But if she was coming back now, she must have gone before, when he was too occupied to notice . . . which meant she must have seen him so occupied.

He hissed like an ocellated lizard, though green wasn't the color he was turning. Toglo got back into her sleepsack without looking either at him or the two Highhead girls. Whatever fantasies he'd had about her shriveled. The best he could hope for come morning was the cool politeness someone of prominence gives an underling of imperfect manners. The worst . . .

What if she starts screaming to the group? he wondered. He supposed he could grit his teeth and carry on. *But what if she complains about me to the Hereditary Tyrant?* He didn't like the answers he came up with; *I'll lose my job* was the first that sprang to mind, and they went downhill from there.

He wondered why Moblay Sopsirk's son couldn't have got up to empty his bladder. Moblay would have been envious and admiring, not disgusted as Toglo surely was.

Radnal hissed again. Since he couldn't do anything about what he'd already done, he tried telling himself he would have to muddle along and deal with whatever sprang from it. He repeated that to himself several times. It didn't keep him from staying awake most of the night, no matter how tired he was.

The sun woke the tour guide. He heard some of the group already up and stirring. Though still sandy-eyed and clumsy with sleep, he made himself scramble out of his sack. He'd intended to get moving first, as he usually did, but the previous night's exertion and worry overcame the best of intentions.

To cover what he saw as a failing, he tried to move twice as fast as usual, which meant he kept making small, annoying mistakes: tripping over a stone and almost falling, calling the privy the campfire and the campfire the privy, going to a donkey that carried only fodder when he wanted breakfast packs.

He finally found the smoked sausages and hard bread. Evillia and Lofosa grinned when they took out the sausages, which flustered him worse. Eltsac vez Martois stole a roll from his wife, who cursed him with a dockwalloper's fluency and more than a dockwalloper's volume.

Then Radnal had to give breakfast to Toglo zev Pamdal. "Thank you, freeman," she said, more at ease than he'd dared hope. Then her gray eyes met his. "I trust you slept well?"

It was a conventional Tarteshan morning greeting, or would have been, if she hadn't sounded—no, Radnal decided, she couldn't have sounded amused. "Er—yes," he managed, and fled.

He knew only relief at handing the next breakfast to a Strongbrow who put away a sketch pad and charcoal to take it. "Thank you," the fellow said. Though he seemed polite enough, his guttural accent and the striped tunic and trousers he wore proclaimed him a native of Morgaf, the island kingdom off the northern coast of Tartesh—and the Tyranny's frequent foe. Their current twenty-year bout of peace was as long as they'd enjoyed in centuries.

Normally, Radnal would have been cautious around a Morgaffo. But now he found him easier to confront than Toglo. Glancing at the sketch pad, he said, "That's a fine drawing, freeman, ah—"

The Morgaffo held out both hands in front of him in his people's greeting. "I am Dokhnor of Kellef, freeman vez Krobir," he said. "Thank you for your interest."

He made it sound like *stop spying on me*. Radnal hadn't meant it that way. With a few deft strokes of his charcoal stick, Dokhnor had picked out the features of the campsite: the fire pits, the oleanders in front of the privy, the tethered donkeys. As a biologist who did field work, Radnal was a fair hand with a piece of charcoal. He wasn't in Dokhnor's class, though. A military engineer couldn't have done better.

That thought triggered his suspicions. He looked at the Morgaffo more closely. The fellow carried himself as a soldier would, which proved nothing. Lots of Morgaffos were soldiers. Although far smaller than Tartesh, the island kingdom had always held its own in their struggles. Radnal laughed at himself. If Dokhnor was an agent, why was he in Trench Park instead of, say, at a naval base along the Western Ocean?

The Morgaffo glowered. "If you have finished examining my work, freeman, perhaps you will give someone else a breakfast."

"Certainly," Radnal answered in a voice as icy as he could make it. Dokhnor certainly had the proverbial Morgaffo arrogance. Maybe that proved he wasn't a spy—a real spy would have been smoother. Or maybe a real spy would think no one would expect him to act like a spy, and act like one as a disguise. Radnal realized he could extend the chain to as many links as his imagination could forge. He gave up.

When all the breakfast packs were eaten, all the sleepsacks deflated and stowed, the group headed over to remount their donkeys for the trip into Trench Park itself. As he had the night before, Radnal warned, "The trail will be much steeper today. As long as we take it slow and careful, we'll be fine."

No sooner were the words out of his mouth than the ground quivered beneath his feet. Everyone stood stock-still; a couple of people exclaimed in dismay. The birds, on the other hand, all fell silent. Radnal had lived in earthquake country his whole life. He waited for the shaking to stop, and after a few heartbeats it did.

"Nothing to get alarmed at," he said when the quake was over. "This part of Tartesh is seismically active, probably because of the inland sea that dried up so long ago. The crust of the earth is still adjusting to the weight of so much water being gone. There are a lot of fault lines in the area, some quite close to the surface."

Dokhnor of Kellef stuck up a hand. "What if an earthquakes should—how do you say it?—make the Barrier Mountains fall?"

"Then the Bottomlands would flood." Radnal laughed. "Freeman, if it hasn't happened in the last five and a half million years, I won't lose sleep worrying that it'll happen tomorrow, or any time I'm down in Trench Park."

The Morgaffo nodded curtly. "That is a worthy answer. Carry on, freeman."

Radnal had an impulse to salute him—he spoke with the same automatic assumption of authority that Tarteshan officers employed. The tour guide mounted his own donkey, waited until his charges were in ragged line behind him. He waved. "Let's go."

The trail down into Trench Park was hacked and blasted from rock that had been on the bottom of the sea. It was only six or eight cubits wide, and frequently switched back and forth. A motor with power to all wheels might have negotiated it, but Radnal wouldn't have wanted to be at the tiller of one that tried.

His donkey pulled up a gladiolus and munched it. That made him think of something about which he'd forgotten to warn his group. He said, "When we get lower into the park, you'll want to keep your animals from browsing. The soil down there has large amounts of things like selenium and tellurium along with the more usual minerals—they were concentrated there as the sea evaporated. That doesn't bother a lot of the Bottomlands plants, but it *will* bother—and maybe kill—your donkeys if they eat the wrong ones."

"How will we know which ones are which?" Eltsac zev Martois called.

He fought the urge to throw Eltsac off the trail and let him tumble down into Trench Park. The idiot tourist would probably land on his head, which by all evidence was too hard to be damaged by a fall of a mere few thousand cubits. And Radnal's job was riding herd on idiot tourists. He answered, "Don't let your donkey forage at all. The pack donkeys carry fodder, and there'll be more at the lodge."

The tour group rode on in silence for a while. Then Toglo zev Pamdal said, "This trail reminds me of the one down into the big canyon through the western desert in the Empire of Stekia, over on the Double Continent."

Radnal was both glad Toglo would speak to him and jealous of the wealth that let her travel—just a collateral relation of the Hereditary Tyrant's, eh? "I've only seen pictures," he said wistfully. "I suppose there is some similarity of looks, but the canyon was formed differently from the Bottomlands: by erosion, not evaporation."

"Of course," she said. "I've also only seen pictures myself."

"Oh." Maybe she was a distant relative, then. He went on, "Much more like the big canyon are the gorges our rivers cut before they tumble into what was deep seabottom to form the Bitter Lakes in the deepest parts of the Bottomlands. There's a small one in Trench Park, though it often dries up—the Dalorz River doesn't send down enough water to maintain it very well."

A little later, when the trail twisted west around a big limestone boulder, several tourists exclaimed over the misty plume of water plunging toward the floor of the park. Lofosa asked, "Is that the Dalorz?"

"That's it," Radnal said. "Its flow is too erratic to make it worth Tartesh's while to build a power station where it falls off the ancient continental shelf, though we've done that with several other bigger rivers. They supply more than three fourths of our electricity: another benefit of the Bottomlands."

A few small spun-sugar clouds drifted across the sky from west to east. Otherwise, nothing blocked the sun from beating down on the tourists with greater force every cubit they descended. The donkeys kicked up dust at every footfall.

"Does it ever rain here?" Evillia asked.

"Not very often," Radnal admitted. "The Bottomlands desert is one of the driest places on earth. The Barrier Mountains pick off most of the moisture that blows from the Western Ocean, and the other mountain ranges that stretch into the Bottomlands from the north catch most of what's left. But every two or three years Trench Park does get a downpour. It's the most dangerous time to be there—a torrent can tear through a wash and drown you before you know it's coming."

"But it's also the most beautiful time," Toglo zev Pamdal said. "Pictures of Trench Park after a rain first made me want to come here, and I was lucky enough to see it myself on my last visit."

"May I be so fortunate," Dokhnor of Kellef said. "I brought colorsticks as well as charcoal, on the off chance I might be able to draw post-rain foliage."

"The odds are against you, though the freelady was lucky before," Radnal said. Dokhnor spread his hands to show his agreement. Like everything he did, the gesture was tight, restrained, perfectly controlled. Radnal had trouble imagining him going into transports of artistic rapture over desert flowers, no matter how rare or brilliant.

He said, "The flowers are beautiful, but they're only the tip of the iceberg, if you'll let me use a wildly inappropriate comparison. All life in Trench Park depends on water, the same as everywhere else. It's adapted to get along with very little, but not none. As soon as any moisture comes, plants and animals try to pack a generation's worth of growth and breeding into the little while it takes to dry up."

About a quarter of a daytenth later, a sign set by the side of the trail announced that the tourists were farther below sea level than they could go anywhere outside the Bottomlands. Radnal read it aloud and pointed out, rather smugly, that the salt lake which was the next most submerged spot on dry land lay close to the Bottomlands, and might almost be considered an extension of them.

Moblay Sopsirk's son said, "I didn't imagine anyone would be so proud of this wasteland as to want to include more of the Great Continent in it." His brown skin kept him from roasting under the desert sun, but sweat sheened his bare arms and torso.

A little more than halfway down the trail, a wide flat rest area was carved out of the rock. Radnal let the tourists halt for a while, stretch their legs and ease their weary hindquarters, and use the odorous privy. He passed out ration packs, ignored his charges' grumbles. He noticed Dokhnor of Kellef ate his meal without complaint.

He tossed his own pack into the bin by the privy, then, a couple of cubits from the edge of the trail, peered down onto the floor of the Bottomlands. After one of the rare rains, the park was spectacular from here. Now it just baked: white salt pans, gray-brown or yellow-brown dirt, a scattering of faded green vegetation. Not even the area around the lodge was watered artificially; the Tyrant's charter ordained that Trench Park be kept pristine.

As they came off the trail and started along the ancient sea bottom toward the lodge, Evillia said, "I thought it would be as if we were in the bottom of a bowl, with mountain all around us. It doesn't really feel that way. I can see the ones we just came down, and the Barrier Mountains to the west, but there's nothing to the east and hardly anything to the south—just a blur on the horizon."

"I expected it would look like a bowl, too, the first time I came here," Radnal said. "We are in the bottom of a bowl. But it doesn't look that way because the Bottomlands are broad compared to their depth—it's a big, shallow bowl. What makes it interesting is that its top is at the same level as the bottom of most other geological bowls, and its bottom deeper than any of them."

"What are those cracks?" Toglo zev Pamdal asked, pointing down to breaks in the soil that ran across the tour group's path. Some were no wider than a barleycorn; others, like open, lidless mouths, had gaps of a couple of digits between their sides.

"In arid terrain like this you'll see all kinds of cracks in the ground from mud drying unevenly after a rain," Radnal said. "But the ones you've noticed do mark a fault line. The earthquake we felt earlier probably was triggered along this fault: it marks where two plates in the earth's crust are colliding."

Nocso zev Martois let out a frightened squeak. "Do you mean that if we have another earthquake, those cracks will open and swallow us down?" She twitched her donkey's reins, as if to speed it up and get as far away from the fault line as she could.

Radnal didn't laugh; the Tyranny paid him for not laughing at tourists. He answered gravely, "If you worry about something that unlikely, you might as well worry about getting hit by a skystone, too. The one has about as much chance of happening as the other."

"Are you *sure?*" Lofosa sounded anxious, too.

"I'm sure." He tried to figure out where she and Evillia were from: probably the Krepalgan Unity, by their accent. Krepalga was the northwesternmost Highhead nation; its western border lay at the eastern edge of the Bottomlands. More to the point, it was earthquake country too. If this was all Lofosa knew about quakes, it didn't say much for her brains.

And if Lofosa didn't have a lot of brains, what did that say about her and Evillia picking Radnal to amuse themselves with? No one cares to think of a sexual partner's judgment as faulty, for that reflects upon him.

Radnal did what any sensible man might have done: he changed the subject. "We'll be at the lodge soon, so you'll want to think about getting your things out of your bags and into your sleep cubicles."

"What I want to think about is getting clean," Moblay Sopsirk's son contradicted.

"You'll each be issued a small bucket of water every day for personal purposes," he said, and overrode a chorus of groans: "Don't complain—our brochures are specific about this. Almost all the fresh water in Trench Park comes down the trail we rode, on the backs of these donkeys. Think how much you'll relish a hot soak when we come out of the park."

"Think how much we'll *need* a hot soak when we come out of the park," said the elderly Strongbrow man Radnal had tagged as someone spending the silver he'd made in his earlier years (to his embarrassment, he'd forgotten the fellow's name). "It's not so bad for these Highheads here, since their bodies are mostly bare, but all my hair will be a greasy mess by the time this excursion is done." He glared at Radnal as if it were his fault.

Toglo zev Pamdal said, "Don't fret, freeman vez Maprab." Benter vez Maprab, that's who he was, Radnal thought, shooting Toglo a grateful glance. She was still talking to the old Strongbrow: "I have a jar of waterless hair cleaner you can just comb out. It's more than I'd need; I'll share some with you."

"Well, that's kind of you," Benter vez Maprab said, mollified. "Maybe I should have brought some myself."

You certainly should, you old fool, instead of complaining, Radnal thought. He also noted that Toglo had figured out what she'd need before she started her trip. He approved; he would have done the same had he been tourist rather than guide. Of course, if he'd arranged to forget his own waterless hair cleaner, he could have borrowed some from her. He exhaled through his nose. Maybe he'd been too practical for his own good.

Something small and dun-colored darted under his donkey's hooves, then bounced away toward a patch of oleander. "What was that?" several people asked as it vanished among the fallen leaves under the plants.

"It's one of the species of jerboa that live down here," Radnal answered. "Without more than two heartbeats' look, I couldn't tell you which. There are many varieties, all through the Bottomlands. They lived in arid country while the inland sea still existed, and evolved to get the moisture they need from their food. That preadapted them to succeed here, where free water is so scarce."

"Are they dangerous?" Nocso zev Martois asked.

"Only if you're a shrub," Radnal said. "No, actually, that's not quite true. Some eat insects, and one species, the bladetooth, hunts and kills its smaller relatives. It filled the small predator niche before carnivores proper established themselves in the Bottomlands. It's scarce today, especially outside Trench Park, but it is still around, often in the hottest, driest places where no other meat-eaters can thrive."

A little later, the tour guide pointed to a small, nondescript plant with thin, greenish-brown leaves. "Anyone tell me what that is?"

He asked that question whenever he took a group along the trail, and had only got a right answer once, just after a rain. But now Benter vez Maprab said confidently: "It's a Bottomlands orchid, freeman vez Krobir, and a common type at that. If you'd shown us a red-veined one, that would have been worth fussing over."

"You're right, freeman, it *is* an orchid. It doesn't look much like the ones you see in more hospitable climates, though, does it?" Radnal said, smiling at the elderly Strongbrow—if he was an orchid fancier, that probably explained why he'd come to Trench Park.

Benter only grunted and scowled in reply—evidently he'd had his heart set on seeing a rare red-veined orchid his first day at the park. Radnal resolved to search his bags at the end of the tour: carrying specimens out of the park was against the law.

A jerboa hopped up, started nibbling on an orchid leaf. Quick as a flash, something darted out from behind the plant, seized the rodent, and ran away. The tourists bombarded Radnal with questions: "Did you see that?" "What was it?" "Where'd it go?"

"That was a koprit bird," he answered. "Fast, wasn't it? It's of the butcherbird family, but mostly adapted to life on the ground. It can fly, but it usually runs. Because birds excrete urea in more or less solid form, not in urine like mammals, they've done well in the Bottomlands." He pointed to the lodge, which was only a few hundred cubits ahead now. "See? There's another koprit bird on the roof, looking around to see what it can catch."

A couple of park attendants came out of the lodge. They waved to Radnal, sized up the tourists, then helped them stable their donkeys. "Take only what you'll need tonight into the lodge," said one, Fer vez Canthal. "Leave the rest in your saddle bags for the trip out tomorrow. The less packing and unpacking, the better."

Some tourists, veteran travelers, nodded at the good advice. Evillia and Lofosa exclaimed as if they'd never heard it before. Frowning at their naïveté, Radnal wanted to look away from them, but they were too pretty.

Moblay Sopsirk's son thought so, too. As the group started from the stable to the lodge, he came up behind Evillia and slipped an arm around her waist. At the same moment, he must have tripped, for his startled cry made Radnal whirl toward them.

Moblay sprawled on the dirt floor of the stable. Evillia staggered, flailed her arms wildly, and fell down on top of him, hard. He shouted again, a shout which lost all its breath as she somehow hit him in the pit of the stomach with an elbow while getting back to her feet.

She looked down at him, the picture of concern. "I'm so sorry," she said. "You startled me."

Moblay needed a while before he could sit, let alone stand. At last, he wheezed, "See if I ever touch you again" in a tone that implied it would be her loss.

She stuck her nose in the air. Radnal said, "We should remember we come from different countries and have different customs. Being slow and careful will keep us from embarrassing one another."

"Why, freeman, were you embarrassed last night?" Lofosa asked. Instead of answering, Radnal started to cough. Lofosa and Evillia laughed. Despite what Fer vez Canthal had said, both of them were just toting their saddle bags into the lodge. Maybe they hadn't a lot of brains. But their bodies, those smooth, oh so naked bodies, were something else again.

The lodge was not luxurious, but boasted mesh screens to keep out the Bottomlands bugs, electric lights, and fans which stirred the desert air even if they did not cool it. It also had a refrigerator. "No ration packs tonight," Radnal said. The tourists cheered.

The cooking pit was outdoors: the lodge was warm enough without a fire inside. Fer vez Canthal and the other attendant, Zosel vez Glesir, filled it with chunks of charcoal, splashed light oil over them, and fired them. Then they put a disjointed lamb carcass on a grill and hung it over the pit. Every so often, one of them basted it with a sauce full of pepper and garlic. The sauce and melting fat dripped onto the coals. They sputtered and hissed and sent up little clouds of fragrant smoke. Spit streamed in Radnal's mouth.

The refrigerator also held mead, date wine, grape wine, and ale. Some of the tourists drank boisterously. Dokhnor of Kellef surprised Radnal by taking only chilled water. "I am sworn to the Goddess," he explained.

"Not my affair," Radnal answered, but his sleeping suspicions woke. The Goddess was the deity the Morgaffo military aristocracy most commonly followed. Maybe a traveling artist was among her worshipers, but Radnal did not find it likely.

He did not get much time to dwell on the problem Dokhnor pre-sented. Zosel vez Glesir called him over to do the honors on the lamb. He used a big pair of eating sticks to pick up each piece of meat and transfer it to a paper plate.

The Martoisi ate like starving cave cats. Radnal felt guilty; maybe ordinary rations weren't enough for them. Then he looked at how abundant flesh stretched the fabric of their robes. Guilt evaporated. They weren't wasting away.

Evillia and Lofosa had poured down several mugs of date wine. That soon caused them difficulties. Krepalgans usually ate with knife and skewer; they had trouble manipulating their disposable pairs of wooden eating sticks. After cutting her meat into bite-sized chunks, Lofosa chased them around her plate but couldn't pick them up. Evillia managed that, but dropped them on the way to her mouth.

They both seemed cheerful drunks, and laughed at their mishaps. Even stiff-necked Dokhnor unbent far enough to try to show them how to use sticks. His lesson did not do much good, though both Highhead girls moved close enough to him to make Radnal jealous. Evillia said, "You're so deft. Morgaffos must use them every day."

Dokhnor tossed his head in his people's negative. "Our usual tool has prongs, bowl, and a sharp edge, all in one. The Tarteshans say we are a quiet folk because we risk cutting our tongues whenever we open our mouths. But I have traveled in Tartesh, and learned what to do with sticks."

"Let me try again," Evillia said. This time, she dropped the piece of lamb on Dokhnor's thigh. She picked it up with her fingers. After her hand lingered on the Morgaffo's leg long enough to give Radnal another pang, she popped the gobbet into her mouth.

Moblay Sopsirk's son began singing in his own language. Radnal did not understand most of the words, but the tune was wild and free and easy to follow. Soon the whole tour group was clapping time. More songs followed. Fer vez Canthal had a ringing baritone. Everyone in the group spoke Tarteshan, but not everyone knew Tartesh's songs well enough to join in. As they had for Moblay, those who could not sing clapped.

When darkness fell, gnats emerged in stinging clouds. Radnal and the group retreated to the lodge, whose screens held the biters away. "Now

I know why you wear so many clothes," Moblay said. "They're armor against insects." The dark brown Highhead looked as if he didn't know where to scratch first.

"Of course," Radnal said, surprised Moblay had taken so long to see the obvious. "If you'll hold still for a couple of heartbeats, we have a spray to take away the itch."

Moblay sighed as Radnal sprayed painkiller onto him. "Anyone want another song?" he called.

This time, he got little response. Being under a roof inhibited some people. It reminded others of their long day; Toglo zev Pamdal was not the only tourist to wander off to a sleeping cubicle. Dokhnor of Kellef and old Benter vez Maprab had discovered a war board and were deep in a game. Moblay went over to watch. So did Radnal, who fancied himself a war player.

Dokhnor, who had the blue pieces, advanced a footsoldier over the blank central band that separated his side of the board from his opponent's. "Across the river," Moblay said.

"Is that what Lissonese name the gap?" Radnal said. "With us, it's the Trench."

"And in Morgaf, it's the Sleeve, after the channel that separates our islands from Tartesh," Dokhnor said. "No matter what we call it, though, the game's the same all over the world."

"It's a game that calls for thought and quiet," Benter said pointedly. After some thought, he moved a counselor (that was the name of the piece on the red side of board; its blue equivalent was an elephant) two squares diagonally.

The old Tarteshan's pauses for concentration grew more frequent as the game went on. Dokhnor's attack had the red governor scurrying along the vertical and horizontal lines of his fortress, and his guards along the diagonals, to evade or block the blue pieces. Finally Dokhnor brought one of his cannons in line with the other and said, "That's the end."

Benter glumly nodded. The cannon (the red piece of identical value was called a catapult) was hard to play well: it moved vertically and horizontally, but had to jump over one other piece every time. Thus the rear cannon, not the front, threatened the red governor. But if Benter interposed a guard or one of his chariots, that turned the forward cannon into the threat.

"Nicely played," Benter said. He got up from the war table, headed for a cubicle.

"Care for a game, either of you?" Dokhnor asked the spectators.

Moblay Sopsirk's son shook his head. Radnal said, "I did, till I saw you play. I don't mind facing someone better than I am if I have some chance. Even when I lose, I learn something. But you'd just trounce me, and a little of that goes a long way."

"As you will." Dokhnor folded the war board, poured the disks into their bag. He replaced bag and board on their shelf. "I'm for bed, then." He marched off to the cubicle he'd chosen.

Radnal and Moblay glanced at each other, then toward the war set. By unspoken consent, they seemed to decide that if neither of them wanted a go at Dokhnor of Kellef, playing each other would be rude. "Another night," Radnal said.

"Fair enough." Moblay yawned, displaying teeth that gleamed all the whiter against his brown skin. He said, "I'm about done over—no, it's 'done in' in Tarteshan, isn't it?—anyhow. See you in the morning, Radnal."

Again the tour guide controlled his annoyance at Moblay's failure to use the polite particle *vez*. At first when foreigners forgot that trick of Tarteshan grammar, he'd imagined himself deliberately insulted. Now he knew better, though he still noticed the omission.

A small light came on in Dokhnor's cubicle: a battery-powered reading lamp. The Morgaffo wasn't reading, though. He sat with his behind on the sleeping mat and his back against the wall. His sketch pad lay on his bent knees. Radnal heard the faint *skritch-skritch* of charcoal on paper.

"What's he doing?" Fer vez Canthal whispered. A generation's peace was not enough time to teach most Tarteshans to trust their island neighbors.

"He's drawing," Radnal answered, as quietly. Neither of them wanted to draw Dokhnor's notice. The reply could have come out sounding innocent. It didn't. Radnal went on, "His travel documents say he's an artist." Again, tone spoke volumes.

Zosel vez Glesir said, "If he really were a spy, Radnal vez, he'd carry a camera, not a sketch pad. Everyone carries a camera into Trench Park—he wouldn't even get noticed."

"True," Radnal said. "But he doesn't act like an artist. He acts like a member of the Morgaffo officer caste. You heard him—he's sworn to their Goddess."

Fer vez Canthal said something lewd about the Morgaffo Goddess. But he lowered his voice even further before he did. An officer from Morgaf who heard his deity offended might make formal challenge. Then again, in Tartesh, where dueling was illegal, he might simply commit murder. The only thing certain was that he wouldn't ignore the insult.

"We can't do anything to him—or even about him—unless we find out he *is* spying," Zosel vez Glesir said.

"Yes," Radnal said. "The last thing Tartesh wants is to hand Morgaf an incident." He thought about what would happen to someone who fouled up so gloriously. Nothing good, that was sure. Then something else occurred to him. "Speaking of the Tyrant, do you know who's in this group? Freelady Toglo zev Pamdal, that's who."

Zosel and Fer whistled softly. "Good thing you warned us," Zosel said. "We'll stay round her like cotton round cut glass."

"I don't think she cares for that sort of thing," Radnal said. "Treat her well, yes, but don't fall all over yourselves."

Zosel nodded. Fer still had Dokhnor of Kellef on his mind. "If he *is* a spy, what's he doing in Trench Park instead of somewhere important?"

"I thought of that myself," Radnal said. "Cover, maybe. And who knows where he's going after he leaves?"

"I know where *I'm* going," Zosel said, yawning: "To bed. If you want to stay up all night fretting about spies, go ahead."

"No, thanks," Fer answered. "A spy would have to be crazy or on holiday to come to Trench Park. If he's crazy, we don't have to worry about him, and if he's on holiday, we don't have to worry about him then, either. So I'm going to bed, too."

"If you think I'll stay talking to myself, you're *both* crazy," Radnal said. All three Tarteshans got up. Dokhnor of Kellef's reading lamp went out, plunging his cubicle into blackness. Radnal dimmed the lights in the common room.

He flopped down onto his sleeping mat with a long sigh. He would sooner have been out in the field, curled up in a sleepsack under gnat netting. This was the price he paid for doing what he wanted most of the time. He knew his own snores would soon join the tourists'.

Then two female shapes appeared in the entrance to his cubicle. *By the gods, not again*, he thought as his eyes opened wide, which showed how tired he was. He said, "Don't you believe in sleep?"

Evillia laughed softly, or maybe Lofosa. "Not when there are better things to do," Lofosa said. "We have some new ideas, too. But we can always see who else is awake."

Radnal almost told her to go ahead, and take Evillia with her. But he heard himself say "No" instead. The night before had been educational beyond his dreams, the stuff people imagined when they talked about the fringe benefits of a tour guide's job. Until last night, he'd reckoned those stories imaginary: in his two years as a guide, he'd never cavorted with a tourist before. Now . . . he grinned as he felt himself rising to the occasion.

The Highhead girls came in. As they'd promised, the threesome tried some new things. He wondered how long their inventiveness could last, and if he could last as long. He was sure he'd enjoy trying.

His stamina and the girls' ingenuity flagged together. He remembered them getting up from the mat. He thought he remembered them going out into the common room. He was sure he didn't remember anything after that. He slept like a log from a petrified forest.

When the scream jarred him awake, his first muzzy thought was that only a few heartbeats had passed. But a glance at his pocket clock as he closed his robe told him sunrise was near. He dashed out into the common room.

Several tourists were already out there, some dressed, some not. More emerged every moment, as did the other two Trench Park staffers. Everyone kept saying, "What's going on?" Though no one directly answered the question, no one needed to. As naked as when she'd frolicked with Radnal, Evillia stood by the table where Benter vez Maprab and Dokhnor of Kellef had played war. Dokhnor was there, too, but not standing. He lay sprawled on the floor, head twisted at an unnatural angle.

Evillia had jammed a fist in her mouth to stifle another scream. She took it out, quavered, "Is—is he dead?"

Radnal strode over to Dokhnor, grabbed his wrist, felt for a pulse. He found none, nor was the Morgaffo breathing. "He's dead, all right," Radnal said grimly.

Evillia moaned. Her knees buckled. She toppled onto Radnal's bent back.

When Evillia fainted, Lofosa screamed and ran forward to try to help. Nocso zev Martois screamed, too, even louder. Moblay Sopsirk's son hurried toward Radnal with Evillia. So did Fer vez Canthal and Zosel vez Glesir. So did Toglo zev Pamdal. So did another tourist, a High-head who'd spoken very little on the way down to the lodge.

Everyone got in everyone else's way. Then the quiet Highhead stopped being quiet and shouted, "I am a physician, the six million gods curse you! Let me through!"

"Let the physician through," Radnal echoed, sliding Evillia off him and to the ground as gently as he could. "Check her first, freeman Golobol," he added, pleased he'd hung onto the doctor's name. "I'm afraid you're too late to help Dokhnor now."

Golobol was almost as dark as Moblay, but spoke Tarteshan with a different accent. As he turned to Evillia, she moaned and stirred. "She will be all right, oh yes, I am sure," he said. "But this poor fellow—" As Radnal had, he felt for Dokhnor's pulse. As Radnal had, he failed to find it. "You are correct, sir. This man is dead. He has been dead for some time."

"How do you know?" Radnal asked.

"You felt of him, not?" the physician said. "Surely you noticed his flesh has begun to cool. It has, oh yes."

Thinking back, Radnal *had* noticed, but he'd paid no special attention. He'd always prided himself on how well he'd learned first aid training. But he wasn't a physician, and didn't automatically take every-thing into account as a physician would. His fit of chagrin was inter-rupted when Evillia let out a shriek a hunting cave cat would have been proud of.

Lofosa bent by her, spoke to her in her own language. The shriek cut off. Radnal started thinking about what to do next. Golobol said, "Sir, look here, if you would."

Golobol was pointing to a spot on the back of Dokhnor's neck, right above where it bent gruesomely. Radnal had to say, "I don't see anything."

"You Strongbrows are a hairy folk, that is why," Golobol said. "Here, though—see this, ah, discoloration, is that the word in your language? It is? Good. Yes. This discoloration is the sort of mark to be expected from a blow by the side of the hand, a killing blow."

Despite Bottomlands heat, ice formed in the pit of Radnal's stomach. "You're telling me this was murder?"

The word cut through the babble filling the common room like a scalpel. There was chaos one heartbeat, silence the next. Into that abrupt, intense silence, Golobol said, "Yes."

"Oh, by the gods, what a mess," Fer vez Canthal said.

Figuring out what to do next became a lot more urgent for Radnal. Why had the gods (though he didn't believe in six million of them) let one someone from *his* tour group get murdered? And why, by all the gods he did believe in, did it have to be the Morgaffo? Morgaf would be suspicious—if not hostile—if any of its people met foul play in Tartesh. And if Dokhnor of Kellef really was a spy, Morgaf would be more than suspicious. Morgaf would be furious.

Radnal walked over to the radiophone. "Whom will you call?" Fer asked.

"First, the park militia. They'd have to be notified in any case. And then—" Radnal took a deep breath. "Then I think I'd best call the Hereditary Tyrant's Eyes and Ears in Tarteshem. Murder of a Morgaffo sworn to the Goddess is a deeper matter than the militia can handle alone. Besides, I'd sooner have an Eye and Ear notify the Morgaffo plenipo than try doing it myself."

"Yes, I can see that," Fer said. "Wouldn't want Morgaffo gunboats running across the Sleeve to raid our coasts because you said something wrong. Or—" The lodge attendant shook his head. "No, not even the island king would be crazy enough to start tossing starbombs over something this small." Fer's voice turned anxious. "Would he?"

"I don't think so." But Radnal sounded anxious, too. Politics hadn't been the same since starbombs came along fifty years before. Neither Tartesh nor Morgaf had used them, even in war against each other, but both countries kept building them. So did eight or ten other nations, scattered across the globe. If another big war started, it could easily become The Big War, the one everybody was afraid of.

Radnal punched buttons on the radiophone. After a couple of static bursts, a voice answered: "Trench Park militia, Subleader vez Steries speaking."

"Gods bless you, Liem vez," Radnal said; this was a man he knew and liked. "Vez Krobir here, over at the tourist lodge. I'm sorry to have to tell you we've had a death. I'm even sorrier to have to tell you it looks like murder." Radnal explained what had happened to Dokhnor of Kellef.

Liem vez Steries said, "Why couldn't it have been anyone else but the Morgaffo? Now you'll have to drag in the Eyes and Ears, and the gods only know how much hoorah will erupt."

"My next call was to Tarteshem," Radnal agreed.

"It probably should have been your first one, but never mind," Liem vez Steries said. "I'll be over there with a circumstances man as fast as I can get a helo in the air. Farewell."

"Farewell." Radnal's next call had to go through a human relayer. After a couple of hundred heartbeats, he found himself talking with an Eye and Ear named Peggol vez Menk. Unlike the park militiaman, Peggol kept interrupting with questions, so the conversation took twice as long as the other one had.

When Radnal was through, the Eye and Ear said, "You did right to involve us, freeman vez Krobir. We'll handle the diplomatic aspects, and we'll fly a team down there to help with the investigation. Don't let anyone leave the—lodge, did you call it? Farewell."

The radiophone had a speaking diaphragm in the console, not the more common—and more private—ear-and-mouth handset. Everyone heard what Peggol vez Menk said. Nobody liked it. Evillia said, "Did he mean we're going to have to stay cooped up here—with a murderer?" She started trembling. Lofosa put an arm around her.

Benter vez Maprab had a different objection: "See here, freeman, I put down good silver for a tour of Trench Park, and I intend to have that tour. If not, I shall take legal measures."

Radnal stifled a groan. Tarteshan law, which relied heavily on the principle of trust, came down hard on those who violated contracts in any way. If the old Strongbrow went to court, he'd likely collect enormous damages from Trench Park—and from Radnal, as the individual who failed to deliver the service contracted for.

Worse, the Martoisi joined the outcry. A reasonably upright and upstanding man, Radnal had never had to hire a pleader in his life. He wondered if he had enough silver to pay for a good one. Then he wondered if he'd ever have any silver again, once the tourists, the courts, and the pleader were through with him.

Toglo zev Pamdal cut through the hubbub: "Let's wait a few heartbeats. A man is dead. That's more important than everything else. If the start of our tour is delayed, perhaps Trench Park will regain equity by delaying its end to give us the full touring time we've paid for."

"That's an excellent suggestion, freelady zev Pamdal," Radnal said gratefully. Fer and Zosel nodded.

A distant thutter in the sky grew to a roar. The militia helo kicked up a small dust storm as it set down between the stables and the lodge. Flying pebbles clicked off walls and windows. The motor shut down. As the blades slowed, dust subsided.

Radnal felt as if a good god had frightened a night demon from his shoulders. "I don't think we'll need to extend your time here by more than a day," he said happily.

"How will you manage that, if we're confined here in this godsforsaken wilderness?" Eltsac vez Martois growled.

"That's just it," Radnal said. "We *are* in a wilderness. Suppose we go out and see what there is to see in Trench Park—where will the culprit flee on donkeyback? If he tries to get away, we'll know who he is because he'll be the only one missing, and we'll track him down with the helo." The tour guide beamed. The tourists beamed back—including, Radnal reminded himself, the killer among them.

Liem vez Steries and two other park militiamen walked into the lodge. They wore soldierly versions of Radnal's costume: their robes, instead of being white, were splotched in shades of tan and light green, as were their long-brimmed caps. Their rank badges were dull; even the metal buckles of their sandals were painted to avoid reflections.

Liem set a recorder on the table Dokhnor and Benter vez Maprab had used for war the night before. The circumstances man started taking pictures with as much abandon as if he'd been a tourist. He asked, "Has the body been moved?"

"Only as much as we needed to make sure the man was dead," Radnal answered.

"We?" the circumstances man asked. Radnal introduced Golobol. Liem got everyone's statement on the wire: first Evillia, who gulped and blinked back tears as she spoke, then Radnal, then the physician, and then the other tourists and lodge attendants. Most of them echoed one another: they'd heard a scream, run out, and seen Evillia standing over Dokhnor's corpse.

Golobol added, "The woman cannot be responsible for his death. He had been deceased some while, between one and two daytenths, possibly. She, unfortunate one, merely discovered the body."

"I understand, freeman," Liem vez Steries assured him. "But because she did, her account of what happened is important."

The militiaman had just finished recording the last statement when another helo landed outside the lodge. The instant its dust storm subsided, four men came in. The Hereditary Tyrant's Eyes and Ears looked more like prosperous merchants than soldiers: their caps had patent-leather brims, they closed their robes with silver chains, and they sported rings on each index finger.

"I am Peggol vez Menk," one of them announced. He was short and, by Tarteshan standards, slim; he wore his cap at a dapper angle. His eyes were extraordinarily shrewd, as if he were waiting for someone around him to make a mistake. He spotted Liem vez Steries at once, and asked, "What's been done thus far, Subleader?"

"What you'd expect," the militiaman answered: "Statements from all present, and our circumstances man, Senior Trooper vez Sofana there, has taken some pictures. We didn't disturb the body."

"Fair enough," the Eye and Ear said. One of his men was flashing more photos. Another set a recorder beside the one already on the table. "We'll get a copy of your wire, and we'll make one for ourselves—maybe we'll find questions you missed. You haven't searched belongings yet?"

"No, freeman." Liem vez Steries' voice went wooden. Radnal wouldn't have wanted someone to steal and duplicate his work, either. Eyes and Ears, though, did as they pleased. Why not? They watched Tartesh, but who watched them?

"We'll take care of it." Peggol vez Menk sat down at the table. The photographer stuck in a fresh clip of film, then followed the two remaining Eyes and Ears into the sleeping cubicle nearest the entrance. It was Golobol's. "Be careful, oh please I beg you," the physician exclaimed. "Some of my equipment is delicate."

Peggol said, "I'll hear the tale of the woman who discovered the body." He pulled out a notepad, glanced at it. "Evillia." A little calmer now, Evillia retold her story using, so far as Radnal could tell, the same words she had before. If Peggol found any new questions, he didn't ask them.

After about a tenth of a daytenth, it was Radnal's turn. Peggol did remember his name without needing to remind himself. Again, his questions were like the ones Liem vez Steries had used. When he asked the last one, Radnal had a question of his own: "Freeman, while the investigation continues, may I take my group out into the Bottom-lands?" He explained how Benter vez Maprab had threatened to sue, and why he thought even a guilty tourist unlikely to escape.

The Eye and Ear pulled at his lower lip. He let the hair beneath it grow out in a tuft, which made him seem to have a protruding chin like a Highhead's. When he released the lip, it went back with a liquid plop. Under his tilted cap, he looked wise and cynical. Radnal's hopes plunged. He waited for Peggol to laugh at him for raising the matter.

Peggol said, "Freeman, I know you technically enjoy military rank, but suppose you discover who the killer is, or he strikes again. Do you reckon yourself up to catching him and bringing him back for trial and decapitation?"

"I—" Radnal stopped before he went any further. The ironic question reminded him this wasn't a game. Dokhnor of Kellef might have been a spy, he was dead now, and whoever had killed him might kill again—*might kill* me, *if I find out who he is*, he thought. He said, "I don't know. I'd like to think so, but I've never had to do that sort of thing."

Something like approval came into Peggol vez Menk's eyes. "You're honest with yourself. Not everyone can say that. Hmm—it wouldn't be just your silver involved in a suit, would it? No, of course not; it would be Trench Park's, too, which means the Hereditary Tyrant's."

"Just what I was thinking," Radnal said, with luck patriotically. His own silver came first with him. He was honest enough with himself to be sure of that—but he didn't have to tell it to Peggol.

"I'm sure you were," the Eye and Ear said, his tone dry. "The Tyrant's silver really does come first with me. How's this, then? Suppose you take the tourists out, as you've contracted to do. But suppose I come with you to investigate while my comrades keep working here? Does that seem reasonable?"

"Yes, freeman; thank you," Radnal exclaimed.

"Good," Peggol said. "My concubine has been nagging me to bring her here. Now I'll see if I want to do that." He grinned knowingly. "You see, I also keep my own interests in mind."

The other Eyes and Ears had methodically gone from one sleeping cubicle to the next, examining the tourists' belongings. One of them brought a codex out of Lofosa's cubicle, dropped it on the table in front of Peggol vez Menk. The cover was a color photo of two good-looking Highheads fornicating. Peggol flipped through it. Variations on the same theme filled every page.

"Amusing," he said, "even if it should have been seized when its owner entered our domains."

"I like that!" Lofosa sounded indignant. "You sanctimonious Strongbrows, pretending you don't do the same things—and enjoy them, too. I ought to know."

Radnal hoped Peggol would not ask how she knew. He was certain she would tell him, in detail; she and Evillia might have been many things, but not shy. But Peggol said, "We did not come here to search for filth. She might have worn out Dokhnor with that volume, but she didn't kill him with it. Let her keep it, if she enjoys telling the world what should be kept private."

"Oh, rubbish!" Lofosa scooped up the codex and carried it back to her cubicle, rolling her hips at every step as if to contradict Peggol without another word.

The Eyes and Ears brought out nothing more from her sleep cubicle or Evillia's for their chief to inspect. That surprised Radnal; the two women had carried in everything but the donkey they'd ridden. He shrugged—they'd probably filled their saddlebags with feminine fripperies and junk that could have stayed behind in their Tarteshan hostel if not in Krepalga.

Then he stopped thinking about them—the Eye and Ear who'd gone into Dokhnor's cubicle whistled. Peggol vez Menk dashed in there. He came out with his fist tightly closed around something. He opened it. Radnal saw two six-pointed gold stars: Morgaffo rank badges.

"So he *was* a spy," Fer vez Canthal exclaimed.

"He may have been," Peggol said. But when he got on the radiophone to Tarteshem, he found Dokhnor of Kellef had declared his battalion leader's rank when he entered the Tyranny. The Eye and Ear scowled. "A soldier, yes, but not a spy after all, it would appear."

Benter vez Maprab broke in: "I wish you'd finish your pawing and let us get on with our tour. I haven't that many days left, so I hate to squander one."

"Peace, freeman" Peggol said. "A man is dead."

"Which means he'll not complain if I see the much-talked-about wonders of Trench Park." Benter glared as if he were the Hereditary Tyrant dressing down some churlish underling.

Radnal, seeing how Benter reacted when thwarted, wondered if he'd broken Dokhnor's neck for no better reason than losing a game of war. Benter might be old, but he wasn't feeble. And he was sure to be a veteran of the last war with Morgaf, or the one before that against Morgaf and the Krepalgan Unity both. He would know how to kill.

Radnal shook his head. If things kept on like this, he'd start suspecting Fer and Zosel next, or his own shadow. He wished he hadn't lost the tour guides' draw. He would sooner have been studying the metabolism of the fat sand rat than trying to figure out which of his charges had just committed murder.

Peggol vez Menk said, "We shall have to search the outbuildings before we begin. Freeman vez Krobir already told you we'd go out tomorrow. My professional opinion is that no court would sustain a suit over one day's delay when compensational time is guaranteed."

"Bah!" Benter stomped off. Radnal caught Toglo zev Pamdal's eye. She raised one eyebrow slightly, shook her head. He shifted his shoulders in a tiny shrug. They both smiled. In every group, someone turned out to be a pain in the backside. Radnal let his smile expand, glad Toglo wasn't holding his sport with Lofosa and Evillia against him.

"Speaking of outbuildings, freeman vez Krobir," Peggol said, "there's just the stables, am I right?"

"That and the privy, yes," Radnal said.

"Oh, yes, the privy." The Eye and Ear wrinkled his nose. It was even more prominent than Radnal's. Most Strongbrows had big noses, as if to counterbalance their long skulls. Lissonese, whose noses were usually flattish, sometimes called Tarteshans Snouts on account of that. The name would start a brawl in any port on the Western Ocean.

Fer vez Canthal accompanied one of Peggol's men to the stables; the Eye and Ear obviously needed support against the ferocious, blood-crazed donkeys inside—that was what his body language said, anyhow. When Peggol ordered him out, he'd flinched as if told to invade Morgaf and bring back the king's ears.

"You Eyes and Ears don't often deal with matters outside the big cities, do you?" Radnal asked.

"You noticed that?" Peggol vez Menk raised a wry eyebrow. "You're right; we're urbanites to the core. Threats to the realm usually come among crowds of masking people. Most that don't are a matter for the army, not us."

Moblay Sopsirk's son went over to the shelf where the war board was stored. "If we can't go out today, Radnal, care for the game we didn't have last night?"

"Maybe another time, freeman vez Sopsirk," the tour guide said, turning Moblay's name into its nearest Tarteshan equivalent. Maybe the brown man would take the hint and speak a bit more formally to him. But Moblay didn't seem good at catching hints, as witness his advances toward Evillia and this even more poorly timed suggestion of a game.

The Eye and Ear returned from the stable without the solution to Dokhnor's death. By his low-voiced comments to his friends, he was glad he'd escaped the den of vicious beasts with his life. The Trench Park staffers tried to hide their sniggers. Even a few of the tourists, only two days better acquainted with donkeys than the Eye and Ear, chuckled at his alarm.

Something on the roof said *hig-hig-hig!* in a loud, strident voice. The Eye and Ear who'd braved the stables started nervously. Peggol vez Menk raised his eyebrow again. "What's that, freeman vez Krobir?"

"A koprit bird," Radnal said. "They hardly impale people on thorn bushes."

"No, eh? That's good to hear." Peggol's dry cough served him for a laugh.

The midday meal was ration packs. Radnal sent Liem vez Steries a worried look: the extra mouths at the lodge would make supplies run out faster than he'd planned for. Understanding the look, Liem said, "We'll fly in more from the militia outpost if we have to."

"Good."

Between them, Peggol vez Menk and Liem vez Steries spent most of the afternoon on the radiophone. Radnal worried about power, but not as much. Even if the generator ran out of fuel, solar cells would take up most of the slack. Trench Park had plenty of sunshine.

After supper, the militiamen and Eyes and Ears scattered sleepsacks on the common room floor. Peggol set up a watch schedule that gave each of his and Liem's men about half a daytenth each. Radnal volunteered to stand a watch himself.

"No," Peggol answered. "While I do not doubt your innocence, freeman vez Krobir, you and your colleagues formally remain under suspicion here. The Morgaffo plenipo could protest were you given a post which might let you somehow take advantage of us."

Though that made some sense, it miffed Radnal. He retired to his sleeping cubicle in medium dudgeon, lay down, and discovered he could not sleep. The last two nights, he'd been on the edge of dropping off when Evillia and Lofosa called. Now he was awake, and they stayed away.

He wondered why. They'd already shown they didn't care who watched them when they made love. Maybe they thought he was too shy to do anything with militiamen and Eyes and Ears outside the entrance. A few days before, they would have been right. Now he wondered. They took fornication so much for granted that they made any other view of it seem foolish.

Whatever their reasons, they stayed away. Radnal tossed and turned on his sleepsack. He thought about going out to chat with the fellow on watch, but decided not to: Peggol vez Menk would suspect he was up to something nefarious if he tried. That annoyed him all over again, and drove sleep further away than ever. So did the Martoisi's furious row over how one of them—Eltsac said Nocso, Nocso said Eltsac—had managed to lose their only currycomb.

The tour guide eventually dozed off, for he woke with a start when the men in the common room turned up the lights just before sunrise. For a heartbeat or two, he wondered why they were there. Then he remembered.

Yawning, he grabbed his cap, tied the belt on his robe, and headed out of the cubicle. Zosel vez Glesir and a couple of tourists were already in the common room, talking with the militiamen and the Eyes and Ears. Conversation flagged when Lofosa emerged from her sleeping cubicle without dressing first.

"A tough job, this tour guide business must be," Peggol vez Menk said, sounding like everyone else who thought a guide did nothing but roll on the sleepsack with his tourists.

Radnal grunted. This tour, he hadn't done much with Lofosa or Evillia but roll on the sleepsack. *It's not usually like that*, he wanted to say. He didn't think Peggol would believe him, so he kept his mouth shut. If an Eye and Ear didn't believe something, he'd start digging. If he started to dig, he'd keep digging till he found what he was looking for, regardless of whether it was really there.

The tour guide and Zosel dug out breakfast packs. By the time they came back, everyone was up, and Evillia had succeeded in distracting some of the males from Lofosa. "Here you are, freelady," Radnal said to Toglo zev Pamdal when he got to her.

No one paid her any particular attention; she was just a Tarteshan woman in a concealing Tarteshan robe, not a foreign doxy wearing nothing much. Radnal wondered if that irked her. Women, in his experience, did not like being ignored.

If she was irked, she didn't show it. "I trust you slept well, free-man vez Krobir?" she said. She did not even glance toward Evillia and Lofosa. If she meant anything more by her greeting than its words, she also gave no sign of that—which suited Radnal perfectly.

"Yes. I trust you did likewise," he answered.

"Well enough," she said, "though not as well as I did before the Morgaffo was killed. A pity he'll not be able to make his sketches—he had talent. May his Goddess grant him wind and land and water in the world to come: that's what the islanders pray for, not so?"

"I believe so, yes," Radnal said, though he knew little of Morgaffo religious forms.

"I'm glad you've arranged for the tour to continue despite the mis-fortune that befell him, Radnal vez," she said. "It can do him no harm, and the Bottomlands are fascinating."

"So they are, fr—" Radnal began. Then he stopped, stared, and blinked. Toglo hadn't used formal address, but the middle grade of Tarteshan politesse, which implied she felt she knew him somewhat and didn't disapprove of him. Considering what she'd witnessed at the first night's campsite, that was a minor miracle. He grinned and took a like privilege: "So do I, Toglo zev."

About a tenth of a daytenth later, as he and Fer carried empty ration packs to the disposal bin, the other Trench Park staffer elbowed him in the ribs and said, "You have *all* the women after you, eh, Radnal vez?"

Radnal elbowed back, harder. "Go jump in the Bitter Lake, Fer vez. This group's nothing but trouble. Besides, Nocso zev Martois thinks I'm part of the furniture."

"You wouldn't want her," Fer replied, chuckling. "I was just jealous."

"That's what Moblay said," Radnal answered. Having anyone jeal-ous of him for being sexually attractive was a new notion, one he didn't care for. By Tarteshan standards, drawing such notice was faintly dis-reputable, as if he'd got rich by skirting the law. It didn't bother Evillia and Lofosa—they reveled in it. *Well*, he asked himself, *do you really want to be like Evillia and Lofosa, no matter how ripe their bodies are?* He snorted through his nose. "Let's go back inside, so I can get my crew moving."

After two days of practice, the tourists thought they were seasoned riders. They bounded onto their donkeys, and had little trouble guiding them out of their stalls. Peggol vez Menk looked almost as apprehensive as his henchman who'd gone to search the stable. He drew in his white robe all around him, as if fearing to have it soiled. "You expect me to ride one of these creatures?" he said.

"You were the one who wanted to come along," Radnal answered. "You don't have to ride; you could always hike along beside us."

Peggol glared. "Thank you, no, freeman vez Krobir." He pointedly did *not* say *Radnal vez*. "Will you be good enough to show me how to ascend one of these perambulating peaks?"

"Certainly, freeman vez Menk." Radnal mounted a donkey, dismounted, got on again. The donkey gave him a jaundiced stare, as if asking him to make up his mind. He dismounted once more, and took the snort that followed as the asinine equivalent of a resigned shrug. To Peggol, he said, "Now you try, freeman."

Unlike Evillia or Lofosa, the Eye and Ear managed to imitate Radnal's movements without requiring the tour guide to take him by the waist (just as well, Radnal thought—Peggol wasn't smooth and supple like the Highhead girls). He said, "When back in Tarteshem, freeman vez Krobir, I shall stick exclusively to motors."

"When I'm in Tarteshem, freeman vez Menk, I do the same," Radnal answered.

The party set out a daytenth after sunrise: not as early as Radnal would have liked but, given the previous day's distractions, the best he could expect. He led them south, toward the lowlands at the core of Trench Park. Under his straw hat, Moblay Sopsirk's son was already sweating hard.

Something skittered into hiding under the fleshy leaves of a desert spurge. "What did we just nearly see there, freeman?" Golobol asked.

Radnal smiled at the physician's phrasing. "That was a fat sand rat. It's a member of the gerbil family, one specially adapted to feed off succulent plants that concentrate salt in their foliage. Fat sand rats are common throughout the Bottomlands. They're pests in areas where there's enough water for irrigated agriculture."

Moblay said, "You sound like you know a lot about them, Radnal."

"Not as much as I'd like to, freeman vez Sopsirk," Radnal answered,

still trying to persuade the Lissonese to stop being so uncouthly familiar. "I study them when I'm not being a tour guide."

"I hate all kinds of rats," Nocso zev Martois said flatly.

"Oh, I don't know," Eltsac said. "Some rats are kind of cute." The
two Martoisi began to argue. Everyone else ignored them.

Moblay said, "Hmp. Fancy spending all your time studying rats."

"And how do you make *your* livelihood, freeman?" Radnal snapped.

"Me?" Flat-nosed, dark, and smooth, Moblay's face was different
from Radnal's in every way. But the tour guide recognized the blank
mask that appeared on it for a heartbeat: the expression of a man
with something to hide. Moblay said, "As I told you, I am aide to
my prince, may his years be many." He had said that, Radnal remembered. It might even be true, but he was suddenly convinced it wasn't
the whole truth.

Benter vez Maprab couldn't have cared less about the fat sand rat.
The spiny spurge under which it hid, however, interested him. He
said, "Freeman vez Krobir, perhaps you will explain the relationship
between the plants here and the cactuses in the deserts of the Double
Continent."

"There is no relationship to speak of." Radnal gave the old Strongbrow an unfriendly look. *Try to make me look bad in front of everyone, will you?* he thought. He went on, "The resemblances come from
adapting to similar environments. That's called convergent evolution.
As soon as you cut them open, you'll see they're unrelated: spurges
have a thick white milky sap, while that of cactuses is clear and watery.
Whales and fish look very much alike, too, but that's because they both
live in the sea, not because they're kin."

Benter hunched low over his donkey's back. Radnal felt like preen-
ing, as if he'd overcome a squadron of Morgaffo marine commandos
rather than one querulous old Tarteshan.

Some of the spines of the desert spurge held a jerboa, a couple of
grasshoppers, a shoveler skink, and other small, dead creatures. "Who
hung them out to dry?" Peggol vez Menk asked.

"A koprit bird," Radnal answered. "Most butcherbirds make a larder of things they've caught but haven't got round to eating yet."

"Oh." Peggol sounded disappointed. Maybe he'd hoped someone

in Trench Park enjoyed tormenting animals, so he could hunt down the miscreant.

Toglo zev Pamdal pointed to the impaled lizard, which looked to have spent a while in the sun. "Do they eat things as dried up as that, Radnal vez?"

"No, probably not," Radnal said. "At least, I wouldn't want to." After he got his small laugh, he continued, "A koprit bird's larder isn't just things it intends to eat. It's also a display to other koprit birds. That's especially true in breeding season—it's as if the male says to prospective mates, 'Look what a hunter I am.' Koprits don't display only live things they've caught, either. I've seen hoards with bright bits of yarn, wires, pieces of sparkling plastic, and once even a set of old false teeth, all hung on spines."

"False teeth?" Evillia looked sidelong at Benter vez Maprab. "Some of us have more to worry about than others." Stifled snorts of laughter went up from several tourists. Even Eltsac chuckled. Benter glared at the Highhead girl. She ignored him.

High in the sky, almost too small to see, were a couple of moving black specks. As Radnal pointed them out to the group, a third joined them. "Another feathered optimist," he said. "This is wonderful country for vultures. Thermals from the Bottomlands floor make soaring effortless. They're waiting for a donkey—or one of us—to keel over and die. Then they'll feast."

"What do they eat when they can't find tourists?" Toglo zev Pamdal asked.

"Humpless camels, or boar, or anything else dead they spy," Radnal said. "The only reason there aren't more of them is that the terrain is too barren to support many large-bodied herbivores."

"I've seen country that isn't," Moblay Sopsirk's son said. "In Duvai, east of Lissonland, the herds range the grasslands almost as they did in the days before mankind. The past hundred years, though, hunting has thinned them out. So the Duvains say, at any rate; I wasn't there then."

"I've heard the same," Radnal agreed. "It isn't like that here."

He waved to show what he meant. The Bottomlands were too hot and dry to enjoy a covering of grass. Scattered over the plain were assorted varieties of succulent spurges, some spiny, some glossy with wax to hold down water loss. Sharing the landscape with them were desiccated-looking bushes—thorny burnets, oleander, tiny Bottomlands olive plants (they were too small to be trees).

Smaller plants huddled in shadows round the base of the bigger ones. Radnal knew seeds were scattered everywhere, waiting for the infrequent rains. But most of the ground was as barren as if the sea had disappeared yesterday, not five and a half million years before.

"I want all of you to drink plenty of water," Radnal said. "In weather like this, you sweat more than you think. We've packed plenty aboard the donkeys, and we'll replenish their carrying bladders tonight back at the lodge. Don't be shy—heatstroke can kill you if you aren't careful."

"Warm water isn't very satisfying to drink," Lofosa grumbled.

"I am sorry, freelady, but Trench Park hasn't the resources to haul a refrigerator around for anyone's convenience," Radnal said.

Despite Lofosa's complaint, she and Evillia both drank regularly. Radnal scratched his head, wondering how the Krepalgan girls could seem so fuzzbrained but still muddle along without getting into real trouble.

Evillia had even brought along some flavoring packets, so while everyone else poured down blood-temperature water, she had blood-temperature fruit punch instead. The crystals also turned the water the color of blood. Radnal decided he could do without them.

They got to the Bitter Lake a little before noon. It was more a salt marsh than a lake; the Dalorz River did not drop enough water off the ancient continental shelf to keep a lake bed full against the tremendous evaporation in the eternally hot, eternally dry Bottomlands. Salt pans gleamed white around pools and patches of mud.

"Don't let the donkeys eat *anything* here," Radnal warned. "The water brings everything from the underground salt layer to the surface. Even Bottomlands plants have trouble adapting."

That was emphatically true. Despite the water absent everywhere else in Trench Park, the landscape round the Bitter Lake was barren even by Bottomlands standards. Most of the few plants that did struggle to grow were tiny and stunted.

Benter vez Maprab, whose sole interest seemed to be horticulture, pointed to one of the exceptions. "What's that, the ghost of a plant abandoned by the gods?"

"It looks like it," Radnal said: the shrub had skinny, almost skeletal branches and leaves. Rather than being green, it was white with sparkles that shifted as the breeze shook it. "It's a saltbush, and it's found only around the Bitter Lake. It deposits the salts it picks up from ground water as crystals on all its above-ground parts. That does two things: it gets rid of the salt, and having the reflective coating lowers the plant's effective temperature."

"It also probably keeps the saltbush from getting eaten very often," Toglo zev Pamdal said.

"Yes, but with a couple of exceptions," Radnal said. "One is the humpless camel, which has its own ways of getting rid of excess salt. The other is my little friend the fat sand rat, although it prefers desert spurges, which are juicier."

The Strongbrow woman looked around. "One of the things I expected to see when I came down here, both the first time and now, was lots of lizards and snakes and tortoises. I haven't, and it puzzles me. I'd have thought the Bottomlands would be a perfect place for cold-blooded creatures to live."

"If you look at dawn or dusk, Toglo zev, you'll see plenty. But not in the heat of the day. Cold-blooded isn't a good term for reptiles: they have a *variable* body temperature, not a constant one like birds or mammals. They warm themselves by basking, and cool down by staying out of the midday sun. If they didn't, they'd cook."

"I know just how they feel." Evillia ran a hand through her thick dark hair. "You can stick eating tongs in me now, because I'm done all the way through."

"It's not so bad as that," Radnal said. "I'm sure it's under 50 hundredths, and it can get above 50 even here. And Trench Park doesn't have any of the deepest parts of the Bottomlands. Down another couple of thousand cubits, the extreme temperatures go above 60."

The non-Tarteshans groaned. So did Toglo zev Pamdal and Peggol vez Menk. Tarteshem had a relatively mild climate; temperatures there went past 40 hundredths only from late spring to early fall.

With morbid curiosity, Moblay Sopsirk's son said, "What is the highest temperature ever recorded in the Bottomlands?"

"Just over 66," Radnal said. The tourists groaned again, louder.

Radnal led the line of donkeys around the Bitter Lake. He was careful not to get too close to the little water actually in the lake at this time of year. Sometimes a salt crust formed over mud; a donkey's hoof could poke right through, trapping the animal and slicing its leg against the hard, sharp edge of the crust.

After a while, the tour guide asked, "Do you have all the pictures you want?" When no one denied it, he said, "Then we'll head back toward the lodge."

"Hold on." Eltsac vez Martois pointed across the Bitter Lake. "What are those things over there?"

"I don't see anything, Eltsac," his wife said. "You must be looking at a what-do-you-call it, a mirage." Then, grudgingly, a heartbeat later: "Oh."

"It's a herd of humpless camels," Radnal said quietly. "Try not to spook them."

The herd was a little one, a couple of long-necked males with a double handful of smaller females and a few young ones that seemed all leg and awkwardness. Unlike the donkeys, they ambled over the crust around the Bitter Lake. Their hooves were wide and soft, spreading under their weight to keep them from falling through.

A male stood guard as the rest of the herd drank at a scummy pool of water. Golobol looked distressed. "That horrid liquid, surely it will poison them," he said. "I would not drink it to save my life." His round brown face screwed up in disgust.

"If you drank it, it would end your days all the sooner. But humpless camels have evolved along with the Bottomlands; their kidneys are wonderfully efficient at extracting large amounts of salt."

"Why don't they have humps?" Lofosa asked. "Krepalgan camels have humps." By her tone, what she was used to was right.

"I know Krepalgan camels have humps," Radnal said. "But the camels in the southern half of the Double Continent don't, and neither do these. With the Bottomlands beasts, I think the answer is that any lump of fat—which is what a hump is—is a liability in getting rid of heat."

"In the days before motors, we used to ride our Krepalgan camels," Evillia said. "Has anyone ever tamed your humpless ones?"

"That's a good question," Radnal said, beaming to hide his surprise at her coming up with a good question. He went on, "It has been tried many times, in fact. So far, it's never worked. They're too stubborn to do what a human being wants. If we had domesticated them, you'd be riding them now instead of these donkeys; they're better suited to the terrain here."

Toglo zev Pamdal scratched her mount's ears. "They're also uglier than donkeys."

"Freelady—uh, Toglo zev—I can't argue with you," Radnal said. "They're uglier than anything I can think of, with dispositions to match."

As if insulted by words they couldn't have heard, the humpless camels raised their heads and trotted away from the Bitter Lake. Their backs went up and down, up and down, in time to their rocking gait. Evillia said, "In Krepalga, we sometimes call camels desert barques. Now I see why: riding on one looks like it would make me seasick."

The tourists laughed. So did Radnal. Making a joke in a language that wasn't Evillia's took some brains. Then why, Radnal wondered, did she act so empty-headed? But he shrugged; he'd seen a lot of people *with* brains do impressively stupid things.

"Why don't the camels eat all the forage in Trench Park?" Benter vez Maprab asked. He sounded as if his concern was for the plants, not the humpless camels.

"When the herds get too large for the park's resource, we cull them," Radnal answered. "This ecosystem is fragile. If we let it get out of balance, it would be a long time repairing itself."

"Are any herds of wild humpless camels left outside Trench Park, Radnal vez?" Toglo asked.

"A few small ones, in areas of the Bottomlands too barren for people," the tour guide said. "Not many, though. We occasionally introduce new males into this herd to increase genetic diversity, but they come from zoological parks, not the wild." The herd receded rapidly, shielded from clear view by the dust it kicked up. "I'm glad we had a chance to see them, if at a distance. That's why the gods made long lenses for cameras. But now we should head back to the lodge."

The return journey north struck Radnal as curiously unreal. Though Peggol vez Menk rode among the tourists, they seemed to be pretending as hard as they could that Dokhnor of Kellef had not died, that this was just an ordinary holiday. The alternative was always looking over a shoulder, remembering the person next to you might be a murderer.

The person next to someone *was* a murderer. Whoever it was, he seemed no different from anyone else. That worried Radnal more than anything.

It even tainted his pleasure from talking with Toglo zev Pamdal. He had trouble imagining her as a killer, but he had trouble imagining anyone in the tour group a killer—save Dokhnor of Kellef, who was dead, and the Martoisi, who might want to kill each other.

He got to the point where he could say "Toglo zev" without prefacing it with "uh." He really wanted to ask her (but lacked the nerve) how she put up with him after watching him at play with the two Highhead girls. Tarteshans seldom thought well of those who made free with their bodies.

He also wondered what he'd do if Evillia and Lofosa came into his cubicle tonight. He'd throw them out, he decided. Edifying a tour group was one thing, edifying the Park Militia and the Eyes and Ears another. But what they did was *so* edifying . . . Maybe he wouldn't throw them out. He banged a fist onto his knee, irritated at his own fleshly weakness.

The lodge was only a couple of thousand cubits away when his donkey snorted and stiffened its legs against the ground. "Earthquake!" The word went up in Tarteshan and other languages. Radnal felt the ground jerk beneath him. He watched, and marveled at, the Martoisi clinging to each other atop their mounts.

After what seemed a daytenth but had to be an interval measured in heartbeats, the shaking ceased. Just in time, too; Peggol vez Menk's donkey, panicked by the tremor, was about to buck the Eye and Ear into a thornbush. Radnal caught the beast's reins, calmed it.

"Thank you, freeman vez Krobir," Peggol said. "That was bad."

"You didn't make it any better by letting go of the reins," Radnal told him. "If you were in a motor, wouldn't you hang on to the tiller?"

"I hope so," Peggol said. "But if I were in a motor, it wouldn't try to run away by itself."

Moblay Sopsirk's son looked west, toward the Barrier Mountains. "That was worse than the one yesterday. I feared I'd see the Western Ocean pouring in with a wave as high as the Lion God's mane."

"As I've said before, that's not something you're likely to have to worry about," Radnal said. "A quake would have to be *very* strong and at exactly the wrong place to disturb the mountains."

"So it would." Moblay did not sound comforted.

Radnal dismissed his concern with the mild scorn you feel for someone who overreacts to a danger you're used to. Over in the Double Continent, they had vast and deadly windstorms. Radnal was sure one of those would frighten him out of his wits. But the Stekians probably took them in stride, as he lost no sleep over earthquakes.

The sun sank toward the spikes of the Barrier Mountains. As if bloodied by their pricking, its rays grew redder as Bottomlands shadows lengthened. More red sparkled from the glass and metal and plastic of the helos between the lodge and the stables. Noticing them made Radnal return to the here-and-now. He wondered how the militiamen and Eyes and Ears had done in their search for clues.

They came out as the tour group approached. In their tan, speckled robes, the militiamen were almost invisible against the desert. The Eyes and Ears, with their white and gold and patent leather, might have been spotted from ten thousand cubits away, or from the mountains of the moon.

Liem vez Steries waved to Radnal. "Any luck? Do you have the killer tied up in pink string?"

"Do you see any pink string?" Radnal turned back to face the group, raised his voice: "Let's get the donkeys settled. They can't do it for themselves. When they're fed and watered, we can worry about ourselves." *And about everything that's been going on*, he added to himself.

The tourists' dismounting groans were quieter than they'd been the day before; they were growing hardened to riding. Poor Peggol vez Menk assumed a bowlegged gait most often seen in rickets victims. "I was thinking of taking yesterday off," he said lugubriously. "I wish I had—someone else would have taken your call."

"You might have drawn a worse assignment," Radnal said, helping him unsaddle the donkey. The way Peggol rolled his eyes denied that was possible.

Fer vez Canthal and Zosel vez Glesir came over to help see to the tour group's donkeys. Under the brims of their caps, their eyes sparked with excitement. "Well, Radnal vez, we have a good deal to tell *you*," Fer began.

Peggol had a sore fundament, but his wits still worked. He made a sharp chopping gesture. "Freeman, save your news for a more private time." A smoother motion, this time with upturned palm, pointed out the chattering crowd still inside the stables. "Someone may hear something he should not."

Fer looked abashed. "Your pardon, freeman; no doubt you are right."

"No doubt," Peggol's tone argued that he couldn't be anything but. From under the shiny brim of his cap, his gaze flicked here and there, measuring everyone in turn with the calipers of his suspicion. It came to Radnal, and showed no softening. Resentment flared in the tour guide, then dimmed. He knew he hadn't killed anyone, but the Eye and Ear didn't.

"I'll get the firepit started," Fer said.

"Good idea," Eltsac vez Martois said as he walked by. "I'm hungry enough to eat one of those humpless camels, raw and without salt."

"We can do better than that," Radnal said. He noted the I-told-you-so look Peggol sent Fer vez Canthal: if a tourist could overhear one bit of casual conversation, why not another?

Liem vez Steries greeted Peggol with a formal military salute he didn't use five times a year—his body went tetanus-rigid, while he brought his right hand up so the tip of his middle finger brushed the brim of his cap. "Freeman, my compliments. We've all heard of the abilities of the Hereditary Tyrant's Eyes and Ears, but until now I've never seen them in action. Your team is superb, and what they found—" Unlike Fer vez Canthal, Liem had enough sense to close his mouth right there.

Radnal felt like dragging him into the desert to pry loose what he knew. But years of slow research had left him a patient man. He ate supper, sang songs, chatted about the earthquake and what he'd seen on the journey to and from the Bitter Lake. One by one, the tourists sought their sleepsacks.

Moblay Sopsirk's son, however, sought him out for a game of war. For politeness' sake, Radnal agreed to play, though he had so much on his mind that he was sure the brown man from Lissonland would trounce him. Either Moblay had things on his mind, too, or he wasn't the player he thought he was. The game was a comedy of errors which had the spectators biting their lips to keep from blurting out better moves. Radnal eventually won, in inartistic style.

Benter vez Maprab had been an onlooker. When the game ended, he delivered a two-sentence verdict which was also obituary: "A wasted murder. Had the Morgaffo seen that, he'd've died of embarrassment." He stuck his nose in the air and stalked off to his sleeping cubicle.

"We'll have to try again another time, when we're thinking straighter," Radnal told Moblay who nodded ruefully.

Radnal put away the war board and pieces. By then, Moblay was the only tourist left in the common room. Radnal sat down next to Liem vez Steries, not across the gaming table from the Lissonese. Moblay refused to take the hint.

Finally Radnal grabbed the rhinoceros by the horn: "Forgive me, freeman, but we have a lot to discuss among ourselves."

"Don't mind me," Moblay said cheerfully. "I'm not in your way, I hope. And I'd be interested to hear how you Tarteshans investigate. Maybe I can bring something useful back to my prince."

Radnal exhaled through his nose. Biting off words one by one, he said, "Freeman vez Sopsirk, you are a subject of this investigation. To be blunt, we have matters to discuss which you shouldn't hear."

"We also have other, weightier, things to discuss," Peggol vez Menk put in. "Remember, freeman, this is not your principality."

"It never occurred to me that you might fear I was guilty," Moblay said. "*I* know I'm not, so I assumed you did, too. Maybe I'll try and screw the Krepalgan girls, since it doesn't sound like Radnal will be using them tonight."

Peggol raised an eyebrow. "Them?" He packed a world of question into one word.

Under their coat of down, Radnal's ears went hot. Fortunately, he managed to answer a question with a question: "What could be weightier than learning who killed Dokhnor of Kellef?"

Peggol glanced from one sleeping cubicle to the next, as if wondering who was feigning slumber. "Why don't you walk with me in the cool night air? Subleader vez Steries can come with us; he was here all day, and can tell you what he saw himself—things I heard when I took my own evening walk, and which I might garble in reporting them to you."

"Let's walk, then," Radnal said, though he wondered where Peggol vez Menk would find cool night air in Trench Park. Deserts above sea level cooled rapidly when the sun set, but that wasn't true in the Bottomlands.

Getting out in the quiet dark made it seem cooler. Radnal, Peggol, and Liem walked without saying much for a couple of hundred cubits. Only when they were out of earshot of the lodge did the park militiaman announce, "Freeman vez Menk's colleagues discovered a microprint reader among the Morgaffo's effects."

"Did they, by the gods?" Radnal said. "Where, Liem vez? What was it disguised as?"

"A stick of artist's charcoal." The militiaman shook his head. "I thought I knew every trick in the codex, but that's a new one. Now we can rub the plenipo's nose in it if he fusses about losing a Morgaffo citizen in Tartesh. But even that's a small thing, next to what the reader held."

Radnal stared. "Heading off a war with Morgaf is small?"

"It is, freeman vez Krobir," Peggol vez Menk said. "You remember today's earthquake—"

"Yes, and there was another one yesterday, a smaller one," Radnal interrupted. "They happen all the time down here. No one except a tourist like Moblay Sopsirk's son worries about them. You reinforce your buildings so they won't fall down except in the worst shocks, then go on about your business."

"Sensible," Peggol said. "Sensible under most circumstances, anyway. Not here, not now."

"Why not?" Radnal demanded.

"Because, if what was on Dokhnor of Kellef's microprint reader is true—always a question when we're dealing with Morgaffos—someone is trying to engineer a special earthquake."

Radnal's frown drew his heavy eyebrows together above his nose. "I still don't know what you're talking about."

Liem vez Steries inclined his head to Peggol vez Menk. "By your leave, freeman—?" When Peggol nodded, Liem went on, "Radnal vez, over the years somebody—has smuggled the parts for a starbomb into Trench Park."

The tour guide gaped at his friend. "That's insane. If somebody smuggled a starbomb into Tartesh, he'd put it by the Hereditary Tyrant's palace, not here. What does he want, blow up the last big herd of humpless camels in the world?"

"He has more in mind than that," Liem answered. "You see, the bomb is underground, on one of the fault lines nearest the Barrier Mountains." The militiaman's head swiveled to look west toward the sawbacked young mountain range . . .

. . . the mountain range that held back the Western Ocean. The night was warm and dry, but cold sweat prickled on Radnal's back and under his arms. "They want to try to knock the mountains down. I'm no geologist—can they?"

"The gods may know," Liem answered. "I'm no geologist either, so I don't. This I'll tell you: the Morgaffos seem to think it would work."

Peggol vez Menk cleared his throat. "The Hereditary Tyrant discourages research in this area, lest any positive answers fall into the wrong hands. Thus our studies have been limited. I gather, however, that such a result might be obtained."

"The freeman's colleagues radiophoned a geologist known to be reliable," Liem amplified. "They put to him some of what was on the microprint reader, as a theoretical exercise. When they were through, he sounded ready to wet his robes."

"I don't blame him." Radnal looked toward the Barrier Mountains, too. What had Moblay said?—*a wave as high as the Lion God's mane*. If the mountains fell at once, the wave might reach Krepalga before it halted. The deaths, the devastation, would be incalculable. His voice shook as he asked, "What do we do about it?"

"Good question," Peggol said, astringent as usual. "We don't know whether it's really there, who planted it if it is, where it is, or if it's ready. Other than that, we're fine."

Liem's voice turned savage: "I wish all the tourists were Tarteshans. Then we could question them as thoroughly as we needed, until we got truth from them."

Thoroughly, Radnal knew, was a euphemism for *harshly.* Tarteshan justice was more pragmatic than merciful, so much so that applying it to foreigners would strain diplomatic relations and might provoke war. The tour guide said, "We couldn't even be properly thorough with our own people, not when one of them is Toglo zev Pamdal."

"I'd forgotten." Liem made a face. "But you can't suspect *her.* Why would the Hereditary Tyrant's relative want to destroy the country he's Hereditary Tyrant of? It makes no sense."

"I don't suspect her," Radnal said. "I meant we'll have to use our heads here; we can't rely on brute force."

"I suspect everyone," Peggol vez Menk said, matter-of-factly as if he'd said, *It's hot tonight.* "For that matter, I also suspect the information we found among Dokhnor's effects. It might have been planted there to provoke us to question several foreign tourists thoroughly and embroil us with their governments. Morgaffo duplicity knows no bounds."

"As may be, freeman, but dare we take the chance that this is duplicity, not real danger?" Liem said.

"If you mean, *dare we ignore the danger?*—of course not," Peggol said. "But it might be duplicity."

"Would the Morgaffos kill one of their own agents to mislead us?" Radnal asked. "If Dokhnor were alive, we'd have no idea this plot was afoot."

"They might, precisely because they'd expect us to doubt they were so coldhearted," Peggol answered. Radnal thought the Eye and Ear would suspect someone of stealing the sun if a morning dawned cloudy. That was what Eyes and Ears were for, but it made Peggol an uncomfortable companion.

"Since we can't question the tourists thoroughly, what shall we do tomorrow?" Radnal said.

"Go on as we have been," Peggol replied unhappily. "If any of them makes the slightest slip, that will justify our using appropriate persuasive measures." Not even a man who sometimes used torture in his work was easy saying the word out loud.

"I can see one problem coming soon, freeman vez Menk—" Radnal said.

"Call me Peggol vez," the Eye and Ear interrupted. "We're in this mess together; we might as well treat each other as friends. I'm sorry—go ahead."

"Sooner or later, Peggol vez, the tour group will want to go west, toward the Barrier Mountains—and toward the fault line where this starbomb may be. If it requires some finishing touches, that will give whoever is supposed to handle them his best chance. If it is someone in the tour group, of course."

"When were you thinking of doing this?" If he'd sounded unhappy before, he was lugubrious now.

Radnal didn't cheer him up: "The western swing was on the itinerary for tomorrow. I could change it, but—"

"But that would warn the culprit—if there is a culprit—we know what's going on. Yes." Peggol fingered the tuft of hair under his lip. "I think you'd better make the change anyhow, Radnal vez." Having heard Radnal use his name with the polite particle, he could do likewise. "Better to alert the enemy than offer him a free opportunity."

Liem vez Steries began, "Freeman vez Menk—"

The Eye and Ear broke in again: "What I told Radnal also holds for you."

"Fair enough, Peggol vez," Liem said. "How could Morgaf have got wind of this plot against Tartesh without our having heard of it, too? I mean no disrespect, I assure you, but this matter concerns me." He waved toward the Barrier Mountains, which suddenly seemed a much less solid bulwark than they had before.

"The question is legitimate, and I take no offense. I see two possible answers," Peggol said (Radnal had a feeling the Eye and Ear saw at least two answers to every question). "One is that Morgaf may be doing this deceitfully to incite us against our other neighbors, as I said before. The other is that the plot is real, and whoever dreamed it up approached the Morgaffos so they could fall on us after the catastrophe."

Each possibility was logical; Radnal wished he could choose between them. Since he couldn't, he said, "There's nothing we can do about it now, so we might as well sleep. In the morning, I'll tell the tourists we're going east, not west. That's an interesting excursion, too. It—"

Peggol raised a hand. "Since I'll see it tomorrow, why not keep me in suspense?" He twisted this way and that. "You can't die of an impacted fundament, can you?"

"I've never heard of it happening, anyhow." Radnal hid a smile.

"Maybe I'll be a medical first, and get written up in all the physicians' codices." Peggol rubbed the afflicted parts. "And I'll have to go riding again tomorrow, eh? How unfortunate."

"If we don't get some sleep soon, we'll both be dozing in the saddle," Radnal said, yawning. "It must be a couple of daytenths past sunset by now. I thought Moblay would never head for his cubicle."

"Maybe he was just fond of you, Radnal." Liem vez Steries put a croon in the guide's name that burlesqued the way the Lissonese kept leaving off the polite particle.

Radnal snapped, "Night demons carry you off, Liem vez, the ideas you come up with." He waited for the militiaman to taunt him about Evillia and Lofosa, but Liem left that alone. He wondered what ideas the two girls from the Krepalgan Unity had come up with, and whether they'd use them with him tonight. He hoped not—as he'd told Peggol, he did need sleep. Then he wondered if putting sleep ahead of fornication meant he was getting old.

If it did, too bad, he decided. Along with Peggol and Liem, he walked back to the lodge. The other militiamen and Eyes and Ears reported in whispers—all quiet.

Radnal turned a curious ear toward Evillia's sleep cubicle, then Lofosa's, and then Moblay Sopsirk's son's. He didn't hear moans or thumpings from any of them. He wondered whether Moblay hadn't propositioned the Krepalgan girls, or whether they'd turned him down. Or maybe they'd frolicked and gone back to sleep. No, that last wasn't likely; the Eyes and Ears would have been smirking about the eye- and earful they'd got.

Yawning again, Radnal went into his own sleep cubicle, took off his sandals, undid his belt, and lay down. The air-filled sleepsack sighed beneath him like a lover. He angrily shook his head. Two nights with Lofosa and Evillia had filled his mind with lewd notions.

He hoped they would leave him alone again. He knew their dalliance with him was already an entry in Peggol vez Menk's dossier; having the Eye and Ear watch him at play—or listen to him quarreling with them when he sent them away—would not improve the entry.

Those two nights, he'd just been falling asleep when Evillia and Lofosa joined him. Tonight, nervous about whether they'd come, and about everything he'd heard from Peggol and Liem, he lay awake a long time. The girls stayed in their own cubicles.

He dozed off without knowing he'd done so. His eyes flew open when a koprit bird on the roof announced the dawn with a raucous *hig-hig-hig!* He needed a couple of heartbeats to wake fully, realize he'd been asleep, and remember what he'd have to do this morning.

He put on his sandals, fastened his belt, and walked into the common room. Most of the militiamen and Eyes and Ears were already awake. Peggol wasn't; Radnal wondered how much knowing he snored would be worth as blackmail. Liem vez Steries said quietly, "No one murdered last night."

"I'm glad to hear it," Radnal said, sarcastic and truthful at the same time.

Lofosa came out of her cubicle. She still wore what Radnal assumed to be Krepalgan sleeping attire, namely skin. Not a hair on her head was mussed, and she'd done something to her eyes to make them look bigger and brighter than they really were. All the men stared at her, some more openly, some less.

She smiled at Radnal and said in a voice like silver bells, "I hope you didn't miss us last night, freeman vez Krobir. It would have been as much fun as the other two, but we were too tired." Before he could answer (he would have needed a while to find an answer), she went outside to privy.

The tour guide looked down at his sandals, not daring to meet anyone's eyes. He listened to the small coughs that meant the others didn't know what to say to him, either. Finally Liem remarked, "Sounds as though she knows you well enough to call you Radnal vez."

"I suppose so," Radnal muttered. In physical terms, she'd been intimate enough with him to leave off the *vez*. Her Tarteshan was good enough that she ought to know it, too. She'd managed to embarrass him even more by combining the formal address with such a familiar message. She couldn't have made him look more foolish if she'd tried for six moons.

Evillia emerged from her cubicle, dressed, or undressed, like Lofosa. She didn't banter with Radnal, but headed straight for the privy. She and Lofosa met each other behind the helos. They talked for a few heartbeats before each continued on her way.

Toglo zev Pamdal walked into the common room as Lofosa returned from outside. Lofosa stared at the Strongbrow woman, as if daring Toglo to remark on her nakedness. A lot of Tarteshans, especially female Tarteshans, would have remarked on it in detail.

Toglo said only, "I trust you slept well, freelady?" From her casual tone, she might have been talking to a neighbor she didn't know well but with whom she was on good terms.

"Yes, thank you." Lofosa dropped her eyes when she concluded she couldn't use her abundantly displayed charms to bait Toglo.

"I'm glad to hear it," Toglo said, still sweetly. "I wouldn't want you to catch cold on holiday."

Lofosa took half a step, then jerked as if poked by a pin. Toglo had already turned to greet the others in the common room. For a heartbeat, maybe two, Lofosa's teeth showed in a snarl like a cave cat's. Then she went back into her cubicle to finish getting ready for the day.

"I hope I didn't offend her—too much," Toglo said to Radnal.

"I think you handled yourself like a diplomat," he answered.

"Hmm," she said. "Given the state of the world, I wonder whether that's a compliment." Radnal didn't answer. Given what he'd heard the night before, the state of the world might be worse than Toglo imagined.

His own diplomatic skills got a workout after breakfast, when he explained to the group that they'd be going east rather than west. Golobol said, "I find the change from the itinerary most distressing, yes." His round brown face bore a doleful expression.

Benter vez Maprab found any change distressing. "This is an outrage," he blustered. "The herbaceous cover approaching the Barrier Mountains is far richer than that to the east."

"I'm sorry," Radnal said, an interesting mixture of truth and lie: he didn't mind annoying Benter, but would sooner not have had such a compelling reason.

"I don't mind going east rather than west today," Toglo zev Pamdal said. "As far as I'm concerned, there are plenty of interesting things to see either way. But I would like to know *why* the schedule has been changed."

"So would I," Moblay Sopsirk's son said. "Toglo is right—what are you trying to hide, anyhow?"

All the tourists started talking—the Martoisi started shouting—at once. Radnal's own reaction to the Lissonese man was a wish that a trench in Trench Park went down a lot deeper, say, to the red-hot center of the earth. He would have shoved Moblay into it. Not only was he a boor, to use a woman's name without the polite particle (using it uninvited even with the particle would have been an undue liberty), he was a snoop and a rabble-rouser.

Peggol vez Menk slammed his open hand down on the table beside which Dokhnor of Kellef had died. The boom cut through the chatter. Into sudden silence, Peggol said, "Freeman vez Krobir changed your itinerary at my suggestion. Aspects of the murder case suggest that course would be in the best interests of Tartesh."

"This tells us nothing, not a thing." Now Golobol sounded really angry, not just upset at breaking routine. "You say these fine-sounding words, but where is the meaning behind them?"

"If I told you everything you wished to know, freeman, I would also be telling those who should not hear," Peggol said.

"Pfui!" Golobol stuck out his tongue.

Eltsac vez Martois said, "I think you Eyes and Ears think you're little tin demigods."

But Peggol's pronouncement quieted most of the tourists. Ever since starbombs came along, nations had grown more anxious about keeping secrets from one another. That struck Radnal as worrying about the cave cat after he'd carried off the goat, but who could tell? There might be worse things than starbombs.

He said, "As soon as I can, I promise I will tell all of you everything I can about what's going on." Peggol vez Menk gave him a hard look; Peggol wouldn't have told anyone his own name if he could help it.

"What *is* going on?" Toglo echoed.

Since Radnal was none too certain himself, he met that comment with dignified silence. He did say, "The longer we quarrel here, the less we'll have the chance to see, no matter which direction we end up choosing."

"That makes sense, freeman vez Krobir," Evillia said. Neither she nor Lofosa had argued about going east as opposed to west.

Radnal looked around the group, saw more resignation than outrage. He said, "Come now, freemen, freeladies, let's head for the stables. There are many fascinating things to see east of the lodge—and to hear, also. There's the Night Demons' Retreat, for instance."

"Oh, good!" Toglo clapped her hands. "As I've said, it rained the last time I was here. The guide was too worried about flash floods to take us out there. I've wanted to see that ever since I read Hicag zev Ginfer's frightener codex."

"You mean *Stones of Doom*?" Radnal's opinion of Toglo's taste fell. Trying to stay polite, he said, "It wasn't as accurate as it might have been."

"I thought it was trash," Toglo said. "But I went to school with Hicag zev and we've been friends ever since, so I had to read it. And she certainly makes the Night Demons' Retreat sound exotic, whether there's a breeze of truth in what she writes or not."

"Maybe a breeze—a mild breeze," Radnal said.

"I read it, too. I thought it was very exciting," Nocso zev Martois said.

"The tour guide thinks it's garbage," her husband told her.

"I didn't say *that*," Radnal said. Neither Martois listened to him; they enjoyed yelling at each other more.

"Enough of your own breeze. If we must do this, let's do it, at least," Benter vez Maprab said.

"As you say, freeman." Radnal wished the Night Demons' Retreat really held night demons. With any luck, they'd drag Benter into the stones and no one in the tour group would ever see—or have to listen to—him again. But such convenient things happened only in codices.

The tourists were getting better with the donkeys. Even Peggol seemed less obviously out of place on donkeyback than he had yesterday. As the group rode away from the lodge, Radnal looked back and saw park militiamen and Eyes and Ears advancing on the stables to go over them again.

He made himself forget the murder investigation and remember he was a tour guide. "Because we're off earlier this morning, we're more likely to see small reptiles and mammals that shelter against the worst heat," he said. "Many of them—"

A sudden little *flip* of sandy dirt a few cubits ahead made him stop. "By the gods, there's one now." He dismounted. "I think that's a shoveler skink."

"A what?" By now, Radnal was used to the chorus that followed whenever he pointed out one of the more unusual denizens of the Bottomlands.

"A shoveler skink," he repeated. He crouched down. Yes, sure enough, there was the lure. He knew he had an even-money chance. If he grabbed the tail end, the lizard would shed the appendage and flee. But if he got it by the neck—

He did. The skink twisted like a piece of demented rubber, trying to wriggle free. It also voided. Lofosa made a disgusted noise. Radnal took such things in stride.

After thirty or forty heartbeats, the skink gave up and lay still. Radnal had been waiting for that. He carried the palm-sized lizard into the midst of the tourists. "Skinks are common all over the world, but the shoveler is the most curious variety. It's a terrestrial equivalent of the anglerfish. Look—"

He tapped the orange fleshy lump that grew on the end of a spine about two digits long. "The skink buries itself under sand, with just this lure and the tip of its nose sticking out. See how its ribs extend to either side, so it looks more like a gliding animal than one that lives underground? It has specialized musculature, to make those long rib ends bend what we'd think of as the wrong way. When an insect comes along, the lizard tosses dirt on it, then twists around and snaps it up. It's a beautiful creature."

"It's the ugliest thing I ever saw," Moblay Sopsirk's son declared.

The lizard didn't care one way or the other. It peered at him through little beady black eyes. If the variety survived another few million years—if the Bottomlands survived another couple of moons, Radnal thought nervously—future specimens might lose their sight altogether, as had already happened with other subterranean skinks.

Radnal walked out of the path, put the lizard back on the ground. It scurried away, surprisingly fast on its short legs. After six or eight cubits, it seemed to melt into the ground. Within moments, only the bright orange lure betrayed its presence.

Evillia asked, "Do any bigger creatures go around looking for lures to catch the skinks?"

"As a matter of fact, yes," Radnal said. "Koprit birds can see color; you'll often see shoveler skinks impaled in their hoards. Big-eared nightfoxes eat them, too, but they track by scent, not sight."

"I hope no koprit birds come after me," Evillia said, laughing. She and Lofosa wore matching red-orange tunics—almost the same shade as the shoveler skin's lure—with two rows of big gold buttons, and red plastic necklaces with gold clasps.

Radnal smiled. "I think you're safe enough. And now that the lizard is safe, for the time being, shall we go—? No, wait, where's freeman vez Maprab?"

The old Strongbrow emerged from behind a big, wide-spreading thorn bush a few heartbeats later, still refastening the belt to his robe. "Sorry for the delay, but I thought I'd answer nature's call while we paused here."

"I just didn't want to lose you, freeman." Radnal stared at Benter as he got back onto his donkey. This was the first apology he'd heard from him. He wondered if the tourist was well.

The group rode slowly eastward. Before long, people began to complain. "Every piece of Trench Park looks like every other piece," Lofosa said.

"Yes, when will we see something different?" Moblay Sopsirk's son agreed. Radnal suspected he would have agreed if Lofosa said the sky were pink; he slavered after her. He went on, "It's all hot and flat and dry; even the thornbushes are boring."

"Freeman, if you wanted to climb mountains and roll in snow, you should have gone someplace else," Radnal said. "That's not what the Bottomlands have to offer. But there are mountains and snow all over the world; there's nothing like Trench Park anywhere. And if you tell me this terrain is like what we saw yesterday around the Bitter Lake, freeman, freelady"—he glanced over at Lofosa— "I think you're both mistaken."

"They certainly are," Benter vez Maprab chimed in. "This area has very different flora from the other one. Note the broader-leafed spurges, the oleanders—"

"They're just plants," Lofosa said. Benter clapped a hand to his head in shock and dismay. Radnal waited for him to have another bad-tempered fit, but he just muttered to himself and subsided.

About a quarter of a daytenth later, Radnal pointed toward a gray smudge on the eastern horizon. "There's the Night Demons' Retreat. I promise it's like nothing you've yet seen in Trench Park."

"I hope it shall be interesting, oh yes," Golobol said.

"I loved the scene where the demons came out at sunset, claws dripping blood," Nocso zev Martois said. Her voice rose in shivery excitement.

Radnal sighed. "*Stones of Doom* is only a frightener, freelady. No demons live inside the Retreat, or come out at sunset or any other time. I've passed the night in a sleepsack not fifty cubits from the stonepile, and I'm still here, with my blood inside me where it belongs."

Nocso made a face. No doubt she preferred melodrama to reality. Since she was married to Eltsac, reality couldn't seem too attractive to her.

The Night Demons' Retreat was a pile of gray granite, about a hundred cubits high, looming over the flat floor of the Bottomlands. Holes of all sizes pitted the granite. Under the merciless sun, the black openings reminded Radnal of skulls' eyes looking at him.

"Some holes look big enough for a person to crawl into," Peggol vez Menk remarked. "Has anybody ever explored them?"

"Yes, many people," Radnal answered. "We discourage it, though, because although no one's ever found a night demon, they're a prime denning place for vipers and scorpions. They also often hold bats' nests. Seeing the bats fly out at dusk to hunt bugs doubtless helped start the legend about the place."

"Bats live all over," Nocso said. "There's only one Night Demons' Retreat, because—"

The breeze, which had been quiet, suddenly picked up. Dust skirled over the ground. Radnal grabbed for his cap. And from the many mineral throats of the Night Demons' Retreat came a hollow moaning and wailing that made the hair on his body want to stand on end.

Nocso looked ecstatic. "There!" she exclaimed. "The cry of the deathless demons, seeking to be free to work horror on the world!"

Radnal remembered the starbomb that might be buried by the Barrier Mountains, and thought of horrors worse than any demons could produce. He said, "Freelady, as I'm sure you know, it's just wind playing some badly tuned flutes. The softer rock around the Retreat weathered away, and the Retreat itself has taken a lot of sandblasting. Whatever bits that weren't as hard as the rest are gone, which explains how and why the openings formed. And now, when the wind blows across them, they make the weird sounds we just heard."

"Hmp!" Nocso said. "If there are gods, how can there not be demons?"

"Freelady, speak to a priest about that, not to me." Radnal swore by the gods of Tartesh but, like most educated folk of his generation, had little other use for them.

Peggol vez Menk said, "Freelady, the question of whether night demons exist does not necessarily have anything to do with the question of whether they haunt the Night Demons' Retreat—except that if there be no demons, they are unlikely to be at the Retreat."

Nocso's plump face filled with rage. But she thought twice about telling off an Eye and Ear. She turned her head and shouted at Eltsac instead. He shouted back.

The breeze swirled around, blowing bits of grit into the tour guide's face. More unmusical notes emanated from the Night Demons' Retreat. Cameras clicked. "I wish I'd brought along a recorder," Toglo zev Pamdal said. "What's interesting here isn't how this place looks, but how it sounds."

"You can buy a wire of the Night Demons' Retreat during a windstorm at the gift shop near the entrance to Trench Park."

"Thank you, Radnal vez; I may do that on my way out. It would be even better, though, if I could have recorded what I heard with my own ears." Toglo's glance slipped to Eltsac and Nocso, who were still barking at each other. "Well, some of what I heard."

Evillia said, "This Night Demons' Retreat was on the sea floor?"

"That's right. As the dried muck and salt that surrounded it eroded, it was left alone here. Think of it as a miniature version of the mountain plains that stick up from the Bottomlands. In ancient days, they were islands. The Retreat, of course, was below the surface back then."

And may be again, he thought. He imagined fish peering into the holes in the ancient granite, crabs scuttling in to scavenge the remains of snakes and sand rats. The picture came to vivid life in his mind. That bothered him; it meant he took this menace seriously.

He was so deep in his own concerns that he needed a couple of heartbeats to realize the group had fallen silent. When he did notice, he looked up in a hurry, wondering what was wrong. From a third of the way up the Night Demons' Retreat, a cave cat looked back.

The cave cat must have been asleep inside a crevice until the tourists' racket woke it. It yawned, showing yellow fangs and pink tongue. Then, with steady amber gaze, it peered at the tourists once more, as if wondering what sauce would go well with them.

"Let's move away from the Retreat," Radnal said quietly. "We don't want it to think we're threatening it." That would have been a good trick, he thought. If the cave cat did decide to attack, his handcannon would hurt it (assuming he was lucky enough to hit), but it wouldn't kill. He opened the flap to his saddlebag just the same.

For once, all the tourists did exactly as they were told. Seeing the great predator raised fears that went back to the days of man-apes just learning to walk erect.

Moblay Sopsirk's son asked, "Will more of them be around? In Lissonland, lions hunt in prides."

"No, cave cats are solitary except during mating season," Radnal answered. "They and lions have a common ancestor, but their habits differ. The Bottomlands don't have big herds that make pride hunting a successful survival strategy."

Just when Radnal wondered if the cave cat was going back to sleep, it exploded into motion. Long gray-brown mane flying, it bounded down the steep slope of the Night Demons' Retreat. Radnal yanked out his handcannon. He saw Peggol vez Menk also had one.

But when the cave cat hit the floor of the Bottomlands, it streaked away from the tour group. Its grayish fur made it almost invisible against the desert. Cameras clicked incessantly. Then the beast was gone.

"How beautiful," Toglo zev Pamdal breathed. After a moment, she turned more practical: "Where does he find water?"

"He doesn't need much, Toglo zev," he answered. "Like other Bottomlands creatures, he makes the most of what he gets from the bodies of his prey. Also"—he pointed north—"there are a few tiny springs in the hills. Back when it was legal to hunt cave cats, a favorite way was to find a spring and lay in wait until the animal came to drink."

"It seems criminal," Toglo said.

"To us, certainly," Radnal half-agreed. "But to a man who's just had his flocks raided or a child carried off, it was natural enough. We go wrong when we judge the past by our standards."

"The biggest difference between past and present is that we moderns are able to sin on a much larger scale," Peggol said. Maybe he was thinking of the buried starbomb. But recent history held enough other atrocities to make Radnal have trouble disagreeing.

Eltsac vez Martois said, "Well, freeman vez Krobir, I have to admit that was worth the price of admission."

Radnal beamed; of all the people from whom he expected praise, Eltsac was the last. Then Nocso chimed in: "But it would have been even more exciting if the cave cat had come toward us and he'd had to shoot at it."

"I'll say," Eltsac agreed. "I'd love to have that on film."

Why, Radnal wondered, did the Martoisi see eye to eye only when they were both wrong? He said, "With respect, I'm delighted the animal went the other way. I'd hate to fire at so rare a creature, and I'd hate even more to miss and have anyone come to harm."

"Miss?" Nocso said the word as if it hadn't occurred to her. It probably hadn't; people in adventure stories shot straight whenever they needed to.

Eltsac said, "Shooting well isn't easy. When I was drafted into the Voluntary Guards, I needed three tries before I qualified with a rifle."

"Oh, but that's you, not a tour guide," Nocso said scornfully. "He has to shoot well."

Through Eltsac's outraged bellow, Radnal said, "I will have you know, I have never fired a handcannon in all my time at Trench Park." He didn't add that, given a choice between shooting at a cave cat and at Nocso, he'd sooner have fired on her.

The wind picked up again. The Night Demons' Retreat made more frightful noises. Radnal imagined how he would have felt if he were an illiterate hunter, say, hearing those ghostly wails for the first time. He was sure he'd've fouled his robes from fear.

But even so, something else also remained true: judging by the standards of the past was even more foolish when the present offered better information. If Nocso believed in night demons for no better reason than that she'd read an exciting frightener about them, that only argued she didn't have the sense the gods gave a shoveler skink. Radnal smiled. As far as he could tell, she *didn't* have the sense the gods gave a shoveler skink.

"We'll go in the direction opposite the one the cave cat took," Radnal said at last. "We'll also stay in a tight group. If you ask me, anyone who goes wandering off deserves to be eaten."

The tourists rode almost in one another's laps. As far as Radnal could tell, the eastern side of the Night Demons' Retreat wasn't much different from the western. But he'd been here tens of times already. Tourists could hardly be blamed for wanting to see as much as they could.

"No demons over here, either, Nocso," Eltsac vez Martois said. His wife stuck her nose in the air. Radnal wondered why they stayed married—for that matter, he wondered why they'd got married—when they sniped at each other so. Pressure from their kith groupings, probably. It didn't seem a good enough reason.

So why was he haggling over bride price with Wello zev Putun's father? The Putuni were a solid family in the lower aristocracy, a good connection for an up-and-coming man. He couldn't think of anything wrong with Wello, but she didn't much stir him, either. Would she have read *Stones of Doom* without recognizing it for the garbage it was? Maybe. That worried him. If he wanted a woman with whom he could talk, would he need a concubine? Peggol had one. Radnal wondered if the arrangement made him happy. Likely not—Peggol took a perverse pleasure in not enjoying anything.

Thinking of Wello brought Radnal's mind back to the two nights of excess he'd enjoyed with Evillia and Lofosa. He was sure he wouldn't want to marry a woman whose body was her only attraction, but he also doubted the wisdom of marrying one whose body didn't attract him. What he needed—

He snorted. *What I need is for a goddess to take flesh and fall in love with me . . . if she doesn't destroy my self-confidence by letting on she's a goddess.* Finding such a mate—especially for a bride price less than the annual budget of Tartesh—seemed unlikely. Maybe Wello would do after all.

"Are we going back by the same route we came?" Toglo zev Pamdal asked.

"I hadn't planned to," Radnal said. "I'd aimed to swing further south on the way back, to give you the chance to see country you haven't been through before." He couldn't resist adding, "No matter how much the same some people find it."

Moblay Sopsirk's son looked innocent. "If you mean me, Radnal, I'm happy to discover new things. I just haven't come across that many here."

"Hmp," Toglo said. "I'm having a fine time here. I was glad to see the Night Demons' Retreat at last, and also to hear it. I can understand why our ancestors believed horrid creatures dwelt inside."

"I was thinking the same thing only a couple of hundred heartbeats ago," Radnal said.

"What a nice coincidence." A smile brightened her face. To Radnal's disappointment, she didn't stay cheerful long. She said, "This tour is so marvelous, I can't help thinking it would be finer still if Dokhnor of Kellef were still alive, or even if we knew who killed him."

"Yes," Radnal said. He'd spent much of the day glancing from one tourist to the next, trying to figure out who had broken the Morgaffo's neck. He'd even tried suspecting the Martoisi. He'd dismissed them before, as too inept to murder anybody quietly. But what if their squawk and bluster only disguised devious purposes?

His laugh came out as dusty as Peggol vez Menk's. He couldn't believe it. Besides, Nocso and Eltsac were Tarteshans. They wouldn't want to see their country ruined. Or could they be paid enough to want to destroy it?

Nocso looked back toward the Night Demons' Retreat just as a koprit bird flew into one of the holes in the granite. "A demon! I saw a night demon!" she squalled.

Radnal laughed again. If Nocso was a spy and a saboteur, he was a humpless camel. "Come on," he called. "Time to head back."

As he'd promised, he took his charges to the lodge by a new route. Moblay Sopsirk's son remained unimpressed. "It may not be the same, but it isn't much different."

"Oh, rubbish!" Benter vez Maprab said. "The flora here are quite distinct from those we observed this morning."

"Not to me," Moblay said stubbornly.

"Freeman vez Maprab, by your interest in plants of all sorts, were you by chance a scholar of botany?" Radnal asked.

"By the gods, no!" Benter whinnied laughter. "I ran a train of plant and flower shops until I retired."

"Oh. I see." Radnal did, too. With that practical experience, Benter might have learned as much about plants as any scholar of botany.

About a quarter of a daytenth later, the old man reined in his donkey and went behind another thornbush. "Sorry to hold everyone up," he said when he returned. "My kidneys aren't what they used to be."

Eltsac vez Martois guffawed. "Don't worry, Benter vez. A fellow like you knows you have to water the plants. Haw, haw!"

"You're a bigger jackass than your donkey," Benter snapped.

"Freemen, please!" Radnal got the two men calmed down and made sure they rode far from each other. He didn't care if they went at each other three heartbeats after they left Trench Park, but they were his responsibility till then.

"You earn your silver here, I'll say that for you," Peggol observed. "I see fools in my line of work, but I'm not obliged to stay polite to them." He lowered his voice. "When freeman vez Maprab went behind the bush now, he didn't just relieve himself. He also bent down and pulled something out of the ground. I happened to be off to one side."

"Did he? How interesting." Radnal doubted Benter was involved in the killing of Dokhnor of Kellef. But absconding with plants from Trench Park was also a crime, one the tour guide was better equipped to deal with than murder. "We won't do anything about it now. After we get back to the lodge, why don't you have your men search Benter vez's belongings again?"

Amusement glinted in Peggol's eyes. "You're looking forward to this."

"Who, me? The only thing that could be better would be if it were Eltsac vez instead. But he hasn't a brain in his head or anywhere else about his person."

"Are you sure?" Peggol had been thinking along the same lines as Radnal. He'd probably started well before Radnal had, too. That was part of his job.

But Radnal came back strong: "If he had brains, would he have married Nocso zev?" That won a laugh which didn't sound dusty. He added, "Besides, all he knows about thornbushes is not to ride into them, and he's not certain of that."

"Malice agrees with you, Radnal vez."

By the time the lodge neared, Golobol was complaining along with Moblay. "Take away the Night Demons' Retreat, oh yes, and take away the cave cat we saw there, and what have you? Take away those two things and it is a nothing of a day."

"Freeman, if you insist on ignoring everything interesting that happens, you can turn any day dull," Toglo observed.

"Well said!" Being a tour guide kept Radnal from speaking his mind to the people he led. This time, Toglo had done it for him.

She smiled. "Why come see what the Bottomlands are like if he · isn't happy with what he finds?"

"Toglo zev, some are like that in every group. It makes no sense to me, but there you are. If I had the money to see the Nine Iron Towers of Mashyak, I wouldn't whine because they aren't gold."

"That is a practical attitude," Toglo said. "We'd be better off if more people felt as you do."

"We'd be better off if—" Radnal shut up. *If we didn't fear a starbomb was buried somewhere around here* was how he'd been about to end the sentence. That wasn't smart. Not only would it frighten Toglo (or *worry* her; she didn't seem to frighten easily), but Peggol vez Menk would come down on him like he didn't know what for breaching security.

All at once, he knew how Peggol would come down on him: like the Western Ocean, pouring into the Bottomlands over the broken mountains. He tried to laugh at himself; he didn't usually come up with such literary comparisons. Laughter failed. The simile was literary, but it might be literal as well.

"We'd be better off if what, Radnal vez?" Toglo asked. "What did you start to say?"

He couldn't tell her what he'd started to say. He wasn't glib enough to invent something smooth. To his dismay, what came out of his mouth was, "We'd be better off if more people were like you, Toglo zev, and didn't have fits at what they saw other people doing."

"Oh, that. Radnal vez, I didn't think anyone who was doing that was hurting anyone else. You all seemed to be enjoying yourselves. It's not something I'd care to do where other people might see, but I don't see I have any business getting upset about it."

"Oh." Radnal wasn't sure how to take Toglo's answer. He had, however, already pushed his luck past the point where it had any business going, so he kept quiet.

Something small skittered between spurges. Something larger bounded along in hot pursuit. The pursuit ended in a cloud of dust. Forestalling the inevitable chorus of *What's that?*, Radnal said, "Looks like a bladetooth just made a kill." The carnivorous rodent crouched over its prey; the tour guide pulled out a monocular for a closer look. "It's caught a fat sand rat."

"One of the animals you study?" Moblay said. "Are you going to blast it with your handcannon to take revenge?"

"*I* think you should," Nocso zev Martois declared. "What a vicious brute, to harm a defenseless furry beast."

Radnal wondered if he should ask how she'd enjoyed her mutton last night, but doubted she would understand. He said, "Either carnivores eat meat or they starve. A bladetooth isn't as cuddly as a fat sand rat, but it has its place in the web of life, too."

The bladetooth was smaller than a fox, tan above and cream below. At first glance, it looked like any other jerboa, with hind legs adapted for jumping, big ears, and a long, tufted tail. But its muzzle was also long, and smeared with blood. The fat sand rat squirmed feebly. The bladetooth bit into its belly and started feeding nonetheless.

Nocso moaned. Radnal tried to figure out how her mind worked. She was eager to believe in night demons that worked all manner of evils, yet a little real predation turned her stomach. He gave up; some inconsistencies were too big for him to understand how anyone managed to hold both halves of them at once.

He said, "As I remarked a couple of days ago, the bladetooth does well in the Bottomlands because jerboas had already adapted to conditions close to these while this part of the world was still under water. Its herbivorous relatives extract the water they must have from leaves and seeds, while it uses the tissues of the animals it captures. Even during our rare rains, no bladetooth has ever been seen to drink."

"Disgusting." Nocso's plump body shook as she shuddered. Radnal wondered how long her carcass would give a bladetooth the fluids it needed. *A long time*, he thought.

Moblay Sopsirk's whooped. "There's the lodge! Cold water, cold ale, cold wine—"

As they had the evening before, the Eyes and Ears and the militiamen came out to await the tour group's return. The closer the donkeys came, the better Radnal could see the faces of the men who had stayed behind. They all looked thoroughly grim.

This time, he did not intend to spend a couple of daytenths wondering what was going on. He called, "Fer vez, Zosel vez, take charge of the tourists. I want to catch up on what's happened here."

"All right, Radnal vez," Fer answered. But his voice was no more cheerful than his expression.

Radnal dismounted and walked over to Liem vez Steries. He was not surprised when Peggol vez Menk fell into step with him. Their robes rustled as they came up to the militia subleader. Radnal asked, "What's the word, Liem vez?"

Liem's features might have been carved from stone. "The word is interrogation," he said quietly. "Tomorrow."

"By the gods." Radnal stared. "They're taking this seriously in Tarteshem."

"You'd best believe it." Liem wiped his sweaty face with his sleeve. "See those red cones past the cookpit? That's the landing site we laid out for the helo that's due in the morning."

"But—interrogation." Radnal shook his head. The Eyes and Ears' methods were anything but gentle. "If we interrogate foreigners, we're liable to touch off a war."

"Tarteshem knows this, Radnal vez," Liem said. "My objections are on the wire up there. I have been overruled."

"The Hereditary Tyrant and his advisors must think the risks and damages of war are less than what Tartesh would suffer if the starbomb performs as those who buried it hope," Peggol said.

"But what if it's not there, or if it is but none of the tourists knows about it?" Radnal said. "Then we'll have antagonized the Krepalgan Unity, Lissonland, and other countries as well, and for what? Nothing. Get on the radiophone, Peggol vez; see if they'll change their minds."

Peggol shook his head. "No, for two reasons. One is that this policy will have come down from a level far higher than I can influence. I am only a field agent; I have no say in grand strategy. The other is that your radiophone is too public. I do not want to alert anyone that he is about to be interrogated."

Radnal had to concede that made sense as far as security went. But he did not like it any better. Then something else occurred to him. He turned to Liem vez Steries. "Am I going to be, uh, interrogated, too? What about Zosel vez and Fer vez? And what about Toglo zev Pamdal? Are the interrogators going to work on one of the Hereditary Tyrant's relatives?"

"I don't know any of those answers," the militiaman said. "The people I spoke with in Tartesh wouldn't tell me." His eyes flicked to Peggol. "I suppose they didn't care to be too public, either."

"No doubt," Peggol said. "Now we have to as normally as we can, not letting on that we'll have visitors in the morning."

"I'd have an easier time acting normal if I knew I wouldn't be wearing thumbscrews tomorrow," Radnal said.

"After such ordeals, the Hereditary Tyrant generously compensates innocents," Peggol said.

"The Hereditary Tyrant is generous." That was all Radnal could say while talking to an Eye and Ear. But silver, while it worked wonders, didn't fully make up for terror and pain and, sometimes, permanent injury. The tour guide preferred remaining as he was to riches and a limp.

Liem remarked, "Keeping things from the tourists won't be hard. Look what they're doing."

Radnal turned, looked, and snorted. His charges had turned the area marked off with red cones into a little game field. All of them except prim Golobol ran around throwing somebody's sponge rubber ball back and forth and trying to tackle one another. If their sport had rules, Radnal couldn't figure them out.

Moblay Sopsirk's son, stubborn if unwise, kept his yen for Evillia and Lofosa. Careless of the abrasions to his nearly naked hide, he dragged Lofosa into the dirt. When she stood up, her tunic was missing some of its big gold buttons. She remained indifferent to the flesh she exposed. Moblay had got grit in his eyes and stayed on the ground awhile.

Evillia lost buttons, too; Toglo zev Pamdal's belt broke, as did Nocso zev Martois'. Toglo capered with one hand holding her robes closed. Nocso didn't bother. Watching her jounce up and down the improvised pitch, Radnal wished she were modest and Toglo otherwise.

Fer vez Canthal asked, "Shall I get supper started?"

"Get the coals going, but wait for the rest?" Radnal said. "They're having such a good time, they might as well enjoy themselves. They won't have any fun tomorrow."

"Neither will we," Fer answered. Radnal grimaced and nodded.

Benter vez Maprab tackled Eltsac vez Martois and stretched the bigger, younger man in the dust. Benter sprang to his feet, swatted Evillia on the backside. She spun round in surprise.

"The old fellow has life in him yet," Peggol said, watching Eltsac rise, one hand pressed to a bloody nose.

"So there is." Radnal watched Benter. He might be old, but he was spry. Maybe he could have broken Dokhnor of Kellef's neck. Was losing a game of war reason enough? Or was he playing the same deeper game as Dokhnor?

Only when the sun slid behind the Barrier Mountains and dusk enfolded the lodge did the tourists give up their sport. The cones shone with a soft pink phosphorescent glow of their own. Toglo tossed the ball to Evillia, saying, "I'm glad you got this out, freelady. I haven't enjoyed myself so much—and so foolishly—in a long time."

"I thought it would be a good way for us to unwind after riding and sitting around," Evillia answered.

She had a point. If Radnal ever led tourists down here again—if the lodge wasn't buried under thousands of cubits of sea—he'd have to remember to bring along a ball himself. He frowned in self-reproach. He should have thought of that on his own instead of stealing the idea from someone in his group.

"If I was thirsty before, I'm drier than the desert now," Moblay boomed. "Where's that ale?"

"I'll open the refrigerator," Zosel vez Glesir said. "Who else wants something?" He cringed from the hot, sweaty tourists who dashed his way. "Come, my friends! If you squash me, who will get the drinks?"

"We'll manage somehow," Eltsac vez Martois said, the first sensible remark he'd made.

Fer vez Canthal had the coals in the firepit glowing red. Zosel fetched a cut-up pig carcass and a slab of beef ribs. Radnal started to warn him about going through the stored food so prodigally, but caught himself. If people fell into the interrogators' hands tomorrow, no need to worry about the rest of the tour.

Radnal ate heartily, and joined in songs after supper. He managed to forget for hundreds of heartbeats what awaited when morning came. But every so often, realization came flooding back. Once his voice faltered so suddenly that Toglo glanced over to see what had happened. He smiled sheepishly and tried to do better.

Then he looked at her. He couldn't imagine her being connected with the plot to flood the Bottomlands. He had trouble imagining Eyes and Ears interrogating her as they would anyone else. But he hadn't thought they would risk international incidents to question foreign tourists, either. Maybe that meant he didn't grasp how big the emergency was. If so, Toglo might be at as much risk as anyone.

Horken vez Sofana, the circumstances man from the Trench Park militia, came up to the tour guide. "I was told you wanted Benter vez Maprab's saddlebags searched, freeman vez Krobir. I found—these." He held out his hand.

"How interesting. Wait here, Senior Trooper vez Sofana." Radnal walked over to where Benter was sitting, tapped him on the shoulder. "Would you please join me, freeman?"

"What is it?" Benter growled, but he came back with Radnal.

The tour guide said, "I'd like to hear how these red-veined orchids"—he pointed to the plants in Horken vez Sofana's upturned palm—"appeared in your saddlebags. Removal of any plants or animals, especially rare varieties like these, is punishable by fine, imprisonment, stripes, or all three."

Benter vez Maprab's mouth opened and closed silently. He tried again: "I—I would have raised them carefully, freeman vez Krobir." He was so used to complaining himself, he did not know how to react when someone complained of him—and caught him in the wrong.

Triumph turned hollow for Radnal. What were a couple of red-veined orchids when the whole Bottomlands might drown? The tour guide said, "We'll confiscate these, freeman vez Maprab. Your gear will be searched again when you leave Trench Park. If we find no more contraband, we'll let this pass. Otherwise—I'm sure I need not paint you a picture."

"Thank you—very kind." Benter fled.

Horken vez Sofana sent Radnal a disapproving look. "You let him off too lightly."

"Maybe, but the interrogators will take charge of him tomorrow."

"Hmm. Compared to everything else, stealing plants isn't such a big thing."

"Just what I was thinking. Maybe we ought to give them back to the old lemonface so they'll be somewhere safe if—well, you know the ifs."

"Yes." The circumstances man looked thoughtful. "If we gave them back now, he'd wonder why. We don't want that, either. Too bad, though."

"Yes." Discovering he worried about saving tiny pieces of Trench Park made Radnal realize he'd begun to believe in the starbomb.

The tourists began going off to their sleeping cubicles. Radnal envied their ignorance of what lay ahead. He hoped Evillia and Lofosa would visit him in the quiet darkness, and didn't care what the Eyes and Ears and militiamen thought. The body had its own sweet forgetfulness.

But the body had its own problems, too. Both women from Krepalga started trotting back and forth to the privy every quarter of a daytenth, sometimes even more than that. "It must have been something I ate," Evillia said, leaning wearily against the doorpost after her third trip. "Do you have a constipant?"

"The aid kit should have some." Radnal rummaged through it, found the orange pills he wanted. He brought them to her with a paper cup of water. "Here."

"Thank you." She popped the pills into her mouth, drained the cup, threw back her head to swallow. "I hope they help."

"So do I." Radnal had trouble keeping his voice casual. When she'd straightened to take the constipant, her left breast popped out of her tunic. "Freelady, I think you have fewer buttons than you did when the game ended."

Evillia covered herself again, an effort almost undermined when she shrugged. "I shouldn't be surprised. Most of those that didn't get pulled off took some yanks." She shrugged again. "It's only skin. Does it bother you?"

"You ought to know better than that," he said, almost angrily. "If you were feeling well—"

"If I were feeling well, I would enjoy feeling food," she agreed. "But as it is, Radnal vez—" At last she called him by his name and the polite particle. A grimace crossed her face. "As it is, I hope you will forgive me, but—" She hurried back out into the night.

When Lofosa made her next dash to the privy, Radnal had the pills waiting for her. She gulped them almost on the dead run. She'd lost some new buttons herself. Radnal felt guilty about thinking of such things when she was in distress.

After a game of war with Moblay that was almost as sloppy as their first, Radnal went into his cubicle. He didn't have anything to discuss with Liem or Peggol tonight; he knew what was coming. Somehow, he fell asleep anyway.

"Radnal vez." A quiet voice jerked him from slumber. It was neither Lofosa nor Evillia bending over him promising sensual delights. Peggol vez Menk stood in the entryway.

Radnal came fully awake. "What's gone wrong?" he demanded.

"Those two Highhead girls who don't believe in wearing clothes," Peggol answered.

"What about them?" Radnal asked, confused.

"They went off to the privy a while ago, and neither of them came back. My man on watch woke me before he went out to see if they were all right. They weren't there, either."

"Where could they have gone?" Radnal had had idiot tourists wander on their own, but never in the middle of the night. Then other possible meanings for their disappearance crossed his mind. He jumped up. "And why?"

"This also occurred to me," Peggol said grimly. "If they don't come back soon, it will have answered itself."

"They can't go far," Radnal said. "I doubt they'll have thought to get on donkeys. They could hardly tell one end of the beasts from the—" The tour guide stopped. If Evillia and Lofosa were other than they seemed, who could tell what they knew?

Peggol nodded. "We are thinking along the same lines." He plucked at the tuft of hair under his mouth. "If this means what we fear, much will depend on you to track them down. You know the Bottomlands, and I do not."

"Our best tools are the helos," Radnal said. "When it's light, we'll sweep the desert floor a hundred times faster than we could on donkeyback."

He kept talking for another few words, but Peggol didn't hear him. He didn't hear himself, either, not over the sudden roar from outside. They dashed for the outer door. They pushed through the Eyes and Ears and militiamen who got there first. Tourists pushed them from behind.

Everyone stared at the blazing helos.

Radnal stood in disbelief and dismay for a couple of heartbeats. Peggol vez Menk's shout brought him to himself: "We have to call Tarteshem *right now!*" Radnal spun round, shoved and elbowed by the tourists in his way, and dashed for the radiophone.

The amber ready light didn't come on when he hit the switch. He ducked under the table to see if any connections were loose. "Hurry up!" Peggol yelled.

"The demon-cursed thing won't come on," Radnal yelled back. He picked up the radiophone itself. It rattled. It wasn't supposed to. "It's broken."

"It's *been* broken," Peggol declared.

"How could it have been broken, with Eyes and Ears and militiamen in the common room all the time?" the tour guide said, not so much disagreeing with Peggol as voicing his bewilderment to the world.

But Peggol had an answer: "If one of those Krepalgan tarts paraded through here without any clothes—and they both ran back and forth all night—we might not have paid attention to what the other one was doing. Bang it . . . mmm, more likely reach under it with the right little tool . . . and you wouldn't need more than five heartbeats."

Radnal would have needed more than five heartbeats, but he wasn't a saboteur. If Evillia and Lofosa were— He couldn't doubt it, but it left him sick inside. They'd used him, used their bodies to lull him into thinking they were the stupid doxies they pretended to be. And it had worked . . . He wanted to wash himself over and over; he felt he'd never be clean again.

Liem vez Steries said, "We'd better make sure the donkeys are all right." He trotted out the door, ran around the crackling hulks of the flying machines. The stable door was closed against cave cats. The militiaman pulled it open. Through the crackle of the flames, Radnal heard a sharp report, saw a flash of light. Liem crashed to the ground. He lay there unmoving.

Radnal and Golobol the physician sprinted out to him. The firelight told them all they needed to know. Liem would not get up again, not with those dreadful wounds.

The tour guide went into the stables. He knew something was wrong, but needed a moment to realize what. Then the quiet hit him. The donkeys were not shifting in their stalls, nipping at the straw, or making any of the other small noises.

He looked into the stall by the broken door. The donkey there lay on its side. Its flanks neither rose nor fell. Radnal ran to the next, and the next. All the donkeys were dead—except for three, which were missing. One for Evillia, the tour guide thought, one for Lofosa, and one for their supplies.

No, they weren't fools. "I am," he said, and ran back to the lodge.

He gave the grim news to Peggol vez Menk. "We're in trouble, sure enough," Peggol said, shaking his head. "We'd be worse off, though, if the interrogation team weren't coming in under a daytenth. We can go after them in that helo. It has its own cannon, too; if they don't yield, goodbye. By the gods, I hope they don't."

"So do I." Radnal cocked his head to one side. A grin split his face. "Isn't that the helo now? Why is it early?"

"I don't know," Peggol answered. "Wait a heartbeat, maybe I do. If Tarteshem called and got no answer, they might have decided something was wrong and sent the helo straightaway."

The racket of engine and rotors swelled. The pilot must have spotted the fires and put on full speed. Radnal hurried outside to greet the incoming Eyes and Ears. The helo's black silhouette spread huge across the sky; as Peggol had implied, this was a military machine, not just a utility flier. It made for the glowing cones that marked the landing area.

Radnal watched it settle toward the ground. He remembered Evillia and Lofosa running around in the landing zone, laughing, giggling, and . . . losing buttons. He waved his arms, dashed toward the cones. "No!" he screamed. "Wait!"

Too late. Dust rose in choking clouds as the helo touched the ground. The tour guide saw the flash under one skid, heard the report. The skid crumpled. The helo heeled over. A rotor blade dug into the ground, snapped, thrummed past Radnal's head. Had it touched him, his head would have gone with it.

The side panel of the helo came down on the Bottomlands floor. Another sharp report—and suddenly flames were everywhere. The Eyes and Ears trapped inside the helo screamed. Radnal tried to help them, but the heat would not let him approach. The screams soon stopped. He smelled the thick odor of charring flesh. The fire burned on.

Peggol vez Menk hurried out to Radnal. "I tried to stop them," the tour guide said brokenly.

"You came closer than I, a reproach I shall carry to my grave," Peggol answered. "I did not see that danger, much as I should have. Some of those men were my friends." He slammed a fist against his thigh. "What now, Radnal vez?"

Die when the waters come, was the first thought that crossed the tour guide's mind. Mechanically, he went through the obvious: "Wait till dawn. Try to find their trail. Pack as much water on our backs as we can and go after them afoot."

"On foot?" Peggol said.

Radnal realized he hadn't explained about the donkeys. He did, then went on, "Leave one man here for when another helo comes. Give the tourists as much water as they can carry and send them up the trail. Maybe they'll escape the flood."

"What you say sounds sensible. We'll try it," Peggol said. "Anything else?"

"Pray," Radnal told him. He grimaced, nodded, turned away.

Moblay Sopsirk's son got through the Eyes and Ears and trotted up to Radnal and Peggol. "Freeman vez Krobir—" he began.

Radnal rolled his eyes. He was about to wish a night demon on Moblay's head, but stopped. Instead, he said, "Wait a heartbeat. You named me properly." What should have been polite surprise came out as accusation.

"So I did." Something about Moblay had changed. In the light of the blazing helos, he looked . . . not like Peggol vez Menk, since he remained a short-nosed, brown-skinned Highhead, but of the same type as the Eye and Ear—tough and smart, not just lascivious and overfamiliar. He said, "Freeman vez Krobir, I apologize for irritating you, but I wanted to remain as ineffectual-seeming as I could. Names are one way of doing that. I am an aide to my Prince: I am one of his Silent Servants."

Peggol grunted. He evidently knew what that meant. Radnal didn't, but he could guess: something like an Eye and Ear. He cried, "Is there anyone in this cursed tour group *not* wearing a mask?"

"More to the point, why drop the mask now?" Peggol asked.

"Because my Prince, may the Lion God give him many years, does not want the Bottomlands flooded," Moblay said. "We wouldn't suffer as badly as Tartesh, of course; we own only a strip of the southernmost part. But the Prince fears the fighting that would follow."

"Who approached Lissonland with word of this?" Peggol said.

"We learned from Morgaf," Moblay answered. "The island king wanted us to join the attack on Tartesh after the flood. But the Morgaffos denied the plot was theirs, and would not tell us who had set the starbomb here. We suspected the Krepalgan Unity, but had no proof. That was one reason I kept sniffing around the Krepalgan women." He grinned. "Another should be obvious."

"Why Krepalga?" Peggol wondered aloud. "The Unity didn't join Morgaf against us in the last war. What could they want enough to make them risk a war with starbombs?"

Radnal remembered the lecture he'd given on how the Bottomlands came to be, remembered also his fretting about how far an unchecked flood might reach. "I know part of the answer to that, I think," he said. Peggol and Moblay both turned to him. He went on, "If the Bottomlands flood, the new central sea would stop about at Krepalga's western border. The Unity would have a whole new coastline, and be in a better position than either Tartesh or Lissonland to exploit the new sea."

"The flood wouldn't get to Krepalga for a long time," Moblay protested.

"True," Radnal said, "but can you imagine stopping it before it did?" He visualized the map again. "I don't think you could, not against that weight of water."

"I think you're right." Peggol nodded decisively. "That may not be all Krepalga has in mind, but it'll be part. The Unity must have been planning this for years; they'll have looked at all the consequences they could."

"Let me help you now," Moblay said. "I heard freeman vez Krobir say the donkeys are dead, but what one walking man may do, I shall." Radnal would have taken any ally who presented himself. But Peggol said, "No. I am grateful for your candor and suspect you are truthful now, but dare not take the chance. One walking man could do much harm as well as good. Being of the profession, I trust you understand."

Moblay bowed. "I feared you would say that. I do understand. May the Lion God go with you."

The three men walked back to the lodge. The tourists rained questions on Radnal. "No one has told us anything, not a single thing," Golobol complained. "What is going on? Why are helos exploding to left and then to right? Tell me!"

Radnal told him—and everyone else. The stunned silence his words produced lasted perhaps five heartbeats. Then everybody started yelling. Nocso zev Martois' voice drowned all others: "Does this mean we don't get to finish the tour?"

More sensibly, Toglo zev Pamdal said, "Is there any way we can help you in your pursuit, Radnal vez?"

"Thank you, no. You'd need weapons; we haven't any to give you. Your best hope is to make for high ground. You ought to leave as soon as you load all the water you can carry. Lie up in the middle of the day when the sun is worst. With luck, you'll be up at the old continental shelf in, oh, a day and a half. If the flood's held off that long, you ought to be safe for a while there. And a helo may spot you as you travel."

"What if the flood comes when we're still down here?" Eltsac vez Martois demanded. "What then, freeman Know-It-All?"

"Then you have the consolation of knowing I drowned a few heartbeats before you. I hope you enjoy it," Radnal said. Eltsac stared at him. He went on, "That's all the stupidity I have time for now. Let's get you people moving. Peggol vez, we'll send a couple of Eyes and Ears back, too. Your men won't be much help traveling crosscountry. Come to that, you—"

"No," Peggol said firmly. "My place is at the focus. I shan't lag, and I shoot straight. I'm not the worst tracker, either."

Radnal knew better than to argue. "All right."

The water bladders would have gone on the donkeys. Radnal filled them from the cistern while the militiamen and Eyes and Ears cut straps to fit them to human shoulders. The eastern sky was bright pink by the time they finished. Radnal tried to give no tourists loads of more than a third of their body weight: that was as much as anyone could carry without breaking down.

Nocso vez Martois said, "With all this water, how can we carry food?"

"You can't," Radnal snapped. He stared at her. "You can live off yourself a while, but you can't live without water." Telling off his tourists was a new, heady pleasure. Since it might be his last, he enjoyed it while he could.

"I'll report your insolence," Nocso shrilled.

"That is the least of my worries." Radnal turned to the Eyes and Ears who were heading up the trail with the tourists. "Try to keep them together, try not to do too much at midday, make sure they all drink—and make sure you do, too. Gods be with you."

An Eye and Ear shook his head. "No, freeman vez Krobir, with *you*. If they watch you, we'll be all right. But if they neglect you, we all fail."

Radnal nodded. To the tourists, he said, "Good luck. If the gods are kind, I'll see you again at the top of Trench Park." He didn't mention what would happen if the gods bumbled along as usual.

Toglo said, "Radnal vez, if we see each other again, I will use whatever influence I have for you."

"Thanks," was all Radnal could say. Under other circumstances, getting patronage from the Hereditary Tyrant's relative would have moved him to do great things. Even now, it was kindly meant, but of small weight when he first had to survive to gain it.

A sliver of red-gold crawled over the eastern horizon. The tourists and the Eyes and Ears trudged north. A koprit bird on the rooftop announced the day with a cry of *Hig, hig, hig!*

Peggol ordered one of the remaining Eyes and Ears to stay at the lodge and send westward any helos that came. Then he said formally, "Freeman vez Krobir, I place myself and freeman vez Potos, my colleague here, under your authority. Command us."

"If that's how you want it," Radnal answered, shrugging. "You know what we'll do: march west until we catch the Krepalgans or drown, whichever comes first. Nothing fancy. Let's go."

Radnal, the two Eyes and Ears, the lodge attendants, and the surviving militiamen started from the stables. The morning light showed the tracks of three donkeys heading west. The tour guide took out his monocular, scanned the western horizon. No luck—dips and rises hid Evillia and Lofosa.

Fer vez Canthal said, "There's a high spot maybe three thousand cubits west of here. You ought to look from there."

"Maybe," Radnal said. "If we have a good trail, though, I'm likelier to rely on that. I begrudge wasting even a heartbeat's time, and spotting someone isn't easy if he wants to be found. Remember that poor fellow who wandered off from his group four years ago? They used helos, dogs, everything, but they didn't find his corpse until a year later, and then by accident."

"Thank you for pumping up my hopes," Peggol said.

"Nothing wrong with hope," Radnal answered, "but you knew the odds were bad when you decided to stay."

The seven walkers formed a loose skirmish line, about five cubits apart from one another. Radnal, the best tracker, took the center; at his right was Horken vez Sofana, at his left Peggol. He figured they had the best chance of picking up the trail if he lost it.

That likelihood grew with every step. Evillia and Lofosa hadn't gone straight west. He quickly found that out. Instead, they'd jink northwest for a few hundred cubits, then southwest a few hundred more, in a deliberate effort to throw off pursuit. They also chose the hardest ground they could find, which made the donkeys' tracks tougher to follow.

Radnal's heart sank every time he had to cast about before they found the hoofprints again. His group lost ground with every step; the Krepalgans rode faster than they could walk.

"I have a question," Horken vez Sofana: "Suppose the starbomb goes off and the mountains fall. How are these two women supposed to get away?"

Radnal shrugged; he had no idea. "Did you hear that, Peggol vez?" he asked.

"Yes," Peggol said. "Two possibilities spring to mind—"

"I might have guessed," Radnal said.

"Hush. As I was saying before you crassly interrupted, one is that the starbomb was supposed to have a delayed detonation, letting the perpetrators escape. The other is that these agents knew the mission was suicidal. Morgaf has used such personnel; so have we, once or twice. Krepalga might find such servants, however regrettable that prospect seems to us."

Horken gave a slow, deliberate nod. "What you say sounds convincing. They might have first planned a delay to let them escape, then shifted to sacrificing themselves when they found we were partway on to them."

"True," Peggol said. "And they may yet be planning to escape. If they somehow secreted away helium cylinders, for instance, they might inflate several prophylactics and float out of the Bottomlands."

Radnal wondered for a heartbeat if he was serious. Then the tour guide snorted. "I wish I could stay so cheerful at death's door."

"Death will find me whether I am cheerful or not," Peggol answered. "I will go forward as boldly as and as long as I can."

Conversation flagged. The higher the sun rose, the hotter the desert became, the more anything but putting one foot in front of the other seemed more trouble than it was worth. Radnal wiped sweat from his eyes as he slogged along.

The water bladder on his back started out as heavy as any pack he'd ever toted. He wondered how long he could go on with such a big burden. But the bladder got lighter every time he refilled his canteen. He made himself keep drinking—not getting water in as fast as he sweated would be suicidal. Unlike the fanatic Morgaffos Peggol had mentioned, he wanted to live if he could.

He'd given everyone about two days' worth of water. If he didn't catch up to Lofosa and Evillia by the end of the second day . . . He shook his head. One way or another, it wouldn't matter after that.

As noon neared, he ordered the walkers into the shade of a limestone outcrop. "We'll rest a while," he said. "When we start again, it ought to be cooler."

"Not enough to help," Peggol said. But he sat down in the shade with a grateful sigh. He took off his stylish cap, sadly felt of it. "It make a dishrag after this—nothing better."

Radnal squatted beside him, too hot to talk. His heart pounded. It seemed so loud, he wondered if it would give out on him. Then he realized most of that beating rhythm came from outside. Fatigue fell away. He jumped up, doffed his own cap and waved it in the air. "A helo!"

The rest of the group also got up and waved and yelled. "It's seen us!" Zosel vez Glesir said. Nimbly as a dragonfly, the helo shifted direction in midair and dashed straight toward them. It set down about fifty cubits from the ledge. Its rotors kept spinning; it was ready to take off again at any moment.

The pilot leaned out the window, bawled something in Radnal's direction. Through the racket, he had no idea what the fellow said. The pilot beckoned him over.

The din and dust were worse under the whirling rotor blades. Radnal had to lean on tiptoe against the helo's hot metal skin before he made out the pilot's words: "How far ahead are the cursed Krepalgans?"

"They had better than a daytenth's start, and they're on donkeyback. Say, up to thirty thousand cubits west of here." Radnal repeated himself several times, before the pilot nodded and ducked back into his machine.

"Wait!" Radnal screamed. The pilot stuck his head out again. Radnal asked, "Did you come across my group heading toward the trail up the old continental shelf?"

"Yes. Somebody ought to be picking them up right about now."

"Good," Radnal bellowed. The pilot tossed him a portable radiophone. He seized it; now he was no longer cut off from the rest of the search.

They sped. The helo shot into the air, sped away westward. The tour guide knew relief: even if he drowned, the people he'd led would be safe.

"Now that this helo's here, do we need to go on?" asked Impac vez Potos, the Eye and Ear with Peggol.

"You'd best believe it, freeman." Radnal recounted the story of the lost tourist who'd stayed lost. "No matter how many helos search, they'll be covering a big area and trying to find people who don't want to be found. We stay in the hunt till it's over. By the way the Krepalgans fooled us all, they won't make things easy."

"Shall we keep resting, or head out now?" Peggol asked.

Radnal chewed on that for a few heartbeats. If the helo was here, that meant the people at Tarteshem knew from its radiophone how bad things were. And *that* meant helos would swarm here as fast as they could take off, which meant his group would probably be able to get supplies. But he didn't want to lose people to heatstroke, either, a risk that came with exertion in the desert.

"We'll give it another tenth of a daytenth," he said at last.

He was first up when the rest ended. The other six rose with enough groans and creaking joints for an army of invalids. "We'll loosen up as we get going," Fer vez Canthal said hopefully.

A little later, panic ran through Radnal when he lost the trail. He waved for Peggol and Horken vez Sofana. They scoured the ground on hands and knees, but found nothing. Rock-hard dirt stretched in all directions for a couple of hundred cubits. "If they pulled up a bush and swept away their tracks, we'll have a night demons' time picking them up again," Horken said.

"We won't try," Radnal declared. The rest of the searchers looked at him in surprise. He went on, "We're wasting time here, right?" No one disagreed. "So here is the last place we want to stay. We'll do a search spiral. Zosel vez, you stand here to mark this spot. Sooner or later, we'll find the trail again."

"You hope," Peggol said quietly.

"Yes, I do. If you have a better plan, I'll be grateful to hear it." The Eye and Ear shook his head and, a moment later, dropped his eyes.

While Zosel stood in place, the other searchers tramped in a widening spiral. After a hundred heartbeats, Impac vez Potos shouted: "I've found it!"

Radnal and Horken hurried to see what he'd come across. "Where?" Radnal asked. Impac pointed to a patch of ground softer than most in the area. Sure enough, it held marks. The more experienced men squatted to take a better look. They glanced up together; their eyes met. Radnal said, "Freeman vez Potos, those are the tracks of a bladetooth. If you look carefully, you can see where it dragged its tail in the dirt. Donkeys never do that."

"Oh," Impac said in a small, sad voice.

Radnal sighed. He hadn't bothered mentioning that the tracks were too small for donkeys' and didn't look like them, either. "Let's try once more," he said. The spiral resumed.

When Impac yelled again, Radnal wished he hadn't tried to salve his feelings. If he stopped them every hundred heartbeats, they'd never find anything. This time, Horken stayed where he was. Radnal stalked over to Impac. "Show me," he growled.

Impac pointed once more. Radnal filled his lungs to curse him for wasting their time. The curse remained unspoken. There at his feet lay the unmistakable tracks of three donkeys. "By the gods," he said.

"They are right this time?" Impac asked anxiously.

"Yes. Thank you, freeman." Radnal shouted to the other searchers. The seven headed southwest, following the recovered trail. Fer vez Canthal went up to Impac and slapped him on the back. Impac beamed as if he'd performed bravely in front of the Hereditary Tyrant. Considering the service he'd just done Tartesh, he'd earned the right.

He was also lucky, Radnal thought. But he'd needed courage to call out a second time after being ignominiously wrong the first, and sharp eyes to spot both sets of tracks, even if he couldn't tell what they were once he'd found them. So more than luck was involved. Radnal slapped Impac's back, too.

Sweat poured off Radnal. As it evaporated from his robes, it cooled him a little, but not enough. Like a machine taking on fuel, he drank again and again from the bladder on his back.

Now the sun was in his face. He tugged his cap over his eyes, kept his head down, and tramped on. When the Krepalgans tried doubling back, he spotted the ruse instead of following the wrong trail and wasting hundreds of precious heartbeats.

By then, the western sky was full of helos. They roared about in all directions, sometimes low enough to kick up dust. Radnal wanted to strangle the pilots who flew that way; they might blow away the trail, too. He yelled into the radiophone. The low-flying helos moved higher.

A big transport helo set down a few hundred cubits in front of the walkers. A door in its side slid open. A squadron of soldiers jumped down and hurried west.

"Are they close or desperate?" Radnal wondered.

"Desperate, certainly," Peggol said. "As for close, we can hope. We haven't drowned yet. On the other hand"—he always thought of the other hand—"we haven't caught your two sluts, either."

"They weren't mine," Radnal said feebly. But he remembered their flesh sliding against his, the way their breath had caught, the sweat-salty taste of their skin.

Peggol read his face. "Aye, they used you, Radnal vez, and they fooled you. If it makes you feel better, they fooled me, too; I thought they kept their brains in their twats. They outsmarted me with the fornication books in their gear and the skin they showed. They used our prudishness against us—how could anyone who acts that way be dangerous? It's a ploy that won't work again."

"Once may have been plenty." Radnal wasn't ready to stop feeling guilty.

"If it was, you'll pay full atonement," Peggol said.

Radnal shook his head. Dying when the Bottomlands flooded wasn't atonement enough, not when that flood would ruin his nation and might start an exchange of starbombs that would wreck the world.

The ground shivered under his feet. Despite the furnace heat of the desert floor, his sweat went cold. "Please, gods, make it stop," he said, his first prayer in years.

It stopped. He breathed again. It was just a little quake; he would have laughed at tourists for fretting over it. At any other time, he would have ignored it. Now it nearly scared him to death.

A koprit bird cocked its head, peered down at him from a thorn-bush that held its larder.

Hig-hig-hig! it said, and fluttered to the ground. Radnal wondered if it could fly fast enough or far enough to escape a flood.

The radiophone let out a burst of static. Radnal thumbed it to let himself transmit: "Vez Krobir here."

"This is Combat Group Leader Turand vez Nital. I wish to report that we have encountered the Krepalgan spies. Both are deceased."

"That's wonderful!" Radnal relayed the news. His companions raised a weary cheer. Then he remembered again his nights with Evillia and Lofosa. And *then* he realized Combat Group Leader vez Nital hadn't sounded as overjoyed and relieved as he should have. Slowly, he said, "What's wrong?"

"When encountered, the Krepalgans were moving eastward."

"Eastw— Oh!"

"You see the predicament?" Turand said. "They appear to have completed their work and to have been attempting to escape. Now they are beyond questioning. Please keep your transmission active so a helo can home on you and bring you here. You look to be Tartesh's best hope of locating the bomb before its ignition. I repeat, please maintain transmission."

Radnal obeyed. He looked at the Barrier Mountains. They seemed taller now than they had when he set out. How long would they keep standing tall? The sun was sliding down toward them, too. How was he supposed to search after dark? He feared tomorrow morning was too late.

He passed on to his comrades what the officer had said. Horken vez Sofana made swimming motions. Radnal stooped for a pebble, threw it at him.

A helo soon landed beside the seven walkers. Someone inside opened the sliding door. "Come on!" he bawled. "Move it, move it!"

Moving it as fast as they could, Radnal and the rest scrambled into the helo. It went airborne before the fellow at the door had it fully closed. A couple of hundred heartbeats later, the helo touched down hard enough to rattle the tour guide's teeth. The crewman at the door undogged it and slid it open. "Out!" he yelled.

Out Radnal jumped. The others followed. A few cubits away stood a man in a uniform robe similar but not identical to the one the militia wore. "Who's freeman vez Krobir?" he said. "I'm Turand vez Nital."

"I'm vez Krobir. I—" Radnal broke off. Two bodies lay behind the Tarteshan soldier. Radnal gulped. He'd seen corpses on their funeral pyres, but never before sprawled out like animals waiting to be butchered. He said the first thing that popped into his head: "They don't look like you shot them."

"We didn't," the officer said. "When they saw they couldn't escape, they took poison."

"They *were* professionals," Peggol murmured.

"As may be," Turand growled. "This one"—he pointed at Evillia—

"wasn't gone when we got to her. She said, 'You're too late,' and then died, may night demons gnaw her ghost forever."

"We'd better find that cursed bomb fast, then," Radnal said. "Can you take us to where the Krepalgans were cornered?"

"This very heartbeat," Turand said. "Come with me. It's only three or four hundred cubits from here." He moved at a trot that left the worn walkers gasping in his wake. At last he stopped and waited impatiently for them to catch up. "This is where we found them."

"And they were coming east, you said?" Radnal asked.

"That's right, though I don't know for how long," the officer answered. "Somewhere out there is the accursed starbomb. We're scouring the desert, but this is *your* park. Maybe, your eye will fall on something they'd miss. If not—"

"You needn't go on," Radnal said. "I almost fouled my robe when we had that little tremor a while ago. I thought I'd wash ashore on the Krepalgan border, ten million cubits from here."

"If you're standing on a starbomb when it goes off, you needn't fear the flood afterwards," Turand said.

"Gak." Radnal hadn't thought of that. It would be quick, anyhow.

"Enough chatter," Horken vez Sofana said. "If we're to search, let us search."

"Search, and may the gods lend your sight wings," Turand said.

The seven walkers trudged west again. Radnal did his best to follow the donkey's trail, but the soldiers' footprints often obscured them. "How are we supposed to track in this confusion?" he cried. "They might as well have turned a herd of humpless camels loose here."

"It's not quite so bad as that," Horken said. Stooping low, he pointed to the ground. "Look, here's a track. Here's another, a few paces on. We can do it. We have to do it."

Radnal knew the senior trooper was right; he felt ashamed of his own outburst. He found the next hoofprint himself, and the one after that. Those two lay on opposite sides of a fault-line crack; when he saw that, he knew the starbomb couldn't rest too far away. But he felt time pressing hard on his shoulders.

"Maybe the soldiers will have found the starbomb by now," Fer vez Canthal said.

"We can't count on it. Look how long it took them to find the Krepalgans. We have to figure it's up to us." Radnal realized the weight on him wasn't just time. It was also responsibility. If he died now, he'd die knowing he'd failed.

And yet, while the searchers stirred through Trench Park, the animals of the Bottomlands kept living their usual lives; they could not know they might perish in the next heartbeat. A koprit bird skittered across the sand a few paces in front of Radnal. A clawed foot stabbed down.

"It's caught a shoveler skink," he said, as if the hot, worn men with him were members of his group.

The lizard thrashed, trying to get away. Sand flew every which way. But the koprit bird held on with its claws, tore at the skink with its beak, and smashed it against the ground until its writhing ceased. Then it flew to a nearby thornbush with its victim.

It impaled the skink on a long, stout thorn. The lizard was the latest addition to its larder, which also included two grasshoppers, a baby snake, and a jerboa. And, as koprit birds often did, this one used the thorn bush's spikes to display bright objects it had found. A yellow flower, now very dry, must have hung there since the last rains. And not far from the lizard, the koprit bird had draped a couple of red-orange strings over a thorn.

Radnal's eyes came to them, passed by, snapped back. They weren't strings. He pointed. "Aren't those the necklaces Evillia and Lofosa wore yesterday?" he asked hoarsely.

"They are." Peggol and Horken said it together. They both had to notice and remember small details. They sounded positive.

When Peggol tried to take the necklaces off their thorn, the koprit bird furiously screeched *hig-hig!* Claws outstretched, it flew at his face. He staggered backwards, flailing his arms.

Radnal waved his cap as he walked up to the thornbush. That intimidated the bird enough to keep it from diving on him, though it kept shrieking. He grabbed the necklaces and got away from the larder as fast as he could.

The necklaces were heavier than he'd expected, too heavy for the cheap plastic he'd thought them to be. He turned one so he could look at it end-on. "It's got a copper core," he said, startled.

"Let me see that." Again Peggol and Horken spoke together. They snatched a necklace apiece. Then Peggol broke the silence alone: "Detonator wire."

"Absolutely," Horken agreed. "Never seen it with red insulator, though. Usually it would be brown or green for camouflage. This time, it was camouflaged as jewelry."

Radnal stared from Horken to Peggol. "You mean, these wires would be hooked to the cell that would send the charge to the starbomb when the timer went off?"

"That's just what we mean," Peggol said. Horken vez Sofana solemnly nodded.

"But they can't now, because they're here, not there." Fumbling for words, Radnal went on, "And they're here because the koprit bird thought they were pretty (or maybe it thought they were food—they're about the color of a shoveler skink's lure) and pulled them loose and flew away with them." Realization hit then: "That koprit bird just saved Tartesh!"

"The ugly thing almost put my eye out," Peggol grumbled. The rest of the group ignored him. One or two of them cheered. More, like Radnal, stood quietly, too tired and dry and stunned to show their joy.

The tour guide needed several heartbeats to remember he carried a radiophone. He clicked it on, waited for Turand vez Nital. "What do you have?" the officer barked. Radnal could hear his tension. He'd felt it too, till moments before.

"The detonation wires are off the starbomb," he said, giving the good news first. "I don't know where that is, but it won't go off without them."

After static-punctuated silence, Turand said slowly, "Are you daft? How can you have the wires without the starbomb?"

"There was this koprit bird—"

"What?" Turand's roar made the radiophone vibrate in Radnal's hand. As best he could, he explained. More silence followed. At last, the soldier said, "You're certain this is detonator wire?"

"An Eye and Ear and the Trench Park circumstances man both say it is. If they don't recognize the stuff, who would?"

"You're right." Another pause from Turand, then: "A koprit bird,

you say? Do you know that I never heard of koprit birds until just now?"
His voice held wonder. But suddenly he sounded worried again, saying,
"Can you be sure the wire wasn't left there to fool us one last time?"
"No." Fear knotted Radnal's gut again. Had he and his comrades
come so far, done so much, only to fall for a final deception?

Horken let out a roar louder than Turand's had been. "I've found it!"
he screamed from beside a spurge about twenty cubits away. Radnal
hurried over. Horken said, "It couldn't have been far, because koprit
birds have territories. So I kept searching, and—" He pointed down.

At the base of the spurge lay a small timer hooked to an electrical
cell. The timer was upside down; the koprit bird must have had quite a
fight tearing loose the wires it prized. Radnal stooped, turned the timer
over. He almost dropped it—the needle that counted off the daytenths
and heartbeats lay against the zero knob.

"Will you look at that?" he said softly. Impac vez Potos peered over
his shoulder. The junior Eye and Ear clicked his tongue between his teeth.

"A koprit bird," Horken said. He got down on hands and knees,
poked around under every plant and stone within a couple of cubits
of the spurge. Before a hundred heartbeats went by, he let out a sharp,
wordless exclamation.

Radnal got down beside him. Horken had tipped over a chunk of
sandstone about as big as his head. Under it was a crack in the earth
that ran out to either side. From the crack protruded two drab brown
wires.

"A koprit bird," Horken repeated. The helos and men would have
been too late. But the koprit bird, hungry or out to draw females into
its territory, had spotted something colorful, so—

Radnal took out the radiophone. "We've found the timer. It is
separated from the wires which, we presume, lead to the starbomb.
The koprit bird took away the wires the Krepalgans used to attach the
timer."

"A koprit bird." Now Turand vez Nital said it. He sounded as dazed
as any of the rest of them, but quickly pulled himself together again:
"That's excellent news, as I needn't tell you. I'll send a crew to your
location directly, to begin excavating the starbomb. Out."

Peggol vez Menk had been examining the timer, too. His gaze kept returning to the green needle bisecting the zero symbol. He said, "How deep do you suppose the bomb is buried?"

"It would have to be pretty deep, to trigger the fault," Radnal answered. "I couldn't say how deep; I'm no savant of geology. But if Turand vez Nital thinks his crew will dig it up before nightfall, he'll have to think again."

"How could Krepalga have planted it here?" Impac vez Potos said. "Wouldn't you Trench Park people have noticed?"

"Trench Park is a big place," Radnal said.

"I know that. I ought to; I've walked enough of it," Impac said wearily. "Still—"

"People don't frequent this area, either," Radnal persisted. "I've never led a group anywhere near here. No doubt the Krepalgans took risks doing whatever they did, but not enormous risks."

Peggol said, "We shall have to ensure such deadly danger cannot return again. Whether we should expand the militia, base regular soldiers here, or set up a station for Eyes and Ears, that I don't know— we must determine which step offers the best security. But we will do something."

"You also have to consider which choice hurts Trench Park least," Radnal said.

"That will be a factor," Peggol said, "but probably a small one. Think, Radnal vez: if the Barrier Mountains fall and the Western Ocean pours down on the Bottomlands, how much will that hurt Trench Park?"

Radnal opened his mouth to argue more. Keeping the park in its natural state had always been vital to him. Man had despoiled so much of the Bottomlands; this was the best—almost the only—reminder of what they'd been like. But he'd just spent days wondering whether he'd drown in the next heartbeat, and all of today certain he would. And if he'd drowned, his country would have drowned with him. Set against that, a base for soldiers or Eyes and Ears suddenly seemed a small thing. He said not another word.

Radnal hadn't been in Tarteshem for a long time, though Tartesh's capital wasn't far from Trench Park. He'd never been paraded through the city in an open-topped motor while people lined the sidewalks and cheered. He should have enjoyed it. Peggol vez Menk, who sat beside him in the motor, certainly did. Peggol smiled and waved as if he'd just been chosen high priest.

After so long in the wide open spaces of the Bottomlands, though, and after so long in his own company or that of small tour groups, riding through the midst of so much tight-packed humanity more nearly overwhelmed than overjoyed Radnal. He looked nervously at the buildings towering over the avenue. It felt more as if he were passing through a canyon than anything man-made.

"Radnal, Radnal!" the crowds chanted, as if everybody knew him well enough to use his name in its most naked, intimate form. They had another cry, too: "Koprit bird! Koprit bird! The gods praise the koprit bird!"

That took away some of his nervousness. Seeing his grin, Peggol said, "Anyone would think they'd seen the artist's new work."

"You're right," Radnal answered. "Maybe it's too bad *the* koprit bird isn't here for the ceremony after all."

Peggol raised that eyebrow of his. "You talked them out of capturing it."

"I know. I did the right thing," Radnal said. Putting the koprit bird that stole the detonator wires in a cage didn't seem fitting. Trench Park existed to let its creatures live wild and free, with as little interference from mankind as possible. The koprit bird had made it possible for that to go on. Caging it afterwards struck Radnal as ungrateful.

The motor drove onto the grounds of the Hereditary Tyrant's palace. It pulled up in front of the gleaming building that housed Bortav vez Pamdal. A temporary stage and a podium stood on the lawn near the road. The folding chairs that faced it were full of dignitaries from Tartesh and other nations.

No Krepalgans sat in those chairs. The Hereditary Tyrant had sent the plenipo from the Krepalgan Unity home, ordered all Krepalgan citizens out of Tartesh, and sealed the border. So far, he'd done nothing more than that. Radnal both resented and approved of his caution. In an age of starbombs, even the attempted murder of a nation had to be dealt with cautiously, lest a successful double murder follow.

A man in a fancy robe came up to the motor, bowed low. "I am the protocol officer. If you will come with me, freemen——?"

Radnal and Peggol came. The protocol officer led them onto the platform, got them settled, and hurried away to see to the rest of the seven walkers, whose motors had parked behind the one from which the tour guide and the Eye and Ear had dismounted.

Peering at the important people who were examining him, Radnal got nervous again. He didn't belong in this kind of company. But there in the middle of the second row sat Toglo zev Pamdal, who smiled broadly and waved at him. Seeing someone he knew and liked made it easier for him to wait for the next part of the ceremony.

The Tarteshan national hymn blared out. Radnal couldn't just sit. He got up and put his hand over his heart until the hymn was done. The protocol officer stepped up to the podium and announced, "Freemen, freeladies, the Hereditary Tyrant."

Bortav vez Pamdal's features adorned silver, smiled down from public buildings, and were frequently on the screen. Radnal had never expected to see the Hereditary Tyrant in person, though. In the flesh, Bortav looked older than he did on his images, and not quite so firm and wise: like a man, in other words, not a demigod.

But his ringing baritone proved all his own. He spoke without notes for a quarter of a daytenth, praising Tartesh, condemning those who had tried to lay her low, and promising that danger would never come again. In short, it was a political speech. Since Radnal cared more about the kidneys of the fat sand rat than politics, he soon stopped paying attention.

He almost missed the Hereditary Tyrant calling out his name. He started and sprang up. Bortav vez Pamdal beckoned him to the podium. As if in a dream, he went.

Bortav put an arm around his shoulder. The Hereditary Tyrant was faintly perfumed. "Freemen, freeladies, I present Radnal vez Krobir, whose sharp eye spotted the evil wires which proved the gods had not deserted Tartesh. For his valiant efforts in preserving not only Trench Park, not only the Bottomlands, but all Tartesh, I award him five thousand units of silver and to declare that he and all his heirs are henceforward recognized as members of our nation's aristocracy. Freeman vez Krobir!"

The dignitaries applauded. Bortav vez Pamdal nodded, first to the microphone, then to Radnal. Making a speech frightened him worse than almost anything he'd gone through in the Bottomlands. He tried to pretend it was a scientific paper: "Thank you, your excellency. You honor me beyond my worth. I will always cherish your kindness."

He stepped back. The dignitaries applauded again, perhaps because he'd been so brief. Away from the mike, the Hereditary Tyrant said, "Stay up here by me while I reward your colleagues. The other presentation for you is at the end."

Bortav called up the rest of the seven walkers, one by one. He raised Peggol to the aristocracy along with Radnal. The other five drew his praise and large sums of silver. That seemed unfair to Radnal. Without Horken, for instance, they wouldn't have found the electrical cell and timer. And Impac had picked up the trail when even Radnal lost it.

He couldn't very well protest. Even as the hero of the moment, he lacked the clout to make Bortav listen to him. Moreover, he guessed no one had informed the Hereditary Tyrant he'd been fornicating with Evillia and Lofosa a few days before they went out to detonate the buried starbomb. Bortav vez Pamdal was a staunch conservative about morals. He wouldn't have elevated Radnal if he'd known everything he did in Trench Park.

To salve his conscience, Radnal reminded himself that all seven walkers would have easier lives because of today's ceremony. It was true. He remained not quite convinced it was enough.

Zosel vez Glesir, last to be called to the podium, finished his thank-you and went back to his place. Bortav vez Pamdal reclaimed the microphone. As the applause for Zosel died away, the Tyrant said, "Our nation should never forget this near brush with disaster, nor the efforts of all those within Trench Park who turned it aside. To commemorate it, I here display for the first time the insigne Trench Park will bear henceforward."

The protocol officer carried a cloth-covered square of fiberboard, not quite two cubits on a side, over to Radnal. He murmured, "The veil unfastens from the top. Hold the emblem up so the crowd can see it as you lower the veil."

Radnal obeyed. The dignitaries clapped. Most of them smiled; a few even laughed. Radnal smiled, too. What better way to symbolize Trench Park than a koprit bird perching on a thornbush?

Bortav vez Pamdal waved him to the microphone once more. He said, "I thank you again, your excellency, now on behalf of all Trench Park staff. We shall bear this insigne proudly."

He stepped away from the microphone, then turned his head and hissed to the protocol officer, "What do I do with this thing?"

"Lean it against the side of the podium," the unflappable official answered. "We'll take care of it." As Radnal returned to his seat, the protocol officer announced, "Now we'll adjourn to the Grand Reception Hall for drinks and a luncheon."

Along with everyone else, Radnal found his way to the Grand Reception Hall. He took a glass of sparkling wine from a waiter with a silver tray, then stood around accepting congratulations from important officials. It was like being a tour guide: he knew most of what he should say, and improvised new answers along old themes.

In a flash of insight, he realized the politicians and bureaucrats were doing the same thing with him. The whole affair was formal as a figure dance. When he saw that, his nervousness vanished for good.

Or so he thought, until Toglo came smiling up to him. He dipped his head. "Hello, freelady, it's good to see you again."

"If I was Toglo zev through danger in Trench Park, I remain Toglo zev here safe in Tarteshem." She sounded as if his formality disappointed her.

"Good," he said. Despite her pledge of patronage before she hiked away from the lodge, plenty of people friendly to Trench Park staff in the Bottomlands snubbed them if they met in the city. He hadn't thought she was that type, but better safe.

As if by magic, Bortav vez Pamdal appeared at Radnal's elbow. The Hereditary Tyrant's cheeks were a little red; he might have had more than one glass of sparkling wine. He spoke as if reminding himself: "You already know my niece, don't you, freeman vez Krobir?"

"Your—niece?" Radnal stared from Bortav to Toglo. She'd called herself a distant collateral relation. *Niece* didn't fit that definition.

"Hope you enjoy your stay here." Bortav slapped Radnal on the shoulder, breathed wine into his face, and ambled off to hobnob with other guests.

"You never said you were his niece," Radnal said. Now that he was suddenly an aristocrat, he might have imagined talking to the clanfather of the Hereditary Tyrant's distant collateral relative. But to talk to Bortav vez Pamdal's brother or sister-husband . . . impossible. Maybe that made him sound peevish.

"I'm sorry," Toglo answered. Radnal studied her, expecting the apology to be merely for form's sake. But she seemed to mean it. She said, "Bearing my clan name is hard enough anyway. It would be harder yet if I told everyone how close a relative of the Hereditary Tyrant's I am. People wouldn't treat me like a human being. Believe me, I know." By the bitterness in her voice, she did.

"Oh," Radnal said slowly. "I never thought of that, Toglo zev." Her smile when he used her name with the polite particle made him feel better.

"You should have," she told him. "When folk hear I'm from the Pamdal clan, they either act as if I'm made of glass and will shatter if they breathe on me too hard, or else they try to see how much they can get out of me. I don't care for either one. That's why I minimize the kinship."

"Oh," Radnal's snort of laughter was aimed mostly at himself. "I always imagined being attached to a rich and famous clan made life simpler and easier, not the other way round. I never thought anything bad might be mixed with that. I'm sorry, for not realizing it."

"You needn't be," she said. "I think you'd have treated me the same even if you'd known from the first heartbeat who my uncle happened to be. I don't find that often, so I treasure it."

Radnal said, "I'd be lying if I told you I didn't think about which family you belonged to."

"Well, of course, Radnal vez. You'd be stupid if you didn't think about it. I don't expect that; until the koprit bird, I thought the gods were done with miracles. But whatever you were thinking, you didn't let it get in the way."

"I tried to treat you as much like everyone else as I could," he said.

"I thought you did wonderfully," she answered. "That's why we became friends so fast down in Trench Park. It's also why I'd like us to stay friends now."

"I'd like that very much," Radnal said, "provided you don't think I'm saying so to try and take advantage of you."

"I don't think you'd do that." Though Toglo kept smiling, her eyes measured him. She'd said she'd had people try to take advantage of her before. Radnal doubted those people had come off well.

"Being who you are makes it harder for me to tell you I also liked you very much, down in the Bottomlands," he said.

"Yes, I can see that it might," Toglo said. "You don't want me to think you seek advantage." She studied Radnal again. This time, he studied her, too. Maybe the first person who'd tried to turn friendship to gain had succeeded; she was, he thought, a genuinely nice person. But he would have bet his five thousand units of silver that she'd sent the second such person packing. Being nice didn't make her a fool.

He didn't like her less for that. Maybe Eltsac vez Martois was attracted to fools, but Eltsac was a fool himself. Radnal had called himself many names, but fool seldom. The last time he'd thought that about himself was when he found out what Lofosa and Evillia really were. Of course, when he made a mistake, he didn't do it halfway.

But he'd managed to redeem himself—with help from that koprit bird.

Toglo said, "If we do become true friends, Radnal vez, or perhaps even more than that"—a possibility he wouldn't have dared mention himself, but one far from displeasing—"promise me one thing."

"What" he asked, suddenly wary. "I don't like friendship with conditions. It reminds me too much of our last treaty with Morgaf. We haven't fought the islanders in a while, but we don't trust them, or they us. We saw that in the Bottomlands, too."

She nodded. "True. Still, I hope my condition isn't too onerous."

"Go on." He sipped his sparkling wine.

"Well, then, Radnal vez Krobir, the *next* time I see you in a sleep-

sack with a couple of naked Highhead girls—or even Strongbrows—
you will have to consider our friendship over."

Some of the wine went up his nose. That only made him choke
worse. Dabbing at himself with a linen square gave him a few heartbeats to regain composure. "Toglo zev, you have a bargain," he said
solemnly.

They clasped hands.

PERSPECTIVES ON CHANUKAH

This one also sees print here for the first time, though it has been heard before. In the fall of 2001, NPR asked me for a 1,500-word sf or fantasy story about Chanukah (for anyone who doesn't know, I am Jewish, though not especially observant) to be read over the air. That's a devilishly hard length for a piece of fiction, unless you're telling a joke or something — you don't have room to do much more. Nothing along those lines occurred to me, but a nonfiction idea did. I asked them if I could write an essay instead. I did, and they ran it, though slightly edited. Though it was written in the aftermath of 9/11, I think it still makes some points worth remembering.

When I was a little boy, Chanukah was, hands down, my favorite holiday. There were presents for eight days, which made me the envy of my Christian friends. There was the excitement of adding one more candle to the menorah each night, till finally every space was filled. And there was the excitement of the story itself, with the heroic Jews beating back the wicked Syrians. My father made me a silver-painted wooden sword to swing in a Sunday-school pageant.

Some years went by. In college, as part of my training as a historian (a good background for a writer, as it luckily turned out—not nearly so good for anything else), I studied the Hellenistic age. After the wars of Alexander the Great's successors convulsed the Balkans and the Near East for more than a generation, three main kingdoms formed in what had been Alexander's empire: the Antigonids in Macedonia; the Ptolemies in Egypt; and the Seleucids in Asia Minor, Syria, Mesopotamia, and, depending on how successful they were at any given moment, various points east.

Antiochus IV (175-164 BCE), the villain of the Chanukah story, was a Seleucid.

What did he think he was doing when he tried to suppress Jewish worship in Palestine? What did the Jews seem like to him? Why did he think they would obey?

Since Alexander's time, a century and a half before, the Seleucids, and, to a lesser degree, the Ptolemies had worked to reshape the culture of the Near East along Greek lines. Greek settlers poured into the area. Greek became the language of administration and culture. Armenians, Phoenicians, Cilicians, Syrians, Babylonians, Egyptians—yes, and Jews—who wanted to get ahead in this new, complex, amazingly cosmopolitan society learned Greek. They went to the theater and watched Greek tragedies and comedies. They wore Greek-style clothes. When they went to the gymnasium to exercise, they did as the Greeks did and discarded those clothes. All of them.

Antiochus was, at that time, the leading representative in that region of what we would have to call Western civilization: of Homer and Hesiod; of Aeschylus, Sophocles, and Euripides; of Socrates, Plato, and Aristotle; of Herodotus and Thucydides; of Pericles and Alexander. The Phoenicians who learned Greek, shaved their beards, and exercised naked in the gymnasium were not far removed from modern business-suited Japanese salarymen who drink scotch and play golf for relaxation. They were hellenized, as so much of the world today is Westernized.

And what of the Jews?

Throughout the Hellenistic age, the Jews and the Greeks didn't understand each other. Neither side tried very hard, either. Alexander went out of his way to talk to the philosophers of India. He never visited Jerusalem, which to him had to seem a backwoods hill fortress of no particular importance.

By Antiochus' time, there was a faction of the Jews living in Palestine that favored assimilation to the Greek way of life, and another faction that resisted. The crisis was precipitated when Antiochus, seeking to unify his own kingdom, tried to institute a single religion within his borders. Most of the kingdom conformed.

In Palestine, he forbade circumcision (which the Greeks thought a repugnant mutilation, viewing it much as the modern West views what is called female circumcision), sacrifices, and the observance of the sabbath, and he installed a statue of Baal in the Temple in Jerusalem. Perhaps this was Baal-Shamen, a Syrian god; perhaps it was Zeus Olympios, with whom Antiochus was closely identified. (Antiochus styled himself Theos Epiphanes—the god made manifest—another vivid illustration of the mental gap between the Greeks, for whom the boundary between the human and the divine was shifting, evanescent, uncertain, and the Jews, for whom it was anything but.)

The Hellenizers in Jerusalem reverenced this image. But rebellion followed, headed by Mattathias and his sons, who fled to the hills and began a guerrilla war. Their first encounter with Antiochus' soldiers was on the sabbath. They let themselves be killed rather than break God's law and defend themselves. After that disaster, Mattathias ordered that they fight, no matter what day it happened to be.

But I want to look at that first massacre. Yes, Antiochus' Greeks won themselves an easy victory. Still, what must they have thought as they slaughtered men who would not resist, who placed obedience to what they saw as God's law above saving their own lives? I have no doubt many of the soldiers laughed as they wielded spear and sword.

But were some of them troubled at the terrible, unyielding purpose those Jews displayed, clinging to their beliefs to death and beyond? Could that spectacle have been as dismaying to them as the spectacle of the fighters in Kunduz who would sooner kill themselves and their comrades than surrender? They grasped the minds of their foes no more than we grasp the minds of ours.

Later in the fight between Jews and Greeks, Judah Maccabee faced an army of Antiochus' under the command of a certain Seron at a place called Beth-horon. Judah's men asked how they could hope to beat the Greeks, who badly outnumbered them. He answered, "It is easy for many to be put in trouble at the hands of a few, and there is no difference in the sight of Heaven between saving the many and the few. Victory in battle lies not in the size of a host, but comes from the strength of Heaven. Those in the host come against us with insolence and lawlessness, to kill us and our wives and children and to plunder us. We fight for our souls and our laws, and He will shatter them before our eyes. Do not fear them." They fought—and they won.

Set in the mouth of a hero twenty-one centuries dead, this sounds noble and inspiring. Set it in a modern man's mouth . . . and one has to wonder who in today's world would be likely to say such a thing.

The truth—and it's a truth the victory of the Maccabees obscures for us—is that my own ancestors in Palestine were as much the Other to the dominant culture of the day, a culture in so many ways ancestral to my own, as the terrorists and suicide bombers of the Muslim world are to inhabitants of today's West. The Greeks in the Hellenistic age were largely blind to Jewish culture and to Jewish literature, which was written in a language they did not know, in an alphabet they could not read, and which ran the wrong way on the page. Can we doubt that most of us in the West are similarly blind to Islam today?

To the Greeks, the Jews' fundamental flaw was their stubborn adherence to their own customs, their refusal to be assimilated into the broader currents of the Hellenistic world, and their even more obstinate devotion to what they believed God expected of them. The Greeks perceived this as fear and hatred of foreigners. True, it was not absolute. By the time of the Jewish revolt from which the story of Chanukah comes, the Old Testament had been translated into Greek for Jews no longer familiar with Hebrew and Aramaic, and there was, as we have seen, a hellenizing party even in Jerusalem. But what happened to the hellenizers after Judah Maccabee's victory? Should we look to the fate of Westernized intellectuals in Teheran after the Ayatollah supplanted the Shah? I would not be surprised.

Absolute or not, however, the rejection of most of Hellenistic culture by most of the Jews was their chief characteristic in Greek eyes. Judaizing elements did not—could not—enter the wider culture of the ancient world until several centuries after the Maccabees defeated Antiochus. Christianity, Judaism's hardy offshoot, flourished and triumphed not least because it proved more receptive to Hellenistic ways of thought than did its parent religion, and made Jewish modes of thought and belief more palatable to what we might call the mass audience of the Roman Empire.

We view the past through the lens of the present. We can't help that; it's the only lens we have. Twenty years ago, the Cold War seemed eternal. Now we know better. Now we have new—and different—problems. But knowledge of the past can also broaden our perspective of the present. I am not always comfortable remembering that Mattathias and Judah Maccabee and their followers were religious zealots along with being freedom fighters, and that Antiochus, like them, was also doing what he thought right and proper. But these truths, no matter how unpalatable, remind me that life, then and now, is not so simple as it seems in stories, and that no man is a villain in his own eyes. And that, it seems to me, is something worth remembering.

UNDER ST. PETER'S

I mostly don't do secret histories, the kind of stories where, though everything works out the way we all remember, the forces creating the working are altogether different from and stranger than the ones we think we understand. I usually prefer to leave the forces and to change the result they produce—another way of saying I write a lot of alternate history. But usually isn't always, and, just as someone who mostly drinks scotch will take a knock of bourbon every once in a while, I did try my hand at one secret history. Here it is. Go ahead, prove me wrong—I dare you.

Incense in the air, even down here behind the doors. Frankincense and myrrh, the scents he remembered from days gone by, days when he could face the sun. Somber Latin chants. He recognized them even now, though the chanters didn't pronounce Latin the way the legionaries had back in those bright days.

And the hunger. Always the hunger.

Would he finally feed? It had been a long time, such a very long time. He could hardly remember the last time he'd had to wait so long.

He wouldn't die of starvation. He couldn't die of starvation. His laughter sent wild echoes chasing one another in his chamber. No, he couldn't very well die, not when he was already dead. But he could wish himself extinguished. He could, and he did, every waking moment— and every moment, from now to forever or the sun's next kiss, *was* a waking moment.

Much good wishing did him.

He waited, and he remembered. What else did he have to do? Nothing. *They* made sure of it. His memory since his death and resurrection was perfect. He could bring back any day, any instant, with absolute clarity, absolute accuracy.

Much good that did him, too.

He preferred recalling the days before, the days when he was only a man. (Was he ever *only* a man? He knew how many would say no. Maybe they were right, but he remembered himself as man and man alone. But his memories of those days blurred and shifted—as a man's would—so he might have been wrong. Maybe he was something else, something different, right from the start.)

He'd packed a lot into thirty-odd years. Refugee, carpenter, reformer, rebel . . . convict. He could still hear the thud of the hammer that drove in the spikes. He could still hear his own screams as those spikes pierced him. He'd never thought, down deep in his heart, that it would come to that—which only just went to show how much he knew.

He'd never thought, down deep in his heart, that it would come to *this*, either. Which, again, just went to show how much he knew.

If he were everything people said he was, would he have let it come to this? He could examine that portion of his—not of his life, no, but of his existence, with the perfect recall so very distant from mortality. He could examine it, and he had, time and again. Try as he would, he couldn't see anything he might have done differently.

And even if he did see something like that, it was much too late to matter now.

"Habemus papam!"

When you heard the Latin acclamation, when you knew it was for you . . . Was there any feeling to match that, any in all the world? People said a new Orthodox Patriarch once fell over dead with joy at learning he was chosen. That had never happened on this trunk of the tree that split in 1054, but seeing how it might wasn't hard. A lifetime of hopes, of dreams, of work, of prayer, of patience . . . and then, at last, you had to try to fill the Fisherman's sandals.

They will remember me forever, was the first thought that went through his mind. For a man who, by the nature of his office, had better not have children, it was the only kind of immortality he would ever get. A cardinal could run things behind the scenes for years, could be the greatest power in the oldest continually functioning institution in the world—and, five minutes after he was dead, even the scholars in the Curia would have trouble coming up with his name.

But once you heard *"Habemus papam!"* . . .

He would have to deal with Italians for the rest of his life. He would have to smell garlic for the rest of his life. Part of him had wanted to retire when his friend, his patron, passed at last: to go back north of the Alps, to rusticate.

That was only part of him, though. The rest . . . He *had* been running things behind the scenes for years. Getting his chance to come out and do it in the open, to be noted for it, to be noticed for it, was sweet. And his fellow cardinals hadn't waited long before they chose him, either. What greater honor was there than the approval of your own? More than anyone else, they understood what this meant. Some of them wanted it, too. Most of them wanted it, no doubt, but most of the ones who did also understood they had no chance of gaining it.

Coming out of the shadows, becoming the public face of the Church, wasn't easy for a man who'd spent so long in the background. But he'd shown what he could do when he was chosen to eulogize his predecessor. He wrote the farewell in his own tongue, then translated it into Italian. That wasn't the churchly *lingua franca* Latin had been, but still, no one who wasn't fluent in it could reasonably hope to occupy Peter's seat.

If he spoke slowly, if he showed Italian wasn't his native tongue— well, so what? It gave translators around the world the chance to stay up with him. And delivering the eulogy meant people around the world saw him and learned who he was. When the College of Cardinals convened to deliberate, that had to be in the back of some minds.

He wouldn't have a reign to match the one that had gone before, not unless he lived well past the century mark. But Achilles said glory mattered more than length of days. And John XXIII showed you didn't need a long reign to make your mark.

Vatican II cleared away centuries of deadwood from the Church. Even the Latin of the Mass went. Well, there was reason behind that. Who spoke Latin nowadays? This wasn't the Roman Empire any more, even if cardinals' vestments came straight out of Byzantine court regalia.

But change always spawned a cry for more change. Female priests? Married priests? Homosexuality? Contraception? Abortion? When? Ever? The world shouted for all those things. The world, though, was a weather vane, turning now this way, now that, changeable as the breeze. The Church was supposed to stand for what was *right* . . . whatever that turned out to be.

If changes come, they'll come because of me. If they don't, that will also be because of me, the new Holy Father thought. *Which way more than a billion people go depends on me.*

Why anyone would *want* a job like this made him scratch his head. That he wanted it himself, or that most of him did . . . was true, no matter how strange it seemed. So much to decide, to do. So little time.

A tavern in the late afternoon. They were all worried. Even the publican was worried; he hadn't looked for such a big crowd so late in the day. They were all eating and drinking and talking. They showed no signs of getting up and leaving. If they kept hanging around, he would have to light the lamps, and olive oil wasn't cheap.

But they kept digging their right hands into the bowl of chickpeas and mashed garlic he'd set out, and eating more bread, and calling for wine. One of them had already drunk himself into quite a state.

Looking back from down here, understanding why was easy. Hindsight was always easy. Foresight? They'd called it prophecy in those days. Had he had the gift? His human memory wasn't sure. But then, his human memory wasn't sure about a lot of things. That was what made trying to trace the different threads twisting through the fabric so eternally fascinating.

He wished he hadn't used that word, even to himself. He kept hoping it wasn't so. He'd been down here a long, long, *long* time, but not forever. He wouldn't stay down here forever, either. He couldn't.

Could he?

He was *so* hungry.

The tavern. He'd been looking back at the tavern again. He wasn't hungry then. He'd eaten his fill, and he'd drunk plenty of wine, wine red as blood.

What did wine taste like? He remembered it was sweet, and he remembered it could mount to your head . . . almost the way any food did these days. But the taste? The taste, now, was a memory of a memory of a memory—and thus so blurred, it was no memory at all. He'd lost the taste of wine, just as he'd lost the tastes of bread and chickpeas. Garlic, though, garlic he still knew.

He remembered the sensation of chewing, of reducing the resistive mass in his mouth—whatever it tasted like—to something that easily went down the throat. He almost smiled, there in the darkness. He hadn't needed to worry about *that* in a while.

Where was he? So easy to let your thoughts wander down here. What else did they have to do? Oh, yes. The tavern. The wine. The feel of the cup in his hands. The smell of the stuff wafting upwards, nearly as intoxicating as . . . But if his thoughts wandered there, they wouldn't come back. He was *so* hungry.

The tavern, then. The wine. The cup. The last cup. He remembered saying, "And I tell you, I won't drink from the fruit of the vine any more till that day when I drink it anew with you in my father's kingdom."

They'd nodded. He wasn't sure how much attention they paid, or whether they even took him seriously. How long could anybody go without drinking wine? What would you use instead? Water? Milk? You were asking for a flux of the bowels if you did.

But he'd kept that promise. He'd kept it longer than he dreamt he would, longer than he dreamt he could. He was still keeping it now, after all these years.

Soon, though, soon, he would have something else to drink.

If you paid attention to the television, you would think he was the first Pope ever installed. His predecessor had had a long reign, so long that none of the reporters remembered the last succession. For them, it was as if nothing that came before this moment really happened. One innocent—an American, of course—even remarked, "The new Pope is named after a previous one."

He was not a mirthful man, but he had to laugh at that. What did the fool *think* the Roman numeral after his name stood for? He wasn't named after just one previous Pope. He was named after fifteen!

One of these days, he would have to try to figure out what to do about the United Sates. So many people there thought they could stay good Catholics while turning their backs on any teachings they didn't happen to like. If they did that, how were they any different from Protestants? How could he tell them they couldn't do that without turning them into Protestants? Well, he didn't have to decide right away, *Deo gratias.*

So much had happened, this first day of his new reign. If this wasn't enough to overwhelm a man, nothing ever would be. Pretty soon, he thought, he would get around to actually *being* Pope. Pretty soon, yes, but not quite yet.

As if to prove as much, a tubby little Italian—not even a priest but a deacon—came up to him and waited to be noticed. The new Pope had seen the fellow around for as long as he could remember. Actually, he didn't really remember *seeing* him around—the deacon was about as nondescript as any man ever born. But the odor of strong, garlicky sausages always clung to him.

When it became obvious the man wouldn't go away, the Pope sighed a small, discreet sigh. "What is it, Giuseppe?"

"Please to excuse me, Holy Father, but there's one more thing each new Keeper of the Keys has to do," the deacon said.

"Ah?" Now the Pope made a small, interested noise. "I thought I knew all the rituals." He was, in fact, sure he knew all the rituals—or he had been sure, till this moment.

But Deacon Giuseppe shook his head. He seemed most certain, and most self-assured. "No, sir. Only the Popes know—the Popes and the men of the Order of the Pipistrelle."

"The what?" The new Pope had also been sure he was acquainted with all the orders, religious and honorary and both commingled, in Vatican City.

"The Order of the Pipistrelle," Giuseppe repeated patiently. "We are small, and we are quiet, but we are the oldest order in this place. We go . . . back to the very beginning of things, close enough." Pride rang in his voice.

"Is that so?" The Pope carefully held his tone neutral. Any order with a foundation date the least bit uncertain claimed to be much older than anyone outside its ranks would have wanted to believe. Even so, he'd never heard of an order with pretensions like that. Back to the beginning of things? "I suppose you came here with Peter?"

"That's right, your Holiness. We handled his baggage." Deacon Giuseppe spoke altogether without irony. He either believed what he was saying or could have gone on the stage with his acting.

"Did my friend, my predecessor, do . . . whatever this is?" the Pope asked.

"Yes, sir, he did. And all the others before him. If you don't do this, you aren't really the Pope. You don't really understand what being the Pope means."

Freemasonry. We have a freemasonry of our own. Who would have thought that? Freemasonry, of course, wasn't nearly so old as its members claimed, either. But that was—or might be—beside the point. "All right," the Pope said. "This must be complete, whatever it is."

Deacon Giuseppe raised his right hand in what wasn't a formal salute but certainly suggested one. "*Grazie*, Holy Father. *Mille grazie*," he said. "I knew you were a . . . thorough man." He nodded, seeming pleased he'd found the right word. And it *was* the right word; the Pope also nodded, acknowledging its justice.

Deacon Giuseppe took his elbow and steered him down the long nave of St. Peter's, away from the Papal altar and toward the main entrance. Past the haloed statue of St. Peter and the altar of St. Jerome they went, past the Chapel of the Sacrament and, on the Pope's right, the tombs of Innocent VIII and Pius X.

Not far from the main entrance, a red porphyry disk was set into the floor, marking the spot where, in the Old St. Peter's that preceded Bernini's magnificent building, Charlemagne was crowned Roman Emperor. Now, to the Pope's surprise, crimson silk draperies surrounded the disk, discreetly walling it off from view.

Another surprise: "I've never seen these draperies before."

"They belong to the Order," Deacon Giuseppe said, as if that explained everything. To him, it must have. But he had to see it didn't explain everything to his companion, for he added, "We don't use them very often. Will you step through with me?"

The Pope did. Once inside the blood-red billowing silk, he got surprised yet again. "I didn't know that disk came up."

"You weren't supposed to, Holy Father," Deacon Giuseppe said. "You'd think we'd do this over in the Sacred Grotto. It would make more sense, what with the Popes' tombs there—even Peter's, they say. Maybe it was like that years and years ago, but it hasn't been for a long, long time. Here we do it, and here it'll stay. Amen." He crossed himself.

"There's . . . a stairway going down," the Pope said. How many more amazements did the Vatican hold?

"Yes. That's where we're going. You first, Holy Father," Giuseppe said. "Be careful. It's narrow, and there's no bannister."

Air. Fresh air. Even through doors closed and locked and warded against him, he sensed it. His nostrils twitched. He knew what fresh air meant, sure as a hungry dog knew a bell meant it was time to salivate. When he was a man, he'd lived out in the fresh air. He'd taken it for granted. He'd lived in it. And, much too soon, he'd died in it.

Crucifixion was a Roman punishment, not a Jewish one. Jews killed even animals as mercifully as they could. When they had to kill men, the sword or the axe got it over with fast. The Romans wanted criminals to suffer, and be seen to suffer. They thought that resulted in fewer criminals. The number of men they crucified made the argument seem dubious, but they didn't care.

As for the suffering . . . They were right about that. The pain was the worst thing he'd ever known. It unmanned him so that he cried out on the cross. Then he swooned, swooned so deeply the watching soldiers and people thought he was dead.

He dimly remembered them taking him down from the cross— pulling out the spikes that nailed him to it was a fresh torment. And one more followed it, for one of the Roman soldiers bit him then, hard enough to tear his flesh open but not hard enough, evidently, to force a sound past his dry throat and parched lips.

How the rest of the Romans laughed! That was the last purely human memory he had, of their mirth at their friend's savagery. When he woke to memory again, he was . . . changed.

No. There was one thing more. They'd called the biter Dacicus. At the time, it didn't mean anything to a man almost dead. But he never forgot it even though it was meaningless, so maybe—probably—the change in him had begun that soon. When he did think about it again, for a while he believed it was only a name.

Then he learned better. *Dacicus* meant *the Dacian*, the man from Dacia. Not one more human in ten thousand, these days, could tell you where Dacia lay—had lain. But its borders matched those of what they called Romania these days, or near enough. And people told stories about Romania. . . . He had no way to know how many of those stories were true. Some, like sliding under doors, surely weren't, or he would have. Considering what had happened to him, though, he had no reason to doubt others.

And now he smelled fresh air. Soon, very soon . . .

"How long has this been here?" the Pope asked. "I never dreamt anything like this lay under St. Peter's!" The stone spiral stairway certainly seemed ancient. Deacon Giuseppe lit it, however, not with a flickering olive-oil lamp but with a large, powerful flashlight that he pulled from one of the large, deep pockets of his black vestments.

"Your Holiness, as far as I know, it's been here since Peter's day," Giuseppe answered seriously. "I told you before: the Order of the Pipistrelle is in charge of what Peter brought in his baggage."

"And that was?" the Pope asked, a trifle impatiently.

"I don't want to talk about it now. You'll see soon enough. But I'm a keeper of the keys, too." Metal jingled as the deacon pulled a key ring from a pocket. The Pope stopped and looked back over his shoulder. Giuseppe obligingly shone the flashlight beam on the keys. They were as ordinary, as modern, as boring, as the flashlight itself. The Pope had hoped for massive, ancient ones, rusty or green with verdigris. No such luck.

At the bottom of the stairway, a short corridor led to a formidable steel door. The Pope's slippers scuffed through the dust of ages. Motes he kicked up danced in the flashlight beam. "Who last came here?" he asked in a low voice.

"Why, your blessed predecessor, your Holiness," Deacon Giuseppe said. "Oh, and mine, of course." He opened the door with the key, which worked smoothly. As he held it for the Pope, he went on, "This used to be wood—well, naturally. That's what they had in the old days. They replaced it after the last war. Better safe than sorry, you know."

"Safe from what? Sorry because of what?" As the Pope asked the question, the door swung behind the deacon and him with what sounded like a most definitive and final click. A large and fancy crucifix was mounted on the inner surface. Another such door, seemingly identical, lay a short distance ahead.

"With Peter's baggage, of course," Giuseppe answered.

"Will you stop playing games with me?" The Pope was a proud and touchy man.

"I'm not!" The deacon crossed himself again. "Before God, your Holiness, I'm not!" He seemed at least as touchy, and at least as proud, as the Pope himself. And then, out of the same pocket from which he'd taken the flashlight, he produced a long, phallic chunk of sausage and bit off a good-sized chunk. The odors of pepper and garlic assailed the Pope's nostrils.

And the incongruity assailed his strong sense of fitness even more. He knocked the sausage out of Giuseppe's hand and into the dust. "Stop that!" he cried.

To his amazement, the Italian picked up the sausage, brushed off most of whatever clung to it, and went on eating. The Pope's gorge rose. "Meaning no disrespect, Holy Father," Giuseppe mumbled with his mouth full, "but I need this. It's part of the ritual. God will strike me dead if I lie."

Not, *May God strike me dead if I lie.* The deacon said, *God will strike me dead.* The Pope, relentlessly precise, noted the distinction. He pointed to the door ahead. "What is on the other side of that?" he asked, a sudden and startling quaver in his voice.

"An empty chamber," Deacon Giuseppe replied.

"And beyond that? Something, I hope."

"Think on the Last Supper, Holy Father," the deacon answered, which didn't help.

He thought of his last supper, which didn't help. Not now, not with his raging hunger. It was too long ago. They were out there. He could hear them out there, talking in that language that wasn't Latin but sounded a little like it. He could see the dancing light under the door. Any light at all stung his eyes, but he didn't mind. And he could smell them. Man's flesh was the most delicious odor in the world, but when he smelled it up close it was always mingled with the other smell, the hateful smell.

His keepers knew their business, all right. Even without garlic, the cross on the farthest door would have held him captive here—*had* held him captive here. He'd tasted the irony of that, times uncounted.

"This is my blood," he'd said. "This is my flesh." Irony there, too. Oh, yes. Now—soon—he hoped to taste something sweeter than irony.

Where would he have been without Dacicus? Not here—he was sure of that, anyhow. He supposed his body would have stayed in the tomb where they laid it, and his spirit would have soared up to the heavens where it belonged. Did he even have a spirit any more? Or was he all body, all hunger, all appetite? He didn't know. He didn't much care, either. It had been too long.

Dacicus must have been new when he bit him, new or stubborn in believing he remained a man. After being bitten, rolling away the stone was easy. Going about with his friends was easy, too—for a little while. But then the sun began to pain him, and then the hunger began. Taking refuge in the daytime began to feel natural. So did slaking the hunger . . . when he could.

Soon now. Soon!

"Why the Last Supper?" the Pope demanded.

"Because we reenact it—in a manner of speaking—down here," Deacon Giuseppe replied. "This is the mystery of the Order of the Pipistrelle. Even the Orthodox, even the Copts, would be jealous if they knew. They have relics of the Son. We have . . . the Son."

The Pope stared at him. "Our Lord's body lies here?" he whispered hoarsely. "His body? He was not taken up as we preach? He was—a man?" Was *that* the mystery at—or rather, here below—the heart of the Church? The mystery being that there was no mystery, that since the days of the Roman Empire prelates had lived a lie?

His stern faith stumbled. No, his friend, his predecessor, would never have told him about this. It would have been too cruel.

But the little round sausage-munching deacon shook his head. "It's not so simple, your Holiness. I'll show you."

He had another key on the ring. He used it to unlock the last door, and he shone the flashlight into the chamber beyond.

Light! A spear of light! It stabbed into his eyes, stabbed straight through his eyes and into his brain! How long had he gone without? As long as he'd gone without food. But sustenance he cherished, he craved, he yearned for. Light was the pain that accompanied it, the pain he couldn't avoid or evade.

He got used to it, moment by agonizing moment. So long here in the silent dark, he had to remember how to see. Yes, there was the black-robed one, the untouchable, inedible one, the stinker, who carried his light-thrower like a sword. What had happened to torches and oil lamps? Like the last several of his predecessors, this black-robe had one of these unnatural things instead.

Well, I am an unnatural thing myself these days, he thought, and his lips skinned back from his teeth in a smile both wryly amused and hungry, so very hungry.

Now the Pope crossed himself, violently. "Who is this?" he gasped. "What . . . is this?"

But even as he gasped, he found himself fearing he knew the answer. The short, scrawny young man impaled on the flashlight beam looked alarmingly like so many Byzantine images of the Second Person of the Trinity: shaggy dark brown hair and beard, long oval face, long nose. The wounds to his hands and feet, and the one in his side, looked fresh, even if they were bloodless. And there was another wound, a small one, on his neck. None of the art showed that one; none of the texts spoke of it. Seeing it made the Pope think of films he'd watched as a boy. And when he did . . .

His hand shaped the sign of the cross once more. It had no effect on the young-looking man who stood there blinking. He hadn't thought it would, not really. "No!" he said. "It cannot be! It must not be!"

He noticed one thing more. Even when Deacon Giuseppe shone the flashlight full in the young-looking man's face, the pupils did not contract. Did not . . . Could not? With each passing second, it seemed more likely.

Deacon Giuseppe's somber nod told him it wasn't just likely—it was true. "Well, Holy Father, now you know," said the Deacon from the Order of the Pipistrelle. "Behold the Son of Man. Behold the Resurrection. Behold the greatest secret of the Church."

"But . . . why? How?" Not even the Pope, as organized and coherent as any man now living, could speak clearly in the presence of—that.

"Once—that—happened to him, he couldn't stand the sun after a while." Deacon Giuseppe told the tale as if it had been told many times before. And so, no doubt, it had. "When Peter came to Rome, he came, too, in the saint's baggage—under the sign of the cross, of course, to make sure nothing . . . untoward happened. He's been here ever since. We keep him. We take care of him."

"Great God!" The Pope tried to make sense of his whirling thoughts. "No wonder you told me to think of the Last Supper." He forced some iron into his spine. A long-dead *Feldwebel* who'd drilled him during the last round of global madness would have been proud of how well his lessons stuck. "All right. I've seen him. God help me, I have. Take me up to the light again."

"Not quite yet, your Holiness," the deacon replied. "We finish the ritual first."

"Eh?"

"We finish the ritual," Deacon Giuseppe repeated with sad patience. "Seeing him does not suffice. It is his first supper in a very long time, your predecessor being so young when he was chosen. Remember the text: your blood is his wine, your flesh his bread."

He said something else, in a language that wasn't Italian. The Pope, a formidable scholar, recognized it as Aramaic. He even understood it: "Supper's ready!"

The last meal had been juicier. That was his first thought. But he wasn't complaining, not after so long. He drank and drank: his own communion with the world of the living. He would have drunk the life right out of him if not for the black-robed one.

"Be careful!" that one urged, still speaking the only language he really knew well. "Remember what happened time before last!"

He remembered. He'd got greedy. He'd drunk too much. The man died not long after coming down here to meet him. Then he'd fed again—twice in such a little while! They didn't let him do anything like that the next time, however much he wanted to. And that one lasted and lasted—lasted so long, he began to fear he'd made the man into one like himself.

He hadn't done that very often. He wondered whether Dacicus intended to do that with him—to him. He never had the chance to ask. Did Dacicus still wander the world, not alive any more but still quick? One of these centuries, if Dacicus did, they might meet again. You never could tell.

When he didn't let go fast enough, the black-robed one breathed full in his face. That horrible, poisonous stink made him back away in a hurry.

He hadn't got enough. It could never be enough, not if he drank the world dry. But it was ever so much better than nothing. Before he fed, he was *empty*. He couldn't end, barring stake, sunlight, or perhaps a surfeit of garlic, but he could wish he would. He could—and he had.

No more. Fresh vitality flowed through him. He wasn't happy—he didn't think he could be happy—but he felt as lively as a dead thing could.

"My God!" the new Pope said, not in Aramaic, not in Latin, not even in Italian. His hand went to the wound on his neck. The bleeding had already stopped. He shuddered. He didn't know what he'd expected when Deacon Giuseppe took him down below St. Peter's, but not this. Never this.

"Are you all right, your Holiness?" Real concern rode the deacon's voice.

"I—think so." And the Pope had to think about it before he answered, too.

"Good." Deacon Giuseppe held out a hand. Automatically, the Pope clasped it, and, in so doing, felt how cold his own flesh had gone. The round little nondescript Italian went on, "Can't let him have too much. We did that not so long ago, and it didn't work out well."

The new Pope understood him altogether too well. Then he

touched the wound again, a fresh horror filling him. Yes, he remembered the films too well. "Am I going to turn into . . . one of those?" He pointed toward the central figure of his faith, who was licking blood off his lips with a tongue that seemed longer and more prehensile than a mere man's had any business being.

"We don't think so," Giuseppe said matter-of-factly. "Just to be sure, though, the papal undertaker drives a thin ash spike through the heart after each passing. We don't talk about that to the press. One of the traditions of the Order of the Pipistrelle is that when the sixth ecumenical council anathematized Pope Honorius, back thirteen hundred years ago, it wasn't for his doctrine, but because. . . ."

"Is . . . Honorius out there, too? Or under here somewhere?"

"No. He was dealt with a long time ago." Deacon Giuseppe made pounding motions.

"I see." The Pope wondered if he could talk to . . . talk to the Son of God. *Or the son of someone, anyhow.* Did he have Aramaic enough for that? Or possibly Hebrew? *How the Rabbi of Rome would laugh—or cry—if he knew!* "Does every Pope do this? Endure this?"

"Every single one," Giuseppe said proudly. "What better way to connect to the beginning of things? Here *is* the beginning of things. He *was* risen, you know, Holy Father. How much does why really matter?"

For a lot of the world, *why* would matter enormously. The Muslims . . . The Protestants . . . The Orthodox . . . His head began to hurt, although the wound didn't. Maybe talking with . . . him wasn't such a good idea after all. *How much do I really want to know?*

"When we go back up, I have a lot of praying to do," the Pope said. Would all the prayer in the world free him from the feel of teeth in his throat? And what could he tell his confessor? The truth? The priest would think he'd gone mad—or, worse, wouldn't think so and would start the scandal. A lie? But wasn't inadequate confession of sin a sin in and of itself? The headache got worse.

Deacon Giuseppe might have read his thoughts. "You have a dispensation against speaking of this, your Holiness. It dates from the fourth century, and it may be the oldest document in the Vatican Library. It's not like the Donation of Constantine, either—there's no doubt it's genuine."

"Deo gratias!" the Pope said again.

"Shall we go, then?" the deacon asked.

"One moment." The Pope flogged his memory and found enough Aramaic for the question he had to ask: *"Are* you the Son of God?"

The sharp-toothed mouth twisted in a—reminiscent?—smile. "You say it," came the reply.

Well, he told Pilate the same thing, even if the question was a bit different, the Pope thought as he left the little chamber and Deacon Giuseppe meticulously closed and locked doors behind them. And, when the Pope was on the stairs going back up to the warmth and blessed light of St. Peter's, one more question occurred to him. How many Popes had heard that same answer?

How many of them had asked that same question? He'd heard it in Aramaic, in Greek, in Latin, and in the language Latin had turned into. He always said the same thing, and he always said it in Aramaic.

"You say it," he murmured to himself, there alone in the comfortable darkness again. Was he really? How could he know? But if they thought he was, then he was—for them. Wasn't that the only thing that counted?

That Roman had washed his hands of finding absolute truth. He was a brute, but not a stupid brute.

And this new one was old, and likely wouldn't last long. Pretty soon, he would feed again. And if he had to try to answer that question one more time afterwards . . . then he did, that was all.

IT'S THE END OF THE WORLD AS WE KNOW IT, AND WE FEEL FINE

My agent and friend, Russ Galen, sent me a book about urban wildlife: the creatures even city folk are likely to see, such as foxes and coyotes and crows and mockingbirds. That's where I first found out about Belyaev's experiments with foxes. By pure happenstance, there was a *National Geographic* article a couple of months later on domestication. That went into more detail about Belyaev and his work, and about its genetic basis. Between the two of them, they gave me the idea for this story.

It's the future. Call it a few hundred years from now. Close enough. Maybe a little more, maybe a little less. Just how much matters less than you think. That's kinda the point, y'know?

What am I talking about? Hang on. You'll see.

Here's Willie. He's lying on the grass in his back yard, playing with his pet fox. The fox's name is Joe. If the fox had a last name, it would be Belyaev. But it doesn't, so don't worry about that. Willie has a last name, one he hardly remembers. You don't need to worry about that, either. Willie sure doesn't.

Willie sits up. He pulls a red, rubbery ball, just the right size, out of a pocket on his shorts. He tosses it into the air. Joe sits there watching, panting, making little excited yappy noises. Willie tosses the ball up again. Joe stares, his dark eyes shining.

Willie throws the ball halfway down the yard. It bounces a couple of times on the grass, then rolls almost to the flower bed at the far end. Joe's after it like a shot. He grabs it in his mouth and shakes his head from side to side as if he's killing it. One of his ears is floppy. It flaps as he shakes the ball.

Then, head high, bushy tail proud, Joe trots back to Willie and drops the ball in front of him. He can't yell *Do it again!*, but every line of his plump little body says it for him. Willie picks up the ball. He doesn't care about fox spit, or much of anything else. I mean, who does, these days?

Away goes the ball. Away goes Joe, fast as he can. Back he comes, ball in mouth. Drop. Wait.

This time, Willie gets cute. He makes the throwing motion, but he hangs on to the ball. Joe's faked out of his shoes, only he isn't wearing any (neither is Willie). The fox bounds across the lawn after . . . nothing. When he gets to about where the ball oughta be, he looks every which way at once, trying to figure out how the hell it went and disappeared on him.

Willie falls out laughing. It's the funniest thing that's happened to him since, well, the last funny thing that happened to him. Which wasn't very long ago, in case you want to know.

When Joe's just about to go, like, totally batshit, Willie calls, "Here it is, silly!" He throws the ball for real. Joe captures it and kills it extra good, as if to pay it back for fooling him. Then he brings it over to Willie. He's ready for more. You bet he is.

They kind of look alike, Willie and Joe. Yeah, and your Aunt Margaret looks like her basset hound, too, after twelve years together. Not like that, though. Like this.

We'll do Joe first. You think fox, you think sharp-nosed chicken thief and bunny cruncher. Joe isn't like that. Sure, his umpty-ump great-grandparents were, but so what? Your Aunt Margaret's basset hound's umpty-ump great-grandparents pulled down moose in the snowy forests right after the glaciers melted. Between them and him, there've been some changes made. And there've been some changes made from those chicken swipers to Joe.

He's plump. I already said that. Partly it's on account of Willie feeds him too much, but only partly. Plump is cute, and cute is what his breeders were after. His floppy ear is also cute. So is a tail that perks up when he sees people. He *likes* people. Since the days of his umpty-umps, liking people's been bred into him.

His fur is longer and thicker and fluffier than your wild woods-running fox's (yes, there still are wild woodsrunners, though not right around here). He has white patches all over, almost like a calico cat. His muzzle is maybe half as long as umpty-ump grandpa's, and quite a bit thicker. His teeth are scaled down, too. They don't have to work as hard as teeth did in the old days.

He's *cute.* I already said that before, too. I know. But he is. I mean, he's *really* cute.

And so is Willie. If you want to get mean about it, Willie looks kind of elfy-welfy. Being mean is *such* an old-time thing, though. He's got big eyes, a snub nose, and features that look as if you left 'em out in the sun a skosh—only a skosh, mind you—too long. Purely by coincidence, he has red hair, close to the color of Joe's. Not even slightly by coincidence, he has a couple of white streaks running through that red hair. Oh, yeah—he's on the plump side, too.

Cute. For sure. USDA prime cute, if you want to know the truth. Not that there's a USDA any more, but you get my drift.

Willie keeps throwing the ball. Joe keeps fetching it. Finally he just wears out, poor little guy. He brings the ball back one last time, drops it out of his mouth, and flops down on the grass, totally beat. He pants and pants, tongue hanging way, way out.

Willie pets him. Joe's tail thumps up and down. He rolls on his back and sticks all four legs in the air. Willie rubs his tummy. Joe wiggles like jello. He doesn't just dig it. He digs it bigtime.

So does Willie. Willie digs everything he does bigtime. If you don't, why do it to begin with?

Here. Wait. I'll show you. Willie waves his hand. Out of nowhere, music starts to play. No, don't ask me how. It's the future. They can do stuff like that stuff here. Take a look at Willie. Is he digging it, or what?

Remember how once, just once, you scored the best dope in the world? Remember how you smoked till your mouth and your throat were all sandpaper and your lungs thought you'd gone down on a fireplace? Remember how you put on your headphones—took three tries, didn't it?—and cranked *Dark Side of the Moon* or "The Ride of the Valkyries" or whatever most got you off all the way up to *eleven*, man? Remember what it was like?

Of course you don't remember. You were wasted, you fool. But you sorta remember how awesome it was, right?

Okay. Willie's like that all the time, only more so. And everybody else in the future is like that, too. And those people don't need to pay big bucks to keep Mexican druglords in supermodels and swimming pools and RPGs, either. They don't need the dope. They're just like that. All the time. Naturally.

How? We're getting there. Trust me.

Belyaev! I just met a fox named Belyaev!
Old Belyaev had a farm, ee-eye-ee-eye-oh!

As a matter of fact, Dmitri Belyaev did. A fox farm. Outside of Novosibirsk, of all places. Even in the future that holds Willie and Joe, Novosibirsk is nowhere squared. Nowhere cubed, even. In the middle of what they called the twentieth century, Novosibirsk was nowhere cubed *and* behind the Iron Curtain.

Belyaev didn't care. Or if he did care, he couldn't do anything about it, which amounts to the same thing. He was trying to find out how people way back when turned wolves into dogs and the aurochs into Elsie the Borden cow and . . . well, and like that.

So he used foxes.

Foxes are—duh!—wild. Or they were when Belyaev started messing with them, anyhow. They don't like people. They're scared of people. A lot of evolution over a lot of years has made sure of that.

But some foxes don't like people less than others. Some foxes are less scared of people than others. Belyaev took the least unfriendly foxes he could find and bred them to one another. Then he did the same thing with the next generation. And the one after that. And the one after that, and the one . . .

Foxes have litters every year. It's a long-term experiment, yeah, but it's not like domesticating sequoias.

Or even people. We'll get there, too. We really will.

You can do stuff like that. Belyaev did it for science. Way back when, Ugh and Mrong and Gronk had no idea they were doing it. They'd never heard of science. They did it anyway. And it worked. If it didn't work, no Pluto. No Foghorn Leghorn. No Elsie, either, or Milky White if you're into musicals, or even Mr. Farnsworth, come to that.

It worked for Belyaev, too. It worked faster than he ever figured it would. By the fourth generation, he had foxes that wagged their tails when people came up. They whimpered for attention. They let people hold them. Hey, they *wanted* people to hold them.

They started looking different, too. Some of them had floppy ears. Some had white patches in their fur. Their tails curled up instead of hanging low. Every so often, some were born with shorter bones or fewer bones in their tails. They got shorter, blunter muzzles. They were turning, yes, cute.

How come? Well, changes in behavior, like, go with changes in biology. Hormones run growth and growth patterns. Hormones run aggression, too. Belyaev's tame foxes had lower stress-hormone levels in their blood. They had more serotonin—the big calmer—in their foxy brains. They were *mellow*, man.

Hormones run growth. And what runs hormones? Right the first time—genes.

Stay tuned. We'll be back.

Willie's taking Joe for a walk. Other people are out and about, too, walking their dogs and foxes and potbellied porkers and what have you. No, nobody's out walking her cat. This is the future, sure. I know. It's not Never-Never Land, though.

Joe says hi to other foxes about how you'd expect. He sniffs 'em here and there to see how they smell interesting and where they smell interesting. He's been fixed, so he doesn't try to hump the foxy female foxes he meets, but he gives 'em an olfactory once-over, all right. He doesn't remember why they smell so good, but he knows they do.

Dogs are a different story. Joe doesn't want much to do with dogs. Once upon a time, dogs were wolves. Something way down deep inside Joe remembers that, too. So does something deep inside the dogs. A lot of them, even ones no bigger than Joe is, think they're supposed to have him for a snack.

It doesn't happen. Willie doesn't let it happen. Neither do the other people. They joke about it, and smile, and laugh, and pat one another on the back or on the arm or on the head. They all kinda look like Willie's cousins. They're short-featured. They're smooth-featured. They're plumpish—not fat, but for sure plumpish. They have streaks and patches of white in their hair.

Dogs and foxes are nothing for them to get their bowels in an uproar about. It's the future. People don't sweat the small stuff. People don't hardly sweat the big stuff, either. What's the point? Ain't no point.

Well, ain't no point unless maybe you're Fritz. Fritz lives down the street from Willie. He's kind of funny-looking. People talk about it all the time, only not where he can hear them. His nose is a little too long and a little too sharp. His chin sticks out a little too much. He looks more like you and me than he's got any business doing, is what I'm saying.

He acts more like you and me than he's got any business doing, too. He's loud. He's brash. He's quarrelsome—he gets into fights, and this at a time and in a place where nobody, and I mean nobody, gets into fights. He has not one but two big, mean dogs. He only keeps them on the leash when he absolutely has to. Otherwise, he lets them run around loose and scare all the other pets in the neighborhood.

They scare the bejesus out of Joe. They would have done worse than that to him one time if he hadn't run like blazes back to his own house. They chased him as far as they could, baying and growling and making like the wolves their umpty-greats were way back when.

They're on the leash now, though. Fritz got into trouble not too long ago. He's walking soft right now. He's trying not to give the mostly automated Powers That Be any more excuse to come down on him. He may be funny-looking, Fritz, but he isn't dumb. He isn't bad, either, not really. He's just . . . different.

He's different the same way his dogs are different, only more so. It's no wonder he has dogs like that, is it? Like draws like, sure as hell.

But he's on his best behavior right now. Joe kinda sits behind Willie's heel, just in case, but Fritz doesn't let his dogs—their names are Otto and Ilse—make any mischief. He smiles at Willie. Even his smile seems odd. His teeth are too big and too sharp, and it looks as though he's got too many of them even if he doesn't.

"How's it goin', Willie?" he rumbles. His voice sounds deeper than it ought to, too.

"It's okay," Willie answers. When is it not okay? Well, it's not so real okay when he has to talk with Fritz, but he can see telling Fritz as much isn't the smartest thing he could do.

"Good. That's good." Fritz on his best behavior is almost harder to take than Fritz being Fritz. You can see the real him peeking out from behind the mask he puts on. He tries to act like everybody else, and the trying shows, and so does the acting.

But Willie is a friendly soul. Not many people these days aren't friendly souls. People like people. People are supposed to like people, and most of them can hardly help liking people most of the time. People are like that. They can't help being like that. So, in spite of seeing the mask, Willie goes, "What's up with you, Fritz?"

"Well, I'll tell you, man," Fritz says. "I've got this chance to bring in some serious cash, only I need me a little front money to help get things off the ground, know what I mean? How are you fixed these days?"

"I'm fine," Willie says, which is true enough. In this day and age, you really have to work at it not to be fine. Some people manage, of course. They may not work quite the same as they did way back when, but nobody's come up with a cure for human stupidity yet.

Take a look at Fritz, for instance. Although with Fritz, like I said before, it isn't exactly stupidity. Fritz just . . . doesn't quite belong where he's at. If he were selling you aluminum siding or something, chances are you'd like him fine. Which is a measure of your damnation, is what it is. And, considering that Fritz is where he's at, it's a measure of his damnation, too.

If he were selling you aluminum siding, you can bet it'd fade and blister in the hot sun. He'd promise you it was top grade, and he'd be long gone, promising other people other things, by the time you found out he was full of shit. The warranty he gave you wouldn't be worth the paper it was printed on, either. Surprise!

So he's sizing Willie up now. He's trying to look like he's being all friendly and everything, but he's sizing him up, all right. So much for best behavior. Sometimes you just can't help yourself, not if you're Fritz. "Listen, man," he says, "with your money and my know-how, we could do all right together, y'know?"

"Maybe," Willie says. He eyes Fritz the same way Joe eyes Otto and Ilse. Joe might like to be friends with them. Only he wonders whether he'll get eaten if he tries. Willie kinda wonders that about Fritz, too. But only kinda. Joe may worry about dogs, but he's fine with people. And so is Willie. People are fine with one another. Most people are, anyhow.

Hey, Fritz is fine with Willie—as long as Willie does what Fritz wants. "Why don't you come back to my place?" he says? "We can talk about it some more there." *I can talk you around there* are the words behind the words.

Willie doesn't hear the words behind the words. Willie is a trusting soul, like darn near everybody else in the future. He's not stupid, either, not exactly. But he's different from people in the old days. So is everybody else in the future. He smiles and goes, "Okey-doke."

Yeah, everybody in the future is different from the way people were back in the old days. Only some are less different than others. Fritz, for instance. He isn't nearly different enough. If he were, his answering smile couldn't have so much barracuda in it. "Come on, then," he says.

"Willie, *no*," a Voice says out of the air. Willie can stop Joe from misbehaving when he talks a certain way. The Voice stops him just like that. Then it goes on, "Fritz, you are sanctioned. Again. Go home. Now. By yourself, except for your dogs."

Fritz's heavy-featured face falls. "Aw, I didn't mean anything by it," he says. "Swear I didn't." He shouldn't be able to protest even that much, but he does.

"Bullshit." The Voice may be automated, but that doesn't mean it came to town on a turnip truck. "The sanction will go up because it's bullshit, too. Go home, I told you. With your dogs. Without Willie. Get moving right this minute, or I'll see what else I can tack on."

Fritz goes. All the other choices are worse. If looks could kill, Willie'd be lying there dead on the sidewalk. So would Joe. And so, especially, would the Voice. It isn't what you'd call corporeal, but Fritz doesn't care.

"I don't think he meant anything bad by it," Willie tells the Voice. It doesn't sigh. It doesn't sound pleased, either. It's not designed that way. It just says, "I know you don't, Willie. That's why I'm here. Nothing's gonna harm you, not while I'm around. And I am."

Not quite *I am that I am*. Close enough for government work. Oh, wait. This is the future. No government, or not hardly, anyway. Willie and Joe go on with their walk. They're happy. Hey, what else are they gonna be?

Genes. It's all in the genes. Once upon a time, a comic with deciduous top cover complained, "They say going bald is in your genes. I *got* hair in my jeans. It's hair on my head I want!"

Usually, what they say is a crock of crap. Not this time. The difference between the hair apparent and the hair presumptive *is* in our genes.

So are lots of other things.

Dmitri Belyaev bred for tame foxes. A long, long time ago, Ugh bred for tame wolves, even though he might not have realized that was what he was doing. Belyaev—and Ugh—got other things, too. They got short tails and floppy ears and white patches of fur and short muzzles and the like. They got them . . . ? Let's hear it, people!

That's right! In the genes.

One of the places they particularly got them was in a DNA sequence near a gene labeled *WBSCR17*. This stretch of DNA shows a lot of differences between wolves and dogs, where most parts of the genome don't.

People have this *WBSCR17* gene, too. Back in the day, when something with it went wrong, the people it went wrong in were born with a genetic disease called Williams-Beuren syndrome. They looked kind of, well, elfy-welfy. The bridge of their nose was abridged, if you know what I mean. And they were the friendliest, most gregarious, most trusting people you ever saw in all your born days. They really, really got into music, too.

In a world where everybody wasn't just like that, they were friendly and gregarious and trusting to a fault. People with Williams-Beuren also had other troubles. Most of them were retarded, some a bit, some more than a bit. They were extra prone to heart disease.

But suppose changes in the human *WBSCR17* gene are a feature, not a bug. You don't need to suppose, of course, on account of that's where we're at. It's where we've been at since the old days turned into what we've got now, however long ago that was. I said it before and I'll say it again—since we are the way we are now, things like how long ago aren't really such a big deal.

After the last Big Fracas, everybody who was left could see that one more fracas and nobody would be left any more. Everybody could see that, if people stayed the way old-time people were, one more fracas was coming, too, sure as God made little green traffic lights.

Human nature doesn't change? Tell it to Belyaev's ghost. Tell it to his foxes, the most popular pets in the not-quite-new world. Change the genome and you change the fox—or the human. Change the human, and you change human nature.

Change *WBSCR17* the way they could after the last Big Fracas, make sure the change goes through the whole surviving population (not too hard, because it wasn't what you'd call big), and what you get is . . .

You get the upside of Williams-Beuren without the downside. No retardation. No heart disease. You get friendly, trusting, considerate, kindly people. All day, every day. They think as well as old-style humans, but not just like 'em. John Campbell would love them and hate them at the same time.

You get Willie, who's every bit as domesticated as Joe, and who likes it every bit as much. John Campbell's been dead one hell of a long time. That's kind of the point, too.

Fritz? Hey, things aren't perfect even in this best (or at least most peaceable) of all possible worlds. Mighty good, but not perfect. Dogs have been domesticated for upwards of 15,000 years. Once in a while, they still come out wolfish. Their genes get a funny roll of the dice, and we call 'em throwbacks. We call 'em trouble, too. If we can help it, they don't get to go swimming in the next gen's gene pool.

And neither will Fritz. The Voice and the other automated safety systems that watch out for things new-model people don't commonly worry about will make sure of that. Nothing cruel, mind you. Fritz can have as much fun as anybody else. But he's the end of his line. If you think that's sad, if his drives remind you of your own, you know what? That's also kind of the point.

Willie and Joe keep walking in the sun. Joe isn't sorry to see the last of Fritz's big old dogs, no sir. Willie is sorry Fritz got sanctioned. He can't imagine that happening to him. Hardly anybody these days can imagine stuff like that. Hardly anybody, but not quite nobody. That's how come the Voice is still around.

Here comes Keiko a little while on, heading his way. Keiko is just the cutest thing Willie's ever seen. Even if you don't look elfy-welfy yourself, you'd think Keiko was hot. Trust me. You would. If you do look like that . . . Willie smiles most of the time any which way. But he *smiles* now. Oh, yeah. So would you, pal.

Keiko's got a little fox on a leash, too. Daisy Mae is as cute a fox as Keiko is a girl. Joe's not supposed to appreciate Daisy Mae the way Willie appreciates Keiko. And he doesn't, not really. But he sortakinda whimpers, way down deep in his throat, as if he almost remembers he's forgotten something.

"Hey!" Willie says, and gives Keiko a hug. She squeezes him back. It feels *so* good. Let's hear it for gregariousness. Yeah!

"What's up with Fritz?" Keiko asks. People have ways of hearing about shit. It's the future. They don't even need smartphones to do it.

Willie was there. It was happening to him. But he doesn't know a whole lot more about it than Keiko does. What he does know, he doesn't hardly understand. If he did . . . Hell, if he did, he'd be Fritz. Bunches of people would be Fritz. And then we'd end up in the soup all over again.

So Willie shrugs a little. "I guess he was kinda on, you know, the selfish side of things." He looks down at his toes when the bad word comes out. I don't care if it's the future or not. There'll always be bad words. Being bad is one of the things words are for. Keiko gasps a little. She knows about Fritz. If you live around there, you have to know about Fritz. That doesn't mean you enjoy thinking about him. Except for gossip's sake, of course. If gossip's not the flip side of gregariousness, what is it?

"Too bad," she says at last. "Oh, *too* bad!"

"Yeah, it is." Willi nods. "But what can you do?" He knows what he wants to do. You bet he does. "Feel like comin' back to my place? We can let the critters run around in the back yard while we fuck." That's not a bad word any more. It hasn't been for a long, long time.

"Sure!" Keiko says. They walk back hand in hand. Some of human nature's changed, uh-huh. Some, but not all. If *that* had changed, there wouldn't be any humans left to have natures any more. There almost weren't. But it's taken care of. It sure is. Look at Willi and Keiko if you don't believe me. Look at their frolicking foxes.

Poor Fritz.

ABOUT THE AUTHOR

Harry Turtledove is an American novelist of science fiction, historical fiction, and fantasy. *Publishers Weekly* has called him the "master of alternate history," and he is best known for his work in that genre. Some of his most popular titles include *The Guns of the South*, the novels of the Worldwar series, and the books in the Great War trilogy. In addition to many other honors and nominations, Turtledove has received the Hugo Award, the Sidewise Award for Alternate History, and the Prometheus Award. He attended the University of California, Los Angeles, earning a PhD in Byzantine history. Turtledove is married to mystery writer Laura Frankos, and together they have three daughters. The family lives in Southern California.

EBOOKS BY HARRY TURTLEDOVE

FROM OPEN ROAD MEDIA

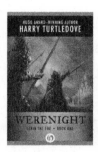

Available wherever ebooks are sold

OPEN ROAD

INTEGRATED MEDIA

Open Road Integrated Media is a digital publisher and multimedia content company. Open Road creates connections between authors and their audiences by marketing its ebooks through a new proprietary online platform, which uses premium video content and social media.